KRESLEY COLE

wicked abyss

London · New York · Sydney · Toronto · New Delhi

A CBS COMPANY

First published in the USA by Gallery Books, 2017
An imprint of Simon & Schuster, Inc.

First published in Great Britain by Simon & Schuster UK Ltd, 2017
A CBS COMPANY

Hardback ISBN: 978-1-4711-5528-4
eBook ISBN: 978-1-4711-5530-7
Australian Paperback ISBN: 978-1-4711-5531-4

This book is a work of fiction. Names, characters, places and incidents are either a product of the author's imagination or are used fictitiously. Any resemblance to actual people living or dead, events or locales is entirely coincidental.

Printed and bound by CPI Group (UK) Ltd, Croydon, CR0 4YY

Simon & Schuster UK Ltd are committed to sourcing paper that is made from wood grown in sustainable forests and support the Forest Stewardship Council, the leading international forest certification organisation. Our books displaying the FSC logo are printed on FSC certified paper.

Dedicated to all those who still dream of fairy tales . . .

EXCERPTED FROM

THE LIVING BOOK OF LORE . . .

The Lore

". . . and those sentient creatures that are not human shall be united in one stratum, coexisting with, yet secret from, man's."

- Most are immortal and can regenerate from injuries.
- Their eyes change with intense emotion, often to a breed-specific color.

The Demonarchies

"The demons are as varied as the bands of man. . . ."

- A collection of demon dynasties.
- The hell demonarchy was the first of all demon kingdoms.

Primordial

"The mightiest of all immortals; filled with power, magics, and majesty."

- The firstborn—or the oldest generation—of a species.

The Møriør

"In the tongue of the Elserealms, Møriør can mean both 'the Dozen' and 'Soul's Doom.'"

- An alliance of otherworldly beings led by Orion the Undoing.
- Have journeyed to our world for reasons unknown.

The Noble Fey of Grimm Dominion

"A warrior nobility who ruled over all the demon serfs in their realm."

- Were called *féodals*, an ancient term for feudal overlords, which became shortened to *fey*.
- Possess supernatural speed and cunning.
- The Sylvan kingdom is ruled by King Saetthan, also known as Saetth.

The Accession

"And a time shall come to pass when all immortal beings in the Lore must fight and destroy each other."

- A kind of mystical checks-and-balances system for an ever-growing population of immortals.
- Three major alliances: the Pravus League, the Vertas Rule, and the Møriør.
- Occurs every five hundred years. Or right now . . .

wicked abyss

PROLOGUE

Listen well to the storyteller, and you'll hear such a tale," Nïx the Ever-Knowing said to her sister Regin as they sat before the fire in their temporary abode. "Once upon a time, two females entered an enchanted forest on opposite ends of the woods. One was a lovely and truehearted fairy princess, born an old soul, with perhaps a bit of a temper. The other was a temptress called the dame of fire, known to be sensual and devious, with perhaps a lack of mercy.

"The princess was fleeing a baneblood archer who'd vowed to wipe out the entire fey royal line. The princess wanted only to live.

"The dame was pursuing a cowardly ruler who'd jeopardized all of his people. The dame wanted only to kill.

"During the princess's journey, she met a mysterious, gorgeous, shifty soothsaying Valkyrie who betrayed her. Next the princess met two sorceresses. They sent her on the adventure of a lifetime, down the rabbit hole to a strange new world, because they knew that not all bad is bad.

"Lastly the princess met a king of beasts with two faces. He could keep her safe from the archer, but first the fairy princess would have to become the beast's bride.

"On the opposite end of the woods, the dame of fire met an ancient and primal force that recognized and rewarded her bravery.

"Next she encountered a wise dragon who admired her audacity, so he decided to grant her one wish.

"Lastly she met a beautiful fairy king, who had offered her his hand in marriage. And everyone knows the best way to become a queen is to marry a king.

"The dame and the princess would meet in the middle of the forest, clashing so violently that even hell trembled. Which one would emerge from the woods? Who would triumph before the clock tolled midnight? The storyteller's companion, one of her Valkyrie sisters, blinked in astonishment at such a tale, then said . . ."

"Uh, Nïx, I just asked if you wanted to go hunt some ghouls." Regin frowned at her sister, wondering how much nuttier the soothsayer could get. After the destruction of the Valkyries' home, her mind was declining even faster than before. "And why are you calling yourself 'the storyteller' and narrating our conversation?"

Nïx smiled vacantly. "The storyteller replied: 'Because I am *telling* a *story*. And besides, no ghouls were harmed during the making of this fairy tale.'"

FITFO. Figure it the fuck out.

—Calliope "Lila" Barbot
princess of the Sylvan fey line

My sire was the devil, and my dam was darkness embodied. I am a shadow that can follow you, even into the night.

—Abyssian "Sian" Infernas
King of Pandemonia and All Hells,
member of the Møriør (A.K.A. the Devil's Own)

ONE

Sylvan Castle
Eleven years ago . . .

As King Saetth leisurely wiped blood off his sword, Lila choked down her fury.

Seated upon his throne, he took his time, keeping everyone in suspense. With two executions complete, only one trial remained.

Mine.

Would she follow her parents' fates?

Through one of the throne room's towering windows, a ray of sunlight beamed over the king. His blond locks and his ornate crown—a wreath of gilded evergreen branches—seemed to glow. Even the sun wanted to touch him.

For all of her thirteen years, Lila had been just as enamored of him.

Off to the side, whispers sounded from her backstabbing royal cousins.

"Saetth's about to behead his child fiancée!"

"The foulmouthed brat got used to being the king's favorite."

"Why isn't the little bitch crying?"

"Or begging for her cursed life?"

Crying or begging? As if. Lila faced Saetth with her chin up and shoulders back, her pampered appearance belying her fortitude.

The perils of this fey court had honed her mettle. Learning from the mistakes of others had sharpened her acumen.

Yet nothing could stifle her unfeylike temper; after all, she'd been betrothed to Saetth since her birth, raised to become the queen of this realm. Rumor even held that she was a princess reincarnated.

Fate *wanted* her to be a queen.

Lila had worn a purple silk gown for this occasion; the color was royal—and defiant.

As the castle's clock tower tolled, Saetth finished cleaning the weapon he always carried, the Ancestors' Sword, the unifying symbol of their royal line. He raised the blade to the sunlight, eyeing the edge with his piercing blue gaze.

Her earliest memories were of sighing over his handsome face, imagining him as her husband and her dollies as the subjects they protected.

Yet now her king suspected Lila of treason?

How could her coldhearted parents have plotted against such a powerful ruler? They'd foolishly trusted an informer, leaving their only child's life hanging in the balance.

Secrecy equals survival in this court.

They'd never cared about her—never pretended she was more than a valuable bargaining chip—which was one of the reasons she'd bonded so strongly with Saetth, who'd at least shown her attention. . . .

He sheathed his sword. Peering down at her, he began her trial with one question: "Why shouldn't I believe you were involved in your parents' plot to steal my crown?"

Lila pinned his gaze with her own uncanny one. Her defense consisted of eight words: "Because it still sits upon your godsdamned head."

Stunned silence reigned.

Saetth's shock turned to amusement. "And that is why you remain my betrothed, Calliope of Sylvan, the queen of my heart." He laughed, his gaze seemingly warm. "If there was ever a girl born to rule, you are she, cousin. But I too was born to rule, and I've kept this crown for millennia because I allow no threats to fester around me." His smile disappeared as if it'd never been. "I hereby exile you from our woodland kingdom."

Leave her beloved Sylvan? Lila would almost rather die. The forests were what separated the Sylvans from the other fey. The splendor of those great trees was equaled only by the shining, meticulous order of life at court.

Just two weeks ago, at a ball in her honor, the lights from a thousand candles had reflected in her jewels as Saetth had led her out to dance. The next day she'd run through the woods alongside bounding deer.

Separating her from this place would be like draining her veins of blood. "To where?"

"The mortal realm."

Gasps sounded; some of her cousins tittered. He might as well have sentenced her to hell.

She would go from proudly displaying everything that made her a Lorean to hiding her very species from prying mortal eyes. From the order the fey so cherished to human chaos.

Saetth said, "We'll see if my hothouse rose can survive among primitive humans."

Lips drawn back from her teeth, she said, "Careful, cousin, this hothouse rose intends to flourish and grow sharp thorns."

More gasps.

Saetth's eyes flickered with excitement. He leaned down and said, "I am counting on it."

"And if the fey-slayer finds me, what then?" Rune Darklight, a homicidal archer and one of the Møriør, was murdering the Sylvan line of succession. Lila was one of only fourteen left.

This castle had a barrier to keep Møriør out; she'd be vulnerable anywhere else.

"Test your new thorns against him," Saetth said. As if any of the monstrous Møriør could be fought! "If you're truly the queen I deserve, you'll figure out something, I'm sure."

"How long until I can return?" Six months? A year?

"Should there come a time when you can prove your loyalty to me through great personal sacrifice, I will provide you the chance to take your rightful place by my side. Until then, wait for my word. . . ."

TWO

The Happiest Place on Earth
Present day . . .

Lila stood on the balcony of the castle in her cornflower blue ball-gown and sparkling tiara, gazing out over the nighttime beauty of her magic kingdom.

As a balmy breeze coaxed light-brown strands from her chignon, the kingdom's symphony started to play below.

She sighed, reliving her last ball. The scent of roses and candlewax had filled the air as Saetth twirled her around the immaculate ballroom.

Closing her eyes, she collected her skirt with a gloved hand and swayed—

"Step into the magic!" a human announced over the PA system, snatching her from her reverie. "The magic of Walt Disney World!"

Too bad Lila's life was all make-believe.

She got paid to dress up like this. Her fairy-esque ballgown was polyester and covered with candy smudge prints from the mortal children who touched it with reverence: *Are you weally a fairwy pwincess?*

I am. I really am. The pointed tips of her ears were expertly hidden beneath her coiffure.

Loreans kept themselves secret—revealing paranormal activity to humans resulted in severe punishments—so a theme park filled with security cameras was an immortal's worst nightmare. To elude Rune the archer, she'd decided to hide in plain sight, taking a gig as a "face character."

After each shift, she came to this balcony in Cinderella Castle and pretended her tiara was real.

Fearing discovery by the archer and by mortals, she maintained no friendships or social life. No love life. Outside of work, she would go running—slowing her natural pace—then hole up in her drab apartment to speed-read or complete another online degree.

A young couple below caught her eye. She sighed with longing when they started making out against a wall. The things she'd seen in this park . . .

She'd never had sex—some part of her must still believe she could become queen—but she'd risked fooling around more and more since she'd started transitioning to her full immortality.

As all of her senses heightened to a supernatural degree, so did her lust. Loreans called this stage "overstimulation." Lila called it "in heat."

Even from this distance, her enhanced eyesight could spy tiny details. The bite of the woman's nails into the man's shoulders, his subtle thrusts against her . . .

Suddenly, the tips of her ears began to twitch. Wariness filled her. Another Lorean neared—

"A fairy princess pretending to be a fairy princess?" a deep voice said from behind her.

Saetth. *Stay cool, stay cool. Calm the hell down!* "Took you long enough, cousin." Turning to him, she craned her head up. Lost her breath.

Dressed in full court regalia, he wore a tailored, fawn-colored suit that highlighted his rangy frame. Amusement lit his riveting blue eyes. Golden blond hair tumbled over his forehead just so. His sword scabbard accentuated his royal air, and his crown still sat proudly upon his head.

He was the epitome of masculine perfection.

Fucker. Take away the fact that he'd exiled her and she'd spent more than a decade cursing him . . . *I'd do him.* Of course, at this point in her development she wasn't very choosy.

"Calliope, you've grown into a vision." His gaze roamed over her. "What's this—do your eyes now match?"

"A contact lens." Her appearance required approval before she was allowed to mingle with park guests. Her mismatched eyes would never make the cut. "Why are you here?" *Take me the hell home. All I want is to go home.*

"How about a proper greeting for your betrothed?"

Betrothed. Was she truly still in the running for queen? Her heart tripped, but not because of any lingering love for him.

Lila was in love with the idea of having as much control over her own life as possible. Of not constantly looking over her shoulder for the Møriør.

Being a ruler would give her the most safety and control she could ever hope for. "*Are* you still my betrothed? I wouldn't know since I haven't heard a fucking word from you."

A hint of a grin played on his lips. "Has little Calliope developed an even tarter tongue since she's been away?"

Tarter? You have no idea, cousin. Her exile had only fueled her temper.

"And yet I wager it will taste so sweet." He grasped her shoulders and drew her closer. To kiss her?

She'd wondered what this would be like for far too long. Especially of late. Even when she'd kissed other guys, she'd dreamed of Saetth, unable to deny he was probably her ideal match, socially, royally—and sexually.

Had he imprinted on her in some way?

He leaned down. As their lips made contact, fireworks exploded.

The eight-o'clock fireworks show. Not so much with the kiss. She'd experienced more heat making out with the mortal who played Goofy.

Saetth groaned, slanting his mouth, touching his tongue to hers.

That was better, but nothing she'd write home about. *Not that I could ever write home, since it's in a different godsdamned dimension and they don't make stamps for that.*

She broke away and pushed against his chest.

He wasn't discouraged at all. Releasing her, he murmured, "Sweet as honey."

So that was the extent of their first kiss? How . . . anticlimactic.

With a smoldering look, he turned and leaned his elbows on the railing to take in the fireworks blazing across the sky.

She'd seen this show so many times that she knew the purple, red, and blue zigzaggy cascades came next.

"Clever to use mortals as your cover from the archer," he said. "And to masquerade as a fairy princess is the boldest choice you could have made. Why am I not surprised?"

I can't believe I just kissed Saetth. "Are you here to take me back or not?"

He straightened and faced her. "I am not."

She bit back a string of insults. *How much longer?*

"I traveled here with a friend to discuss something with you. Ah, here she is now."

A stunning black-haired female with golden eyes strolled out onto the balcony. She rocked a scarlet sheath dress. A live bat perched on her shoulder like an accessory.

Was the creature eating a tuft of cotton candy? A package of it jutted from the woman's messenger bag.

Saetth said, "Calliope, this is Nïx the Ever-Knowing, the Valkyries' soothsayer."

Nïx? She was one of the most famous—or infamous, depending on your alliance—immortals alive. "I've read about you in my *Book of Lore*." Lila's only connection to the immortal world, the book updated itself with every major battle or power shift. "It's a pleasure to meet you."

Though Nïx was a crucial leader in the Vertas alliance, the Valkyrie was also rumored to be crazy. By way of greeting, Nïx said, "Have you ever wanted to dance with the devil in the pale moonlight?"

Huh?

Saetth said, "I think what Nïx means to ask is if you've ever wanted to strike back against the Møriør."

Also known as the Bringers of Doom. "Of course." Rumor held that those tyrants were journeying from their side of the universe to invade this one. Their archer had already arrived in advance of them.

Since she'd been old enough to understand what a bogeyman was, she'd lived in fear of them all.

Growing in lockstep with her fear was fury, the two emotions seeming entwined. "Not a minute goes by that I don't think about them. I've forfeited so much to remain hidden from their threat." She pointedly added, "During my *exile*."

Saetth arched a blond brow. "I told you that you could return home once you'd made a great personal sacrifice to prove your loyalty. Are you ready to?"

Lila stilled, working to calm her heart rate. She would do *anything* to live in Sylvan again.

Anything. "Yes, how?"

"Nïx has assured me that victory against the Møriør on a battlefield is impossible, but she's also provided us a unique opportunity to deal that alliance a blow."

Nïx drew a dossier from her bag and handed it to Lila.

King Abyssian Infernas, the Devil's Own. He was the primordial demon of the Møriør alliance. Lila flipped through the pages of the file, skimming a description:

Physically flawless . . . the phrase "handsome as the devil" came about because of comparisons to his notoriously seductive sire . . . aggressively pursued by females . . .

Under the miscellaneous section, she read:

The oldest living demon . . . proficient in all weapons, but has carried the same battle-ax for ten millennia . . . can fell an entire army on his own . . . newly crowned king of Pandemonia, A.K.A. hell.

That fabled realm had always intrigued Lila to a curious degree. "What do you expect from me?" She closed the file. "I've never shot a bow or wielded a sword." Though she didn't possess fighting skills, she had *read* widely on the subjects of battle, survival, and weapons.

She could do everything from orchestrating an ambush to constructing a trebuchet—in theory.

"You have three innate advantages that are even more valuable," Nïx said. "You can read and write his language." Among many others. They came easily to her. "You developed mental blocks against mind reading when growing up." For protection at the insidious fey court. "And you are his mate."

Shock gut-punched Lila. *Mate???* She reeled on her feet, latching onto the balcony railing. "No way. There's no way fate would connect me to one of those monsters." The thought arose: *Maybe my fascination with Pandemonia isn't so curious.* But she quashed it.

"You're the Devil's Own's own," Nïx said, her eyes glimmering. "You'll go to hell and use that connection to garner information from him—plans for upcoming battles, details about his alliance, and so on. I'm especially keen to learn about Orion, the Møriør's leader."

Go to hell? Reading about and visiting were in no way the same.

Saetth said, "As soon as you've uncovered weaknesses, we will extract you."

Lila's palm sweated through her opera glove as she gripped the dossier. "You want me to be a spy? This mortal realm is bad enough, but at least I'm not *damned*." And mated!

How could fate have screwed her over like this? Lila's tiara must be on too tight. She'd cut off circulation to her brain or something.

Saetth's lips thinned. "When I first heard Nïx's plan, it sounded as if I'd be sending a lamb into the lion's den. But the demon will be compelled by his instinct to protect and care for you."

"And also to claim me." Nausea churned at the thought.

Nïx said, "I've assured Saetth that the demon cannot and will not hurt you. Abyssian's tender feelings for you will make it easy to coax secrets from him." She tapped her chin with a pink claw. "Of course, you might have to encourage those feelings. . . ."

"Encourage? You want me to *seduce* a monster, one among a group of them that I've hated and feared my entire life? This just gets better and better!"

"You don't have to go *all* the way." Nïx winked. "Just a great deal of the way."

Aghast, Lila asked Saetth, "You wouldn't mind another male's hands all over me? A Møriør touching your future queen?"

He exhaled, as if he found her attitude tiresome. "Perhaps if I were a demon myself. But I'm better than that. I know this is the only logical course, and I'm not ruled by primitive instincts."

Nïx collected more cotton candy for the bat. "Speaking of instincts, Abyssian might be turning a *jot* more demonic of late. But with the Accession coming around, who isn't—am I right? Just be sure to stay feisty with him. He'll like that."

Feisty? At times, Lila nearly choked on her rage toward the Møriør.

Saetth said, "If there were any alternative, I would undertake it."

Nïx's gaze flashed to him, and Lila could have sworn a spark of . . . animosity lit the Valkyrie's eyes.

It passed so quickly, Lila thought she'd imagined it. "I just wanted to come home," she said, though the opportunity to plot against the bogeymen did hold some appeal.

When she thought of the endless nightmares she'd had about them—waking to her own scream, still feeling the fey-slayer's arrow in her chest—fury surged.

And Saetth shared much of that blame. He'd sent her to the mortal realm with only a few belongings. No ID, no money, no way to contact him.

Early on, she'd rationalized his behavior: *My parents* did *try to kill him.*

But lately, she'd decided to call a dick a dick.

"Accomplish this mission," Saetth said, "and you will come home. As my queen."

Lila had three pie-in-the-sky dreams: to live safely in Sylvan, to be the queen, and to start a family that would also live in safety. A distant fourth was the hope that she'd fall in love one day.

Saetth could make three of her dreams come true. He was a means to an end.

All she had to do was give up any sappier hopes. *As a calculating fey royal, I should have no problem doing that.*

"You know we will do well together," Saetth said. "With your ingenious mind and my ruthlessness, we will be unstoppable. Which means *Sylvan* will be unstoppable." Gazing down at her, he said, "We'll celebrate your success with a wedding. You've always wanted your own family. You could welcome our babe before the year is out. We'll get started on that upon your return."

"My *return*." Like a glass of cold water tossed in her face. "From seducing the oldest demon alive." Her groping sessions with furries notwithstanding, Lila wasn't exactly seductress material.

Nïx pouted. "But you don't have to go *all* the way." Then the soothsayer grew abruptly serious, and a lightning bolt fractured the sky in a spectacular display. The crowds below gasped, thinking it was a part of the show. Thunder boomed with such force that the castle shuddered. "I've foreseen this future—if you journey to hell, you will save Sylvan from the Møriør. Because of your sacrifice, your people will be protected. *For an eternity of eternities*."

Dramatic much?

"I've also foreseen that if you *don't* journey to hell, the Møriør will declare war on Sylvan—imminently. Just as they leveled my home, they will destroy yours. Then the archer will use his new foothold in the fey realm to uncover more of the royal line."

Lila didn't care about any of her cousins; they ran the gamut from scummy to vile. She'd only ever cared about her own survival and maybe Saetth's. "If the demon knows I'm one of the archer's specific targets, he could turn me over to his ally despite his . . . matehood with me." A sentence she'd never thought she'd say. "I might not get a chance to *encourage* anything." *Don't vomit.*

Nïx shook her head. "With your human accent and ballsy ways, he'll never suspect you're a princess of anything—just as long as you don't let on that you know you're his mate."

Sylvan's destruction versus a throne and a family.

As Lila had struggled to survive over these years, she'd at least had the hope of returning to her beloved kingdom. Would she allow its ruin because she wasn't ready to sacrifice for her people?

Isn't sacrifice what queens do? "How would I begin?"

Nïx said, "Go about your regular daily life—it's an excellent cover. We'll arrange for the infiltration."

"How?"

The Valkyrie's gaze grew unfocused. *Seeing the future?* "I've informed the hell king that his mate is somewhere in the universe, ready for the taking, and provided a description of you. He's already put out a bounty. When the time comes, I'll make sure you're captured and safely delivered to him. Of course, you'll have no idea when, since the capture must look real."

This plot sounded more and more dangerous. "*If* I agreed to this, I'd have to wait until I'm fully immortal." The females in Lila's family usually transitioned around twenty-three, so she was long overdue. Until that happened, she was as vulnerable to harm as a mortal. Going toe-to-toe with immortals would be idiotic. "Maybe in a few weeks."

"Events are building with the Møriør," Nïx said. "I can't give you that much time."

Saetth told Lila, "You've been out of the Lore, so you don't know how bad it's gotten."

"I've read the *Book of Lore*, keeping up to date with the Møriør's major battles." If those one-sided slaughters could be considered battles.

"What goes on behind the scenes is just as important." Brows drawn, he said, "The cowardly fey-slayer sprung a sneak attack on me recently. He destroyed the Ancestors' Sword."

"Are you shitting me?" Lila's gaze dropped to the scabbard on Saetth's hip. Looking more closely, she could see he wore another sword—not the king's blade. This shocked her as much as everything else she'd learned tonight.

The sword that had beheaded her parents was no more.

The Møriør had struck home yet again. Was Lila going to hide while they continued their assault on the kingdom?

Never.

She faced Nïx. "When would the . . . capture happen?"

"Sooner rather than later."

Lila's ears twitched. She narrowed her eyes at the Valkyrie's blasé expression. "I need to know the duration of my stay in hell and the details of my extraction."

"You'll stay until the demon tells you what I want him to, and we'll extract you as soon as you need us to."

Lila shook her head. "You have to give me more than that."

"No."

"No?"

"Yes." The soothsayer shrugged, flustering her bat. "Some details are above your feygrade."

"Feygrade? Did you really just say that?" *Do not pop the Valkyrie in the mouth.*

Saetth took Lila's hand, drawing her attention back to him. "You have to trust in Nïx's plan. She knows what's best for Sylvan. Cousin, I wouldn't expect this of you if the alternative weren't so dire."

"You *expect* me to go into a Møriør stronghold."

"All will be well," he said. "Remember, a demon cannot hurt his mate."

THREE

Graven Castle
The dimension of Pandemonia

I plan to torture her till she begs for mercy," Sian said as he twirled his great battle-ax. "Make her pay for all her treachery in her past life."

He and Uthyr, his dragon ally, stood on a terrace high in Sian's castle. A league below them, demon legions clamored for war.

Sian was feeling just as bloodthirsty. "*If* Princess Kari's even been reincarnated." Merely thinking about the perfidious bitch made his muscles tense. "I have only the word of a soothsayer."

But he'd always believed. . . .

Uthyr rested on his hind legs and wrapped his spiked tail around his gigantic body. Like all Møriør, he could communicate telepathically: *—Your female probably doesn't even know she's a reincarnate, could go her whole life without remembering a previous existence. She might have no memory of a betrayal. What then?—*

Sian hoped she did remember. If not . . . "I have more than enough memory for both of us."

Uthyr gave a dragonic sigh, a lazy stream of flame tumbling from his lips. *—Will you not tell me your mate's crimes?—*

Even after so long, Sian couldn't speak about her actions without going into a rage. When he gripped the handle of his ax, he could feel Uthyr studying him.

The dragon shifter had decided to take a sabbatical in Pandemonia, saying he planned to "work on his chess game and visit with the local dragon population." Most likely he was here to monitor Sian's declining self-control and increasing aggression.

Sian didn't care what the shifter did, as long as he didn't get in the way. "All you need to know is that she betrayed me and every demon of this realm." Because of her, Sian had been left maimed for ten millennia. Inwardly, he'd been scarred much, much worse.

For eons, he had awaited his revenge, not only on his mate, but on her entire hated species.

Uthyr scratched his neck with the claws of a back paw, shedding a metallic blue-gold scale. *—You've never doubted she would be reborn. What made you so certain?—*

Because he'd had no choice. "When I learned of her death, I vowed to live long enough to see her return." How else could he have gone on?

He would never forget falling to his knees beside the river of fire, roaring and clawing at his chest, grief and hatred blistering him inside.

—No word on your bounty?—

"Immortals are scouring the universe for her. If she retains her species and her unique appearance"—a fey with one amber eye and one violet—"she will be found." If not, he would take over the hunt between his next two wars.

In the first campaign, he would fight off an invasion of trespassers. In the second, he would launch his own invasion.

Nothing pleased Sian so well as a good, meaty war, and he was grateful to have conflicts to distract him. Otherwise he would've gone mad since learning of his mate's possible reincarnation.

And since he'd been struck by the hell-change curse.

Upon his brother's recent death, Sian had reluctantly returned to Pandemonia to assume the crown—and all its disadvantages. He'd started to transform from a male of striking good looks into his most monstrous self.

Whoever ruled hell slowly *became* hell. The last time Sian looked at his reflection—months ago—a hideous stranger had stared back at him.

His formerly smooth, tanned skin was dark red with glowing glyphs over his chest. His chiseled features had become blunter, more brutal. Mystical hell metal pierced his skin—bars at the bridge of his nose and through his nipples, not to mention other parts of his body.

He'd grown a pair of massive wings that resembled a bat's. Long black claws tipped his fingers and the toes of his beastlike feet.

For ten millennia, he'd gone without horns—thanks to Kari—but now a new, larger pair had emerged, more menacing even than before. A wide swath of skin surrounding his eyes was darkened like a demonic mask. Only the color of his green irises remained the same—unless they went black when he was in the grip of rage.

The hell-change heightened his aggression until he could barely *think* at times, his most primal demon instincts at the fore. Like him, hell was in turmoil. Ever since Sian had learned his mate might be alive, the realm had been plagued with firestorms and lava floods. Ash choked the air. The skies churned.

He rubbed his hand over his still-unfamiliar face. Even if she retained memories of her previous life—unlikely—she wouldn't recognize him.

All those years ago, he'd believed his mate had felt some measure of attraction to him. Now she would be repelled.

Only one thing could return him to his previous form. But to even contemplate it could bring on madness. . . .

The dragon's watchful gaze was upon him. *—If you can learn to manage these rages, what will looks matter? We Møriør have a mission, demon. We live lives of service.—*

"Is that the point of our unending existences?" Sian's life seemed to be one long wait, measured by an hourglass that gave up a grain of sand every few centuries. "Is service what makes you rise in the mornings?"

—That and television.—

Sian lifted a brow. "Alas, those two enticements have little effect on me."

—Then what does affect you?—

"A challenge. I can't remember the last time an enemy landed a blow against any of us." The Møriør—not even at full strength—continued to rout any opposition with ease. "Our power is vast, but life is long without challenge. I would give my ax to find a worthy opponent."

Would he ever know a hard-won victory again?

Uthyr shrugged his large wings. *—Your thoughts have been grim ever since you learned of your mate's possible return.—*

"I've felt this way for some time, but the idea of her resurrection has brought much into glaring relief."

He'd waited ten thousand two hundred and thirty-four years, three months, and seventeen days for his female to return to him.

What if she truly had? What would happen to him after his vengeance was done?

What would happen *to her*?

As if it were yesterday, Sian recalled the day he'd met Princess Karinna of Sylvan. He'd been outside the newfound Pando-Sylvan portal when he'd caught her maddening scent from the other side. He'd hurried through the rift to track the thread to its source, suspecting he would find his mate.

The unfiltered sun had stung his eyes, temporarily blinding him. His first sight of heaven had been her face, the first sound her voice. She'd been twenty-four, a practiced flirt, and entrancingly lovely.

He'd been a pup of sixteen. *I never stood a chance against her.*

He'd trusted in a manipulative, traitorous female and nearly felled a kingdom—

A wave of déjà vu hit him, so strong his body reeled. He could almost scent Kari, as if he were back in Sylvan on that first day so long ago.

How could it be? Did he dream?

His muscles tightened as they did before battle. This was no dream. "By all the dark gods . . ."

Uthyr lifted his snout. —*What is it?*—

Sian's lips drew back from his fangs. "The bitch's scent."

FOUR

The Happiest Place on Earth

Hey, somebody want to let me in?" Lila called outside the concealed employee door.

All she wanted was to get back to her apartment and process everything Saetth and Nïx had told her tonight. Yet some chucklehead had locked Lila out.

Yanking off her tiara, she waved at the camera above the door. "Yoo-hoo." This costume dress weighed more than a dozen pounds; she itched to peel it from her tired body. "Hellooo! Fuckers!"

She gazed around. Probably wouldn't be good if some visitor videoed Cinderella cussing like a sailor. Grumbling, "Still, fuckers," she started toward another entrance. She was hungry and exhausted, but still keyed up from that meeting.

Carried away in the moment and high on the promise of striking back, she'd told Saetth, "I won't rest until I discover a way to hurt Abyssian Infernas." *In other words, keep that extraction team at the ready.* "I'll figure out what his weaknesses are and how to exploit them. I'll do anything I can to destroy him."

Now doubts about this plan crept in. Too many questions and variables remained. *Note to self: be in charge of future political plots or be excluded from them.*

Hindsight. Twenty. Whatever.

She peeled off her opera gloves, stuffing them into her secret pocket, then pulled out her hidden phone to order takeout. Her fake "real life" would continue, and she planned to speed-read a new series of how-to books.

Her ears twitched and her fingers paused on the dial screen when a grating screech sounded, like metal on metal. The nearby frog song and insect chatter went silent.

The screech came again. "Is somebody there?" she called, though she knew anyone who'd ever asked that question was already in deep shit.

Quiet answered her. *No, no, just my imagination.* Still, she pocketed the phone and hastened down the pathway.

Of course she was jumpy. She'd lived in a hypervigilant state for so long, and now she had a capture to anticipate.

Sooner rather than later.

Apparently, she *would* do anything to get back to Sylvan—even act as a bounty hunter's quarry in order to infiltrate a primordial demon's home in hell.

The only problem about waiting for an "infiltration setup"? Lila might be leaving herself vulnerable to the archer—

Two women materialized on the path not ten feet from her. *Loreans.*

One had black hair; the other was a redhead. Both were gorgeous. They wore Sorceri garb—metal bustiers, heavy gold jewelry pieces, and claw-tipped gauntlets.

Had one of them clawed the pathway railing to produce that screech? *To spook me?* It was working. Lila had no powers to defend herself; her only asset was her speed.

They stood in front of a shimmering portal. On the other side was a huge stone keep. Silken material lay pooled on the floor, as if the Sorceri had tossed it through the rift.

Wait . . . that was Lila's pink chemise! How had they gotten it from her apartment?

The redhead raised one gauntlet, rapping her claws together. In a sinister voice, she said, "This is the part where you run."

On it! Lila whirled around, her full skirts whipping from the movement, and darted away.

Sorceri couldn't trace—teleport—and could never outrun a fey like Lila. If she could reach a group of mortals, the pair would back off.

Her updo came undone. Were her ears visible? She swatted her hair off her face.

Midstride, she chanced a glance over her shoulder. *Lost them!* Just over a footbridge was a ramp to the main park. She could already hear guests laughing—

Her stomach lurched, her feet suddenly above her head. She was tumbling down an embankment. How? She'd never seen . . .

SPLAT.

She landed face-first in a shallow retention pond. Spitting mud, she scrambled to get free, but the muck sucked off her shoes and coated her gown.

The Sorceri strolled to the bridge, laughing as if this was all good-natured fun. The black-haired one said, "Good one, sis. Making the path appear to move. Didn't you pull a similar illusion when you crashed Rydstrom's car?"

The redhead chuckled. "It never fails. Why do people always think what they see is real?"

They'd distorted Lila's vision! She clawed at the embankment, but her bare feet caught in her skirts like spinning tires. She fell on her face again.

Ugh! Swiping filth from her eyes, she snapped, "You'll do this with security cameras around? Have you lost your minds?"

"Of course not," the redhead said. "I've made this all invisible."

Just as Lila got loose and tensed to flee, the black-haired female said, "Climb to this bridge, fey. Come stand in front of us. Without making another sound." Her words were laden with sorcery! A mind-controller? Lila fought to repel the command but found herself climbing toward the Sorceri.

When she stood before the two females, the black-haired one said, "I'm Melanthe. This is my sister, Sabine."

Sabine created an illusion out of thin air of a girl who looked exactly like . . . Lila. "I'd say this fey is our bounty."

The infiltration! They were about to put her in Abyssian's castle. *Sooner rather than later, Nïx?*

Sabine erased her illusion. "We've caught ourselves Hell's Most Wanted."

"So here's the situation," Melanthe said to Lila. "My beloved husband, Thronos, and I are the rulers of the Vrekener clan. I'm sure you've heard of us."

Vrekeners were winged demons, fanatical about morality. Angel lore was based on them. What was a *sorceress* doing as their queen?

"Well, Thronos and I kind of trespassed in Pandemonia. A scoch. I'd call it trespassing-*ish*. And we might've brought to hell an entire population of angels. Ish." Melanthe continued, "But if I turn you over to Abyssian Infernas for a bounty, then he probably won't unleash his demon legions to destroy my people." She placed one hand protectively over her belly. "So you are going to be our ace in the hole. As a matter of fact, let's just call you Ace from now on."

Sabine said, "We're about to cash in on you, Ace."

"Nothing personal." At Lila's ear, Melanthe added, "By the way, Nïx had a final message for you: *Never trust a Valkyrie*. Now, sleepwalk, Ace."

Lila resisted, but sleep overtook her.

FIVE

Sian could perceive any entry into—or exit from—Pandemonia. A portal had opened, in his own throne room no less. Kari's scent emanated from there.

He traced to the room. A pink garment lay on the floor. He snatched up the tiny piece, shuddering at the silk against his palm. The chemise was similar to the shift he'd once stolen from her.

Was this a jest? He turned to face the portal. Dropped his jaw. On the other side, in some distant realm, was . . . his mate.

Though mud covered her, Sian could tell her fine-boned features and full lips were the same. Which meant she would be breathtaking when not filthy.

Eyes closed—would they be mismatched again?—she stood motionless between two Sorceri females. Was she bespelled?

The black-haired sorceress pressed one claw from her gloves against Kari's jugular. Most likely a poisoned tip. The Sorceri were known toxinians. Some poisons could kill even an immortal.

Sian grated, "You have my attention." He eased closer to the portal. *Damn it, a one-direction rift.* He couldn't simply snatch Kari.

He tried to read the Sorceri's thoughts, but the females had blocks in place. "Who are you?" He probed Kari's mind as well, yet even in this stupor, she maintained her own blocks.

The black-haired female gazed up at him, and a tremor passed over her, no doubt at Sian's horrifying appearance. "I'm Melanthe, queen of the Vrekeners. And this is my sister, Sabine, queen of Rothkalina." The redhead gave a careless wave.

"You have a lot of bloody nerve contacting me." The Vrekeners were the ones who'd invaded his realm! He'd get to that soon enough. For now, his eyes couldn't stray from Kari.

The tips of her pointed ears poked out from her mane of damp brown hair. So she was fey once more. As before, she stood a little over five feet. Her mud-coated dress revealed the same willowy figure.

He hadn't expected a replica.

When he realized he was gripping that pink chemise, he used magic to make it disappear to his chambers. "What is wrong with your captive?"

"I commanded her to sleepwalk."

"I've heard of your powers." Melanthe could control minds and create portals between worlds. Her sister could make a victim see anything she wished. Their talents would be particularly valuable for bounty hunting. "Why not attempt to ensorcell me?"

"Something tells me you've developed an immunity over your long life."

True. It would take more than a fledgling sorceress to control his mind. "Why is your bounty covered in mud?" He wanted to see Kari's face clean.

Melanthe said, "She *fell* for our ruse." Both Sorceri chuckled at that.

"How did you locate her? Nïx?"

"It doesn't matter how," Sabine said. "Just know that your reincarnated mate is in play."

"Nïx plots my downfall. If the soothsayer wants me to have Kari, perhaps I should resist acquiring my mate."

Resisting Kari was *not* Abyssian Infernas's strong suit.

Which Nïx must know. In his last encounter with the soothsayer, she'd warned him, "Hold on to your ass." She'd also told a group of gathered Møriør, "To win this war, I'll use every trick in my tricksy little bag of tricks."

The Valkyrie has begun.

Melanthe said, "Your mate's name is Calliope now. Not Kari."

"I don't give a fuck what her current name is."

"You put a Lorewide bounty on this female. Will you not honor it?"

"Perhaps I would have if you and your husband hadn't taken over one of hell's mountains and declared it a sovereign territory." The winged Vrekeners might technically be demons, but they acted . . . angelic.

In hell?

It wasn't to be borne! "Not to mention the havoc you wreaked on my subjects." She and her husband had freed the legions—the most warmongering of Pandemonia's demon population—from their interminable labors of hell.

Melanthe waved his comment away. "So we freed thousands of demons from unending strife. Ish."

"They were to be punished for an uprising against my sire." Though Pandemonia hadn't been actively ruled for ages, Sian's father and brother had set up controls. This self-governing dimension was filled with protections to punish intruders and to keep its unruly inhabitants in check. "They are bloodthirsty. Now they hunger to war on you."

"You either want your female or not." Melanthe tapped that claw against Kari's neck.

While he applauded the sorceresses' daring, he wouldn't be trapped by it. Sian shrugged. "Keep the bitch. We war. I'll destroy you, then take her."

"You'd risk her?" Melanthe said. "So apparently you *didn't* love her during her previous life."

I adored her, would have done anything for her. "I want her for revenge only."

Sabine exhaled. "All the best with that."

Melanthe shook her head. "I've ensorcelled her to die within the hour—unless I release her from my commands. Your mate's perished once already."

Sabine added, "You won't get a *third* chance with her, I assure you."

"What do you want?" Sian demanded of Melanthe.

She pressed her advantage. "The mountain we've settled, two thousand leagues in all directions from it, and your vow never to attack our kingdom of New Skye."

Even her sister raised her brows at the greedy demand.

"That range would encompass *my* keep, sorceress. If you think I'll hand over Graven Castle, you're as mad as Nïx."

"I recently learned that the king of Pandemonia becomes one with the realm, manipulating it like a god."

Nïx had to be giving them information. Few knew that the king and the kingdom were connected, his mind shaping the world, and the world controlling his appearance. The soothsayer was proving to be a wily adversary.

Then leave your female alone, Sian. Refuse the godsdamned bait.

"You can make the dimension as large as you want," Melanthe said. "Add territory between us. Keep your own lands as they are, but expand ours."

He could. His magic in hell was limited only by the level of his life force. But the process would temporarily deplete him, and he needed his strength for the Møriør.

"Time's a-wasting," Melanthe said. "If your mate dies, so does your chance for offspring."

Though Sian fucked—irregularly since his transformation—he had never spilled seed. He never would unless he claimed his mate. Just once was all he needed to rid himself of his demon seal. He could then have offspring with a different female, one he chose for himself, instead of fate's insane match for him.

A loud boom sounded behind the Sorceri. He narrowed his eyes as fireworks lit the sky in the distance; beneath them he spied a fine castle. "What land are you in?" He'd always believed he would find Kari in *Gaia*—Earth and all its connected dimensions.

With a snicker, Sabine said, "We're in the Magic Kingdom."

Sian had been to thousands of realms, but he didn't know that one. "Is she a royal in this life?"

"Hardly," Melanthe said. "In fact, she appears to be a nine-to-fiver."

"A what?"

"You're running out of time, demon," Sabine said with an edge to her tone. "Make the deal, or we'll send you her corpse so you can bury her."

Sian bared his fangs, his demon instincts erupting like the countless volcanoes of his lands. He'd been unable to save Kari before—but now Sian had power.

He could preserve her life in order to punish her. If Nïx wanted to play, he could outwit the Valkyrie, out-*trick* her. He was the devil's son; trickery was in his blood.

"Our time is valuable." Melanthe began opening another portal. "A shame we couldn't do business."

Sabine laughed. "Two portals at once? Bravo, sister." They steered Kari toward the new rift.

"Stop." Claws gone sharp, he told the Sorceri, "In exchange for her, I vow to the Lore that I will give you your lands and a promise never to attack them." The presence of a sovereign kingdom in his dimension would rankle! "Now retract your commands and send her through the portal."

"Very well." Melanthe turned to Kari. "Wakey wakey."

The fey's eyes blinked open—they were both amber this time—but she was slow to shake off the sorcery. "Did I fall asleep?"

Gods, her dulcet voice was the same. Her first words to him rang through his memories: *"I am Princess Karinna, and I shall be your guide to Sylvan. Are all demons so handsome?"* She'd smiled at him, her dual-colored eyes sparkling. His heart had thundered, and he'd cringed to feel his horns straightening uncontrollably. . . .

"What of the other command, sorceress?"

"Ah, yes. Shed all of my orders," Melanthe told her captive. Laughing, she told Sian, "Have fun"—the two Sorceri shoved Kari into Pandemonia—"with your beauty, *beast*."

"Foul fucking witches!" he yelled, but they'd already escaped through the other portal.

When Kari stumbled, still seeming drugged, Sian snatched her against him. He would deal with those Sorceri later. For now, he savored this moment, his glyphs blazing from his sense of triumph.

I have Kari in my home. I own *her, bought and soon to be paid for. After lifetimes of waiting, she is mine.*

He wrapped his wings around her and nearly groaned from the feel of her cheek against his chest.

SIX

Recognition came slowly to Lila. She was tucked against the body of some kind of creature. Hadn't the Sorceri sisters threatened her? *My mind's so foggy.*

Warmth cocooned her, and she felt . . . safe. She hadn't felt this way since she'd first learned an archer loved to hunt her kind.

She forced open her eyes and drew her head back. An instant passed before she realized she was gazing at skin. Lots of bloodred skin with glyphs that resembled illuminated raised scars. They coiled in ancient-looking patterns on the chest of some towering creature.

The being's scent was like fire—and male.

Leather straps crisscrossed his mighty chest. Both of his nipples were pierced with thin metal bars. She glanced over her shoulder. By the light of those glyphs, she saw the wings that had wrapped around her.

Wings???

They retracted with a swooping sound. She faced forward and tilted her head up and up. . . . Her mind turned over.

A monster.

It was more than seven feet tall with jutting horns. A band of black radiated out from fathomless onyx eyes, down its cheeks and above its heavy brow.

She swallowed thickly. "Demon?" This could *not* be Abyssian Infernas.

Its features were rough and sneering. *"Demon."*

When those wings closed around her once more, she loosed a scream that had been building for all her life.

Sian traced his shrieking captive to one of the seven great towers of Graven. Once an amusement hall for hell's orgies, the decrepit top floor in this tower would make an ideal prison.

Forty chambers surrounded a central court and a broken fountain, yet no doors led into the castle.

There were zero comforts, just crumbling stone, thick cobwebs from poisonous blood-meal spiders, and toxic fire vines.

Those red vines forked out across the walls and covered the exterior of the tower as well. If Kari tried to climb down from this height, she'd be in for a nasty surprise.

The only light came from lava oozing down neighboring volcanoes. Shadows slithered along in constant motion.

She squirmed against him. He'd been a teen when he'd seen her last, but now he responded as an adult demon male, his body tensing.

Fighting harder, she twisted in his arms. He didn't want to hurt her too badly—yet—so he released her, dropping her without care as he teleported to the other side of the courtyard.

She bounced on the stone floor, dust and ash rising to blend with the mud covering her. Sian was tempted to toss her in a bath.

Coughing, she sprang to her feet, then sprinted from him. With her fey speed, she was a blur as she charged from one room to the next.

Each one had celebrated a different sexual facet. If she could read the lurid Demonish inscriptions covering most of the walls, she'd probably expire. He crossed his arms, waiting for her to discover the lack of exits.

She finally slowed, stopping across the courtyard from him. "Where have you taken me?" She breathed wisps of airborne ash, coughing.

"To hell. I am Abyssian Infernas, the king of it. Do you remember me?"

"*You* are . . ." She shook her head. "I've never met you before, but I've heard of you. You're the oldest demon alive, and one of the Møriør."

She truly had no memory of him? "This tower is your prison and will be for the rest of your immortal life."

"Why would you keep me captive?" She coughed again, her eyes watering. "What have I done to be locked up in hell?"

"You will pay for wrongs done to me in your past life. And for wrongs you and Nïx no doubt have planned."

"Whoa, whoa, whoa. Past life? You clearly have the wrong woman. I'm not a reincarnate, and I don't know anyone named Nïx."

He traced to her, clamping her slim arm in his fist. "And yet here you are." He teleported her to the tower balcony, a spacious stone terrace. At the run-down railing, he gestured to the legions teeming below.

Freed from their punishments, demons of all species had filed in from Slaughter Gorge for the Vrekener battle, one that would never be. But he could promise them another. . . . "If you try to escape my castle, my legions will catch you, and they will not oblige you with a death. They'll keep you alive for their use."

The tips of her pointed ears flattened against her head.

"If you wish to survive here, you will obey my every command. Any hesitation to heed an order will be considered a refusal. Any command only half obeyed will be considered a refusal. Any lie will be considered a refusal. Do you understand me?"

Her gaze narrowed. Instead of shrinking from him, she looked like she'd briefly lost her footing, but had managed to right herself. "You have no right to take away my freedom and threaten me, Møriør!"

"Might makes right. Now, answer me: Do you understand my commands?"

"I understand them."

He relaxed a fraction, until she added, "And I reject them."

SEVEN

A jot *demonic, Nïx?*

Lila watched the rage building in the king's expression as one might watch a roller coaster plummeting off a track.

His pronounced jaw clenched, and his wings unfolded in an ominous display. They must be fifteen feet wide! Their shape was jagged, like a bat's.

How could this animal be Abyssian? He was supposed to be an insanely hot king. *Insane* was the only descriptor that applied to this demon.

Females fought over *him*?

He'd said nothing about Lila being his mate. If he found out for certain she was a spy, he'd kill her.

And why was he harping on about a past life? Surely Nïx would have told Lila if—

Or not. Never trust a Valkyrie. *Lesson learned, bitch.*

"Any female with sense would show respect to her new master!" All the muscles in his long, lean body tensed. "Do not test me—I have eons of wrath at the ready."

While she had a lifetime of entwined fear and fury toward the Møriør.

All the things she'd given up . . . all the nightmares . . . all the times she'd looked over her shoulder in terror . . .

Now this demon was throwing some vague, baseless accusation at her? Wrongs done *in a past life*? "What specific crimes are you accusing me of?"

His monstrous face was difficult to read, but he seemed confounded that she wasn't cowering. Then his fists clenched, his arm muscles like whipcords. "Treachery against the hell demonarchy."

"That's all you'll tell me?"

"If you want to know more, then *remember*." His voice was deep, his Demonish accent thick. "You'll have plenty of time to search your memory."

Was she a reincarnate? There'd been that rumor. . . . "Why not just kill me?"

"You deserve an unending life in hell full of constant torments. But if your torture ceases to amuse me, I will behead you. You'll never know when I might appear as your reaper." He reached down to the ax sheathed at his side and ran his revolting black claws over the blade.

This male wasn't exactly keen to *protect and care for* her.

She'd signed on to coax secrets from a hot demon heartbreaker. A get-cozy job. Instead, Lila was in a bid for survival, with an upside of *damnation*.

Nïx had burned her. But why?

Had Saetth known?

Lila didn't react well to being set up. She had anticipated living in Sylvan, not dying in hell.

All bets are off, Valkyrie. If Nïx wanted her inside this castle, then Lila refused to remain here. *I'll escape this dump.*

One of her six online degrees was in structural engineering, and she had a wicked imagination. No prison could hold her. Certainly not with a stupid brute like this demon as jailor.

She crossed her arms over her chest and surveyed her surroundings. She gave her escape a week. Tops.

For now, she told Abyssian, "This heap is your 'castle'? Why am I not surprised?"

"You dare to provoke me?" His wings flared again.

She'd been left at the mercy of the Møriør. *Burned.* "After the day I've had, I *do* dare."

He lunged forward, gripping her upper arm to teleport her again.

She swayed on her feet, getting her bearings as her new bout of dizziness faded. He'd taken her to some kind of darkened cavern. Channels of lava surrounded a pool of steaming water. "This hovel is *exactly* where I'd expect you to live."

Those markings on his chest glowed brighter. "Clean the filth from your body."

"There is no way in this hell I'll bathe in front of you."

"Then you just refused my order? You'll learn who commands you."

"You can take your fucking *commands* and shove them up your demonic—"

He lifted her and tossed her into the water.

Prick! She struggled toward the surface, but the hem of her heavy dress caught on something. She kicked, then harder a second time . . . couldn't get free! She panicked, attacking the zipper, but it stuck.

The demon appeared beside her in the water, ripping the dress away and shoving her to the surface.

She sucked in lungfuls of air. "You asshole! You could've killed me." She'd escaped one danger, but now she had a new one: she wore only a strapless bra and boy-short panties, and the demon's huge hands circled her waist. "Let me go. *Now.*"

He traced them to a shallower spot, then released her.

When she stood, his avid gaze dipped to her breasts, their shape outlined in her bra. She ducked down and submerged herself to her neck.

He shook his head hard and flared his wings again, but he'd seemed to put his fury on hold. Could he feel bad about almost killing her? If she was his mate—and that was a big *if* right now—he should.

With a wave of his hand, he conjured a cloth from thin air. The demon possessed magics too? *Not in the godsdamned dossier, Nïx!*

He grabbed Lila's nape and brought the cloth to her face. "Look at me," he grated.

She raised her chin, but only to glare. While some of his rage was fading, her temper still simmered. "Do you get off on throwing me around like a doll?"

"Shut up." The beast brushed the cloth over one of her cheekbones, stunning her to silence.

Had she gone into shock? Maybe she was dreaming all this. She could be lying unconscious in a retention pond in the Magic Kingdom.

He lightly pinched her chin to start on the other side of her face, his brows drawn with concentration. He cleaned the tips of her ears, which made them twitch. He even scooped water over her head to rinse her hair.

She watched drops stream down his marked torso, the sight hypnotic. *Yes, I'm still in shock.* "Are you finished?" she demanded of the Møriør monster.

"Why were you so dirty?" Tending to her like this seemed to extinguish what remained of the demon's anger. His gaze roamed over her face, lingering on each of her features.

The way he looked at her . . . maybe she *was* his mate. Maybe that part was true. "Because your lackeys made me bust my ass in the mud."

"You speak like a human. Did you live among them in the Magic Kingdom?"

Did he think the theme park was a *real* kingdom? What had those Sorceri told him? "Why should I tell you anything about myself?"

As she spoke the cloth descended to her neck, then lower, his heavy-lidded eyes following the path.

She jerked away. "You've got to be kidding! Are you going to try to rape me now?" A male of his size would kill her.

"Hardly." He dragged his gaze back to hers, his anger rising once more. "Never forget—*I* am not the villain here."

"But I am? Because of my alleged past-life crimes? Do you *hear* how screwed-up that sounds?" She met his onyx eyes. "Understand me, demon: if you release me now, I might be persuaded to leave this pathetic excuse for a castle standing. If not, I'll bring it down around your ears."

EIGHT

Why was she *not* afraid of Sian? In his new form, he terrified most beings. No one had ever naysaid him.

And he'd been fully demonic, bellowing at her as his horns had straightened from lust and anger.

Even the powerful Melanthe had flinched at his appearance. Sian's mate was *threatening* him. "Are you deranged in this life? You must be." Then how would he control her? She'd already refused an order, calling his bluff on his promise to kill her.

And he would never thrash a female, regardless of how much she deserved it. His gut had clenched just to see her struggling in the water, even though an immortal couldn't drown to death.

"I'm not deranged. I'm pissed off to be treated this way." Her language might be coarse, but her imperious tone still sounded like a princess's. With her chin raised, she looked like one too.

Her outrage sat ill with him. There was a possibility—however minuscule—that she had no idea about any of this. Nïx might be using her as an unwitting pawn.

No matter. He'd still punish Kari for the past.

He grabbed her arm to teleport her again. They arrived back in the tower, dripping water. He released his grip on her—only to catch her when her legs buckled.

"Damn it, stop tracing me, demon!"

He stepped away, letting her drop to her knees. He shook his hair out and sluiced water from his skin.

She stayed down, pressing the back of her hand against her mouth to stifle her coughs.

At the sight of his mate in naught but tiny scraps of pink silk, he shuffled his feet apart to keep himself standing.

Though Kari had teased him in the past, allowing him a sliver of hope that she would be his, she'd never offered him a glimpse of her body.

His eyes drank her in, blood pooling in his groin. She was a touch slimmer than she'd been before, but still entrancing.

Her bra molded to her breasts and nipples, highlighting more than concealing. His fists opened and closed, the urge to knead her nigh overwhelming him. Cock gone hard as stone, he raked his gaze down her torso, then lower.

Gods almighty. The thin material of her panties clung to her, giving him maddening hints of what her sex would look like. His horns straightened as he imagined tonguing his mate, tasting her orgasm at last. . . .

He took a step back to see her from behind. Her panties had ridden up to reveal the taut cleft of her ass. He barely stifled a growl.

"Enjoying the view of my ass, demon?" She scrambled to stand.

He had to clear his throat before he could speak. "It's adequate."

"Then you'll have no trouble tearing your gaze away."

He faced her, daring her to say something about his swollen shaft, but she refused to look at him. "When were you born, female?" If he'd found her mere months ago, he would've still possessed his old looks, would've been a physical match for such a beauty.

She didn't seem to hear him—or she was ignoring him. She backed up to lean against a wall, only to scream and stumble forward. Tears welling, she glanced wildly behind her. She'd brushed against one of the fire vines. The contact had left a burn on her skin, as if it'd been a flame.

"Those are fire vines. They cover the exterior of the tower as well, in case you're stupid enough to attempt climbing down."

Her fists balled, as if she were willing back her tears.

"I'm told the pain is intense, even for an immortal. You'll sicken from that poison over the night."

Misery radiated off her. Despite his hatred, he still struggled against his primal need to care for his mate.

So he recalled some of the last words Kari had ever spoken to him. As blood had streamed down his face, she'd said, "You almost look like a person now."

Rage seethed. *Punish her.* His gaze darted. Perhaps she'd retained phobias from her previous life. "Do you still have a deathly fear of spiders?" Her shudder told him *yes.*

Ah, a tool to use against her. He waved a hand, conjuring a spinning wheel and a chair. "Harvest all the cobwebs in this tower and spin them into thread before dawn."

She glanced from the wheel to him and back. "Are you joking? I don't know how to spin."

Using magic, he dragged down a matted wad of webbing from a doorway. As if an invisible person manned the wheel, the pedal began to move, the wheel to turn. Bits of the thick web attached to a starter length of thread. "Finish all of the webs before sunrise, or their inhabitants will return to wrap you in silk. Blood-meal spiders are quite large—and poisonous."

Her face paled even more. "I'll jump." Her coughing started up again.

"If you want to meet my legions, all you have to do is ask." Before he traced away, he said, "Take care not to prick your finger on the spindle."

When he returned to the throne room, Uthyr awaited him.

—That could have gone better.— With his acute senses, the dragon would've heard everything. He probably knew as much of the castle's intrigues as Sian did. *—You believe she's working for Nïx?—*

"Yes, wittingly or not." Pacing in front of his marble throne, he said, "My mate satisfies me not at all! She is senseless." Kari had been one of the most intelligent beings he'd ever known. He'd expected the same of her in this life.

What a disappointment.

—Or she is bold. Demon, your mind is suffering from your change, and your thoughts are in chaos. If you mistreat her, she will come to hate you. Have you not even considered a fresh start with her? Forgiveness?—

"I'll forgive my mate as soon as you shift back to a man." Why the dragon refused to return to his humanoid form baffled Sian.

—It will not and cannot happen.—

"Precisely. I want revenge only. She deserves nothing more."

—Immortals so love their vengeance.— Uthyr sighed, a flame gusting from his lips, scorching another wall. *—But not often at the expense of matehood.—*

Sian gave a bitter laugh. "Don't you understand, dragon? Matehood is an impossibility." He had once asked Rune, his closest friend, what having a mate was like. Rune had answered, "I get more happiness in one second of loving Josie than I did in seven thousand years of life without her."

Sian had accepted he would never experience such satisfaction. At times he imagined that some other trickster demon had stolen into his body to replace Sian's heart with a cold lava rock. What had once been fiery and alive was now crumbling and black.

"Even if I didn't despise my female—even if she isn't Nïx's bait for my downfall at best and a spy at worst—do you really believe a fey that exquisite could accept me in this form?" When he'd signaled his interest, she'd sneered, *You've got to be kidding.* "Or survive in hell? Her kind don't belong in Pandemonia." The ash had made her cough after mere minutes here. "And how do you predict she'll feel about me when I wage war on the fey?"

Sian had hungered for vengeance against Sylvan for ages, but Orion had asked him to wait till this Accession. Finally, that time had come. "I might as well get some sport out of my mate." He'd made sure she could never finish spinning. Yes, he loved trickery and games, but in the end the jest would always be on him—he would never know a mate's bond.

He traced to the terrace railing to survey his legions.

Uthyr joined him. Though each of the great dragon's steps shook the terrace, he could move with a catlike grace when he wanted to, a boon whenever he used his other talent: chameleon cloaking to the point of invisibility. *—I can give you counsel, friend, but I need to know more about your past. What made you hate her?—*

Sian didn't answer. Couldn't. Not yet.

—Why would you even have met her so long ago? Fey and demons didn't run in the same circles.—

Back then, the fey had still been known as elves, and Sian's twin, Goürlav, had just inherited the crown of Pandemonia. "An explorer discovered a portal between our kingdoms, but wariness rose on both sides, the species having nothing in common. So the king of Sylvan agreed to foster me in his realm for a season."

A spell had enabled Sian to speak Elvish. For security reasons, it had also bound his abilities to trace and mind-read.

No spell in existence could have helped Sian understand the elves' stifled emotions, calculating ways, and superior airs. Many considered the demons little better than beasts.

Yet Goürlav had ordered him to go, wielding his power over his twin for the first time, infuriating Sian. . . .

"Why can we not simply attack these uncanny newcomers?"

"Your thoughts are forever turned to conflict." Goürlav exhaled. "We can always *go to war with them. Yet a chance for peace is fleeting. I should at least try*

for it before the hell-change robs me of reason." He clamped Sian's shoulder. "If this works, if you help *me make this work, we could all know prosperity as never before. Our realms need each other's resources; with trade, we could better the lives of all elven- and demonkind. . . ."*

Sian had resisted right up until he'd scented Kari on the other side.

Uthyr said, *—At least tell me, demon: Why make her spin?—*

"Because she can never complete her task, and it will please me to watch her fail."

The dragon winced, his scales rippling. *—Sometimes you forget there's a difference between trickery and cruelty.—*

"That female taught me much about cruelty." She'd used his feelings for her to manipulate him, digging for demon weaknesses without a qualm—because she'd seen him as a lesser being. Her bigoted parents had taught her that *all* beings were vastly inferior to the elves.

Sian recalled when Kari had asked if demons formed bond pairs. He'd figured she would need to know all of the details about demon matehood—graphic though they were. . . .

"A male can sense a female is his. Yet the only way to be absolutely certain is through intercourse." Pulling on his collar, he said, "A demon cannot spill seed for the first time with any but his fated female. Some males bed many with this hope. It's called attempting*."*

"How convenient," she sniffed. "And primitive."

Though the elves formed bond pairs, no physical limitations constrained them; they could marry where they pleased. With so much control over their emotions, they could repress any instinctive drives.

He'd found them to be like unfeeling shells. But Kari was different.

She asked, "And if attempting is successful, do demons wed?"

"Only royals. But marriage is just a formality. If a male finds his mate, he will mark her neck. That is a lifelong pledge."

"Mark?" Realization flashed in her dual-colored eyes. "A demon would . . .

bite *a female?" She was appalled. "Like those disgusting vampires? How barbaric!"*

"Have you ever even spoken to a vampire, Kari?"

She blinked in confusion. "Talk to a vampire? Why would I bother?"

He'd told himself that he would introduce her to other species, expanding her views—that once she was separated from her parents, she could shed their narrow-mindedness. He hadn't realized how deeply ingrained her beliefs had been.

Kari's reincarnation was fey once more, so he had little doubt she'd been raised the same way.

And her godsdamned eyes matched.

All the same flaws—yet none of the charms.

NINE

It might take me more than a week to crack this prison.

Other than stone, Lila hadn't found anything she could use to attack her captor—no materials to create a projectile, or a sneak blade, or a trap.

Nor could she find a single door leading into the castle. That large archway to the terrace was the tower's only opening.

Taking care to avoid those excruciating fire vines, she crossed to the railing once more. She gazed out from what must be a league in the air and surveyed hell, disbelieving she was here.

The landscape boggled her mind. The night sky was black and choked with ash. In the distance, a gigantic volcano spewed lava. A river of it coursed through the valley below. Was that the legendary Styx?

The air reeked of misery, ruin, and death. Like a horror theme park on steroids.

A dense wave of fire vines did in fact crisscross the tower's exterior. She'd have no chance of avoiding them if she climbed down.

Even if she could reach the ground, the "legions" below would seize her. There must be thousands of demons gathered. If she somehow outran them, she'd be hemmed in by that lava river. The heat didn't seem to bother all those shirtless warriors, but she would be burned alive.

Lava *rapids*? She truly was in hell.

Nïx, you bitch. Why would she have betrayed Lila? Only Saetth had incentive.

Lila was the next in line for the throne, and her parents hadn't been the only ones grumbling about his inability to protect the royal house from the Møriør. Lila's cousins might mount a coup, especially now that he'd lost the sword.

But she couldn't believe he'd send her to hell just to be rid of her. If he'd felt threatened, he would simply keep her exiled or kill her.

The Valkyrie must have duped him as well.

Lila shivered in her damp underwear. Night grew chilly in hell? Her captor hadn't provided blankets or dry clothes. No food. Only orders.

For all her bluster, Lila was about to have . . . doubts.

What "wrongs" did the demon think she'd committed? If Abyssian came in the night as her reaper, would he behead her the way Saetth had her parents? One clean swipe? Maybe she'd go to sleep and never wake up.

Lila would fight to get free, but right now she needed to focus on her immediate task. She *did* fear spiders—didn't most people?—but more than that she feared a challenge stumping her. It'd be a first.

Her life motto was *FITFO*. Because as far as a problem went, she always figured it the fuck out.

She gazed up at the sky, trying to determine how long till sunrise. The lengths of days and nights varied from world to world, and she'd read that hell's stretched longer than most. But if dawn arrived sooner than she expected—

A gust of ash-laden wind rushed over her. As she hurried inside, she went into another coughing fit, brushing against a fire vine. *Damn it!*

Eyes watering, she crossed to the wheel that he'd conjured with a wave of his hand. Having been away from the Lore for so long, she wasn't used to *real* displays of magic.

Was spinning a cobweb even possible? It sounded so fairy tale–esque. But then, she *was* a fairy princess.

She sat and replayed the earlier demonstration. Tamping the floor pedal would make the wheel spin. A measure of thread had already been started. Apparently, she was to attach sections of thick cobweb to the end of that length, pulling it straight as the wheel dragged it in.

She hesitated to touch the pile of cobwebs. But she had to, else meet the web's spinners.

When she reached for the webbing, it stuck to her fingers. "Ugh!" With clumsy movements, she began to work, coughing all the while.

A couple of false starts slowed her down, but she learned from her mistakes and found a rhythm. The tensile thread was surprisingly strong.

Her monotonous task gave her too much time to think. Sooner or later the demon would discover her real identity, and without warm and fuzzy feelings toward his mate, he'd turn her over to the Møriør archer for assassination—if Abyssian didn't do it himself.

Rumor held that Rune Darklight, A.K.A. Rune the Baneblood, had once been a slave in the broiling fens of Sylvan, horribly abused by the ruler during his time: Queen Magh, who was both Saetth's mother and an ancestress of Lila.

Rune had sworn to stamp out Magh's entire line. Which meant Lila as well. If she didn't escape this place before she was found out . . .

I now have a deadline, emphasis on dead.

She recalled the grueling tension at court whenever the archer assassinated another royal. With each execution, the noose tightened, the odds of survival growing slimmer. For months after, everyone would appear haunted and hollow-eyed.

She'd been too young to grasp all the ramifications, but she'd known one thing for certain: *The bogeyman is real. . . .*

In her lifetime, Rune had murdered four of her cousins, all of them caught outside the fortified safety of Sylvan Castle, all of them despicable.

But I'm *not.*

The tips of her pointed ears began to twitch. Foot paused on the pedal, she rubbed the back of her neck and gazed around the dim area.

She heard the scurrying of . . . *things* in every dark place, but she never caught sight of them. Probably for the best.

Yet she was certain she was being watched.

TEN

Reclining on the bed in his lavish chambers, Sian held a looking-glass—not to see his own reflection, never his own—but to spy on Kari. In hell, he could use mirrors to view any scene in the present.

He'd observed her as she'd first investigated her surroundings. She'd appeared to be freezing in her flimsy lingerie.

And Sian cared not at all.

She'd crossed to the balcony and surveyed his lands, her eyes growing stark at the sight.

He didn't care.

Ashy wind had gusted into the tower; as she coughed, she'd brushed up against another fire vine.

But he could not care less.

When she'd sat at the wheel, she'd looked shell-shocked. *Good.*

Though his instincts screamed at him to protect her, warm her, clothe and feed her, he refused. He'd once followed his instincts with her, and look where that had left him.

With the help of his hell-change aggression, he buried those impulses deep, deeper—until a filter seemed to cover his gaze, red from his hatred.

Crimson haze in place, he didn't even see her as his mate. She was simply a desirable prisoner.

Once she'd spun all of the webbing he'd provided, she rose and warily approached another large cobweb. *Dark gods, that body.* Her curves were graceful, her form proportionately flawless.

Her long, light-brown hair had dried into loose, shining curls. The dainty points of her ears poked out through the heavy fall of those tresses.

He still couldn't believe Kari was here in his keeping. Under his control. He wondered yet again if he was dreaming.

Considering Nïx's involvement, he'd likely pay for this pleasure.

His prisoner reached for the webbing. When it stuck to her hands and wrapped around her arms, she gave a cry, and the tips of her ears flattened against her head.

He'd once been fascinated by her ears, had never seen anything like them. The tips had twitched whenever she'd been unsettled and had flattened on the few occasions she'd been anxious—such as when he'd been about to kiss her for the first and only time.

That kiss. Her sweet lips had slain him, and he was still trying to recover.

Kari returned to her wheel and resumed spinning, her movements hypnotic. As he stared, his thoughts spun as well, tumbling back millennia. . . .

Sian swept Kari around the ballroom during yet another tedious function. He had to fight not to clasp her close to his body.

Could her hands be any softer? Her scent any more alluring?

He might have questioned why a large hell demon like himself would be paired with such an airily delicate mate—if her body didn't heat his blood like nothing else.

Since he'd laid eyes on Kari, his adolescent desires had only ratcheted up. He'd experienced the most powerful culmination of his life—with her stolen silk shift around his member.

Yet he craved her not only for physical reasons. His female's mind was a mystery greater than any of the ones in the magical realm of hell.

If only he could read her thoughts! Right now, her mind seemed a million leagues away. She danced with him, but she wasn't looking *at him.*

"What are you contemplating, Kari?" he asked, knowing she'd never tell him. He hated it when her gaze grew distant. Though every one of his thoughts revolved around her, she lived in a world kept separate from him.

"This and that," she murmured.

She was leading him to insanity! At times she encouraged him to woo her, only to turn around and snicker at him behind her fan with her toadying friends.

But whenever he doubted her feelings, she would tease him or allow him some new liberty, such as pressing a kiss to her wrist or holding her closer while dancing.

"Will you confide your musings to me, princess?"

Finally she gazed up at him. "You're soon to leave us."

Not without you. *If he could teleport in this realm, he would be tempted to steal her. "Does the idea of us parting aggrieve you whatsoever?"*

She shrugged.

Shrugged! He inhaled for calm. Sian had only so long before he was dispatched back to hell—and before she was wed. The king of the Draiksulian elves pursued her hand ardently.

Sian scowled in the male's direction. The king was tall and fair-haired, an ideal elven specimen. Sometimes Kari gazed at him as if she were infatuated.

Sian scarcely prevented himself from baring his fangs at the male. But Kari grew appalled at his every loss of control, deeming these displays "savagery." She'd once told him, "You're as unthinking as a red-eyed vampire."

"Demon, your grip."

His hands had tightened on her. Easy, Sian. *She was a fragile elf, and still vulnerable to harm. "Pardon me."*

He'd been racking his mind for a way to win her affections. He'd never told her she was his mate—she'd taken his explanation of demon matehood . . . poorly—but perhaps 'twas time to confess all?

Or mayhap he should try seduction? As a handsome prince of hell, he had scant experience coaxing a female to bed—he'd always been plagued with females pursuing him*—but how difficult could it be?*

Kari would become fully immortal soon and must be needing a male's touch to see her through this time of transition. After he claimed her and they shared that pleasure, she would never doubt they were fated to be together.

He told her, "I myself would be deeply aggrieved if we were parted. Which is why you're coming with me to Pandemonia."

She sighed. "Oh, am I?"

He drew her closer. "You will be mine, Kari. For all time. I will never be separated from you."

She rolled her eyes. "You are infatuated with me, young demon. It will pass once you return home and surround yourself with fawning demonesses."

"What I feel for you is no mere infatuation."

With a challenge in her gaze, she demanded, "What aside from my looks draws you?"

"You are the cleverest female—nay, the cleverest being *I have ever known. You can't be bothered to read or study, but you make fools of all the elven courtiers who live by their considerable wits. You are merry whenever you allow yourself to let down your guard with me." She loved hearing about Pandemonian legends of old, would grow relaxed as he spun tales. "And you are fiercely protective of those you love." Her snobbish family. "If I could but earn that fierce love for myself."*

Casting him a soft look that made his heart punch his chest, she murmured, "You are the first male ever to answer that question adequately." Yet then she tensed once more, and her tone turned flippant. "Clearly we are meant to be together."

Was she jesting? "Why do you play games with me, little female?"

"I don't know what you're talking about."

"You burn hot and cold."

He thought he spied a flicker of something like . . . scheming in her dual-colored eyes. Gone so quickly. "I burn hot, my darling, then realize you do not return the tender regard I feel for you."

"I am mad for you!"

Her gaze darted at his outburst. Dancers nearby glared at him.

He glanced over her shoulder. Her parents looked on with distaste, as usual.

In a lower tone, he asked, "Can you truly not know of my feelings?" He hadn't bothered hiding them. He'd sneaked into her room to leave her gifts, and he'd danced with her at all of these ridiculous balls she adored. He'd even written bloody poems to her!

"Then why do you not trust me?" She sounded sad. "You tell me tales of old about Pandemonia, but never anything about your kind. You want to take me to your dimension, but how can I go there to be with you when you refuse to reveal details about it?" She gazed away, tears welling.

He had not thought of these things! Of course she would be nervous about living in a new world.

Out of loyalty to his kind, he'd withheld information. But if he could win this female, she would become *his kind.*

The dance ended. "I will tell you anything you want to know, Kari." He curled his finger under her chin, lifting her face. "Anything at all." Yes, Sian had been racking his mind for a way to win her affections; he decided on seduction. "For a kiss."

Her eyes widened. "You are overbold, demon."

"Steal away with me, and give me a single kiss."

She worried her bottom lip, then whispered, "When the clock tower strikes three, meet me beside the lake."

Anticipation made him nigh light-headed. Somehow he forced himself to release her. "With pleasure."

Millennia later, Sian watched her spinning, seeming lost in thought herself.

He conjured her silk shift, bringing it to his face. As he inhaled her scent, his member shot hard as stone.

He considered calling for one of his royal concubines, but he couldn't drag his gaze from the mirror.

Over all these long ages, he'd known countless females, purging himself of his need for his mate. But he had always wondered what his fated female would look like unclothed, trembling beneath him—

She tugged up her bra again, which pulled the material taut over her pert breasts and stiffened nipples.

He growled in response. How many times had he imagined what shade those peaks would be? And if she'd moan to have them sucked?

How many times had he come, teeth gritted with frustration because he was squeezing his cock instead of kneading those mounds of creamy flesh?

Frustration now; frustration then. Wondering if he'd ever be free of it, he recalled their meeting by the lake. . . .

Arriving an hour early, he'd paced the water's edge as he awaited her.

The little witch had danced the rest of the ball with that king. As the pair had glided over the dancefloor, everyone murmured about how perfect they looked together. Kari had gazed up at the male with a besotted expression.

Sian's fists had clenched until he'd realized her game. She was meeting him, *which meant she wanted* him, *which meant she was only trying to make her demon jealous.*

It was working!

He stilled when he scented her approaching down the woodland path to the water.

She wore a dark cloak, drawing back the hood as she neared. "I cannot believe I agreed to meet you."

Flashing a cocky grin, he wasted no time closing in on her. "Perhaps I am not the only one keen for a kiss."

She took a step back. "I want you to tell me of your kind, and then *I shall kiss you."*

He stalked closer, backing her up against a tree. "A kiss should always come first." His shaft was already hardening.

She craned her head up. "What are you doing, Abyssian? Stop being silly." With her spellbinding eyes locked on his mouth, she wetted her full lips.

Her gaze rose to his horns. Smooth and black, they curved back from his temples. He was proud of them. A demon's horns were used for fighting—but they also brought sexual pleasure. She would learn to love them, to caress the sensitive lengths for him.

When they straightened even more as she stared, her ears flattened against her head. Anxious? Did she find his most demonic feature distasteful?

No, she couldn't. Fate would never have paired them. He cupped her face. "Princess, you are my mate."

Sian unlaced his pants and freed his cock. In his hell-change, the flesh had become pierced as if he were a demon of old—yet another part of himself rendered unfamiliar.

He dismissed the idea of a concubine, wanting nothing to distract him from this memory, one he'd replayed infinite times. With his mate near, his recollection was even more vivid. . . .

"Yours? You do not mean . . ."

"You are the only one I will love, the only one who can rid me of my demon seal, so I can give you younglings." He grasped her arms, drawing her closer. Her trembling body yielded to his so sweetly, her soft breasts pressing against him. "Kari," he rasped. "I plead: let me take your lips, as I've dreamed about."

Those lips parted in surprise.

Sian desired her no less now than he did then: desperately. He wrapped her shift around his member, and all of a sudden he was sixteen again, his body stricken with lust for her. Would this craving never end?

His breaths were ragged. Moisture beaded the head of his cock, the closest he'd ever gotten to producing seed. *Oh, yes, she is mine.*

Though he wasn't physiologically able to ejaculate, he knew he was about to orgasm harder than he had since his time in Sylvan, when he would come with her scent fresh in his mind. . . .

Savoring the feel of her against him, he said, "Fate gave you to me." As he gazed down at her heartbreakingly lovely face, his chest tightened. He felt connected *to her—as if he'd been awaiting her from his first breath. Nothing else mattered but her. "I know you want me too." He leaned down, and his mouth covered hers.*

She parted her lips for him! When their tongues touched, pinpoints of light exploded behind his lids. Her kiss was like a lightning strike combined with a wave crashing over him.

Electrifying, sending him off balance.

Or righting *his balance for the very first time.*

He groaned with bliss. This is the way of it. Of matehood. *He finally understood.*

Sian didn't cherish her because he desired her; he desired her because he cherished her.

When he deepened their soul-shattering kiss, she gasped against his lips. Her innocent surprise would have stolen his heart had he not already given it to her.

At the memory, Sian began to culminate. His heels dug into the mattress, his fist flying up and down his shaft. His wings contracted, then flared.

His lungs emptied on a bellow, so loud his tower rocked. The mirror cracked. Volcanoes all over his lands erupted with each pulse of his cock as the pleasure went on and on. . . .

With a last shudder of his wings, he sprawled across the bed, catching his breath. Tension melted from him. He felt like he floated, like he'd been drugged.

He'd just come harder than he had as an adult male.

Now that his lusts had been slaked, his hatred returned. Their one kiss had lasted only a brief time because she'd drawn back to tell him,

"The Draiksulian king trusts me; perhaps I should save my kisses for him."

Sian hadn't been able to reveal information to her fast enough. He must have given her all she'd needed to know that night; the next morning, she'd severed him from her life completely.

Treacherous bloody female!

Yet still his body floated. . . .

She was the key to his release, in more than one sense. For all of Sian's power, he was denied something so simple: spending.

Over his lifetime, he'd grown more and more obsessed with the idea. A couple of months back, on a night when Sian and Rune had shared too much demon brew, Sian had asked his friend, "What is it like to spill seed?"

After eons of waiting, Rune had recently lost his own demon seal to his mate, a phantom/vampire halfling named Josephine. "There is no describing it," Rune had said. "Before I met Josie, I had total control over myself for thousands of years, could fuck for hours on end, days even." He'd leaned in to admit, "I lasted two thrusts inside her before I exploded. Came so hard my vision blurred. It's . . . mind-altering."

Sian must know what this felt like! Snapping his fangs, he threw Kari's shift across his room.

Now that she'd returned, the intensity of all his emotions made him realize he'd been sleepwalking through his eternal life.

If he hadn't had the Møriør . . .

He redressed, then used magic to repair the mirror. He would have to deal with the gathered legions sometime today. But for now, he watched his prisoner go about her futile labor.

At the last moment, Sian *might* let her complete her task—but only so he could see how she reacted to new stimuli. . . .

ELEVEN

Lila had just finished gathering the last of the webs when the first spider crawled in from a hole in the roof.

Early. It wasn't dawn yet.

The size of a punch bowl, the arachnid had red and silver splotches across its bulbous body and long bushy legs. *Yes, demon, I* do *fear spiders.*

Seeming to focus all of its eyes on her, the spider skittered along the ceiling, then paused. *It's waiting for me to fail.*

She'd read about the mystical labors in hell; was she now immersed in one?

Keeping the new threat in sight—and inwardly screaming—she continued her chore. *Focus, Lila.* But she was even more unnerved than before because she'd heard a roar from somewhere across the castle.

Abyssian's roar. It had to have been. And for some reason, it'd sounded . . . sexual.

Despite her overstimulation, she shuddered to think of the demon as a sexual being. He was too big, too violent, and apparently he lost all control in the throes, roaring like a beast.

So much for insta-love toward his long-lost mate. While torturing

Lila, he was screwing someone else—probably some lusty, big-boned demoness with claws and ponderous breasts. Had that roar scared the female?

Or delighted her?

Lila supposed Abyssian's body as a whole wasn't *un*attractive. But she still couldn't comprehend why females would pursue him.

The subject was forgotten when another spider crawled in to join the first. Then another. And another, until a dozen had gathered. Did they plan to wrap *her* in their silk at dawn?

Focus. Time moved at a sluggish pace here. She could finish before daybreak if she kept her eye on the ball—

They began scuttling back and forth. It took her a few panicked moments to realize they were creating *new* webs. "No, no, no!" She would have to outrace them, then somehow harvest the additional webs!

The faster she spun, the faster they did—until they'd cloaked nearly every chamber entrance.

She was failing. Already, blood dripped from her fingers and sweat from her skin. Her head pounded. Each time she coughed on ash, the tower seemed to spin. That devil had told her she would sicken from the vine burns.

A hazy light grew outside. Dawn? She wasn't through! Would those creatures attack as one—

Abyssian appeared. Or two of him did. Her vision had turned double.

"You barely finished in time."

I . . . did? She glanced up. The spiders and the new cobwebs receded into the walls, only the wheel and thread remaining.

"You've earned your breakfast." He conjured a tray of food, setting it on the edge of the broken-down fountain. "To merit a respite, you'll complete another task." With a wave of his hand, he produced a broom and a mop.

Or as she liked to call them, *the beginning of my arsenal.*

"Clean each of these rooms by nightfall," he ordered. "Or the spiders will return." He vanished.

Prick! She cursed him in multiple languages.

The king intended these tools to be a part of her punishment? *Mistake, demon. I'll repurpose them to strike back in some way.*

She would finish this chore; then during her *respite*, she'd plot.

A desperate need for energy made her investigate the food. *Demon* food. The contents of one bowl were merrily swimming around. Nausea churned.

She'd have to get through the day on nothing but sheer will. Knotting her hair atop her head, she squared her shoulders, then started sweeping.

Cleaning this place appealed to her fey sense of order. Not that she'd ever tell him that.

In several rooms, she found stone bed frames, but no mattresses. Statuary of obscenely erect demons, fauns, and vampires had fallen throughout the tower. Most had lost their focal point—carved stone dicks littered the floors. She piled them up in the corners of a few chambers.

Words had been etched into the tower walls from top to bottom. Demonish.

In her quest to read ever more about this dimension, she'd taught herself the language.

No longer could she deny the obvious: a past-life history with Abyssian would explain her unusual interest in Pandemonia. More evidence that she was a reincarnate. . . .

She made out some of the archaic spellings, raising her brows as comprehension took hold. This tower had been some kind of sex den, and each room had been devoted to a particular act or position.

Though intrigued, she needed to concentrate on her task. Using her fey super speed, she cleaned until sweat drenched her body, pausing only when coughing spasms seized her. Barefooted, she couldn't avoid stepping on the fire vines. With each hour she grew weaker.

Right now, I hate that Valkyrie almost as much as Abyssian.

By the time Lila had finished with the broom, blood stained the handle from ruptured blisters. Dust and ash coated her skin and hair.

In one of the forty chambers, a grate covered the floor with a drain beneath, and a warm cascade poured through a pipe in the roof.

Water for mopping. How fortunate for her.

Lila promised herself that she would soak her sore body under that stream when finished.

For now, she rolled her head on her neck, then got back to it. The poison from the fire vines and a lack of sleep were making her delirious, but dusk was slow to come.

When she stumbled into the last room, the light of day had just begun fading. She pushed past the pain in her muscles, her feet, her bloodied palms, and toiled.

Then . . .

Done! She surveyed the drying floors with a sense of triumph. *Set to rights, check, check.*

She limped to the bathing chamber, lurching under the water. Ignoring the blisters in her palms, she scrubbed her body and hair, washing her underwear as well as she could. Then she merely soaked.

Her lids grew so heavy. Maybe she should close her eyes . . . just for a second. . . .

Her eyes shot open. She'd dozed off standing up!

Wringing her hair out, she headed to the central courtyard. She drew up short.

Somehow she'd missed a room. Thank gods, she had some spare time. Dashing for the broom and mop, she cleaned. But then she found another dirty room.

Was she going crazy? How could she not have seen those?

She squinted. No, not going crazy; this was a freaking trap. The demon king had set her up to fail.

The second time she'd been set up in as many days.

There was no way to FITFO; the logical solution and orderly completion her fey mind craved had been denied.

How dare he! He would return soon, shouting and threatening. Yet he'd never even given her the *chance* to succeed.

He was treating her like a . . . plaything.

She heard a voice booming from the valley below. She headed outside to the terrace railing and gazed down. *Speak of the devil.* Abyssian stood atop a monolith of stone, addressing his legions.

Her immortal senses were definitely coming online. Even from this distance, she could make out differences among the demons. Some had wings, others had hooves. The shape and color of their horns varied. All were shirtless and armed.

Shirtless must be a thing here.

The lava river illuminated Abyssian's features. His forbidding face and horns. That fathomless gaze. The glinting of his white fangs and teeth.

The skin glyphs across his broad chest burned just as brightly as the river. At his side, he wore that large battle-ax. His intimidating wings stretched wide. Each one had a curving claw atop the largest joint and at the bottom of the outermost one.

King Abyssian Infernas emanated pure power.

Saetth wanted her to spy? Her report: *We're about to get our asses kicked. Seek terms.*

From what she could make out, Abyssian was banishing all the demons back to "their punishments." With each moment, he became more aggressive, his voice rising and his muscles tensing. Even the landscape grew more unsettled.

Tornadoes of ash swirled in the valley. The lava river swelled, consuming more rock.

Again, the brutal king was spinning out of control. So what would happen when he returned to this tower and found her chore incomplete? Even if he had no imminent plans to kill her, he could accidentally harm her.

Unless she struck first. Maybe she'd actually been sent here to *assassinate* a Møriør.

How delicious an idea.

Her gaze darted. He would laugh if she brandished a sharpened broom handle. Stone debris abounded, but she wouldn't be able to hurl it hard enough.

She crossed to her pile of spun thread. The stuff seemed as strong as Titanian steel. She could use the lines against the demon—but how?

A spring trap? She'd studied them enough in her survival books. The mechanics were similar to a trebuchet. But how to create a trigger and a counterweight?

The answer came to her, and she grinned evilly.

Her fingers flew as she began to knot the thread, creating a net. On the other end of the line would be a snare.

She could picture the trap so clearly. The mop handle would serve as a manual trigger; a net full of obscene statuary would provide the counterweight.

Once she'd lured Abyssian into place, she would snap the handle, loosing the weight, which would then tighten the snare around his ankle.

The end result: Abyssian plummeting toward the lava river, tethered to a net filled with stone penises.

The promise of this visual gave her a shot of energy. She set up her trigger and snare, then she loaded the net with dicks until the trigger threatened to snap.

Once she'd concealed the snare with ash, she glanced from her trap down at Abyssian. This wouldn't be enough. He'd need to be too dazed/injured to trace away when her contraption yanked his demonic ass off the terrace.

So a trap *and* a weapon for herself. A sneak weapon.

Her gaze lit on the spinning wheel, on the spindle. Shame it wasn't cursed to put him to sleep—

Wait . . . Abyssian had provided her a source of poison. She could coat the spindle and stab him.

All she had to do was overcome a lifelong phobia.

With grim determination, she collected the broom. When fear threatened to undermine her, she told herself: *You can be a plaything to a hateful demon for the rest of your life or you can be a badass slayer of Møriør. Choose.*

Resolved, she headed toward one of the spider holes to begin her grisly new task. . . .

TWELVE

"My lazy fey slave," Sian grated when he appeared before her. She wasn't even trying to finish the last few rooms? He clenched his fists, that crimson haze covering his eyes.

Craning her head up, she met his gaze. "I'm not lazy—you set me up so I would fail. Tell me why you're doing this to me."

He stalked closer, having no idea what his next move would be. His rationality continued to decline; tyrannizing his subjects only worsened his condition.

She backed toward the edge of the terrace. "Can you even see me, you blank-eyed beast? Hear me?"

Why would she ask that? "You knew the consequences should you not finish your chores."

At the railing, she whispered, "But I've hurt myself, demon."

Her voice rocked him. Though he'd willed himself to be blind to her needs, he now fought back against the animal aggression taking him over.

Once he'd cleared the filter from his vision, he saw that her pale skin was abraded in several places. Burn marks from the fire vine lashed her flesh.

She wasn't regenerating. Which meant she wasn't immortal yet. Which meant she was very, very young.

Rune had mistakenly thought Josephine was in her mid-twenties. By all the gods, this female might be younger even than that.

Sian's instinct to care for his vulnerable mate raged inside him. The only demon instinct stronger than the one to mate was the one to protect.

Right now he needed to fulfill *both*.

He traced to her, coiling an arm around her back. His bare torso pressed against her scantily clad body. Flesh met flesh. Electricity sparked through every point of contact.

Even she looked surprised.

Her scent made him light-headed . . . her racing heartbeat drummed in his ears. . . .

Worry turned into crushing need, his emotions in chaos. When she gazed up at him with those lustrous eyes, he drew her even closer, his shaft straining against her.

He needed to taste her lips. Just once in this lifetime. To see if their kiss could be as intense as he remembered.

Lost in her, he barely perceived the movements of her hands. But he felt three pricks in his neck. He released her to pat his skin . . . the spindle was jutting from his throat?

"What the fuck is this?" With her speed, she'd struck him multiple times, like a little viper! Lust dwindling, he pulled out the spindle. "Stupid female! Do you really think something like this could hurt me?"

"No. Which is why I coated the point with freshly milked spider venom."

His lips parted. This amount of venom wouldn't kill an immortal, but she didn't know that! Was she *trying* to murder him?

"If you strike out at me, I'll hit you twice as hard!" With a haughty smile, she kicked a piece of wood at the railing. A handle?

A line constricted around his ankle. He met her gaze for a split second. "You bitch—"

His feet . . . yanked out from under him . . .

Some force had flung his body over the railing and off the terrace. Stunned realization: this was the first time an enemy had landed a blow against him—*in ages.*

Too astounded to react, he plunged toward the river.

The king's expression right before he went over the edge was one of the most rewarding sights Lila had ever witnessed. But her satisfaction didn't last long.

Swoop . . . swoop . . . swoop . . .

The sound of his wings reached her ears. "Oh, shit." He was flying back.

The venom hadn't slowed him down at all! Now what?

He reached the terrace's height, then hovered menacingly before her, his fangs bared. Those monstrous wings extended, slowly sculling the air to hold him aloft. His fists clenched, his onyx eyes promising pain.

Fuck! Where to run?? As she whirled around toward the interior, she heard him land behind her.

Her gaze rose to the roof overhang above the terrace. If she could reach it before he caught her, she could scrabble across the roof, then down another side of the tower, fire vines or not. She had no other option.

Pumping her arms, she sprinted across the stone. She vaulted for the overhang, pulling herself up—

His roughened hand clamped her ankle. He tugged on her leg, but she clawed to hang on, kicking at him. As she dangled, he wrapped his arms around her body, his head level with her waist. His face pressed against her midriff.

She couldn't fight from this position, could only squirm, which made his lips graze her belly. His warm breaths ghosted over her damp skin.

Each sweep of his lips seemed to weaken her resistance. The unyielding muscles of his chest and arms flexed, his skin so hot against hers. When she shivered from the sensations, he groaned.

He'd trapped her utterly, was now supporting her. What was he going to do? She couldn't see—

His tongue flicked her skin.

She froze, stunned. His rumbling growl made her belly tighten.

When he dipped his tongue to her navel, her lids went heavy. Damn him, it wasn't *un*pleasant. She couldn't see his wrathful face, could only hear him and feel. . . .

He adjusted his grip, moving his hands. She jolted again. Under her panties, he cradled her ass, each of his splayed fingers heating her skin like a brand.

With another groan, he rubbed his face against her, then his horns. Reminded that a barbaric demon king was groping her, she brought her knee up. "Stop this!"

He kept kissing, didn't seem to have heard her. Still holding her aloft, he removed one hand. *What is he going to do with that hand?*

Her eyes went wide when he hooked his fingers around the waist of her panties and began to lower them. . . .

THIRTEEN

Against all reason, the fey's attack had only fueled Sian's arousal.

He couldn't remember the last time he'd felt this *alive.* His heart pumped; his breaths heaved. Her scent and taste put him into a lather. When he'd first cradled her taut ass in his palms, he'd feared he would spontaneously come.

In this state, drawing down her panties and licking between her silken thighs seemed the perfect idea. Licking his mate till she came upon his pointed tongue—

"Stop this, demon!"

He nuzzled below her navel. *Stop?*

She'd begun squirming again. "You said you *weren't* a villain."

Comprehension hit him. With a will he'd never known he possessed, he somehow relinquished his prize, lowering her down his body. Her skin rubbed his pierced nipples, her mons sliding past his swollen cock.

He shuddered when he set her on her feet.

As she backed away, she stared at his groin. His shaft strained against his leather pants, his balls aching like they'd been struck with a forge hammer.

She looked spooked—but her own nipples were hard.

Gods almighty. When he pictured her haughty, insolent, sexy smile just before she'd sent him flying, he almost grabbed her again.

To cool his need, he recalled his last fateful meeting with her in her previous life—the day of her wedding. Her words echoed in his mind: *I could never love you. . . .*

He had clutched his head in anguish, unable to do anything as she'd set off to marry another male.

One she'd loved all along.

Wrath renewed, Sian began to circle her. She pivoted to face him.

"How old are you?" She looked to be in her early twenties. She must soon be turning immortal, which meant she would be suffering from overstimulation. At the possibility, his pulse quickened even more.

"Twenty-four." Her answer had a knife's edge to it, as did her question: "When did you first realize you were a sadist?"

"When I ran afoul of you in the past." Still he circled her. "Were you trying to kill me with that poison?" *And why does picturing your haughty smile make my cock harder?*

"Ideally." Each brusque query and reply was like a blow between sparring partners. "How old are you?"

"Ten thousand. How did you learn to build traps?"

"Reading—you should try it sometime. Did you like my use of stone dicks?"

"If you wanted rock-hard, you needn't have looked farther than me," he said with a smirk. "Where is the Magic Kingdom?"

"Right between Rivendell and Narnia, asshole. Shouldn't an ancient relic like you have more control over yourself?"

Relic? "You bring out the very worst in me. How did you overcome your fear of spiders?"

"I reminded myself that they're less repulsive than you are."

Little bitch! Fists clenched, he rammed his horns against the nearest wall, and the tower rocked.

She swallowed, but she didn't flinch. "You have no right to keep me here, demon! No right to make me your plaything! What do you imagine I've done to you?"

"In this life, you were sent here by Nix as a spy. If you want to know your past crimes, then *remember*."

"I'm no spy. And this Nïx person can go fuck herself." She crossed her arms over her chest. When he failed to keep his gaze from dropping, she made a sound of frustration. "Are you ever going to give me clothes?"

He told her breasts: "I find myself particularly incentivized *not* to do so."

She bristled.

Leave her, Sian. Nothing good could come from this interaction.

He almost wished he hadn't cowed his demon warriors so easily. After calling off the battle against the Vrekeners, he'd ordered those legions back to their interminable punishments—with only a vague promise of a future war against the fey. He'd hoped for a mutiny.

But when Sian, now the primordial of their species, had stretched his wings and bared his fangs, even the bravest of those hell demons had fallen quiet and retreated.

Not so this female.

He recalled his threat to throw her to the legions. After this attack, he thought it more appropriate to threaten the legions with her.

Find something else to occupy you. He could go pay the Vrekener queen her land bounty, but he was in no hurry. The process of building land, hell manipulation, was grueling.

He could go on another doomed search for the fabled hellfire. *That way lies madness. . . .*

Wind gusted into the tower, and airborne sparks fluttered around them like snowflakes of ember. When his prisoner had finished coughing, her eyes watered. "*You* belong here. *I*—do—not. Release me now!"

This creature seemed to have a demonic temper when provoked

enough. So unlike his mate in the past. For all that he'd once adored her, Princess Karinna had been the mistress of sneering indifference.

His gaze lit upon the untouched food tray in the courtyard. "Why should I provide you food if you're not going to eat it?"

"I can't stomach things that are still moving."

"You will learn to." Those dishes were delicacies from the Stygian Marsh, enjoyed by only the wealthiest demons of Pandemonia. "Or should my servants change their menus to tempt a fey prisoner?" The idea was ludicrous. "Once you get hungry enough, you'll eat. If you enter into a battle of wills with me, you will lose."

"If you have a grove or an orchard, I could pick my own food."

"There are no groves or orchards! Have you forgotten the location of your new home? This isn't some sort of fairy woodland. This is *hell*."

"Then let me work in the kitchen. I could find something to eat there."

Angling to get out of the tower? "You actually think to escape me. You were sly with your trap, but I'm far too strong for you to defeat." Damn it, he should be furious at her insolence and gall! *Not secretly hoping she will strike again.*

"Demon, there is one thing I can absolutely guarantee: I will escape you. Save yourself the embarrassment and free me."

Considering her outrage and her desire to get away from him, she might *not* be Nïx's pawn. If this fey was complicit, shouldn't she be seducing him to win his good favor—instead of stabbing him with a poisoned spindle?

Unless Nïx had sent her here to kill him.

Sian was struck by how little he knew about his mate's current existence. He hadn't cared who her family was or where she'd been born, because she was still Kari and his history with her was all that mattered.

But this new version was throwing him. He decided to send spies, his three best generals, to the Magic Kingdom to find out more about her.

She pinched her temples, swaying on her feet. She'd neither slept nor eaten since she'd gotten here. She was sick from the fire vines and injured.

Gods, what would this little firebrand be like at full strength?

He could enchant her with a healing spell, using some of his life force to improve hers, but she didn't deserve that consideration after attacking him. Instead, he grew vine all over the castle's roof—which she definitely deserved.

He refused to allow pity—or his instincts—to curtail his vengeance. Her pain wasn't a fraction of the misery she'd brought down upon him. Upon all of the demons in hell. Her labors weren't enough punishment. *She'd had no pity for me.*

He bared his fangs at her. "I look forward to our next meeting, female."

"Whatever, demon." She rubbed her eyes, plucking something from one.

She'd been wearing a colored contact lens. Her eyes were mismatched again.

FOURTEEN

For the past four days, Sian had run through the wilds of hell in the pouring rain. His emotions remained chaotic.

My mate finds me "repulsive." He roared with frustration, increasing his pace.

He'd gone from being one of the most irresistible males in the universe to one his female could scarcely stand to look upon.

He didn't even want her for his queen, but he wanted to *be* wanted. By her.

Months ago, he'd lamented to Rune that his new visage would keep females from flocking to him—which had meant fewer substitutes to blunt his need for Kari. Even if only for a brief time.

Has my need ever *been blunted?* He'd told himself he was using other females to purge himself of his obsession. *Then why is it even stronger?*

Hardly trusting himself around his prisoner after their last encounter, Sian had remained away, refusing even to watch her through the mirror.

Fate must have been jesting to pair a lovely fey with a bitter monster. Maybe Nïx's plan was to madden Sian until he became a less effective warrior.

When the brush grew thicker, he drew his battle-ax from its holster.

All but an extension of him, the weapon had a solid-black blade, the metal forged in hellfire. His sire, King Devel, had given it to him when Sian had been a pup, with a word of advice: *Only hit hard if you aim true, son.*

The fey prided themselves on their Titanian steel, but this razor-sharp hell metal was indestructible.

Sian hacked his way through the dense brush. Strange, even with his current turmoil, the landscape wasn't as restless as it'd been before his female had arrived.

The rains were easing the drought and tamping down the airborne ash. Even the Styx was subsiding to normal levels of lava.

At times, he took pleasure in seeing the lands react to his moods, one of the few aspects he liked about being king. Otherwise, the crown of Pandemonia was just a weighty responsibility that fell to him—but held no benefit.

A king's power? As a primordial, he'd already been infinitely powerful.

Having legions to command? With nothing more than this ax, Sian had felled armies all on his own. Plus his Møriør alliance could wreak more havoc than millions of trained warriors.

No, he hadn't yet found any real benefits to this throne—only one horrific liability: the hell-change.

That curse had warped Goürlav all the way up to his recent defeat in a death match. Each year for eons, his appearance had deteriorated.

So too will mine. Though Sian's transformation differed from his fraternal twin's—each becoming a separate brand of monster—he could *feel* himself worsening. A low, constant hum reverberated along his spine, as if some engine powered his decline.

He ran harder. He'd bloody *liked* his former face. It'd stared back at him from the mirror for ten thousand years, was part of his identity.

Take away my face, what happens to my sense of self?

When he dreamed, he looked as he once had. When he fantasized about taking his mate, his body wasn't hulking and monstrous.

If I could just find the hellfire . . .

He remembered the last time he'd seen his dam, darkness personified. After hundreds of millennia, her life force had run its course. An outline of a faded shadow by then, she'd wanted to pass on advice to her sons. . . .

"Your sire won't survive long once I return to the ether." Speaking over her sons' pleas for her to stay, she told Goürlav, "Like King Devel, you shall inherit the crown and be cursed with the hell-change."

Taking that bit of news better than Sian would have, Goürlav asked, "Will you finally tell us how he halted his curse?" Their sire was handsome.

She'd brushed Goürlav's golden hair from his brow. "Find the fire, and your appearance will be pleasing."

Sian frowned. "The hellfire?" Legend held that their ancestor had spied a colored flame across the black vastness of space. It'd lured him to this dimension, but proved elusive forever after. Sian and Goürlav had hunted for the fire, digging up clues, determined to solve the puzzle. "We cannot locate it."

She gave him a weak smile. "If your sire could, then anyone can."

Goürlav quietly said, "Why will he not tell us where it is?" His expression was wounded.

"Because the search prepares you for what is found. . . ."

To this day, despite countless desperate attempts, no one ever had uncovered the hellfire. Searching for it was futile, hopes of it ridiculous. Before Goürlav had left this dimension, he'd scoured it, draining himself of magic—only to become even more disillusioned.

Sian had searched no less. He could see every inch of hell in his mind, could picture everything from a crooked step in the castle to a dragon separated from its pack, but he couldn't spy the source of that flame.

It'd probably faded to an ember, or extinguished entirely. *Desperate. Futile. Ridiculous.* Sian *knew* that.

So why had he been out here looking even now?

He burst into a clearing, startling a pack of hellhounds. They cowered before the king of hell. All creatures in Pandemonia—including demons—recognized Sian's horns. But not all creatures recognized his dominion.

Like the mysterious Lôtān, now extinct.

Sian pushed on. He passed traps intended to snare trespassers. Apparently the Vrekener queen and her king had escaped two of them during their Pandemonian exploration.

Sian would devise new ones. That would help settle his mind.

He wondered what traps his mate would come up with. He couldn't decide what was more aggravating: that she'd gotten the better of him, or his continued arousal over the memory.

As he headed into the great moonraker forest, uneasiness warred with his frustration. Maybe he shouldn't have left her alone. After so long without her, he half-expected her to disappear again.

Or die. He'd been unable to prevent her first death—from childbirth.

Sian had never understood why her . . . husband hadn't waited a few months or even a year for Kari to become invulnerable before getting her pregnant. Those two had had all the time in the worlds to start a family.

Why the urgency? Why hadn't Kari insisted on waiting?

When he'd been sixteen, her needless death had leveled him. Unrelenting rage, jealousy, and grief had overwhelmed his young mind.

All these years later, he roared to the sky, unable to handle it better.

Even so, the pull to return to her was intense. He fought it. He'd told Uthyr he would be out in the wilds for a couple of months.

She was safe in her tower. Food automatically appeared for her. As long as she was within the bounds of Graven, she was protected from all the dangers of hell.

But she also seemed to be a magnet for trouble. And she wasn't yet immortal.

Once Sian eventually returned, he would give her a ring bespelled to accelerate her healing until her immortality took over. With that in place, he could relax away from her.

He slowed his steps. Then shouldn't he return and do it now?

No, until he'd wrested more control in this form, *he* might be the biggest danger to her.

Damn it, he didn't trust his own judgment! He rammed his horns into a massive moonraker tree, toppling it.

Before he acted, he would confer with the dragon. His ally was here for just this purpose.

Sian closed his eyes to sense Uthyr's location. . . . *Got you, dragon.* Though Uthyr usually hunted far afield, he'd been sticking close to the castle, was just behind the nearest mountain.

If Sian traced that close to home, he'd be foolish not to check on his prisoner at the same time. Telling himself he was *not* rushing back to his mate, Sian appeared at Uthyr's location.

The dragon was nowhere to be seen.

Sian detected his ally's invisible presence. Uthyr was crouched behind a boulder to pounce on his unsuspecting prey—a large reptile the size of a hellhound.

Uthyr said, *—Do not spook my meal, demon, or you'll* be *my meal.—*

Clenching his jaw, Sian waited.

The dragon's camouflaged tail swished side to side. Like a shot, he vaulted forward, snaring his quarry between his forepaws.

Shaking off his invisibility, Uthyr snapped the creature's neck, then tossed the carcass above his head. He seared it with fire until it landed, roasted, in his mouth.

GULP. *—Ahh. Medium well.—* He stifled a belch with his bloody forepaw.

"I could have provided you a feast of those creatures."

—Hunting keeps a dragon shifter young.— Uthyr turned back toward the castle along a canyon trail.

Sian fell in beside him. "I want your counsel about my prisoner."

—I'm surprised to see you so soon. Not quite the two-month absence you predicted.— The dragon smirked. *—I gave you a week. Seems we both overestimated your willpower.—*

That smirk raised Sian's hackles. So much for an ally's wise counsel. "I returned because I might place protective magics over her. You'll have to excuse my hypervigilance since this female has already died once!"

Uthyr kicked a boulder along as they walked. *—Yet you somehow survived the loss.—*

What was the dragon getting at? "Luckily I hadn't claimed her." Sian had never heard of a demon who wouldn't greet death if his claimed mate perished. His own sire had. Somewhere in the Elserealms, Devel had led the front in an impossible battle—an immortal's version of suicide.

Massive neck stretching, Uthyr craned his head toward Sian, making him feel like a laboratory animal under inspection. *—Plus your hatred numbed what you felt for her and kept you from comprehending the magnitude of what you'd lost.—*

Not helping Sian's anxiety.

—To sever that lifeline of hate after so long would be like cutting off a limb.—

Or horns! "Why sever it when I've no doubt she'll give me new reasons to hate her?"

—Such as her trap?—

"You know about that?" Was there anything his ally didn't know about?

—I might *have been observing the terrace that night.—*

Sian bared his fangs. "Worthless dragonic spy!"

—I wanted to make sure you didn't do anything drastic when you were fresh from a legion gathering. Picture how crazed you must've looked to her. She protected herself. Quite resourcefully, I might add.—

"Know that she will not seize the upper hand again," he said with all confidence, even as he felt a whisper of disappointment over that fact.

Uthyr's lips drew back from rows of pointed teeth, his version of a smile. *—Imagine my surprise to see you plummeting from your own tower while leashed to a . . . what's the modern phrase? Ah, yes, a* bag of dicks.— He laughed at his own joke, emitting puffs of smoke.

Sian grated, "You've developed quite a mastery of modern phrasings."

—I learned much from Rune's memories.—

All of the Møriør were supposed to have slept during their five centuries of travel from the Elserealms to this side of the universe—except for Rune, who'd worked as their spy in Gaia.

Whenever a Møriør woke, he or she would delve into Rune's mind to learn what history had passed and to pick up new words and speech patterns.

Sian hadn't slept during the journey. Instead he'd lain in a kind of twilight, tormenting himself, wondering if this Accession would return his mate to him. . . .

Golden eyes alight, Uthyr said, *—Plus the Vrekener queen, our new Pandemonian neighbor, has glorious television recordings! I secretly watch through her window.—*

"That trespassing territory thief?" Melanthe had taken advantage of Sian, and he would punish her for it, somehow, someway. Speaking of territory . . . "Do you know where the Magic Kingdom is? My prisoner said it lies between Rivendell and Narnia."

—These places sound familiar. I'll think on it.— When Sian conjured a rag and began to clean his ax, the dragon said, *—Searching for the hellfire again?—*

Why had Sian confided his mother's words to Uthyr?

Stopping along the path, the dragon placed a paw in front of Sian. *—You need to accept that you will never find it. Acknowledge your curse and work within the confines of it.—*

How easy for him to say! Uthyr voluntarily chose his shape.

Sian would kill to be a shifter. He'd even dreamed about shifting from his hell-change form to his previous guise and back.

—That's your only chance for a lasting future with your female.—

"Lasting future? I despise her. I could never again trust her. Even so, any male would want to be attractive to his mate." They continued on.

—If raised differently, Kari could be changed from before. Nature versus nurture, demon.—

"In this we agree. In fact, no longer will I call my prisoner Kari. This fierce new version, *Calliope*, is in a class all her own." Because she wasn't a royal in this life?

Maybe a princess's restraint had been ingrained into Kari from birth. The same restraint that had curbed Kari's temper could have controlled her sexuality.

Calliope had an explosive temper. Would her lusts be just as volatile?

"Turn Princess Kari feral . . . and you have Calliope." Could that also mean she wasn't narrow-minded and heartless? "Unless she's playing games with me. The possibility remains that she's a planted spy."

—Games? Mayhap you're attributing your own traits to her.— Uthyr flicked his tail, a movement he often made just before saying "checkmate." *—I'm surprised you haven't decided to seduce her.—*

Sian glowered at the dragon. "I'm sure you heard what she makes of my appearance." He waved at himself. "She finds me repulsive."

—What did you want most out of life? Ah, yes, a challenge.—

"An attainable one." But hadn't Sian also lamented never knowing a hard-won victory? If he could seduce her in this guise . . .

—Considering her age, she might be feeling the effects of overstimulation.—

Her senses would be growing ever sharper, bombarding her with stimulation, her desires increasing in time.

—I remember my own transition. I would have tupped a sweet-talking ghouless for relief.—

"You think I could use her new lusts against her?"

—I don't like the conniving gleam in your eyes.—

Sian had been in battle. He'd suffered physical agony and horror. He'd lived through the amputation of his horns. But nothing had hurt him like the hole Kari had left in his chest. He needed to make her experience the same! He wanted her to fucking ache for *him*.

To think of nothing but *him* for the next ten thousand years.

"If someone who looks like me used and tossed her away, she'd be humiliated." He might be able to punish her worse than the labors he'd planned.

—This was not *the direction I'd hoped your mind would go. And how could you mate and discard her? You'd have to withhold your claiming bite. Is any demon male strong enough to resist marking his mate's neck in the throes of first spending?—*

If Sian did mark her with his fangs, she would irreversibly become the queen of hell. "A strong enough demon male? How about the primordial"—Sian pounded a fist against his chest—"of the entire godsdamned species?"

Uthyr gave him an unimpressed look.

"I'll think on this, dragon. For now, let's see how my captive reacts to amusing new torments." Amusing for him alone, of course.

Before Sian could trace away, Uthyr said, *—I've seen some of your recollections of her.—*

Not surprising. As bonded as a family, the members of the Møriør were telepathically linked, with few secrets between them. Though he trusted his allies with his life, Sian had shielded certain memories from them. Yet snippets always slipped through. "When we all communicate, we learn much about each other." A fact of life.

—True. And I might have dug a bit.—

Sian bared his fangs again. Digging into masked memories was taboo! If Uthyr saw Sian's shameful pleas to Kari . . . "I've killed for lesser slights. Have I tried to find out why you refuse to shift back to your human form? No. But I will now."

Uthyr shrugged his wings. *—I investigated so I might be of more service to you, friend. I must know the history.—*

There was a reason Sian didn't want the others to know. Unbidden, his thoughts turned to the past.

After he'd revealed to Kari everything about his kind, she'd avoided him for weeks, refusing any contact with him. He'd been helpless to do anything as a future with his mate slipped from his panicked grasp.

Separated from his twin for the first time and without a single friend in that world, he'd walked around in a daze, doubt his only companion: *Was I too rough with her, too demonic?*

Maybe she'd had trouble accepting the totality of their fated connection. Or she'd been spooked by it. But surely she could never doom him to an existence with no female or family.

Then he'd heard the announcement of a surprise wedding between her and the Draiksulian king—set for that very afternoon. Sian had sprinted to the castle to stop her. He couldn't lose both of his parents *and* his fated female in the space of a year! He climbed through her window. . . .

Surrounded by her handmaidens, she stood on a dais, dressed in a white gown. Her beauty stole his breath.

"What are you doing in here?" she demanded, giving him a look of distaste. "Get out now."

He ran his hand over his face, comprehending his own appearance. He hadn't shaven, and his garments were a mess. "I won't leave until you talk to me."

She dismissed her attendants. Something about her was different. She seemed both older and colder.

"What are you doing, Kari? Are you wedding that king to take yourself out of my reach?"

With zero emotion, she said, "I am marrying my fiancé because I want him. *I have loved him since I was a little girl."*

Sian's stomach lurched as if it'd been punched. "Do not do this, Kari. You love me*!" Hadn't she told him as much?* The tender regard I feel for you . . .

"I do not—and could never—love an animal with horns." She returned her attention to her reflection.

He gaped in disbelief. But their kiss . . . the way she'd responded . . . their plans . . .

Adjusting a lock of her shining hair, she asked, "Can I make it any plainer, prince of beasts?"

His actions later that day would shame him for the rest of his unending life. . . .

—*Demon?*— Uthyr's gaze narrowed on Sian's clenched fists.

He'd dug his claws into his palms until they dripped blood.

—*At least tell me how Kari died. It must have been before she became fully immortal.*—

Sian grated, "She died at twenty-four, giving birth to the child of another male." He turned his mind from that enraging memory lest he trace to Calliope and do something dire. "Ask me no more about it. Just go, Uthyr. Fly with the other dragons."

—*I'm not a dragon; I'm a dragon shifter. But that juvenile pack* is *fun to spar with. If you refuse all of my advice, I might as well go.*— He paused. —*One thing, though . . .* —

"What?"

—*If history often repeats itself, and she's on the cusp of immortality . . . could she* currently *be pregnant?*—

To lose her again?

The king of all hells threw back his head and yelled until the whole realm quaked.

FIFTEEN

You can do this! Lila peered down at the bowl of . . . soup. She could swear this one was more animated than the last, but she needed the nourishment.

She'd been imprisoned for six days, had scratched as many slashes into a wall.

Trays of food appeared for each meal, always with demon dishes. The only good thing about her hunger and exhaustion: a subdued sex drive.

After her last encounter with Abyssian, Lila had berated herself for responding to a Møriør. For some inexplicable reason, she'd felt . . . *chemistry* with that crazy demon. Lots of it.

Far more than I felt with Saetth.

Just minutes ago, Abyssian's roar had echoed over the kingdom again, though this one sounded more enraged than sexual. What had set him off this time? Would he take it out on her?

Anticipation of a blow could sometimes be as bad as the hit. She would know. Nightmares of the archer had plagued her since childhood—but never as badly as they had here.

If she could fall asleep. She often got the sense of being watched, keeping her on edge. Most nights, she huddled for warmth on the stone floor, listening to hell's soundtrack. While spiders skittered inside the castle walls, dragon calls and the howls of distant hellhounds drifted in from the wilds.

Other times, she'd watched the dramatic storms. Last night, rain had poured while electric-blue lightning forked above the tops of nearby volcanoes. Lava had steamed in the downpour, solidifying into bizarre shapes.

None of the tales she'd read could convey how surreal Pandemonia was. . . .

During the days, Lila had paced along a narrowing trail between fire vines, conceiving and discarding escape plans. Despite all of her reading, she didn't have enough knowledge about this realm to plot her exit from it. And she needed to build up her strength.

With that in mind, she sat on the edge of the fountain and dipped a spoon into the soup.

Though she hadn't eaten since her last sandwich in the employee lounge, she'd lost zero weight. Was she so close to immortality that her figure had already frozen forever? Next would come tingling regeneration. Then she'd become bulletproof. Few things could kill her other than a beheading.

Stop stalling, Lila. Soup. She lifted the spoon. The dish smelled appetizing enough, but small creatures that resembled jellyfish fluttered in the warm broth.

How did one go about this? Swallow a jellyfish whole? Crush it up first?

Chew it . . . live?

She could drink the broth, but she needed protein. Scrunching her eyes closed, she eased the spoon toward her mouth. For good measure, she pinched her nose. She wavered when she heard a flutter and a tiny splash in her spoon.

The jellyfish wasn't going down without a fight. Literally.

Inhale. Exhale. Here goes. Her hand trembled. With a whimper, she parted her lips, only to gag—

Her ears twitched. She sensed another presence, heard heaving breaths. Her eyes flashed open, her spoon clattering back into the bowl.

Abyssian had appeared not twenty feet from her, looking as demonic as ever. His longish black hair was tousled, his fangs bared. His wings unfurled behind him. He wore only low-slung leather pants and scuffed boots.

Her heart sank. What impossible task would she face today? Moving an ocean with a leaky cup?

She abandoned her attempt at lunch and stood, conscious of her own clothing—underwear so ripped and frayed the material bordered on transparent.

When she tugged up her bra, he watched her movements avidly, then seemed to shake himself. "Are you with young, female?"

What a random question. "Why would you ask me that?"

"ANSWER ME!"

She swallowed. "Not that I know of."

Some of the tension left his lean muscles, but then his masked eyes narrowed again. "Could you be?"

"No."

He waved a hand, and a gold ring appeared between his thumb and forefinger, looking minuscule in his grasp. "I will tolerate no disobedience from you," he told her in his rough voice. "Remember that you are to obey all my commands, such as the one I now give you: don this ring without argument."

He tossed it to her. Her hand shot out reflexively to catch it. "What is this?"

"It is the ring your king commanded you to wear. You will do whatever I order, whenever I order it. You have yet to understand your place here."

"My king is Saetth of the Sylvan fey." *Unless he screwed me over.*

"That arrant coward?"

He was a lot of things, but she didn't think he lacked courage. Everyone was always talking about his skill with a sword. "He's no coward."

"Then why won't he answer Rune's challenges?"

"What are you talking about?"

"The Møriør's archer has challenged Saetth to a sword fight, one on one—even though a sword is not Rune's weapon. If Saetth wants to save his line, then why not fight to rid his people of the fey-slayer?"

Saetth had told her, *If there were any alternative, I would undertake it.* Had there been? "Rune must be older and stronger. Hardly fair."

"They're near in age and half brothers. There is no better-matched fight."

"Brothers?" *For fuck's sake, am I related to Rune??*

"They share a father."

Then half related at worst. And generations must separate her and the archer.

"Rune destroyed Saetth's sword recently—when your spineless king chose to target Rune's female in a sneak attack."

"Why should I believe anything you say?" she asked, though she couldn't come up with a reason why Abyssian would lie about that.

"Don't give a damn if you do or don't." He jerked his chin at her hand. "The ring, princess."

She stiffened. "Why would you call me that?" Oh, gods, had he figured out her true identity?

"In your previous life, you were a fey princess of Sylvan."

Could Lila truly have been reborn into the same royal line? *Fate wants me to be a queen.* At least the demon still didn't know she was a princess now as well. She wasn't in the archer's sights.

Yet.

"In my *alleged* previous life." She sat again and gazed at the ring, assessing its power. Most fey possessed innate—but rarely developed—

magic. She could sense a spell attached to this band. "I won't put it on until you tell me what you've bespelled it to do."

His fangs sharpened at her impertinence. The broad planes of his chest swelled, drawing her gaze to his pierced nipples. His golden markings began to glow. Against his red skin, those coiled patterns looked like . . . flames.

Hypnotic.

"Wrong answer." Before she could blink, he'd traced to kneel beside her. "I'll force it on your finger if I have to. Though I'll probably break something of yours in the process."

"No!" She made a fist around the band, shoving her hand behind her back.

With a growl, he leaned forward, arm snaking around her waist, wings all but enclosing her.

His scent surrounded her. He smelled like a sun-warmed evergreen that had just caught fire. She hadn't imagined the heat of his skin before; it seemed to sear her.

Right in front of her mouth was one of his piercings. When she turned her head away, he leaned over her even more. His rippling chest rubbed her breasts. A gasp left her lips when that piercing raked across her own nipple.

His breaths grew ragged, tickling the tip of her sensitive ear, and she nearly moaned. She had the insane urge to snatch his long black hair and yank him down for a kiss.

What is happening to me?

She was so distracted by these sensations that he easily snagged her hand. He sat back on his haunches, dragging her fist to his chest. Prying open her fingers, he retrieved the ring. Yet then he stilled, seeming transfixed by their hands. Hers looked small and pale next to his huge claw-tipped one.

Breaking his stare, he tried to shove the band onto her finger.

She struggled. "Stop it, you brute! I don't want it!"

"You'll wear whatever I command you to," he said, his voice even huskier than usual.

He flattened her hand against his chest, straightening her fingers. He didn't seem to notice that he'd placed her palm right over a nipple. Her lips parted, her attention dipping.

His impossibly large dick was hard again. Stunned by the sight, she stopped fighting for just a moment; he slid the ring on, and it tightened around her finger.

"Damn you!" She'd never be able to remove it.

Pinning her gaze with his own, he shifted her hand on his chest. And again. Oh, yes, he'd noticed the placement of her hand, and now he was forcing her to pet him.

Her overstimulated body responded, loving the feel of his chiseled muscles. No, he was a monster! "I don't want to touch you."

He peered at her stiff nipples straining against her threadbare bra. "Do you not?" How could three words sound so arrogant? Smirking, he rubbed his tongue over one fang; his tongue was pointed! He looked like he was about to lean in and suckle her.

She'd never had her nipples kissed before. Her breaths shallowed as she imagined what his lips would feel like closing over a peak. His mouth would be so hot. His pointed tongue would flick the tip, circling it. . . .

"Hmm." The satisfied sound rumbled from his chest, doing strange things to her belly. "I think in this context, you would very much like to be *my plaything*, Calliope."

Gripping her wrists with one hand, he lowered his other to rest upon one of her thighs. He inched it higher . . .

Higher . . .

She bit back a whimper, battling the urge to rock her hips in invitation. "Never."

"Then why do I scent your arousal, little female?"

SIXTEEN

Her body needs mine! Sian wanted to bellow with triumph. The first time he'd ever elicited her arousal scent, and he was in this form!

The mouthwatering honey of her sex would've maddened a lesser demon. Blood rushed to his groin, swelling his cock till he thought it'd rip free of his pants.

Her mismatched irises began to glow, both turning a bright, shimmery teal. He'd never seen them change color before! But surely she must have felt some kind of sharp emotion around him during the four months he'd been in Sylvan.

Her thigh trembled beneath his palm, her breasts rising and falling with her panting breaths. Her hard nipples begged for his attention.

His tongue flicked in his mouth. He'd fantasized infinite times about sucking her breasts, rubbing his stubble over them, tonguing her nipples till she came for him.

Was he about to have his fantasy?

I could cover her right now. His gaze flashed to her supple neck. Could he possibly resist marking this female as his own?

She raised her chin. "If I am aroused, it isn't for you, beast. *Never* for you. I'd had stirring thoughts *before* you arrived."

His excitement dimmed to nothing. He'd been enjoying the effects of her impending transition and nothing more.

Of course.

He gazed at his large demon hand upon her thigh. His black claws were stark against her alabaster flesh. Before he could choke back the words, he'd asked, "Then what does arouse you?"

"At the bottom of my turn-ons list: fuckface demons who abuse me."

With a harsh curse, he released her and traced to the other side of the tower, willing his erection to wane.

Another loss of control, another close call. He'd nearly rutted her on the floor.

Earlier, the idea of his mate bearing another's young—and possibly dying again—had made Sian lose his mind. But she wasn't pregnant, and she now wore a healing ring. No disaster loomed. So why couldn't he force himself to leave her? "Had you a male?" *Say no. . . .*

A female this lovely must have. Maybe a lover who'd been helping her through the transition? At the thought, Sian almost rammed his horns into the wall again.

"I *have* a fiancé."

I'll gut that fuck. "A fey, no doubt." She didn't deny it. "I absolve you of your agreement with him. In this world, you have no one."

"Why do you care if I'm engaged? And why would you suddenly ask me if I was pregnant?"

"You died in childbirth in your last life."

She glanced away sharply—from the shock of what he'd told her, or was there more?

"I will not let anything get in the way of my revenge, not even your death. Which is why I imbued the ring with a healing spell." His life force depleted to defend hers. *Welcome to the world of matehood.*

"I thought the option of killing me was on the table. If my torture ceased to amuse."

"I've concluded you will be endlessly entertaining."

"Why do you keep . . . trying things with me?" Her cheeks reddened. Could she be a virgin? Then her fiancé was an idiot. "Don't you have a really old female in your life, one even a relic like you can be with?"

Another jab about age? He'd never thought that might be a detractor. Immortals grew stronger with longevity. But they could also grow mentally unstable. "I have *twelve* females. My harem of concubines keeps me very satisfied," he lied—not about the number, but about the satisfaction.

Had Sian ever been even *remotely* satisfied since she'd ruined him with that one perfect kiss?

In any case, he'd never been with any of those concubines, had inherited them along with the crown.

Calliope bit out, "Then go dally with your harem."

"I like variety. And a challenge."

"You think I'd ever sleep with you? Now you're just being ridiculous. The only place I'd ever sleep with you is in your dreams." She shook her head, and her silken hair danced over her shoulders.

Her scent muddled his thoughts. He inhaled it like a drowning man's next taste of air. *Not helping my erection.*

Damn it, he'd done what'd he come to do; he should leave now. Yet his feet felt rooted to the spot. He wished he had other pressing kingdom concerns to distract him.

Absolute power didn't *corrupt* absolutely; it *bored* absolutely.

Seducing her would keep me occupied. He stifled the idea. She was right: he was just being ridiculous.

She said, "If you'd told me the ring was for healing, I probably wouldn't have resisted you."

"Perhaps in your realm, a king explains his wishes to lowly prisoners; not in this one."

She cast him a measured glance, as if trying to predict what he'd do next.

Good luck. *He* didn't even know. He felt the need to be around others, yet Uthyr had taken his advice and flown off. The rest of Sian's family—the Møriør—weren't available.

For now, Orion the Undoing, leader of their alliance, slept in a godlike hibernation, building strength for the Accession. Rune honeymooned with Josephine. Blace, the oldest vampire, investigated Josephine's mysterious vampire father.

Darach Lyka and their alliance's witch, Allixta, remained in Tenebrous, the Møriør's moving realm, but Sian wouldn't return there yet. Minutes in Tenebrous could equal hours or even days elsewhere, and he didn't want to let Calliope out of his sight for that long.

She crossed her arms over her chest. "Even lowly prisoners usually know why they're being punished. So what will it be tonight?" she demanded, eyes flashing. "Maybe you'd like to chase me around and lick my torso some more?"

Admittedly, not his finest moment—but he couldn't seem to *think* anymore! "Take care, little firebrand; the next part of you I lick will *not* be your torso."

She gasped, her ears flattening.

Sian's gaze clocked the movement. Rune hated the fey so much that he despised pointed ears, even his own. He'd avoided bedding any females with that feature. So had Sian—but now he was right back to being fascinated by his mate's delicate ears. He wanted to discover how sensitive they were.

Hadn't she trembled when he'd exhaled against one tip? *Could* she be seduced? For whatever reason, she had responded to him.

If Uthyr had nearly tupped a ghouless in his transition, Calliope might turn to Sian.

Get this idea out of your head, demon. Even if seduction were a sound idea—which it wasn't, at all—a demon with his strength couldn't take a fragile female like her until she'd turned immortal. "When do the women in your line reach immortality?"

"I'm way overdue. If this ring makes me heal, how will I know if I've turned?"

"Every month I will remove it and test you," he said.

Her lips thinned. "Every month."

Was the duration of her imprisonment just sinking in? "Why didn't you confess your age and weakness in the beginning, then beg for mercy from your tasks?" Even with her two lives added together, she was only in her forties. "I might have been moved to grant it."

"*Beg* for mercy?!" She charged forward, breasts bouncing—again, not helping his erection—to stand in front of him. "I would rather bite out my tongue and bleed to death than beg."

Her talk of dying checked his arousal. "You're quick to choose death."

"You're quick to threaten me! And since you won't tell me what my 'crime' was, why shouldn't I believe you've set me up? Maybe you get off torturing young females so much that your deluded brain makes up excuses to justify your twisted needs!"

She continued to make him into the villain. Yes, she was young, but he had been as well, a mere sixteen years old. Yes, he'd been harsh with her, but no permanent harm had been done—unlike his own mutilation. "You are either very stupid or crazed to continue challenging one like me." Evidence mounted that she was simply maddened.

And that she was no spy.

Between Sian and Calliope, only one of them was considering seduction.

If he could somehow get her in bed with him, he'd rut her till he'd slaked his need, then discard her, cutting *her* from his life completely. He'd leave her to rot in this tower.

The only drawback to his plan? He didn't know how to seduce. For most of Sian's life, his only difficulty with finding a partner had been getting rid of her amorous friends, since he never slept with more than one at a time.

Hands balled into fists, she said, "All I keep hearing about is my *supposed* former life, when I *supposedly* wronged you. You're a demon who lives in hell and a Møriør on top of that; something tells me you're not the most trustworthy male!"

"Since when have the Møriør been known as untrustworthy?"

"Since they decided to invade *our* universe and conquer everyone in Gaia."

"Someone needs to rule you because you are all doing a bloody bad job of ruling yourselves." Especially under Nïx's guidance. Why didn't they realize she was leading them to an apocalypse?

"I've hated and feared all of the Møriør since I was a girl. Now that I've met you, I see I was right to."

"Hated and feared? Then you know nothing of my alliance."

"I know the one thing that counts."

He grated, "And what's that?"

She held his gaze. "You're all monsters."

SEVENTEEN

Day seven in hell.

As warm water ran over her underwear-clad body, Lila rolled her head on her neck. She'd just taken the edge off with a quick orgasm—her first since arriving here—while trying to avoid thoughts of Abyssian.

But the ring was a constant reminder.

She glared at it. "Fucker." Healing wasn't unwelcome—all of her bruises, burns, and abrasions had mended—but she had no idea what other spells the ring might carry.

Plus it felt like a mark of possession, a tiny slave collar.

Despite her healing, she was fading overall. Her head ached, her muscles were stiff from sleeping on the floor, and she still hadn't eaten. Nor had she figured out an escape. Which meant she didn't know enough.

She raised her face and rinsed her mouth. Perhaps she shouldn't antagonize the demon king—a source of information—if he returned?

She exited the makeshift shower, wringing her hair out, and almost stepped on an encroaching runner of fire vine. Before long, she would be hemmed in at the center of the tower.

Yesterday she'd used the edge of a food tray to sever a branch, and four more had taken its place, like a hydra's head.

How to defeat it? As she pondered solutions, she scratched another slash on the wall to mark her captivity.

Two spiders poked out from holes to watch her.

They no longer terrified her, thanks to her immersion therapy. She'd named that pair Chip and Dale and fed them jellyfish-soup-creature-thingies.

None of the others would approach her, still pissy because of her venom harvesting.

How different life here was from her life in Sylvan Castle when she had strolled out to her private garden and coaxed fawns to eat lilies from her hand. She must be missing her home badly; she'd dreamed of a deer last night.

In her reverie, she'd been sprinting circles in the tower when a fawn came bounding into the courtyard, its tiny hooves *clickety-clacking* on the stone floor.

Bits of grass had dotted its muzzle, the young fawn still a clumsy forager. Lila had gazed around, mystified by how it'd gotten into a tower with no doors. And what would a woodland creature be doing in hell?

She'd breathlessly eased closer to it, inching out a hand. . . . Just as she'd been about to pet its head, it'd disappeared.

Was her subconscious trying to tell her about a possible exit from this place?

Focus, Lila. Fire vine. She began to pace. The threat of the vine was like a puzzle devised to test her. How to conquer a poisonous vine that spread nonstop but couldn't be cut?

Maybe she could build a stone barricade out of the remaining relics. A bulwark of raunchy statues. Lovely.

The ancient inscriptions on the walls were just as dirty as those statues. She'd read some, everything from *She seized his horns, guiding his mouth to her nether lips, demanding the wonder of his tongue* to *In a frenzy of possessiveness, he rubbed his aching horns all over her breasts, marking her with his scent* to *Licking the pierced head, she sucked him greedily, awaiting the heat of his promised seed.*

Judging by the bulk of them she'd read, demons were obsessed with horns, claws, piercings, and—

A loud splashing sound carried from the lava river below.

She meandered around vines to the edge of the terrace. At least the ash had started to settle outside. She hadn't coughed a single time today, and the foreboding feeling of this place had lifted somewhat.

She gazed over the railing. Blinked.

A dragon—multiple times bigger than any she'd ever seen—was swimming in the lava. Metallic blue-gold scales covered its gargantuan body, and two rows of black horns protruded from its head.

Must be Uthyr, one of the Møriør. If he was visiting, would the baneblood archer show up here too?

She rubbed her hand over her chest. After her dream of the fawn, she'd had yet another nightmare about the fey-slayer.

The dragon took a mouthful of lava and spurted it up like a fountain.

Dragons. Swimming in lava. Of course.

This demonic world was foreign to her, but by all the gods, she would figure out how to survive here until she could escape.

She would adapt. She always did. When she'd been cast into the mortal realm with only a bag of clothes and a *Book of Lore*, Lila had been as good as doomed.

Until she'd figured it the fuck out.

She'd learned to live without luxuries and order and servants. Without knowing where her next meal would come from. Without any promise of safety.

Fearing human detection, she'd learned to accept her loneliness and pour her energies into educating herself.

At fifteen, she'd finagled a way to buy the one tool she'd coveted: an ID. After that, she'd set about exploiting weaknesses in the mortals' financial and social structure to pay for her education.

Just as Lila had promised Saetth, she flourished with every hardship she survived, like the fire vine that grew with each cut—

Her eyes went wide. *That's it!* Suddenly she knew how to defeat the vine.

She laughed at the solution, stamping her feet. By not *defeating* it at all. . . .

EIGHTEEN

Sian's spies had returned with their first cursory report on Calliope, leaving him with more questions than answers.

In the ten days since her capture, his curiosity about his mate burned ever hotter. His gaze fell on the hand mirror. *Want to see her.*

He considered his addiction to watching her a major failing. Over the last few nights, he hadn't slept, just gazed at her even when she slumbered.

Once she drifted off, nothing could wake her. And she had an active dreamlife, her expressive face evincing emotion after emotion, her limbs and ears twitching.

Was she dreaming about her past life? Would she ever admit if she were?

He succumbed to the need, snatching up the mirror and summoning the scene in the tower. He raised his brows at the sight.

She was talking to two spiders that seemed to be following her around the central courtyard. Fascinating. Was she no longer afraid of them?

She crossed to one of the walls and reached toward a fire vine. Then she . . . pressed her palm against it!

Why would she burn herself? To trick him in some way! To get sympathy?

She gritted her teeth against the pain. Then she did it to her *other* hand. To the backs of her wrists as well.

His instincts screamed to protect her. Even from herself.

She paused, eyes watering, then *repeated* the process. When tears spilled down her cheeks, he tensed to trace there and demand answers—

Realization struck him, and he stilled.

"Immunity." She was building up her tolerance to the vine, so she could escape down the side of the tower. Torn between the need to kiss his ingenious mate and the urge to throttle her, he muttered, "You clever girl."

He found himself almost pulling for her. Yet a wave of his hand imbued her ring with a confinement spell. As long as she wore it, she could never leave the castle.

She burned her forearm in vain. "Motherfucker fuckity fuck!"

His brows rose. Definitely not the language of a princess.

Calliope had gotten inside a Møriør hold; a spy would not be this desperate to get *out* of one.

Damn this thread of hope. Even if she proved true in this life, she hadn't in her last. He could never trust her. The day he'd lost his horns he'd lost forever any hope of a future with her. A traitorous voice whispered, *You grew new horns.*

Unsettled, he traced to the River Styx to find Uthyr basking in lava again, backstroking with his wings. His golden eyes were heavy-lidded. —*There is* nothing *like Pandemonian lava. Demon, if you could bottle this* . . . — He sucked in a mouthful and spurted it into the air. —*How is Calliope?*—

Sian paced the stony riverbank. He kicked a black lava rock—cold and crumbling like his heart—into the river, watching it melt. "She's doggedly trying to escape. And scratching slashes on the wall for each day of imprisonment."

—Not typical spy behavior.—

"My thoughts as well." He couldn't hold in what he'd seen her do. "She was purposely making contact with the fire vine, burning herself to build immunity." His tone held a note of pride.

—So she can climb out of the tower! Your mate's a cunning female. And you thought her stupid.— Uthyr lifted his scaled brow. *—I wonder how else you've misjudged her.—*

So did Sian. "My own spies have returned from their first foray into her background. Apparently the Magic Kingdom is a gathering place for mortals. Calliope worked there for years as a *face character*, whatever that is."

The contents of her apartment were sparse and gave scant insight into her personality—aside from the books stacked against every wall from floor to ceiling. The subjects ranged from introductory Japanese to Sumerian artifacts.

If she liked reading, then Graven's Tower of Learning would leave her agog. *Pity she'll never see it.* "She was abducted from her place of employment by the Sorceri bounty hunters."

The hunters he still owed. Though Sian disliked having a debt hanging over him, he wasn't looking forward to a bout of hell manipulation.

He'd have to put himself into a trance, envisioning the changes he would make to the lands—but he'd actually be forcing his own consciousness to expand.

Such an undertaking would deplete his life force in a way it hadn't been in ages.

If Calliope could enliven his mind and combat his stupefying boredom, she might be worth that price.

—No wonder your mate is so indignant. She likely had a life she was enjoying. A career. Maybe even a lover. It seems Nïx is playing with you both.—

Sian gnashed his fangs. "My mate had a . . . fiancé."

Uthyr cringed. *—That's less than encouraging. What of her family?—*

"I believe she has none. No blood ties were uncovered on Earth."

—I pity young Calliope. Cooping up a fleet-footed fey is beyond cruel.—

Her species loved to run. Did she miss it? What would she give for a bout of freedom?

—And imagine how confused she must be. She's starving, imprisoned, and friendless in a strange new dimension. If you won't bring her food she can tolerate, I'll toss some game in there. Maybe keep her company. You could conjure a chess set for us.—

Sian scowled.

—She is bold, but that doesn't mean she won't be afraid at times.—

Sian's mate. Afraid.

Damn Uthyr for plucking that instinct string!

Over his endless lifetime, Sian had pondered one question more than any other: *What if she returns . . . different?*

Already she seemed to be.

—She's affecting you, demon. Your rages are much less severe.—

Mates were thought to center each other, bringing clarity and steadiness. Was she neutralizing his uncontrollable aggression?

—You won't even attempt to seduce her?—

Sian shook his head.

—Why not?—

"Because it will end in failure."

—What would you lose by trying? This strikes me as abysmal, Abyssian.—

"Damn it, dragon, I don't know *how*. Before my transformation, my seduction arsenal consisted of one tried-and-true move: a crook of my finger. I beckoned, and females fought over me." Everyone except his mate. "I never needed anything more. Yet you think someone like me could tempt an exquisite fey?"

—I will assist your endeavors with seduction. In the form of a man, I was quite good at it.—

Was Sian actually about to take advice on this subject from a fucking dragon? Before he could stop himself, he'd grated, "What would be your first move?"

—I'll help you, but only if you swear off the cruelty. I won't put forth the effort just to have you undermine it.—

"Very well. I swear off the cruelty. For now."

Nod. *—First, you need to provide her with comforts. If you give her a bed, she will think of you favorably whenever she's in it. The same with clothes. Then you invite her to dinner. Afterward the two of you could explore the castle, and you'd let her pick out treasures for herself.—*

Graven was a type of time capsule. The thousand rooms throughout the seven towers were filled with mystical goods—art, jewels, weapons, clothing, and more—preserved since his foresires had first created this castle.

As boys, Sian and Goürlav had played among those rooms, calling them the attics of the gods.

The two brothers had once been inseparable. After Sian's return from Sylvan, they'd never been as close. How could they have been? Yet another thing Kari had stolen from him. . . .

—You could delight your mate with the marvels here.—

Reminded of his rage, Sian snapped, "She deserves no delight."

Uthyr tapped his chin with a long talon, innocently asking, *—Didn't she call your home a "pathetic excuse for a castle"?—*

The little witch had. She must've compared Graven to the stately castle in that Magic Kingdom and found the demons' seat of power lacking. But so far she'd seen only a derelict tower and a cavern here.

He scrubbed his hand over his nape, recalling an exchange between himself and Kari:

"Do your kind truly burrow in the ground?" she asked with a shudder.

"Some live in the underworld of the Abyss." As his ancestors had before Graven had been completed. "But we also have temples of solid gold and a grand castle."

"Grand?" She scoffed. "I suspect your definition of the word does not match my own."

Sian stopped pacing. "If you were a talented seducer as a man, that would have been millennia ago. What do you know of modern females?"

Uthyr cast him a fang-filled grin. *—I watch soaps.—*

NINETEEN

Need a weapon.

Lila, Chip, and Dale had scoured the tower top to bottom but hadn't found anything she could use to protect herself once she climbed down to the ground.

Because she *would* be climbing down—even if she had to burn every inch of herself on vine to become immune. But then what? She had no weapon, survival gear, currency, or a map.

She didn't even have clothes.

Figuring someone might have lost a piece of jewelry in the fountain drain—a diamond could come in handy—she crawled into the basin. Chip and Dale hung out on the edge to oversee the job.

She told them, "If I get stuck in this well, go find Timmy." Ass sticking in the air, she wedged her arm into the drainage pipe, patting around for anything loose.

Nothing. She pulled her arm out, then eyeballed the drain. "Fuck, fuck, fuck." Her voice echoed down the pipe.

Chip started to skitter like crazy.

She raised her head. "What? What are you looking at? No, seriously, what are you looking at? I can't tell with all your eyes." The rest of the unseen spiders skittered in the walls . . . like a warning.

She sensed the heat of a gaze on her upturned ass. *Must be Abyssian.* She whispered to Dale, "Fuckface is right behind me, isn't he?" She gracefully made it to her feet and turned to the demon.

As usual, he wore no shirt, just low-slung leather pants. His horns were straightened, his eyes black. Surprise, surprise—he was hard.

Had the demon been leering at her on all fours, imagining what he would do to her?

A shiver raced over her at the thought. She was reminded of another inscription on the wall: *Horns flaring, he mounted her from behind, wedging his great shaft into her wetness.*

Her cheeks flushed. Damn it, she could not be viewing *Abyssian Infernas* in a sexual light. No female could be that hard-up.

Without a word, he began pacing in front of her, his large, scuffed boots pounding the stone floor. Trying to get himself under control?

She sat on the fountain edge between the spiders, and the three of them stared as he strode back and forth.

When the demon frowned at her colleagues, she said, "Meet Chip and Dale. Guys, this is His Highness, the evil tyrant of hell."

Still Abyssian said nothing. *Pacing, pacing.* Finally, he grated, "What is a face character?"

He must've had his own spies check her backstory. "A greeter of sorts at Disney World." At his blank look, she said, "It's an amusement park with rides and games."

"The castle I saw at that . . . park was a facsimile?"

She nodded.

"Then the Magic Kingdom is a place of trickery," he said, seeming keyed up at the idea.

"People know they're getting tricked. They like it." She tilted her head. "I'd call it more make-believe."

"And this place was built for amusement?"

Unable to resist, she said, "Mortals also go there to worship a mouse god. His likeness is everywhere. There's a duck demigod too. I could show you around."

He gestured at himself. "Go into the mortal realm?"

With his horns, glyphs, and dark red skin? That wide mask of black around—

Her lips parted. His eyes had turned green. He'd grown calm enough for them to revert to their natural color.

A vivid, blazing green. *Whoa.*

Inner shake. "The mortals would, um, think you were in costume."

"And then you could use your speed to flee among them."

She should've concealed her super speed. All fey were fast, but the royals were the fastest. Some said that was how they'd gotten to be royal to begin with.

Since this was the calmest she'd ever seen Abyssian, she tried to reason with him: "Will you just trace me somewhere I can use a phone? If I miss any more days without calling in, I'm going to get shit-canned from my job." She knew she could never work there again—her hiding place had been blown—but it'd be nice to give her supervisor a heads-up. Oh, and then to use her speed to flee the demon among the mortals.

He leaned against a wall, the sinews in his torso flexing. His wide shoulders tapered down to those narrow hips.

She might've expected the king of hell to have a bulky, no-neck build. Instead, his seven-foot-plus frame had been blessed with long, lean muscles and not a spare ounce of flesh anywhere.

He was oblivious to the fire vines on the wall. In fact, they peeled away from him, as if *he* was too hot.

Could she produce heat to tame them? Her immunity efforts were slow-going and painful.

"You work in a park devoted to make-believe and *games*," he said, his gaze keen. "Did you go to school to learn your trade?"

No school necessary for her gig, but . . . "I went to college in the mortal realm." Courtesy of her fake ID and Papa Disney. Without any kind of social life to distract her from studies, she'd completed her first degree with a triple major in under three years.

On graduation day, she'd started on her second degree. She collected them.

"You were a princess in a former life; I can't see you with your nose in a book. I imagine you fixated on baubles and laces, dreaming about ball gowns."

"I used to be like that."

"What happened?"

She gazed past him. "It was time to stop being a silly girl."

Her beautiful but unfeeling mother used to tell her, "No matter what trials you face, you must *be as you've always been*: a princess of the blood."

In the mortal realm, Lila had realized that if she didn't adjust, she'd be culled from that world before she reached her immortality.

Her mother had said, "You are the boulder in a stream, standing immovable against constant pressures." But Lila had told herself, "I'm a tree in the woodlands. I can't expect the sun to come find me; I'll stretch to reach the light." Determined to fit in, she'd dressed like mortals, talking and behaving like them.

The demon snapped, "Godsdamn it, what are you thinking about?"

"Huh? Nothing important."

In Demonish, he muttered, "Maddening female." She got the impression that he hated her but was helplessly intrigued by his mate.

When would he admit that she was his? She might have disbelieved it, but there were times . . . "I was just recalling a watershed moment in my life that shaped me as a person. But I'd never share it with someone I distrust so much."

He glowered. "Why did you disguise your eyes?"

She shrugged. "I wish they matched."

"They do when they turn."

"My eyes don't turn."

"Bright teal. A lover never told you that?" His voice dropped lower. "Hasn't your fiancé brought you to come?"

Her cheeks grew hot. She was used to blunt talk, but his interest was . . . dark. "Why would *my* orgasms be any of *your* business?" *Because I'm your . . . starts with an M . . .*

He didn't take the bait. Standing fully, he investigated her food tray. "You truly can't stomach these dishes?" When she shook her head, he strode outside, gazing back at her.

Expecting her to follow?

Picking a spot on the terrace where the railing had broken off, he sat with his long legs hanging off the edge.

She sidled closer.

"Sit, Calliope." He waved beside him.

"So you can push me off?"

"I can do that anyway."

True. She cautiously joined him, catching a hint of his scent. Fire, evergreen, and male.

There they sat, overlooking hell together. They hated each other, but apparently they'd called a temporary truce.

She wanted information from him; what was his reasoning?

As he gazed out at the rugged terrain, tension seemed to seep from him. His eyes even grew a touch heavy-lidded. He clearly loved it here.

She tried to see it from his point of view. Now that the ash had cleared, the sun shone brighter, and the landscape was alive with color. The black of the mountains only made the lava river more vivid. Gold and silver stripes ran down cliff faces. Did molten ore simply spill out?

She pointed to the largest volcano far in the distance. "What is the name of that one?"

"Mount Volar."

"The name of the river?"

"The Styx."

"When I was younger, I would read tales about this dimension. Are there really traps in the wilds of hell?" *What will I face out there?*

"Countless. Which should appeal to you." He turned to look at her. "A net from spider silk was crafty. But the crowning touch was using phallic carvings for a weight."

"*You* are the one who imprisoned me in this tower. Besides, if anyone should be brought down by faun erections, it's you, King Abyssian. You deserved that and more."

Green eyes lively, he asked, "Are you planning on *more*?"

"I'm just getting warmed up."

For some reason, her answer seemed to please him. "A wiser female would use her wiles, instead of coming at me head-on."

"I don't possess wiles."

His gaze roamed over her. Voice dropping to a husky timbre, he said, "Oh, little firebrand, I beg to differ."

Stifling the impulse to fan herself, she tucked her hair behind her ear. "I would never depend on wiles anyway. I depend on my mind. It's served me well in the past; it will with you."

"You propose to *outwit* me?" He grew animated, as if this was the most exciting thing he'd heard—in centuries. "Be forewarned, I'm a master of trickery. I could match even Loki, the greatest trickster ever to live."

"I've experienced your trickery with those labors." Reminded of those interminable hours, she said, "But I don't expect anything more from you; trickery is for the weak-minded and lazy."

He looked to be on the verge of laughing. "Calliope, I would very much like to spar with you. I wager I'll be up for the mental challenge."

"Demon, I win this round just by virtue of one fact."

"Which is?"

She held his gaze. "You didn't even know we've already begun."

His expression turned to one of fascination. Then he seemed to harden himself. "You were bright in your past life as well."

"Who do you believe I was?"

He hesitated, then said, "You were once Kari of Sylvan. A treacherous princess."

"Why are you so certain?"

"A soothsayer confirmed it." No doubt Nïx. "And you are nigh identical to Kari in looks."

"According to your ten-millennia-old recollection? I'm not convinced. Shouldn't I have memories of my past life?"

"Some do; some don't. The most visceral memories are the ones that might remain. Often they come in dreams."

"I suppose I would have had an inkling of one by now. If I were going to."

"Perhaps nothing was visceral enough for you to retain," he grated, his ire at the ready.

She was still on edge, her ire just as much so. In a pointed tone, she said, "Perhaps one has to sleep *comfortably* to dream. I myself sleep on the floor, huddled for warmth." When he didn't respond, she said, "Tell me about that princess's crimes." Lila was determined not to be equated with some long-ago fey.

"*You* betrayed me. Then you . . . died."

The mix of emotions he attempted to conceal made her stomach knot. Despite the passage of so many years, he still grappled with yearning, hatred, and grief.

In all her confusion about this reincarnation business, she hadn't given much thought to his loss. This hint of vulnerability made him seem less of a villain.

At least he *believed* he had motives to torment Lila. "You said she died in childbirth." *If I'm reincarnated, could I—she—we—have an immortal kid out there? Or a line of my own?* "Did the baby survive?"

Abyssian shook his head. Staring out over hell, he murmured, "Lost with you."

If Lila recovered Kari's memories, would she relive dying? And the death of her child? She shivered. "Who was the father?"

Without looking at her, the demon gave a curt shake of his head. *Lay off.*

Still too affected? At some point, she was going to have to ask if

Kari was his mate. *Not* posing the question would become as incriminating as blurting out her knowledge. "How big is this castle?" she asked, changing the subject.

He seemed relieved. "Immense. It has seven towers, each with hundreds of rooms, all filled with treasures."

"It sounds like a city."

"In a mystical realm, the structure grew and changed in unforeseen ways. It's steeped in magic. Some say it has a mind of its own."

"What do you mean?"

Her interest clearly pleased him. "If Graven likes an individual, it will give him or her gifts, even steering one's steps."

She recalled the fanciful stories she'd read about magical palaces and charmed keeps. Under different circumstances, she might've liked to explore this place.

"The heart of the castle is all but alive, a moving labyrinth. Yet you think to escape?" He shook his head. "Finding your way outside could take you days, or even years. And if Graven didn't want you to leave, you never would."

Given enough time, she could prison-break anything. *You're running out of time, Lila.* Her deadline approached. "I wager I could. Set me loose inside, and let's see."

"Escaping the castle would only catapult you into more danger. The lava river tides are unpredictable. Time it poorly, and you'd be incinerated. And what do you think my subjects would do with an alluring fey wandering around hell?" Maybe help her escape? "Say you made it past them and the fire river, you'd then have to contend with traps and predators. Hellhounds would rip you to pieces, if the reptiles didn't get you first. And in the end, you'd still be trapped in this dimension."

If she could find one sympathetic demon in the realm, she could talk him into teleporting her. But if not . . . "I read that there's a portal leading to my homeland, the Pando-Sylvan rift."

Did tension steal over him? "It's closed forever."

"Maybe I could open it."

"That would be an unequaled feat. It's been sealed for millennia with the strongest magics."

"You've presented problems that need solutions. I like solving things. My motto is FITFO."

"Pardon?"

"Figure it the fuck out. I'll do it over and over again out there."

He was getting exasperated with her. "A tender female like you wouldn't make it five minutes."

"You'd be surprised. My talent is adapting."

"In your past life, you expected the universe to bend to *your* will. Now you talk about adapting with pride."

"I do it well." Didn't mean she *liked* to. One day she'd have power over her own destiny.

"Such as when befriending spiders?"

She gazed over her shoulder. Chip and Dale peeked around the upper corners of the terrace doorway like two songbirds from a fairy tale. She faced Abyssian. "Whatever it takes, demon."

"How well you adapt won't matter if you get attacked by any of the beasts out there. What if history repeats itself and you die before you become immortal? Even if you avoid pregnancy, you could still be killed. And that ring can't heal a lethal wound."

She wanted to scream, *Your archer buddy will sink an arrow into my heart!* Instead she said, "You're right. I should just sit here and starve. Or wait for a maniacal demon to come be my reaper."

"I told you I won't kill you." He gazed out at the mountains. "Perhaps I'm done punishing you. Maybe I got the worst of my anger out of my system." He slid her a sideways look. "Plus evidence begins to suggest you are not a spy. I'm not convinced, but for now I'll withhold judgment on that count. For the rest, imprisonment will suffice."

"Now I feel *so* much safer. I'll sleep like a babe tonight the second my head hits the pillow. Oh, wait. I don't have a pillow. But as long as I'm not being punished . . ."

A clean breeze blew over them, toying with strands of her hair. She lifted her head to take in the new scents. "There's a sea nearby?" Even the sea breeze carried a hint of fire.

The air smelled like Sylvan in the fall, when gardeners used to burn leaves. All around the castle, plumes of smoke would funnel upward. That night there'd be an autumn feast.

Will I never return home?

His gaze took in her face. "The Mercury Sea. The shore is on the other side of the castle."

Shore. She felt another pang. She used to love swimming in Sylvan's streams and ponds. When she'd lived in Florida, the land of easy swimming, she'd never been able to risk revealing her ears.

"My chambers overlook the water."

Must be nice. "How did the sea get its name?"

"When calm, the silver water reflects the sky. On stormy days, it looks like mercury."

It sounded spectacular. "You're proud of your home."

He grated, "There is *much* to be proud of." His wings unfolded, drawing her attention.

Both times he'd closed them around her she'd been too freaked out to register how they felt.

"Never seen wings before? The demon slaves in Sylvan must be wingless breeds."

"They're not slaves. They're *serfs*."

"Are you jesting?" He gave a bitter laugh. "Whatever you have to tell yourself, princess."

Lila had been exiled young. Had her understanding of the fey realm been skewed?

Frustration clear in his expression, he asked, "Why do you have such strong mental blocks?"

"So crazy demon kings can't tap into any more of my nightmares and make them come true—"

Her stomach growled; he stiffened at the sound.

"I won't be *endlessly entertaining* to you when I curl up on the ground from weakness and never get up. Is that what you planned?"

Seeming to make a decision about her, he said, "Perhaps not." He raised his palm, twirling his other hand over it. An orange appeared!

As he peeled it, her mouth watered at the scent, her gaze following his fingers. They were surprisingly dexterous, but those claws . . . Could he retract them even more? How did he touch females?

He caught her gaze. "What would you do for this?"

She gave him her most arrogant smile. "Not a fucking thing, demon."

Had his lips quirked? Seeming pleased by her answer, he held out the orange atop his flattened palm—as she'd once fed deer.

Now *she* was the creature being coaxed closer. When she swiped the orange, their fingers brushed, and a current seemed to pass between them. Hell demons must give off sparks. "Is it poisoned?"

"If you doubt it, return it."

MINE. With her first bite, she rolled her eyes with pleasure. Even her taste buds were becoming more sensitive. "Thank you," she said between bites. As she ate, energy poured into her, her headache fading.

When juice dripped onto one of her boobs, his gaze grew heavy-lidded. In Demonish, he said, "I find myself desperately craving orange juice."

She reminded herself to act as if she didn't understand him. "It's bad manners to speak a different language in front of those who don't know it." Once she'd finished her orange, she asked, "Do you eat fruit?"

"Demons need meat." With a significant look, he said, "But I'm also tempted by sweet things."

Changing the subject . . . "How much magic do you wield?"

He hiked his broad shoulders. "In this plane, I can do nigh anything."

"You have power over everything here?" *Such as my life . . .*

He exhaled. "Total and utter."

"You sound as if you regret that fact, which confuses someone like me—who has zero power."

"Life is long without a challenge," he said. No wonder hers had sped by! "And you do wield power. It can reside in beauty and desire. You possess the former, eliciting the latter from me." He openly admitted to desiring her?

Before she could reply, he conjured a pomegranate. She caught herself grinning at his magic. "Those are my favorite."

He used a claw to slice it open, then handed half to her. "I know. You loved them in the distant past."

How many people loved pomegranates above every other fruit? She'd been able to dismiss his knowledge of her spider phobia, but not this.

Taken with those rumors of her reincarnation, it might be time to accept the evidence.

Weren't reincarnates usually brought back to right some wrong? So why would Lila have been reborn?

Maybe to bring down the Møriør.

She believed in fate; the idea of a greater cosmic purpose for her existence appealed to her in so many ways. . . .

She scooped out the seeds from one of the sections, moaning with delight. Yet then he gestured for her to return it.

But . . . but . . . She gazed from the fruit to the demon.

He had a tricksy look in his eyes, as if he'd just made a chess play and was wondering if she could predict all the moves ahead.

He didn't expect her to hand it back to him. So she forced herself to.

His lips curled. Then he hurled the fruit toward the Styx.

"Hey! Nooo." She glared at him. "Dick."

"Am I?" He traced away.

What did that mean? Sighing, she stood and returned to her tower. Inside, she drew up short. New things filled one of the rooms!

She rushed closer. He'd given her a mattress with luxurious bedding. A rug warmed the space, and a mirror hung on the wall. A gift box sat atop the new bed.

She knew all this had come because she'd handed back her pomegranate. Tricksy, tricksy demon.

The point wasn't lost on her. *Give a little to get.*

But what else did he want her to give?

Glancing around at the inscriptions on the chamber walls, she frowned. Of all the rooms Abyssian could have chosen—such as the fellatio room or the "wheelbarrow" one—he'd picked for her the room that celebrated a demon's claiming bite.

He, for one, believed they had a fated connection. So why wouldn't he cop to it?

Atop the gift box lay a note, handwritten with a bold scrawl:

Join me for dinner at nightfall.

A

This must be more trickery, a trap of some sort. But if knowledge was her only weapon, seeing more of the castle would benefit her.

She opened the package, finding a gown of dazzling gold silk. It was strapless, with a stiff, low-cut bodice. Goldwork embroidery adorned the wide ballroom skirt. Maybe the gold thread had been spun from straw.

Also in the package were matching pumps, a corset, hose and garters, toiletries, and a bathrobe.

Would the king expect to sleep with his dinner date? What if those twelve concubines were in attendance?

She could skip dinner, using the bedding material to shield her skin as she climbed down the fire vines.

Or she could accept the invitation . . . *and* carry out her escape. She surveyed all the gifts—her new arsenal. *Oh, Abyssian, you just fucked up royally.*

Lila grinned. She would join him for dinner, on her way somewhere else.

TWENTY

Determined not to watch her in the mirror, Sian roamed his castle halls. The echoing sound of his boots seemed to mock him.

Absolute power boring me absolutely.

At least Calliope made his life unpredictable. *How bloody long until dinner?*

He'd decided to invite her simply to discover more about his mate's current life. He would order Sylvan dishes for her and a sweet wine to loosen her tongue.

If he could keep his temper—and lust—in check, he would compliment her and make her more comfortable.

His only concern: that *he* would be seduced again, softening toward her. Earlier, they'd had an almost normal conversation, and damn him, he'd enjoyed it.

Merely sitting next to her had soothed his anger. He'd experienced an acute satisfaction to gaze out at his lands with her.

As she'd surveyed his realm, there'd been no distaste in her expression—more like curiosity. He'd imagined her looking at his body in a like manner. Seeing it anew. *Accepting* it.

If she could grow used to hell, could she possibly grow accustomed to *him*?

Sian was hell; hell was Sian. . . .

Maybe he should call for a concubine to while away his time. Strange that he hadn't even considered that option when he'd brought himself release earlier. Fresh from visiting his mate, he'd come with a shock wave's intensity, biting his arm bloody to muffle his destructive roar.

His concubines had written, beseeching him to join them in their tower. But he preferred females who would lie with him because of desire—not royal duty. Which meant he'd been with few females in general since he'd started changing.

He'd told himself that he'd diluted his memories of his mate with each female he bedded, but who was he kidding? He'd never taken another without fantasizing his mate's trembling body was beneath him.

In his dark imaginings, she'd wrung every culmination from him for ten thousand years.

If Calliope was the key to his pleasure, would he make do with lackluster substitutes for the rest of his life? Before, he'd had no choice because he'd lost her. Now . . . how could he discard her when she was in his keeping?

He'd have to. Even if she could somehow see past his "repulsive" looks, he could never accept her as his queen and the mother to his heirs. Fey and demon parents begat banebloods—creatures whose very blood was poisonous.

No, Sian wanted Calliope only to break his demon seal. Afterward, he would send her away to another prison, far from him.

Then he'd make some demoness his queen and have a hundred red-blooded heirs with her.

Damn it! The prospect of a substitute left him cold.

Yet so did the prospect of a future *with her*. He could never forget how skillfully she'd manipulated him into offering up hell's weaknesses.

Kari's kingdom had desired slaves. Her father had learned from her where and how to get them.

Because of Sian, scores of demons had lost their freedom forever. His fists clenched, his lifeline of hatred firmly in hand, his crimson filter at the ready.

Again Sian's mind turned to seduction. Why should he deny himself sport with Calliope? He was king of this realm; if he was to be cursed in form, he might as well revel in his power here.

He traced back to his tower and grasped the hand mirror, calling up her new room. He'd chosen a chamber devoted to a sex act he'd not yet enjoyed, an inside joke—with Calliope on the outside.

He frowned at her expression. The female had a cagey, foxlike look about her. *Up to something.*

Her gaze bounced from the wall mirror to the rug to the bed. Then she began to move with such speed that he could barely follow her actions. . . .

She broke the mirror, using a shard to cut the rug. She set up another shard to refract sunlight toward a runner of fire vine. She ransacked the bedding and pillows, then tore apart her new corset to get to the boning.

When he realized what she was planning, the unfamiliar urge to laugh nearly overtook him. "Wily little fey."

What a . . . surprise.

Calliope was *already* matching wits with him. In spite of all he'd told her about the dangers of hell, she was still going to attempt an escape.

He couldn't decide what aroused him more: the fact that the firebrand was using all those gifts against him or her stubborn bravery.

Her preparations complete, Lila collected her toiletries and hurried into the bathing chamber.

Brushing her teeth proved to be a religious experience; her shower with scented bath oil was a sensual indulgence.

As she braided locks atop her head, she automatically started to cover her ears. She grew giddy when she realized she didn't have to.

After donning the garters and hose, she rechecked the box for a shift or panties, but found none. Maybe demonesses didn't wear panties? She glanced at her own frayed ones, but couldn't bring herself to wear them again.

When she stepped into the gown, the material sighed with each of her movements. The decorative ties were in the front, so she was able to lace herself. Luckily she didn't need the corset she'd trashed. She slipped on the pumps, which fit perfectly.

Dressed, she took in her reflection with the single remaining shard of mirror on the wall.

Well, then.

The low bodice pushed her breasts far above the crisp edge, making them look larger, all but revealing her areolas. The gown tucked in around her waist, flaring at her hips.

She'd never worn such a decadent dress. She looked womanly, *felt* womanly.

She felt . . . sexual. And she was all too aware of her lack of panties.

Would Abyssian like this dress on her? Not that she would care, since a dozen concubines would probably be joining them.

She tilted her head, attention on her eyes. Did sharp emotions—anger, glee, lust—really turn her irises teal?

As the sun set, she grabbed the drawstring gear bag she'd fashioned from a pillowcase and rug tassels. She reached under her dress to strap it to her thigh. Her skirts concealed it.

At nightfall, she exited her room into the courtyard, expecting Abyssian to materialize soon—instead a patch of the wall in front of her started to shimmer. A door appeared where none had been a moment ago.

She cautiously opened it and crept out to a landing. A winding candlelit stairway awaited her.

Not even a servant or guard to escort her? Would her escape be easier than she'd hoped? She descended, her heels loud on the stone.

Abyssian's description of this castle had set her imagination aflame. *Steeped in magic . . . a mind of its own . . . all but alive.*

As she made her way down stair after stair, the magnitude of this labyrinthine palace struck her. The demon hadn't exaggerated its size.

From the staircase, she stepped into a corridor. A gilded door at the end groaned open. She headed through it into a new hallway, and the door behind her closed.

Ah, so that's how Abyssian would keep his mouse in the maze: no door would open until the previous one closed, which gave her zero avenues for escape.

That was okay. She'd prepared for a confrontation.

As she traveled deeper into the castle, that feeling of being watched returned. Sensations danced over her skin, and the faintest whispers sounded in her ears. At one point, she could have sworn a breath ghosted across her nape.

The castle *did* seem alive, simmering with secrets, mysteries—and loneliness.

Because its master was lonely? Why *wouldn't* Abyssian be if he'd lost his mate? He clearly still longed for Kari.

For me?

She passed a blue chamber with a large mural of hellhounds and dragons hunting. Her ears twitched, and she glanced over her shoulder at the mural—then shivered. Were the eyes of one of the hellhounds following her?

Shake it off, Lila. Soon she came upon yet another set of steps. She was halfway down them when the entire staircase began to move, sweeping her to another landing. She grabbed the railing, laughing with excitement.

Next she entered a gallery with gargoyle statues and ancient tapestries lining the walls. Trenches of moving lava meandered through the expanse, lighting and heating the area, dispersing the chill of the other corridors.

At the end were two massive doors. They must be fifty feet tall, made of what looked like solid gold. When she stood before them, she craned her head up, feeling small and insignificant.

Etched across the surface were scenes of demonic battles, filled with more hellhounds, dragons, storms of flame, and horned warriors attacking some gigantic reptilian creature.

These scenes evoked hell's storied past, trials and punishments in an unforgiving and mysterious world.

So what would she face beyond these doors?

When they started to open, she squared her shoulders, knowing one thing for certain: whatever awaited her . . . Lila would adapt.

She stepped into a grand dining room, her heels clicking on the polished marble floors. A fire crackled in a large hearth along one wall. A candlelit chandelier descended from a soaring ceiling.

Abyssian sat at the head of a long table set for two. Only he and she would be dining?

He stood at her arrival, acting the gentleman. She hadn't expected manners from a brute like him. That wasn't her only surprise.

The king's appearance was . . . improved.

His crown was made of fire, its shape wider in the back, then tapering to two sharp ends over his forehead. He wore fine tailored clothes: black leather breeches and a crisp white tunic embroidered with gold symbols that matched his glyphs. A wide, red sash circled his waist. His dark boots shone.

Did he have feet like a man or paws? Hooves? And how did he wear a shirt? The back must be modified for his wings. He'd folded them down until they were barely visible past his broad shoulders.

His long hair was secured in a queue, and his irises looked impossibly green against the darkened skin around his eyes. Yet as his penetrating gaze roamed over her, that green wavered to glowing black.

When a curl escaped her updo and she tucked it behind her ear, his eyes clocked the movement and lingered. Though pointed ears were the most unmistakable trait of the fey, this demon seemed to like hers.

Tracing to the other end of the table, he pulled out a chair for her. Abyssian's behavior was improved along with his looks? His concessions tonight struck her as *respectful.* Obviously he was setting her up for some elaborate trick.

Wary, she glided forward.

Had he just inhaled the scent of her hair? In a roughened voice, he said, "Your beauty pleases me, Calliope."

Her cheeks grew hot. But she was still a princess; if the king put forth the effort to be civil, at least on the surface, she'd reward him with the same. "Thank you, King Abyssian."

His welcoming and gracious efforts were working. She felt herself relaxing a touch—

"Now, if you will be so kind as to lift your skirts. . . ."

TWENTY-ONE

Calliope narrowed her eyes at him. "What did you say?"

In that dress, she resembled Kari more than ever. Good. Sian needed to be reminded of her treachery.

Because right now she tempted him beyond reason.

He'd watched her approach through the castle, chest tightening to see her eyes bright and her cheeks pinkened with exhilaration as she'd explored his home. With each of her shallow breaths, her plump breasts had threatened to spill from her bodice.

He'd been so enthralled with her looks, he'd almost forgotten about all the weapons she carried. "You can lift your skirts, or I will do it for you," he said. "And I won't be as considerate of the fact that you might not be wearing undergarments."

To her credit, she remained unfazed, even sighing. "What are you going on about now, demon?" She gave him an assessing glance.

For the first time in ages, he'd taken care with his appearance, having a valet help him since he refused to look at his reflection. Sian thought he'd detected her approval earlier. "I'm talking about your abuse of my gifts."

"You were *spying* on me?"

Constantly. But once she had finished with her escape preparations, he'd given her privacy to bathe and dress. "I can scent something is amiss with you."

She turned from him with an irritated huff, then raised a dainty foot to the chair. After reaching beneath her skirts, she turned to toss her hidden bag onto the table.

He reached inside it and pulled out a weapon: a shard of glass with cloth wrapped around the base to create a handle. "A fair enough knife."

She jutted her chin.

A smaller drawstring bag held an ashy powder. "I suspect you used the mirror and sunlight to cook the fire vine into a portable toxin. Had you intended to throw that in my eyes?"

Shrug.

He pulled free a set of sharpened sticks that she'd threaded into a swath of cloth for accessibility. "You used the boning from your corset to make throwing sticks."

She crossed her arms over her chest.

With a wave of his hand, he disposed of her bag and implements. "Save yourself any future efforts at escaping. Your ring"—he pointed to the gold band on her finger—"has a confinement spell as well as healing. As long as you wear that, you can't exit the castle."

She scowled at the ring, then at him. "All you've done is give me a problem to solve."

The little firebrand *was* just getting warmed up. His pulse quickened at the idea.

Smoothing her hair, she asked, "What are you going to do to me now?"

"Nothing. Though I won this round, I'll replace these items in your room, and we can start this evening over."

What's his game?

The demon had just caught her red-handed, yet he wanted to continue their dinner? "Sure. Why not?" What else could she do? All her efforts had been wasted.

And sneaky fucking Abyssian had shoved at least two spells into her ring. She could have burned herself on the fire vine for weeks, and she still wouldn't have been going anywhere.

But she had to believe another chance to escape would come her way. Tonight she would learn as much as she could. Tomorrow she would regroup.

After seating her, he traced to his chair at the opposite end of the long marble table. Even the table surface had chiseled Demonish inscriptions. Would he notice if she read them? "Is all the furniture stone in this castle? And the doors gold?"

He nodded. "We have only one slow-growing forest here, with trees so large lumber production would be difficult. But we have limitless igneous rock and ore." As a golden goblet appeared before her, he said, "Try the wine. Unless you'd prefer demon brew." He raised his own cup.

"I don't drink." She'd never been able to afford a misstep in the mortal realm.

With steel in his tone, he said, "You do tonight."

Pick your battles. She took a sip. Nice enough wine, she supposed. She gazed around the room, then back at him. In the firelight, he looked less monstrous. Surprisingly, she found aspects of the king . . . not off-putting.

The flash of white teeth against his reddened skin. His prominent cheekbones. The clarity of his gaze.

Even his large black horns were striking. They emerged from his temples to flare back along his head. Ridged at the base, the lengths grew smoother toward the tips.

Naturally the king of hell would look to his best advantage by firelight.

He might be beastly, but he had pride in his bearing. He should; he was a king, a primordial—and a member of the most powerful alliance in existence.

A Møriør sat right down the table from her. Though she was boldly assessing him, he said nothing, letting her look her fill.

His lips even curled. "That color suits you."

Compliments and wine? Again, he was putting forth an effort to make her more relaxed. At any moment, she expected him to say, *And for my next trick . . .* Her gaze flicked upward. "The crown of the hell demonarchy is understated." Unlike Saetth's fey crown.

"Because it serves little purpose. The demons of Pandemonia instinctively recognize and revere a monarch's horns. Mine are identifiable to them above all others."

She'd never read that. "I'm surprised His Highness invited me tonight. We didn't seem to get off on the right foot." She bit her lip and took a sip of wine. *He might not have feet, Lila.*

"I want you to call me Abyssian."

Another order. "Very well, Abyssian." She had a brief thought that he was trying to seduce her—he must want to be free of his demon seal—but she dismissed the idea. She'd made no secret of her hatred of him.

"I am curious about my prisoner." With a wave of his hand, he made the table shorter, teleporting her chair closer.

"Oh!" She blinked.

He noticed her hand shaking on her cup. "Nervous?"

"I'm suspicious. Before the night's through, you'll probably make me run for my life from hellhounds or something."

"You're in no danger this evening. I vow to the Lore that you'll be safely returned to your tower after dinner," he said, adding, "And there's no outrunning hellhounds."

Dick. "Good to know."

"Where did you live before your current home?" He sampled his drink. For a sinister demonic king, he had nice lips.

She dragged her focus back to his intense green eyes. "I was born in Sylvan."

"Are you close to your parents?"

"I wanted to be." Her upbringing had been so different from the ones she'd read about among other species. Maybe that explained why she wanted children so much: to shower them with the love she'd been denied. "But it wasn't in the cards," she said, her voice sounding sad, even to herself. Her scheming and cold parents had been consumed with acquiring ever more power. "They died years ago."

"How *many* years?" Abyssian asked, as if the number was significant.

"Eleven."

"You were thirteen when they ceased guiding you? Then what happened?"

"I went to the mortal realm to live." Wanting away from this subject, she asked him, "What were your parents like?"

Tone abruptly curt, he said, "I've already answered this question for you in a past life."

She drew back her head. "So am I never going to discover more about you? If so, I guarantee you'll hear nothing more about me."

Seeming to grind his fangs, he finally said, "My sire was a warrior and explorer, known for his wiliness. My dam was darkness personified."

"What does that mean?"

"It means she was beyond most beings' comprehension." He drank from his goblet, his unreadable gaze taking her in. "She was a creature of shadow, born from the ether."

How wild. "Is that where you came by your magic?"

"Possibly some, but this realm fuels the king's magic, tying it to the ruler's life force. The king in turn controls the land. Pandemonia and I are symbiotic."

Fascinating. "So you don't wield magic off-plane?"

"It's a luxury I enjoy in my own kingdom—one I have no need of in others."

"Did Kari come to this realm? Is that how you met her?"

He shook his head, seeming to debate how much he'd reveal. At length, he said, "When I was sixteen, that rift between Sylvan and Pandemonia had just been discovered. Back then, the fey were known as elves. They and the demons were such dissimilar species that mistrust simmered on both sides. So the king of Sylvan and my brother, King Goürlav, agreed that I would be fostered in the elven dimension for a season, learning about their culture. Kari was to be my guide."

"And then what happened?" Would he finally tell her how she'd "betrayed" him? She braced for his answer.

His claws lengthened around his goblet. "You were a devious spy for Sylvan."

Oh, shit. Her deadline had just gotten real. If he found out Lila's ill-fated mission . . .

"You manipulated me into revealing my realm's weaknesses to you. I told you how defenseless the outland demons were, how they'd rarely learned to teleport or mind-read, preferring a simpler way of life. I admitted how vulnerable Goürlav was, his new powers still developing." Abyssian's fangs sharpened. "And you reported those secrets to your father, the king. Armed with that knowledge, he broke his treaty of honor and launched a surprise attack against Pandemonia."

"Why?"

"To capture and enslave outland demons. Because of your treachery, Goürlav was forced to seal the portal for good—like a tourniquet to stem blood from a ruined limb—abandoning those demons." No wonder Abyssian had tensed earlier when she'd brought up the rift. "Families were torn apart."

Realization dawned. "You're talking about Princess . . . *Karinna*."

Nod.

"That's not the story I was taught."

"This I must hear."

"According to the history books, when the Pando-Sylvan rift

opened, a demon prince found Karinna playing with her friends. He abducted her, dragging her back to hell." Myths of Persephone and Hades were said to have arisen from Karinna's legend. "A demonic army invaded Sylvan for more females and treasures, but Karinna figured out their weaknesses and escaped. Back in Sylvan, she gave her father all the information he needed to protect the realm. The worst of the captured marauders were enslaved as punishment."

Karinna had been a rallying cry for millennia, a type of fey martyr. Her name was a reminder never to forget the mindless violence demons were capable of.

Am I *Karinna?*

Abyssian bit out, "The *fey* history books have it wrong. The elves attacked us."

"Why should I believe you?" she asked, though she . . . did, despite her feelings about Abyssian. He had no reason to lie, would just baldly say, *Yes, we struck.*

And Sylvan had a long history of enslaving invaders. Strange, though: for a pastoral realm with few natural resources, Sylvan had been "invaded" *constantly.*

"Believe me because I was there. And if I'd abducted a female and dragged her to hell—she'd fucking still be in hell."

Instead Karinna had gotten pregnant by another male and died. "Who did she marry?" Lila had never read anything on her husband.

Abyssian drank deeply. "A king of another fey realm."

If—when—this demon found out about Lila's betrothal to a fey king, he would lose his shit.

"And now you know your past crimes." His version of the story did make the princess sound treacherous.

Even so, Lila was *sick* of paying for others' sins.

Because of her parents, Lila had been exiled. Because of Karinna's actions, Lila had been captured by a Møriør. Because of Magh, she'd been hunted all her life by Rune.

While Lila could understand the archer's vendetta, she didn't want to pay for it with her life. Her worst crimes had been snobbery and ignorance, and she'd shed those weaknesses in her teens.

I *never did anything to the archer.*

She would take responsibility for her own actions, but she was done shouldering undue blame. At least in this life, she *was* trying to hurt someone—yet only to strike back against an enemy. "What happened to you back then?"

"A trusted general smuggled me back here just before Goürlav sealed the portal."

"If what you say is true, then I'm surprised you've never retaliated against Sylvan in all this time."

"I made a vow to wait for this Accession. The Møriør's attack is imminent."

Just as Nïx had said. Lila had to warn Sylvan. Her escape just became that much more critical. "In this conversation, you've revealed weaknesses to me. Aren't you afraid history will repeat itself?"

He bared his fangs. "Don't you understand? I *want* a fey invasion. The weaknesses of old no longer exist, and my power is vast. If your kind step into hell, they'll be trapped in torment." At his words, the lands rumbled.

She swallowed. "Why would you confide in Karinna? Were you two lovers?"

"We were . . . not. Fey and demons don't belong together."

"Why?"

Her question seemed to take him off guard. "Because they beget dark fey."

Also known as banebloods, those poisonous creatures had demon fangs and fey ears. Their logical minds warred with their base instincts. "Dark fey like the Møriør's archer? I wager he's glad his parents didn't feel the way you do."

"The way *everyone* does."

Not her. She hated Rune for what he threatened to do, not for what he was. And more, Lila believed in fate. If a theoretical demon was destined for a theoretical fey—and the fey *accepted* the bond—then fate intended for banebloods to be born.

Abyssian asked, "Would *you* mate with a demon?"

She said nothing, because she didn't want him to get any ideas. She would never accept a bond with Abyssian Infernas.

"I have no idea what you're thinking, and it vexes me to no end. You must've practiced constantly to hone your blocks. Why would you have?"

Because her cousins used their demon servants to mind-read at court. She shrugged, which just made Abyssian madder.

"If you're so blameless, open your blocks to me."

"Sure thing." She did for a split second, blasting out one thought.

He raised his brows. "I'd be happy to *get fucked*. Are you offering? If so, I'm accepting."

It was disturbingly easy to picture Abyssian in the sexual positions described on the tower walls. Pandemonia was getting to her. Or overstimulation!

She refused to be attracted to a Møriør who'd tormented her and kept *concubines*. "I'd have to be dead first."

"To fuck me?"

"To open my blocks. Because *I* don't trust *you*."

"So fucking is still on the table." Eyes gleaming, he said, "Or perhaps fucking on the table is still on?"

Though his play on words turned her imagination to a sizzling scenario—him, naked over her on this table, pistoning between her thighs—she managed a bored look. "Pass."

"You doubtless want to stay faithful to your former intended." Abyssian steepled his large fingers. "Tell me about this male who inspires such devotion. Does he live in the mortal realm?"

"In Sylvan."

"How did you meet him?"

"My parents introduced us."

"And you were enthralled with his looks."

"Looks aren't everything."

"Sayeth the beauty." The demon's lips curled into a smirk that other females—not her—would consider sexy. "Had you planned to have offspring with your fey male?"

Abyssian's voice made her ears twitch. She didn't have a lot of experience with demon kings, but this one was jealous. "We've talked about it. I want a large family."

What kind of father would Saetth be? She still debated whether he had set her up. *Why not just kill me . . . ?*

With each moment she floundered in hell, her lifelong dream of being queen of Sylvan grew more distant.

No. She'd still fight for that future. She would be a good ruler, had absorbed so much knowledge growing up at court. She'd taken her first steps amid power scuffles; her teething ring had been tasty intrigues. She'd learned to dance at the same time she'd grasped political footwork.

Her first word: *queen.*

Then her experiences in the mortal realm had given her a broader mind-set.

She'd once read descriptions of the different types of ruling styles, everything from benevolent father to tyrannical dictator. She'd liked the *protector of the realm/service to the people* style.

"Now what are you thinking about? Your eyes went distant."

"This and that."

Her answer clearly irritated the demon. "You were thinking of *him.*" Abyssian's eyes flickered. "Two perfect fey with their perfect feylings. Sounds like a match made in hell to me."

TWENTY-TWO

"You've asked me a lot about my personal life, but what about yours?" Calliope leaned back in her chair, her breasts straining against her bodice.

The sight *enthralled* him. His arousal had been simmering since he'd first seen her in that gown. Even speaking of her betrayal hadn't dimmed his need.

Ten days ago, he'd been sleepwalking; now everything felt so visceral.

She followed his gaze and tugged up her bodice in a vain attempt to cover more flesh. Kari would've worn that dress like a second skin, using the garment to play up her beauty—her favored weapon.

If this fey ever recalled her wiles, Sian would be doomed. "What do you wish to know about my personal life?"

"Do *you* want a wife and kids?"

"I do want pups," he said honestly, "but a male like me needs his mate for such things. At least for the first time. Do you know about a demon male's seal?"

"Vaguely."

"I won't spill semen until I claim my destined female. But after my seal is gone, I can plant my seed in *any* field—except a fey's."

"Because of banebloods."

Sian nodded. For millennia Rune had cursed his nature. When members of the Møriør had delved into the archer's mind to be brought up to speed with this time, Rune couldn't conceal the depth of his frustration and shame over his black blood.

Sian's looks might be repulsive, but Rune had been poisonous to everyone, always on his guard not to harm another by accident.

Now the archer's entire existence had changed. "My friend Rune believed he would never have a mate, but he has found his female at last."

"Another dark fey? I thought they were rare."

"They are." Banebloods were usually killed at birth. "But his mate is a halfling who is immune to him." Rune's vampiric female couldn't get enough of the black blood running through his veins.

"And you never found your mate in all this time?"

Sian waved to the seat at his right. "Do you see a queen by my side?"

"What if you never find her?"

"I could wed. I might make some lucky demoness my queen through a binding ceremony." Would Pandemonians recognize another female as queen while his mate still lived? Would his red-blooded heirs be recognized?

Not that Calliope herself would ever be. The Vrekeners might accept a sorceress for their queen, but the hostile hell demons would never—*could* never—show fealty to a monarch without horns.

In an impudent tone, Calliope said, "Or perhaps you prefer to stick to your harem?"

"I plan to wed *and* keep my harem of twelve."

Her lips thinned.

Nettling her amused him to a surprising degree. "Do you oppose the institution?"

"Of marriage?"

"Of harems."

Her eyes flashed. "In your case, I find it—how should I put this?—predictably antiquated."

"Antiquated?"

With a challenging arch to her brow, she said, "It seems that servicing twelve females would require a lot of time and devotion. *If* satisfying them was a priority." She leaned in and added in a confiding tone, "But then, older males don't often aspire to impossible goals."

His lips twitched. "I can provide references from them, if you're inclined to join their number."

Her haughty smile made his cock stiffen even more. "You must expect this very dimension to freeze over."

He had to raise his goblet to disguise his grin.

"I'd never share a male like that."

He shrugged. "Pity."

"How would that work anyway? Would you put your wife into the rotation?"

"Depends on how much she pleasured me," he said.

"Would you take your concubines to your marriage bed?"

"No need. I'd go to them. They occupy one of Graven's towers, living in luxury." He assumed.

"Can we cut to the chase? Why did you invite me to dinner?"

Because absolute boredom drains my life force more than anything else. Because it enlivens my decaying mind to be near you. "I told you. To learn more about my prisoner. And I didn't issue an invitation. I issued a command."

"You can learn all you want, but you'll always despise me just for being a fey."

"Maybe, Calliope, I'm looking for reasons *not* to despise you."

She clearly hadn't expected that answer. "Then maybe, Abyssian, I'll look for reasons not to despise you as well."

"Now that we have that settled, shall we dine?" At his words, dishes materialized in front of them, a bounty of food.

"Are you wielding magic to create this dinner?"

"I do have servants." Though an army of them had cooked this feast, magic summoned the fare to appear here.

"These are all . . . fey dishes." She gazed at him with a soft expression that would've made a lesser demon shudder with pleasure.

Kari had once cast him that same expression. He was ashamed to admit how much it'd affected him. He'd fantasized about earning that look again as much as he had about claiming her.

"Thank you, Abyssian."

Not trusting his voice, he inclined his head. Damn her. *Do not get seduced, Sian.*

She began to eat, nearly purring over the herb salad. The taste of buttery bread drizzled with honey made her lids grow heavy.

He had no appetite for this foreign food, so he downed his demon brew and watched her savoring love affair with her meal.

Transitioning immortals were sensation seekers, constantly testing their new perceptions; this one's body seemed to be vibrating as she sampled one dish after another. Her chest was flushed, her nipples stiff against the silk of her gown.

He pulled at his collar. Did she realize how erotic she appeared when eating? He had his answer when she licked honey from her thumb with a sheepish grin.

No, she did not. Her sensuality was innate.

For the main course, a platter of pheasant and roasted vegetables materialized. With her first bite, she gave an audible moan that made him shift in his seat.

Over the last hour, the agreeable ache in his shaft had escalated into unenjoyable pressure. "I suspect you're in the grips of overstimulation, are you not?"

Her cheeks went red. Even the tips of her ears pinkened. "What makes you say that?"

He found he liked stealing blushes from her. "Oh, not a thing."

"Any other suspicions about me you'd like to voice?"

"That you're a virgin."

Her face blazed in confirmation.

"Your former male failed to seduce you."

"Why are you so certain he tried to?"

"Because in his position, I would do naught else." How easy life would prove if he'd been born a fey like her. He'd once been ready to look like her kind, act like them. He would've sacrificed anything for her.

"Can we change the topic from my sex life to one more suitable for dinner?"

"Certainly. As long as we follow up after dessert." Glare. "You have a stout appetite for so slight a creature." Smirking over his cup, he said, "Of course, when one plans to escape from hell, one needs to build up strength."

"When one doesn't know if one will receive another edible meal, one eats more." She took a large bite, chewing with exaggeration.

He just stopped his lips from curling. He liked this boldness in her. Yet it differed from Kari's. The princess's had come from the absolute belief in her own superiority. Calliope simply got so mad she grew heedless of consequences, her temper truly demonic.

Which appealed. He wanted to kiss her when her eyes went teal with fury.

She said, "You seem to be drinking more than eating."

He raised his cup. "Sylvan fare is not my preference." In Demonish, he murmured, "Though I hunger for a certain fey's honey upon my tongue."

Had she blushed again? Surely she couldn't understand his language. He'd never met a Sylvan who spoke the "cant of slaves." She must've reacted to the tone of his voice.

Dessert proved to be an agony. She would dip a strawberry in cream, then subtly suck the cream off the tip.

Gods almighty. She would be dining at his table every night.

In a throaty voice, she said, "Has anything ever tasted so good?"

He slanted her a look. "Your lips, I'd wager."

She cast him a sassy grin. "A fool's bet, because you will never know."

Challenge accepted, firebrand.

Between bites, she said, "Thank you again for this food. Not that you gave it to me out of kindness. I know you have some agenda."

"Hmm. What do you think it could be?"

Her brows drew together. Whatever thoughts whirred behind those spellbinding eyes killed her appetite. She pushed her plate away.

Curiosity hammered him.

Her gaze grew distant, and all of a sudden he felt as if he were sixteen again, strangling inside to know her mind was elsewhere—to know she didn't find him interesting enough to stay engaged with him.

He'd solved mysteries of the godsdamned universe, but her mind was forever unknown to him.

Magic cleared the dishes and refilled her cup. "I don't have to ask if you've enjoyed yourself," he said to reclaim her attention.

Facing him again, she said, "The wine and food were excellent."

But not the company? "We're not without comforts in hell. Still, you must despise it here."

She shrugged her pale shoulders. "The atmosphere is improving, so that's a plus."

"Because the ash is settling?"

"It's more than that. I don't know how to explain it. I got a sense of misery and ruin. Death. Now that sense has lifted."

Because of changes within me?

"How long have you been king of this realm?"

"A new position. Goürlav, my brother, died recently."

"Were you close?"

"We were at one time." The worse Goürlav's appearance had become, the more he'd closed himself off—despite Sian's efforts over the ages. "He and I were fraternal twins."

"I don't see how he could die. Was he as strong as you?"

"Stronger." Goürlav had become known as the Father of Terrors—because eventually his very blood began to spawn monsters. *Will mine?* "He lost a death match to a powerful vampire." Sian had considered vengeance, but the fight had been fair.

"Why would he enter one?"

Goürlav had led Sian to believe that he'd neither wanted nor needed friendship, creating his own solitary lands. After giving up the search for the hellfire, he'd abandoned Pandemonia, leaving the realm running as if it were a clockwork factory. Yet apparently he'd been lonely enough to seek a companion. "He intended to win the hand of a young sorceress, one who'd volunteered to wed the victor." Regardless of who—or what—prevailed.

Sian shook his head at the absurdity. He felt huge and ungainly next to Calliope's small perfection; what in the hells had Goürlav been thinking?

Loneliness must have driven him into that death-match ring. *My twin died because he was hideous—yet still yearning.*

Sian's gaze took in Calliope's fine-boned face. *My fate as well?*

At the end of Goürlav's life, few would have looked at his gruesome appearance and believed he'd once been a gentle soul with a dream of peace and commerce.

The bloody betterment of all elven- and demonkind!

Changing the subject, Sian said, "I'm surprised you haven't asked me anything about the Møriør. If you hail from Sylvan, you must have heard much about my alliance."

"From my earliest memories. You're the bogeymen that bring about the end of the worlds. Fey children have nightmares about the savage hell demon, the fire-breathing dragon, the bloodthirsty vampire, and more. Especially the fey-slayer."

"Did you have nightmares as a child?"

"You think they ended just because I grew up? Now my nightmares have come true. I've been captured by the hell demon and imprisoned in his lair."

"I haven't wet my ax with a Sylvan's blood in millennia. And our archer doesn't slay your kind indiscriminately. He only kills the royals from Queen Magh's line."

"Why?"

"He vowed to stamp out her descendants. Saetth is Magh's son, and the rest of his kin are like him—evil and vicious. The whole tainted root needs to be destroyed. The worlds will be a much better place without those degenerates."

She narrowed her eyes. "I'm to believe Rune only kills royal fey? And only those guilty of viciousness? Is he so infallible as judge, jury, *and* executioner?"

"Yes, you're to believe that. There's little about the fey that he doesn't know."

"I read in the *Book of Lore* that you and your alliance fought the ice demonarchy recently, laying waste to their whole army. Is that true?"

"No. Only four out of our alliance actually fought them." Allixta had twiddled her thumbs with boredom, her magic unneeded in that conflict.

"According to the book, the archer shot a shock-wave arrow that turned bones to dust. Across the battlefield, demons writhed on the ground like worms, never to regenerate. You were no less deadly, taking out battalions with your ax."

"That demonarchy was attempting to awaken a malevolent god who once tried to bury all of Gaia in ice. But none of you are old enough to remember that. The Møriør *are*." If those demons had succeeded, the apocalypse would be a lot sooner than any in the Lore expected. "We warned them what would happen should they stand against us. We *always* warn them."

She tilted her head, as if she didn't know whether to believe him.

"What else have you heard about my alliance?"

"Rumor says Orion the Undoing can detect weaknesses in everything and everyone."

True. "Is that the rumor?" Sian would never give this female information that wasn't commonly known. And he'd reveal no weaknesses—history wouldn't repeat itself—but then, the Møriør had very few. "Our leader's powers are unimaginable. Any who challenge him are doomed to failure."

"The Møriør's base is supposed to be a dimension that moves through space and time."

"It's called Tenebrous, and that's no secret." The war room in Perdishian—Orion's black-stone castle there—had a wall of glass through which one could see worlds flashing by.

"Many believe the Møriør's dragon can incinerate an entire realm."

Also true. "King Uthyr is a long-term visitor here at the castle."

Voice scaling higher, she said, "Do the others visit often?"

"They rarely travel to Pandemonia," he told her, noting the relief in her expression. She *should* be afraid of them. But . . . "You are currently with the Møriør who poses the greatest threat to you."

She shot him another glare. "I have heard a lot about your alliance, but I could never determine one thing: what do the Møriør want?"

"To stop the apocalypse."

"Stop it? You *bring* the doom."

He shook his head. "We herald it. The Vertas alliance is led by Nïx the Ever-Knowing, a madwoman who seems bent on destroying this universe. She foolishly believes she can match Orion in power." Her counterintuitive maneuvering left the Møriør scratching their heads. If Orion was known as the Undoing, Nïx should be known as the Unpredictable. "Yet so many in Gaia—including the fey—foolishly trust her. We will stop her. We will right the balance."

"By enslaving us all? By annihilating our way of life and burning our realms to the ground?"

"By defeating and governing you. We journeyed from the Elserealms to Gaia solely for that purpose."

"Do you intend to *govern* us like you did the legions who'd gathered below? I think the word you're looking for is *oppress*."

Irritation simmered. "I might have . . . intimidated them so they would return to Slaughter Gorge, to resume their interminable punishment."

"That sounds dire."

"It should be. They took part in an uprising against my sire, so Devel punished them diabolically."

"How so?"

"He divided them into two armies, banishing half to an inferno on one side of the valley and half to an abyss on the other. Each of their strongholds contained a locked portal that led out of hell and a golden key."

"Let me guess: the key only worked on the opposite army's portal."

Sian was impressed. "Just so. Their desire to leave hell embroiled them in eternal strife. They've battled each other every night for millennia." At least until the Vrekener queen had somehow stolen *both* keys. All Melanthe had wanted was the godsdamned gold.

"Millennia? You didn't think they'd served a long enough punishment?" Calliope asked, incredulous. "So you sent them back for more?"

"Eternal means *eternity*." Sian had replaced the keys, starting the whole thing back up again.

"What about forgiveness? Or peace?"

"Demons don't forgive, and peace is overrated. War is what I live for. I have the disposition for battle and a body designed for killing." He took a drink. "Let me guess: you don't believe in war."

"Only when it can't be avoided and it *ends* in peace. You're planning to invade Sylvan, but you don't *have* to. Is there anything in the universe that I could do or say to keep you from attacking?"

Careful, Calliope, you could give a demon dangerous ideas. What did he want more? Payback against Sylvan, or its former princess in his bed?

He intended to have both. "I will enjoy my long-awaited revenge."

"Then fey children are right to be afraid of you." Did younglings truly fear them all? "What will you do when you conquer the kingdom?"

"So certain of my victory?"

She rolled her eyes.

He liked that she understood his might. "After wiping out any resistance, I will free the demons of that land, then enslave the fey nobility. I daresay you're a member of the Sylvan gentry."

"I daresay I'm already a slave."

Gods, her insolence was sexy. Excitement continued to burn away his ennui.

"I would support your first decree," she said.

"Would you indeed?"

She nodded. "If I were queen, I'd liberate all the demons."

"You mean those *serfs*?"

Her cheeks flushed, his barb hitting home. "I was young when I left the kingdom. I might not have understood Sylvan as well as I'd thought."

Her admission surprised him. "But you wouldn't support my second decree? Do you not think the fey overlords deserve a like punishment for enslaving others?"

"If you did that, you would be duplicating the worst thing that kingdom ever did."

"*Your* actions were critical to the success of that slave raid!"

"I'm *not* Karinna." Seeming to rein in her temper, she said, "You don't have to be that kind of ruler. Don't do this, Abyssian."

"What do you know of ruling? Or of anything?"

"What do *you* know? You've been king for just a short while, and your first decree is war? No, wait—that's your second. Your true first was doubling down on an eternal punishment." Tone dripping with sarcasm, she said, "Your royal record will be unmatched in history."

If Sian hadn't fucked up so dearly in the past, Goürlav's record would've been historic. After his brother had been forced to abandon all those subjects, the young, idealistic king had lost any desire he'd had to make changes.

He'd shouldered all the blame for families being torn apart, and for what had happened to Sian. *"Dear gods, brother, how could they have . . . your horns were . . . ?"* Goürlav hadn't even been able to say the word: amputated. *"They will never grow back . . . and I forced you to go there."* Sian had handed Goürlav his bloodied horns, telling him, *"Cast these away. I never want to see them again."*

To this day, he had no idea what Goürlav had done with them.

Calliope said, "If you're going to defeat and govern, then decree instead that the fey and demons live in peace together. Make the kingdom an example of what could be."

"The Sylvans would never live like that. They consider every other species inferior. Did your family not raise you to believe that?"

"I can think for myself." Five words Kari would *never* have uttered.

"Come, you must believe the practices of other species are savage. For instance, a demon's claiming bite."

"I'd say it's fairly common. The Lykae and vampires do it too."

"If you were mate to a Lykae, would you let him mark your flesh?"

"If I loved and trusted him, I would," she said, astounding Sian. "But . . ."

"But what?" Of course she would qualify such a statement.

"I don't think it's fair. Why don't females ever get to bite? If I wore a mark, I'd make my man get a tattoo or something."

"A *tattoo*," he rasped. "To make things *fairer*."

"Was that too progressive for a relic like you?"

Imaginings ran riot in his mind. Her baring her neck to receive his fangs . . . while he plunged his shaft inside her . . . on the brink of spilling for the first time . . .

The visual had made him hard as hell metal, his fangs now aching along with his cock. He scrubbed his palm over his mouth. Calliope dredged up hopes best left buried.

How had he gone from his plan to use and discard her to fantasizing about claiming her as his own?

What if she returns different?

He shook his head hard. What was more likely—that his mate would welcome a male's bite or that she was weaving a web of deception even now?

Had she figured out she was his? He hadn't exactly concealed his attraction, yet she'd never brought up the possibility. "If you have your own views on other species, what do you make of demons?"

"If I based my opinion on my experiences with you, I would assume all demons are violent and unnecessarily cruel. But I don't believe in wholesale hate, attributing the deeds of one to many."

Who *was* this creature? "Violent and cruel?" What had Uthyr said? *There's a difference between trickery and cruelty.* "Guilty as charged. I come by both honestly; I *am* the king of hell."

She sighed. "I used to think that way."

"What way?"

"That we can only be *as we've always been*. Maybe in time your mindset might expand."

"And if I'm satisfied with how I am?"

"Then you'll never grow."

He drank, masking his reaction to her. Talking to her like this made his heart speed up. Being with her made the years fade away, until he felt . . . young.

But *young* meant *trusting*, which he would never be again. "You're one to speak of growing," he bit out. "You were the most intolerant female I've ever met."

"How old was Karinna when she died?"

"Twenty-four. Your age," he said, only to frown. *Yet you plan to send her away, outside of your reach?* That would also mean outside of his protection. At the thought of losing her, his wings tensed. He yearned to have his mate safeguarded within them.

"How do you know she wouldn't have changed in her thirties? Her forties? Her hundreds? Karinna died before she ever had the *chance* to grow."

His mind began to race. Could a young female like Calliope be shaped into the queen he wanted and deserved? Perhaps she'd been returned to him for just that purpose!

What if he could teach this adaptable fey? Bend her to *his* will? He swallowed. A future might still be possible. "On the surface you seem different in this life. Though this could be an act." How could he shape what he couldn't even get his arms around? "For all I know, you've remembered the past and are deceiving me right now. You were an exceedingly skilled liar."

Temper erupting, Calliope shoved back from the table and shot to her feet. "I'm not that fucking princess!" Her eyes blazed teal.

He opened his mouth to protest, but she cut him off: "Even if I share a soul with her, I'm *not* her. I don't remember that life, don't want to. And I'm sick of taking the blame for others' actions."

"Why should I believe anything you say?" He wished she could pass some test to allay his suspicions. At that moment, he realized Uthyr was right. Sian did have a stranglehold on a lifeline of hate. For all these ages, it'd kept him sane.

So what will happen if I release my hold?

She strode to the hearth. As she paced in front of the fire, flames reflected off her golden gown. "I'm sorry you and others were hurt by Princess Karinna. But that's your past, not mine. I don't claim it. My name is *Calliope*. Lila to my friends."

"Lila." He liked the way her pet name felt on his tongue.

As if she hadn't heard him, she said, "Since I haven't done anything, you don't have the right to hold me here against my will."

"Might makes right," he said, because he had no credible counter to her words.

"Might won't keep me imprisoned—because wits always win."

He stood, staring her down. "Calliope, understand me: you will never escape this realm."

She boldly held his gaze. "Abyssian, understand *me*: I will escape you, and when I do, *I will leave rubble in my wake*!" As she spoke, the fire flared behind her, twin spires above her head that resembled horns.

His breath left him. She looked like a queen.

A queen of hell.

TWENTY-THREE

Casting off blame felt amazing! Like a catharsis. So why was Abyssian staring at Lila as if he'd seen a ghost?

Dinner with him had been enlightening. Once she'd gotten used to his brusque tone, his crass crowing about his harem, and his whiplash moods, she'd been able to detect more of those tiny hints of vulnerability.

And more of his loneliness.

Abyssian had traveled to Sylvan at only sixteen, returning with all his dreams extinguished. Even after everything he'd done to her, she pitied the boy he'd been.

Suddenly his vivid green irises turned black. He advanced on her, forcing her to back up against the wall. He reached for her, covering her nape with his palm.

Stunned, she craned her head up.

He was gazing at her with a wild yearning, his stern brow furrowed. His features were harsh, even brutal, but she found his face starkly magnetic. Despite his fierce expression, he cupped her neck gently.

He grazed his knuckles over her cheekbone, treating her like she was the most delicate thing he'd ever touched. "I feel torn apart, Calliope, as if two souls war within me. Part of me believes it possible to forgive you. Part of me wants to hate you for another eternity." A quake somewhere deep in the ground punctuated his statement.

This warrior king's unexpectedly tender touch made her breaths shallow. Something about him called to her, drawing her in.

"You're trembling."

"Because every time you get this close to me, those claws of yours sink into my skin." Which was only partly true.

"I won't hurt you again." He sounded so different when he wasn't yelling or sneering. With his Demonish accent and deep pitch, his voice was . . . sexy.

Really sexy.

He leaned down and nuzzled her ear.

She shivered against him, biting back a moan at the surge of pleasure.

He nuzzled her other one. "Your pretty little ears drive me mad. I imagine licking them, nipping them, murmuring wicked words just to make them twitch." He moved to the tip . . . he flicked her pointed ear with his pointed tongue.

This time she couldn't stop her moan.

He gripped her sides with his big hands, his thumbs stretching around just under her breasts.

She was panting. Could he feel her racing heartbeat?

"Your eyes are bright teal." He rested his forehead against hers, their breaths mingling. "My kingdom for a kiss, Lila."

Sexy demon! "I don't . . . I can't lose control with you."

"I'll take care of you. I'll bring you the release you crave." He stroked his thumbs upward, grazing her nipples. "The pleasure you *need*."

Her eyes nearly rolled back in her head. "Oh, gods. . . ."

He groaned. "Want my mouth on your stiff nipples." He grazed his thumbs again, then rested them over the hard peaks. The pads of his thumbs lightly kneaded.

She was levitating! She tried to speak but only managed a breathy cry.

"Does my little fey like that?" he asked, his eyes promising wicked things.

Likes? No, loves! She nodded eagerly.

"We can go slow, beautiful."

She hadn't thought he had this much control over his inconceivable strength, but he was gentle.

Her brows drew together. Which meant he'd simply chosen *not* to be gentle before.

That thought broke whatever spell she'd been under. This was the Møriør who'd tormented her, the one who'd probably bedded a dozen demonesses today.

The male who wanted her to *join their number.*

Gaze locked on her mouth, he leaned down. In Demonish, he said, "Wanted your kiss for so long."

He didn't *deserve* her kiss. Just before their lips met, she slapped him—hard. Pain flared in her wrist. "Ow! Godsdamn it, that hurt!"

He released her, his eyes returning to green, as if he were just waking up. His brows drew together, his expression somehow both unsurprised and confused. "I . . . the ring will heal that."

Ugh! "Get this through your blockhead: whenever I'm injured—from your claws or your bruising grip or from warding off your unwanted advances—it still hurts."

A muscle ticked in his prominent jaw as he clearly struggled for control of himself. He grasped her elbow, then teleported her back to that cursed tower.

Over dinner, she'd been able to pretend she was merely a guest of the king. Back in her prison, she felt like a shafted Cinderella after the ball.

She yanked her arm away, and he released her. "So that's how it works between us? When I don't succumb to your seduction, you return me here as punishment?"

He drew his head back. "That's not what I intended."

"You dress me up, let me out, then put me away again? I'm not some doll that you can bring out to play with whenever you feel like it."

He scrubbed a palm over his face, as if he hadn't expected this anger.

Which just made her madder! "Tonight you've shown me that you *can* be gentle with me—which means you've decided *not* to be over these last few days." Her wrist throbbed. "Which makes you an even bigger prick than I'd first thought!"

He scowled at his hands. At his claws? Facing her, he said, "Calliope, the way I've been recently is not how I usually am. You might adapt well, but I do not."

"What does that mean?"

He parted his lips to speak, then closed them. Another try: "My existence has been the same for ten millennia. Now my life is in flux. Having such limited experience with change, perhaps I haven't reacted well to it."

"Reacted well? Is *that* how we're describing your behavior?" *The nerve of this asshole!* "And to believe I'd started to pity you for being so lonely."

TWENTY-FOUR

"Pity *me*?" Sian had once been one of the most perfect male specimens in all the worlds!

Desired. Pursued. Coveted.

His ego took yet another blow. He felt it all the more because she was right. He *was* lonely. But he hadn't been before her return—because he'd drifted through his life like a sleepwalker.

Now she was awakening things in him best left dead.

That stubborn pride of his made him lie: "I'm hardly lonely. My concubines cater to my every filthy desire."

"Then you can take *them* from the cupboard."

"You will dine with me each eve."

"I'd rather eat dirt."

"That can be arranged," he grated. "Again, this isn't an invitation. You've received a command from your king."

She bit out: "Not—my—king."

He inhaled for calm, reminding himself of the illusion he'd seen in the fire.

In hell, mystics read flames. Sian's own mother had been a pyromancer.

He didn't know if the castle had spoken, declaring Calliope its mistress, or if Sian's subconscious had supplied the vision, but either way, he knew better than to ignore it.

Tomorrow night at dinner, he would harness his temper. He would treat her as if she were made of glass.

He gazed down at his long, sharp claws. In those first days, he'd been crazed with the fragile fey. How many times had he hurt her?

There had to be a way to retract his claws fully. He'd been in this form for so short a time, he still didn't understand all the facets of his evolving—*de*volving—body.

He pictured his claws retracting even more—and they did! He was about to call her attention to it, but she appeared to be reaching her limit with him.

"Now that you've put away your doll, you can leave."

He exhaled. Even if he'd treated her like his queen, Calliope could never accept a life in hell. Much less his monstrous appearance. She would attempt to escape him again and again, for the rest of her life.

The odds of her return had been hundreds of billions to one. Right now the odds of any kind of understanding between them seemed far less likely.

Even if he could discover a way around all their obstacles, she would never forgive his upcoming invasion of her home. Still he said, "Calliope, I don't want to fight with you anymore."

"No, I'm well aware of what you'd rather be doing with me." Hands balled into fists, she snapped, "You've imprisoned, starved, and abused me. As you told me less than an hour ago, you're the Møriør who *poses the greatest threat* to me. Why in the gods' names would I ever kiss you?" She was shaking even more.

Any female who'd trembled near him in the past had quivered from desire—all females save the one linked to him by fate. She'd hated and feared him since she was young.

Picturing Calliope as a little girl afraid of monsters, he scrubbed his palm over his face. His *repulsive* face.

Wait . . . His brows drew together as he recalled her words: *Why in the gods' names would I ever kiss you?*

Among all the reasons for not kissing him . . .

She'd never mentioned his appearance. Could they get past it? As he gazed down at her, he felt as if some constriction around his throat was loosening.

She turned from him, all but dismissing him, then headed to her new room.

Biting back commands, insults, questions, he traced away. In his quarters, he stared at the hand mirror lying on his bed as an opium addict would a pipe.

Was the mirror a new lifeline? With a curse, he surrendered to his compulsive need to watch her. She paced at the end of the bed.

He winced at the lewd writing surrounding her. She was an innocent, yet he'd put the female in a former sex den, his idea of a joke.

She glared at her ring, then made her way to the balcony railing. She stretched her right hand past it. When she tried to do the same with her left hand, the ring wouldn't pass the invisible barrier.

She muttered, "Sneaky fucking Abyssian." Her eyes shimmered as her tricky mind plotted retaliation. He welcomed it, enjoyed the games they played.

As long as she couldn't escape.

In the past, Sian had felt as if he'd stared at that miserly hourglass, willing a single grain of sand to drop. The hours he'd just spent with her had sped by faster than any before them. His loneliness ebbed whenever he was simply near her. Even when they fought.

I want her.

He wasn't ready to release his lifeline and let himself free-fall—how could he ever bring himself to trust her?—but he knew beyond a doubt that he couldn't live without her passion.

He would possess her for his own; he could *try*.

Just as Goürlav had done, Sian would bravely enter the godsdamned ring.

He would investigate possibilities, pouring his energy into a potential future with his mate—which meant he needed to clean up his life so he could focus on her.

Right now he had twelve too many concubines and a debt to the Sorceri hanging over his head. Picturing the ordeal to come, he ripped off his shirt, then stretched out on his bed.

Damn. This is going to hurt.

TWENTY-FIVE

Lila ran through the Sylvan forest, darting in and out of dense fog banks. A shadowy form stalked her.

The fey-slayer.

No escaping him; even with her speed, she could never run fast enough.

An owl swooped down in front of her, making her scream and stumble. Nooo! *Her ears twitched at the twang of the bowstring. The arrow's feathers whistled as it zoomed toward her. She whirled around.*

The arrowhead pierced her chest. Unbearable pain radiated out from her heart.

She collapsed to the ground. The fawn from her dreams peeked out from behind a nearby fern. They met eyes until her vision left her. . . .

Lila shot upright in bed, choking back a cry. She heard the spiders milling about in the walls, the dragon calls and hellhound howls. The lava from the closest volcano cast a soft glow inside. Just a nightmare. Nothing to fear.

Yet.

She lay back, relishing her pillow. She'd barely gotten to sleep earlier—because of serious overstimulation.

After Abyssian had left, she'd discovered new bedding in her room and also a negligee and robe of white silk. She'd eagerly changed out of her dinner dress into the nightgown. The silk had glided over her body, stiffening her nipples.

She'd hopped atop her bed, moaning at the softness. She'd gone from frayed underwear and a stone floor to lavish sleepwear and a feather-tick mattress. *The life!*

Under the covers, her sex drive had ramped up yet again as she'd replayed what the demon had done to her earlier.

Kissing her neck. Nuzzling her sensitive ears. Stroking her nipples.

Part of her had regretted making him stop. Lying there, she'd considered taking the edge off with a quick orgasm, but she'd again had that sense of being watched.

Eventually, she'd passed out. Until now.

The skittering from the walls intensified. A warning? She shot upright again. One of her ears twitched, then the other.

Something was wrong in hell.

Static electricity made her hair stand on end, and the entire dimension started to quake. Dust rained from the ceiling.

Even over all these sounds she heard a faint *clickety-clack* on the stone floor.

She turned and found the fawn from her dreams! It was standing in her room, mere feet from the bed.

Am I losing my mind??? As she'd done in Sylvan, she held out her palm. The shy creature sidled closer along the side of the bed . . . until she could feel its warm breath on her hand.

The fawn vanished just as Lila's bespelled ring slipped off her finger.

Deep in a trance, Sian envisioned the mountain the Vrekeners had settled upon. Then he pictured the terrain between that peak and his castle expanding.

Body straining on his bed, he enlarged New Skye one league at a time. He built up land until he'd re-created mountains. He duplicated ravines and rivers.

One for them, one for me.

He drained his magic, his very life force. Sweat beaded his skin, nearly rousing him from his trance, but he held on until the territory was as vast as he'd promised the sorceress—and his own was the same size as before.

But New Skye was like a scourge in his realm, in his mind. His trickster nature urged him to test the boundaries of his vow to the sorceress, to punish her extortion. But how . . . ?

Test the boundaries.

Of course.

He could cut New Skye free of Pandemonia, leaving the new dimension whole, but unanchored. He'd re-create hell's borders—without New Skye inside.

The Vrekener inhabitants wouldn't know anything was amiss until someone tried to trace there and couldn't find the moving dimension.

He who laughs last, Melanthe.

But gods, the process would deplete him, would be like severing a part of himself.

Bracing himself, he envisioned ripping away the new realm. He dug into his consciousness to mentally tear at New Skye.

His breaths heaved, his muscles knotting . . . finally he perceived the total excision of the Vrekener realm. Using the last of his strength, he sealed both planes.

When he managed to open his eyes, the room tilted. *I've erred. Spent too much magic.*

Over these months, as his appearance transformed, his sense of self had grown unstable, his identity eroded. Tonight, in the midst of this upheaval, he'd reached deep into himself and altered something that equaled his very being.

Like a snapped rubber band, his mind still resounded. Pandemonia was left weakened.

Just like the king of hell.

TWENTY-SIX

Lila didn't know if the fawn was a waking dream, a hallucination, or magic.

She didn't know why her ring had loosened right when hell was acting wonky.

But she did know that without that ring, she could now bail over the terrace edge, escaping the tower to get to Sylvan.

Would she jeopardize her life out in Pandemonia to warn her kingdom about the Møriør's invasion?

Yes. Maybe they could evacuate or call on every Vertas ally to mount a defense. Maybe *this* was why Lila had been reincarnated.

All she needed was one sympathetic demon in this realm. . . . Ready to undertake this mission, she got busy.

In a blur, she ripped and tore and sewed. Not even half an hour later, she'd crafted coverings for her arms, hands, and feet out of the bedding, and a protective apron from the rug.

Once she'd completed her preparations, she changed into her dinner dress, the skirt now shortened to her knees, and fastened the rug shield over it.

Chip and Dale gazed on with curiosity. "I know how ridiculous I look," she told them. "But desperate times . . ." She stuffed her pumps into her makeshift bag, along with her remaining fire-vine powder.

One last detail. She used ash to scribble a message on the back of Abyssian's invitation to dinner. Then she left the note and the ring on her stripped bed.

With a final look around, she headed to the terrace railing. A fall from this height would prove deadly, but the risk didn't deter her.

She saluted Chip and Dale, who skittered with disapproval, then swung her legs over. When she grasped the nearest vine, she gritted her teeth as she waited for the familiar pain to sear through her. . . .

Nothing! Her improvised mitts and footwear were working, protecting her from burns.

She began to climb down, picking her way among the crisscrossing tangle. Once she grew accustomed to the various strengths of the vines, she quickly descended the rest of the way.

On the ground, she wanted to scream her victory. Free! *I told you I would escape, Abyssian.* She would never go back to that tower. Never.

She drew her shoes out of her bag and slipped them on. After removing her mitts and rug apron, she stuffed them into the bag. They might come in handy again.

She surveyed her surroundings, spying not a single soul, nor any animals. Everything looked so different from down here. Matching landmarks against her memory, she headed along a black rock path to the lava river.

A three-way divide greeted her. Left would take her toward the sea Abyssian had spoken of. Right would take her in the direction of eternally punished demons. They couldn't free themselves from this place much less her. Hoping for a happy medium, she chose straight, the path wending alongside the river.

She followed it for leagues, the rocky terrain turning into silvery grasslands. Wispy shrubs with razor-sharp thorns lined the trail, and the river tapered.

Still no sign of demons.

If she couldn't find someone to teleport her, maybe she could locate the Pando-Sylvan rift. How big could hell be anyway? She'd only read estimates of its size.

After her confinement, she was eager to run. She stowed her cumbersome shoes, then took off down the trail. The farther she got from the castle, the more the skies cleared.

A full moon hung heavy in the sky, lighting her path as the prairie grasslands gave way to volcanic mounds covered with strange plant life.

I'm entering the wilds of Pandemonia.

Hell seemed eager to show Lila all its wonders. She zoomed past huge flowers with black petals, their blooms the size of satellite dishes. Giant ferns unfurled their glittering silver fronds. Dragonflies as big as eagles darted overhead. Smaller streams of lava crisscrossed each other like red-hot braids.

High in the sky, silhouettes of dragons raced across the moon.

Though completely foreign to her, this realm didn't intimidate her. She craved hell's wildness; it seemed to well up inside her and demand a release.

Tonight, so many aspects of Pandemonia reminded her of . . . sex. The scent of flames. The bold colors. The constant pressure, friction, and *eruptions.*

The lava was fiery and vivid, like Abyssian's hypnotic skin.

Where had *that* thought come from?

The sky grew brighter. Tiny insects hovered in the air, each one carrying a minuscule tendril of flame, as an ant would carry a leaf.

Real fireflies! She couldn't contain a laugh, crying, "More!"

Pandemonia obliged. Pent-up volcanoes rumbled, and the fireflies swirled.

She'd assumed the wilds of hell would be, well, hellish. Not *awesome*. Out here, she felt alive, her senses sparking as never before. She was brimming with energy, and her blistering speed increased even more.

Her arousal was off the charts.

She felt immortal. No, like a goddess. Confidence surged inside her—

A roar sounded, echoing over the dimension.

Abyssian.

His mate was loose. In hell.

Something had set off the spiders in Calliope's tower, tearing him from his stupor. But she wasn't in any of the rooms.

How had she gotten free? *How?* Had his protections failed during the hell manipulation? *Can't lose her again!*

He traced to her bed. Beneath her ring was a message written in ash:

This round goes to me, demon. I left your castle standing (though your pride should be in rubble right about now).

C

He scented the air, but she wasn't in the vicinity. Which meant she was likely dead.

No. Never. Never again. His claws and fangs shot longer. *Control yourself, or lose her forever.*

He closed his eyes, searching his realm. Searching . . .

There! He sensed her close to hell's forest. Normally, he would use magic to secure her, but his life force was too low. He traced, appearing on a peak that overlooked the region.

How had she gotten this far from Graven? He spotted her in the distance. Still alive!

She was running full bore, her feet barely touching the ground, her legs a blur. She headed toward several traps.

"Calliope, STOP!"

She slowed, searching the night for him. She gazed up and turned to face him. Whatever she saw in his appearance made her raise her brows. She tensed to run again.

If he traced after her, he would lose sight of her for a precious instant. By the time he'd reached her last position, she could have already raced away.

"There are traps all around you," he called. "Bottomless pits and quicksand bogs. If you come with me now, I'll give you your freedom."

"Right," she called back, her sarcasm carrying. "I'm going to believe that."

"You'll come with me, or you'll die out here tonight."

She smiled at him. "I've never felt more alive. And I've got things to do."

He held up his palms. "Calliope, I am asking you to return with me."

"Are you *inviting* me?"

"Yes!"

"Consider this my RSVP." She raised her middle finger.

He had tried to bargain with her. His only other option: threats. "If you don't stop where you are, I will—"

"Get fucked, Abyssian," she interrupted.

"Godsdamn it, this isn't a game!"

"Then why is it so fun?" She blew him a kiss and charged away.

He traced to a point ahead of her on the path, but she'd already blown past him. He pivoted and trailed her through the brush.

How had she escaped? The castle might have helped her. If so, he could never let her out of his sight again—unless he could figure out some way to keep her in hell of her own volition. Sensing a trap ahead, he yelled, "There's a pitfall!"

A split second later, she teetered along the edge. "Abyssian!" she screamed, her arms pinwheeling. "Help me!"

He traced, diving for her. *If I don't reach her* . . . He materialized in midair. Frowned.

She was gone; to the sound of her laughter, he shot headfirst into the pit.

TWENTY-SEVEN

"Sucker!" The trickster had fallen for such an old trick?

Somehow sensing exactly where to place her feet, Lila continued on. The flowers and ferns gave way to spindly trees, and she neared a dark wall of some kind.

No, not a wall. Moonrakers: enormous trees often found in demon dimensions.

She raced into the murky forest, gaping at the size of the trunks. They made redwoods look like twigs. Face raised, she spun as she ran. The leaves were silver, the bark as black as Abyssian's eyes.

Reminded of his pursuit, she increased her pace. Light cascaded from a clearing ahead. What would hell show her next? She burst into the clearing and stopped short.

In a silver-grass glen, a cascade of . . . gold flowed. An illuminated *gold*fall.

Molten ore—the same shade as her dress—poured from a cliff into a large steaming pool. "My gods." She wanted to stare at such a scene forever. But he closed in on her; she could hear his breaths.

Abyssian appeared mere feet behind her. He lunged for her, snaring her bag. She twisted, shimmying from the strap, then took off.

He tossed away the bag, yelling, "Enough, female!"

She hurried past the pool—then skidded to a stop. Dead end. The tree trunks were all grown together. The demon had cornered her.

She ran behind the fall of gold, slowing along the pool's edge.

He scowled at her from the opposite side. When he went to her right, she fled left. He adjusted his course; so did she. They both slowed, gauging what the other would do.

"How did you get the ring off?" he demanded.

"Like it was hard?"

"You could have been killed a dozen times over out here. Is your captivity so unbearable that you'd risk your life? Or are you bent on getting to Sylvan?"

She raised her chin.

"Do you really believe warning your kingdom will save them from me?"

"Instead I should sit in that tower and do nothing? You might not give a shit about the inhabitants of Pandemonia—other than devising ways to punish them—but I care about my fellow fey."

"You've already sliced your cheek open . . ." He trailed off. "Calliope . . . it's *healing*. The wound is mending without the ring."

She reached for her face; the tingle of regeneration was unfamiliar, but pleasant.

He exhaled a gust of breath. "You're an immortal now."

It'd finally happened! No wonder she felt so supercharged.

I am *supercharged.*

"But even an immortal can die out here. Calliope, do you want this to be the last night of your life?" he asked, his gaze stricken.

Oh, yes, his interest in her was about so much more than revenge. Some part of her had hoped Nïx was wrong, that no tie between Lila and Abyssian existed. His expression left no doubt in Lila's mind.

I'm his mate.

He offered his hand. "I will take you home, and we will discuss this. Can we not be reasonable?"

She straightened. "I'm not going back to that tower."

Seeming to reach the end of his patience, he clenched his big fists. "I'm king of this realm—you'll go wherever I bloody tell you to."

Ha! "You'll have to catch me first." As if he could. "And you're looking worn out there, relic. The old-timer didn't have his nap today?"

The sculpted muscles of his bare torso tensed. "You're going to pay for that one, female."

"Threats, Abyssian? What're you going to do? Lock me up?"

Voice gone husky, he said, "Maybe I'll toss you into my bed, and we won't leave it for years."

She hated how smug and arrogant and *sexy* he made those words sound. Her attention shifted down. *Whoa.* "You've got a hard-on. Shocking. You get off on the chase?" She sidled to her left.

He eased that way also, so she edged back to compensate. "If so, I'm not the only one. I can scent how much you enjoyed my pursuit."

She followed his gaze as it dipped to her bodice. The gold material clung to her breasts, outlining her hard nipples. "Overstimulation." She was in heat. Couldn't be helped.

"How long will you use that excuse?"

"As long as I'm still suffering from it." Even now, she was torn between the impulse to throat-punch Abyssian and the urge to explore his glyphs. With her tongue.

His eyes flickered from green to black and back. "Want to hear a secret that most young Loreans don't know? Overstimulation never lets up. You simply learn to deal with it better over the years."

"You're lying." In this state, she could barely think! She'd assumed there was a set time limit. If this lust went on indefinitely . . .

"Not at all. The years will bear that out, and I look forward to them. But first I need to get you out of danger. I'm about to trace, little fey. I've got a fifty-fifty shot of predicting which way you'll go."

"Whatever you're going to do, you better be quick about it. Because I'm faster than I've ever been."

He lunged to her left; she skirted right—

Arms snagged her waist. The demon had faked her out and tackled her!

The force sent them hurtling across the glen. His wings closed around her, and he twisted to take the impact as they landed.

She was . . . unharmed? He'd handled her like a crystal vase someone had beaned at him.

He released her from his wings, but only to flip her onto her back in the silvery grass. Levering himself above her, he pinned her wrists above her head.

Neither of them moved. Their breaths sounded loud, even over the bubbling pool. As his body loomed over her, his massive size registered in a way it never had before. *He's a lethal warrior.*

His scent—clean sweat and fire—hit her. Overstimulation left her dazed. The molten gold lovingly highlighted his features, the color matching his glyphs.

Light played over his straightened horns. His sweat-slicked skin. His brutal but mesmerizing face.

When had he grown as captivating as the rest of this world? Rugged terrain; rugged demon.

He looked like hell's version of a sex divinity.

Inner shake. This was a Møriør holding her. She thrashed against him, didn't gain an inch.

"I scent your arousal, female. If it's anything like mine, you're frantic for release." He wedged his hips between her thighs, propping himself over her. Only their clothes and a slight space separated their bodies.

She was high from her immortality, from exploring Pandemonia. If overstimulation lasted forever, her chances of resisting him grew dim.

What was he about to do? Better question: what was *she* about to do? Urges racked her.

She wanted to lick his lips, to clutch his generous pecs. Her fingers opened and closed as she imagined sinking her nails into his narrow hips and yanking him against her.

His smoldering gaze raked over her body. "You're so fucking sexy." He rubbed his pointed tongue over one of his fangs.

The sight made her shiver. Helpless to resist, she rocked her hips. She sucked in a breath when her pussy briefly pressed against his hard dick. The unreal heat of it reached her through their clothes.

"Lila, *yes*!" He shuddered, but he didn't grind against her, just held himself there. "Again . . ."

Staring into his onyx eyes, she wantonly undulated for more of his addictive heat. Her skirt hiked up, almost exposing her, but she didn't care.

Not now. Not on the first night of her immortality.

Sian wanted to roar with triumph. He'd gone from believing his mate would die tonight—to discovering she was a true immortal.

If she would let him protect her further, history would *not* repeat itself.

And now she lay beneath him, looking like an offering. Her loose hair streamed out across the grass, those locks shining in the goldlight. Her cheeks were flushed, her tapered ears pinkened. Her heavy-lidded eyes were blazing teal.

She bit her bottom lip, clearly debating whether to undulate again.

"Do it, female," he rasped. "You *want* to do it." He could scent her lush wetness. "Didn't it feel good?"

She rubbed up against him, making him dizzy with pleasure. "I saw the way you looked at me earlier, demon. See the way you're looking at me now." She repeated the sensuous movement, beginning to pant. "This is more than revenge. You were either in love with Karinna or she was your mate."

Between breaths, he said, “I’ve hated Kari—you—for ten millennia.”

“Deny it, then.” She rocked upward again, but he needed more contact between them.

He wanted more of his mate. He thrust against her, drawing a moan from her throat. *Not enough.*

When he reached for her skirt, her eyes went wide. “No! I don’t want you to fuck me.”

“I’m not. *Yet.*” He grasped her skirt, searching her expression.

She hesitated, then nodded.

He raised the material to reveal her mouthwatering sex. Atop her mons, she had a small patch of sandy-brown curls. Her little clitoris pouted for his touch—for his tongue—and the trimmed curls around her lips were soaked.

His horns shot straighter, his body in a lather for that wetness. “Gods almighty.”

He tore open his pants, wincing when his cock sprang free. His pierced shaft thickened even more when he laid it over her clit. At the contact, he hissed in a breath between his teeth.

Moisture beaded the crown, a maddening hint of the ejaculation his mate would give him. Catching her sultry gaze, he commanded her, “Use it.”

Lila whimpered when his ridiculously big dick pressed down on her.

Her bunched-up skirts kept her from getting a look at it—and maybe that was a good thing.

When she felt his searing flesh throb against her, she moaned, *“It’s so hot.”* She writhed, rubbing her slick pussy along his shaft.

Wait . . . was he pierced? She undulated again, perceiving uniform ridges along the underside, like metal barbells. They felt *unbelievable.* "Oh, my gods!" Her release grew closer, her moisture spreading over him.

His eyes were fully black. *"More."* His wings extended, his magnificent body gone rigid with tension.

She gave him more—rocking faster and faster with short snaps of her hips.

His jaw slackened as he watched her. "Can't even see your movements . . . just a blur! What the fuck . . . are you doing . . . to me?" He sounded dazed. "Ahh! Use it, Lila. Use it to come."

She did, uncaring of anything but her approaching orgasm. At this point, she would've let him shove that pierced dick inside her.

Between ragged breaths, he said, "About to come! It's so good . . . so fucking good. Do *not* stop." His length pulsated over her.

With a moan, she increased the tempo.

In Demonish, he rasped, "You make me insane. Madden me! Never get enough of you. *Never.*"

The ground rumbled; pillars of stone erupted behind him! His horns and wings cast wicked shadows against that backdrop.

He was godlike. A primordial in the throes.

She felt like she was witnessing something forbidden, something no mere Lorean like her should see.

Just as the thought occurred, he grated, "You *are* my mate. *Mine.*" His eyes held a proprietary gleam. "For all time. Mine to pleasure and possess."

"Oh, gods, oh, gods." His words pushed her past the brink. "I'm going to—"

Bliss engulfed her body.

Wet.

Scorching.

Boundless.

Her head thrashed as she dug her fingers into the grass. His beast-like growls ratcheted up her orgasm till she couldn't contain her screams. . . .

"Yes, Lila, *yes*!" He could barely believe what he was seeing—his female mindless from lust.

Her screams rang in his ears, the sweetest sound he'd ever heard. She bucked and writhed, using his cock to draw out her ecstasy.

First time to come with my mate. He was going to release so hard he feared for his sanity. "Fuck, female!" *Too* hard. Too crazed—

The scent of her orgasm wrenched his culmination from him.

A godsdamned detonation.

"AHHHH!" His muscles seized. His back bowed. The ravaging pleasure forced a roar from his lungs. Waves of it made his body quake like his lands. *"Lila!"*

The dimension shook. Over and over and over . . .

A final groan. A last shudder. Nigh comatose, he collapsed to his side.

"Abyssian?" she murmured.

Head lowered against her chest, he raised a finger. "Moment." He tried to keep his weight off her. To catch his breath. To right his mind.

He'd known that pleasure with a mate was far different from a meaningless round with any other female. He'd heard males boasting about the sexual fortune a fated one had brought them. He'd predicted that coming with Calliope would be an experience like no other.

But this . . . this was like every release over his lifetime had combined into one—then been multiplied exponentially.

He reached down and swiped his thumb over the head of his cock, shocked at the amount of pre-cum he'd produced for her.

Soon she would free his seed; if he didn't go crazed in the process, all would be well.

After this encounter, nothing could keep him from enjoying more of her sizzling passion. He would go to any lengths to have her in his bed. And he needed her not to escape again.

As he fastened his pants, an idea arose. She'd asked him if there was anything she could do to prevent him from attacking Sylvan. *As a matter of fact, firebrand . . .*

His allies would be furious, but in time, they would understand—

Sudden pain flared in his head. "Damn it, woman!" She'd bashed him in the skull with a rock.

TWENTY-EIGHT

Lila had just scrambled to her feet when his hand clamped her ankle.

Yank. He snatched her back, catching her before she hit the ground. "You little witch!"

Despite this confusing detour with Abyssian, she still needed to escape. "No! Let me go!" She couldn't believe she'd just gotten off with the universe's primordial demon. "If you take me back to that tower, I'll kill you!"

"You're in no position to threaten me, female. Your speed only helps when you're free."

And she wasn't. Not now. For how long could she stand more of that confinement?

Dragging her against him, he teleported her from the glen.

They appeared in a firelit room. When he released her, she smoothed her ruined dress into place and surveyed her new surroundings.

An oversize bed with a stone headboard dominated the room. Opened terrace doors allowed in moonlight and a cool breeze. The fur of some quadruped sprawled in front of a large fireplace.

Mounted on the wall above the mantel was the head of a giant reptilian creature with slitted pupils, scaly green skin, and serpentlike fangs the size of her arms. This was the beast depicted on the gold doors outside the dining room! "Where are we?"

"My chambers." He rubbed his head.

She hadn't even drawn blood. *A shame.* "Why would you bring me here?" She pulled grass sprigs from her hair.

"You told me you didn't want to go back to your tower," he said, his voice roughened from his roars.

She made her way to the fireplace. With him standing not far away, she felt as if she were flanked by two fires. His heat . . . his scent . . . Her thoughts grew muddled. Had she really just ground against him till they'd both come?

And had he truly admitted she was his mate?

Stalling to regain her composure, she pointed to the trophy over the mantel. "What is that thing?"

"The Lôtān, a Leviathan—half dragon, half kraken, with venom that could kill even an immortal."

"I thought the Leviathan was a sea creature."

"It sprang from the sea but lived on land as well, swimming in lava."

"You keep its head . . . here? In your bedroom?"

Shrug. "My ancestor battled it to claim this dimension. This trophy is sacred in hell."

She raised her face when a sea breeze filtered in through the opened doors. Hadn't he said his room overlooked the Mercury Sea? She headed outside to a tower terrace similar to the one she knew so well. Only this one looked unscathed by time.

Beyond the railing was the water! *Whoa.* The pale moonlight danced over the waves. She could hear them crashing all the way up here.

He followed her out and joined her at the railing.

She sensed that he wanted her to remark on the view. So she didn't.

"An improvement from your previous lodgings, no?" He faced her.

"Are you offering me the use of your room going forward? If so,

I accept, but you'll have to throw a sheet over that thing above the mantel."

"Not quite." He crossed his arms over his chest and leaned against the railing. "Obviously, I need to keep an eye on you. We will be *sharing* my room."

Ridiculous. "I'm not going to *live* with you."

"I've decided you'll also be sharing my bed."

"Become your concubine?" She scoffed. "The demon has jokes! Just a few hours ago, I let you know how I felt about that prospect. Hell freezing over? Ringing a bell, relic? I would never have sex with you after your treatment of me."

No matter how frenzied he'd just made her.

She shivered to recall the sight of his mighty body as he'd roared . . . those primal shadows . . .

Even now—in the moonlight, with the wind ruffling his midnight black hair—she found him . . . compelling.

"My treatment of you? Then perhaps I'll do as you did and simply declare myself a different person now. I'll disavow my past actions—as you did Kari's."

"That's not the same." *It's kind of the same.*

"I'll never hurt you again, Calliope."

"*Never hurting me again* shouldn't be a selling point; it should be a given," she said, wondering why they were still discussing this subject. "I might be your mate, but that doesn't make you mine."

A muscle ticked in his wide jaw. His voice dropped to a menacing level. "Trust me when I say that you—as Kari—made that fact *abundantly* clear."

Because Karinna was his mate. All evidence pointed to Lila being her reincarnation. *I'll have to . . . process that later.* "Why didn't you tell me?"

"I plotted revenge for the past."

"More reason why I don't want anything to do with you."

"Do you not? You came quickly enough against my cock."

Her face heated. "You're the most arrogant asshole I've ever met. Have you forgotten that I have a fiancé?"

Tick, tick, tick went that jaw muscle. "In hell, you have no one but me."

"There's nothing you can say to convince me to become your concubine. *Nothing.*"

"No? How about peace for Sylvan? If you became mine, the Møriør would refrain from attacking."

Her lips parted.

"Each hour I'm here enjoying you is an hour I'm not warring against the fey."

"And how long will that last?"

"A standard demonic concubine contract lasts for a minimum of a thousand years."

A millennium? With this fucker?

"However, since you are my mate I'm interested in securing you . . . *indefinitely*. I will make you my queen."

She gaped at him.

"You were willing to risk your life to warn your kingdom about my invasion. Wed me, and you can end the specter of war entirely."

Marrying him would mean surrendering forever all of her pie-in-the-sky dreams: to live safely in Sylvan, to be the queen of that realm, to start a family that would also live in safety, and possibly to fall in love.

What if Saetth was innocent in all this? If she could get back to him, she could have a wedding and coronation this very season. They could start having kids right away.

Her fey children would run the forests as she had.

Even if Saetth had dicked her over, she could find someone else for herself. *Anyone* else.

A male who was normal. Who knew what a phone app was. Who didn't accessorize with a battle-ax. Who wouldn't cringe to picture the kids they'd have together.

Abyssian squared his shoulders. "For as long as you are my wife, I vow to the Lore that the inhabitants of Sylvan are safe from my alliance. None will fall by a Møriør's hand."

She drew back her head in disbelief. A vow to the Lore was unbreakable, yet she knew how badly he wanted to punish her kingdom. "Ah, I see, the master of trickery is playing with me. You'll figure some way out of your vow, and make me a victim of your games yet again. You're illustrating why I could never trust you!"

"The time for games has passed."

"You're . . . serious? Then this is coercion."

He shook his head. "A mutually beneficial arrangement."

If she was bound to Abyssian, Rune would have to back off.

Was she actually considering this marriage? How could she not when it would save her people *and* herself? "You'd vow to keep me safe from any threat to my life? Any at all?"

"Yes. I easily make that pledge."

Eventually he'd find out she was Magh's descendant. His vow would force him to protect her—even from Rune! "Maybe if you didn't demand sex—"

"Not an option," he said, tone unyielding.

"We aren't physically compatible. I'm too small compared to you." When he'd loomed over her in that glen . . . "You're well over a foot taller than I am. With your wings, you must have three times my weight, and you've got to be ten thousand times stronger."

He'd begun shaking his head before she'd even finished. "I promise you, we will be compatible."

Sex. With Abyssian Infernas. She ignored the spike in her pulse. "You said you wouldn't hurt me. Losing my virginity with you will hurt." Despite her new immortality.

And he'd need to bite her during the claiming. She recalled his reaction at dinner when she'd said she would accept a mate's bite. Abyssian had looked like he'd forgotten how to blink.

Perhaps in that past life, she—or Kari—had rejected the possibility. Lila had been truthful, though. If she were mated to a male she loved—and trusted—she would bare her neck, taking her medicine.

Loving and trusting Abyssian weren't in her future.

"I would be as gentle with you as possible."

Her lifelong aspiration to be Sylvan's queen faded from distant hope toward wistful memory. But if she kept the Møriør from attacking her people, she could do more for them than any other ruler before.

Isn't sacrifice what queens do?

When she imagined Abyssian's ax raised against the Sylvan army . . . or one of Rune's arrows piercing her heart . . .

Dear gods, she was going to have to surrender to the king of hell.

Dear. Gods.

She'd wondered whether fate had some kind of cosmic plan in store for her. Lila's mind flashed to a memory of playing with her dolls, pretending they were her subjects in need of protection. Maybe she'd been reborn to sacrifice herself—damning herself to hell—for Sylvan.

"I will have your answer now," Abyssian said. "I understand you'll be giving up certain . . . things to live here. But through your actions, Sylvan will be spared for an eternity of eternities."

The exact phrase Nïx had used.

Realization struck. This had all played out according to the Valkyrie's plan. *That bitch.*

I was a pawn to save Sylvan, in ways I never even suspected.

Had Saetth been in on the plan? She'd questioned why her fiancé wouldn't simply order her assassination; maybe because he'd known she needed to be alive for this sacrifice? "Fine. I'll do it."

Abyssian exhaled, as if he'd been holding his breath. "Very good. Just so we understand each other: as my wife, you'll serve me in every way, doing my bidding."

Frustrations that had compounded all her life boiled to the surface. She met Abyssian's gaze. "I hate you."

In a lover's voice, he said, "And I you. That's why our marriage will work. Neither of us will expect anything more than pleasure between us."

Expediency was key.

Fearing Calliope would back out from their agreement, Sian hadn't even given her a chance to change her clothing for the wedding. He'd hastily teleported her into his empty court, appearing in front of the throne dais for the simple hand-fasting ceremony.

Her pupils had dilated to the size of coins.

Part of him was just as shocked. *She agreed to wed me?* Her decision made him grudgingly respect her more. Like Kari, Calliope was nothing if not loyal.

The marriage rite was straightforward. He would wrap a sacred tie of leather made from the hide of the last Lôtān around their clasped hands as they repeated vows.

He asked her, "Are you ready?" He'd told her what she would say, a basic pledge of self.

She hesitated, then nodded.

Curling his finger under her chin, he lifted her face. Brows drawn, she bit her bottom lip.

What he wouldn't give to know her thoughts *now*. As he gazed down at her, the millennia faded away until he felt as if he'd held her in his arms just yesterday at a dance in Sylvan.

"What are you contemplating, Calliope?" he asked, though he suspected she'd never answer.

She surprised him by saying, "How I will live without everything I'm giving up."

The idea of her pining for her fiancé sent Sian's jealousy skyrocketing. "You'll simply have to find other things to satisfy you." He would make her forget that prick if it killed him.

"I won't hold my breath." Gesturing at her filthy dress, she said, "Not exactly how I imagined my wedding. But this is just how I would imagine yours."

He supposed young females cared about such things. "Perhaps if you please me as a wife, I will grant you a more formal coronation."

"Be still, my beating heart. You're really sweeping me off my feet, demon."

Undaunted, he conjured the Lôtān tie, then took her hand. As he wrapped the binding around his wrist, then hers, Calliope's gaze rested on his long claws. Their hands looked as mismatched as the rest of their bodies.

Yet fate said she was the only female with whom he could feel complete.

When he retracted his claws, her attention shifted to his wings, then to his fangs, then his horns. His mate was sizing him up, no doubt wondering how they would be together sexually.

Her behavior struck him as heartening. The real problem would be if she refused to look at him at all.

He'd asked himself what Goürlav had been thinking to imagine a future with a beauty. Wouldn't Goürlav ask him the same?

Sian didn't care. For lifetimes, he'd dreamed about what could have been with this female. For better or for worse, he had to know.

TWENTY-NINE

Déjà vu hit Lila the second they'd appeared in this throne room. Had she seen this place in a dream? How could she have? She'd never been here before.

Shaking off that odd sense, she focused on getting through this wedding. *Her* wedding.

She had yearned for control over her life—yet she was about to have less of it than ever before. She would be under the thumb of a dominant demon.

Who was an enemy.

She doubted an immortal as old as Abyssian held modern marriage views. Talk about a male set in his ways.

But she'd secured a measure of protection for her people. She needed to take comfort in that.

She wondered what Saetth would do when he found out she'd married Abyssian. Nïx would no doubt tell him—especially if they'd been in league for that portion of the plot. . . .

Abyssian began his vows. In his deep, accented voice, he promised to treasure and protect her.

She tensed when a marble throne started to materialize on the dais beside his. Was the castle providing it for her?

Once the demon concluded, he gave her hand a squeeze.

Oh. My turn.

She delicately cleared her throat and recited her vows. As she finished—"This I promise until the end of time"—her throne appeared fully.

Engravings marked the back of it. She skimmed some of the Demonish words: *Mistress of this castle, lady of flames, dark queen of this land.*

Fate had always wanted her to be a queen.

Memories of hard-won political lessons from her childhood surfaced. Here she would be hated by a united populace—just because of her species. She'd probably have more than Rune to worry about.

"I'm to kiss you now," Abyssian said, leaning down.

She averted her face.

He didn't complain, just pulled her against his body and grazed his lips over her cheek.

There. They'd done it.

Her ears twitched when hounds howled from the brush. Lightning flared outside, and volcanoes rumbled.

The dimension seemed to go askew. Her skin grew even more hypersensitive; chills raced over it.

In those lightning bursts, Abyssian's features appeared more demonic. Something was happening here—much more than a wedding.

Yet he didn't behave as if anything was different.

Lila sensed that *hell* was happy about the marriage. She felt as if this realm was . . . welcoming her.

Crazy, right?

She'd been so busy concentrating on her new groom that she hadn't given much thought to the other aspects of this union. She would be making her home in a land that was as fierce as it was mystical.

For an eternity of eternities.

He drew back. "You are now Queen Calliope the first, of Pandemonia and All Hells." Thunder boomed, and the castle quaked.

Too much to process. I turned immortal. I got off with a demon. Did I really just get hitched to a Møriør*? How could someone like me be the queen of hell? Don't have anyone I can talk to about this.*

Unlike Persephone, Lila would live in hell permanently. Which meant she needed to figure this realm—and her new husband—the fuck out.

Fast.

He traced them back to his bedroom. What would happen now? He waved his hand, and that familiar gold band appeared between two of his fingers. "I want you to wear this. I exchanged the confinement spell for contraception."

"Whatever." She snatched the ring and shoved it on. With that consideration taken care of, would he just toss her on the bed and do it? A shiver of dread coursed up her spine. "Now what?"

"You and I will take a bath."

"I figure I can stumble my way through one on my own."

"Alas, I cannot," he said with a smirk she longed to slap off his face. "In this realm, a wife is expected to wash her husband."

He took her elbow and guided her down a hallway toward a golden door that opened automatically for them.

Inside, steam wafted from a full copper bathtub the size of a small pool. Positioned atop a raised stone platform, the tub had submerged benches. *Hell's hot tub.* A few glass containers of bath oils and salts lined the dais.

A large modern shower took up the opposite side of the room. Lava flowed down one wall like an indoor water feature, heating the area and providing light. A stack of towels was at the ready, and an elegant silk robe hung beside the tub.

The demon stood before her and stroked the backs of his claws over her cheek. "You may undress now."

Sian enjoyed watching her choke back a thousand retorts. Nettling his mate was becoming his favorite pastime.

Her behavior had fascinated him from the beginning, and now he would get to investigate new facets of her. Sooner or later her demonic temper would overwhelm her, but how much could he vex her until then?

She stepped back. "Though I thought I would be a wife, you're ordering me around like a slave." Looking as if she faced a firing squad, she started to unlace her bodice.

She was cooperating? He'd expected her to tell him again to get fucked. Then they would bicker. Then he would toss her in the tub.

Instead, she was about to remove her dress for him. She must love her kingdom very, very much.

Some strange emotion churned in his chest. Guilt? He so rarely felt it he couldn't be sure.

Perhaps he could have finessed this situation more. His female was young, and she'd only get one wedding night. Yet she would have no flowers, finery, or well-wishers—just a demon she hated ordering her to strip.

Over this night, he'd been in conflict.

Whenever he softened toward her, he would remember their past.

Whenever he was harsh with her, he would grow uneasy about their future.

Eyes gone teal with fury, she said, "I guess I should expect commands since you pretty much bought me. But I want you to know that if the stakes weren't so high, if you and your alliance of monsters weren't about to murder my kind, I would never screw you, not in a million years."

He ground his teeth. Maybe he *didn't* want her to tell him her thoughts.

Like the concubines, Calliope would lie with him only out of duty. "Just for that, I vow I won't fuck you until you *ask* me to."

Instead of snapping a reply, she tilted her head. "So I'll have some control over the first time I have sex?"

He exhaled. "You call me a monster, but at least in that, you won't find me so."

She held her dress against her chest, hesitating to bare her breasts. He doubted the virgin had been naked with a fey male before, much less a demon enemy. She would need encouragement. He could give a little to get. "Delight me, Lila. Show me your stunning body."

Chin raised, she let the material fall to her waist.

He hissed in a breath. Her flawless breasts were upthrusting and pale, with rose-pink nipples and raised areolas. They swelled right before his rapt gaze, beckoning his mouth.

In Demonish, he rasped, *"Exquisite."* Less than an hour ago, he'd come harder than ever before, yet his cock grew painfully stiff.

Her breaths had shallowed, those breasts rising and falling.

The realities of his situation hit him. His mate was stripping for him. She was immortal. She would be his for all time. In a barely recognizable voice, he said, "You are so godsdamned lovely. I must see more."

She let the dress drop the rest of the way to the floor.

The sight left him unsteady on his feet. He'd known her figure was willowy, with graceful curves—that tiny waist flaring to the softness of her hips. He'd known her legs were shapely. He'd briefly seen the sandy-brown curls on her mons.

But altogether, her naked body rendered him thunderstruck.

Abyssian Infernas had waited ten thousand two hundred and thirty-four years, three months, and seventeen days for his female to return to him.

He met her gaze. *"You were worth the wait."*

THIRTY

The demon's husky voice made Lila's belly clench. His brows drew together, and his claws sank into his palms. His erection jutted like a steel rod in his pants.

But somehow she forced herself to stand bare before him. She'd expected him to leer at her or smirk.

Instead, he looked . . . awed. He'd sounded it too.

He made her feel beautiful—and powerful.

So he'd been right. There *was* power in desire. A small fey could affect one of the strongest beings in the Lore. She did have some sway over him, and it would only grow.

She found her shoulders rolling back.

When they met gazes, an understanding seemed to pass between them. She was reminded of the pomegranate. She'd given to him, and his expression told her he would reward her again and again and again.

He stood beside the tub, holding his hand out for her. Surprising herself, she took it and stepped into the deep water.

She caught his intoxicating scent, and her heart tripped.

Her first bath as an immortal felt heavenly—despite the fact that she'd have to share it.

He began to undress, so she looked away. She'd rather not see her future. . . .

Once he'd entered the water, she faced him. "What now?"

He reached for her, pulling her into his arms. "I'll start by washing you." He sat on one of the tub's benches and settled her sideways on his lap. She tensed when his hard dick pressed against her hip.

After selecting a bottle from the dais, he conjured a cloth, pouring oil on it. Lifting one of her arms, he drew the cloth from her wrist to her shoulder. His gaze roamed along with that cloth, rapt as he washed more of her body.

He discovered her ticklishness under her arms. He showed her the surprising sensitivity of her neck and collarbone.

With each moment, her resistance faded. She was growing more convinced that he would be gentle during sex, sparing her pain. But could it be . . . *good*?

What would an experienced demon king like sexually? As he began to massage one of her hands, she gazed at his chest. Those hypnotic glyphs moved across his flesh like the golden tips of flames.

She'd bet that raised skin was responsive. Would his heart pound if she flicked one with her tongue?

She recalled snippets she'd read on the walls in the tower. How would Abyssian react if she grabbed his horns and steered him to lick between her legs . . . ?

He kneaded her other hand, relaxing her even more. With a sigh, she leaned back against his arm.

Like this, she found his body less intimidating. Maybe she could get used to it in time.

They had nothing but time. *I'm immortal.*

"So this is the key to taming my firebrand queen?" he said, but his tone wasn't snide. "She likes to be petted." He threaded their fingers together. "Your little pink nails fascinate me as much as your ears. I'll have you digging these nails into me when you come. Scoring my back . . . my chest . . ."

Her cheeks heated yet again.

He noticed. "When you blush, the tips of your ears pinken." He nuzzled one, his hot breaths hardening her nipples and slicking her pussy.

She was about to come before he'd even gotten to her breasts! She gasped when his big, roughened hand covered one.

He made a strangled sound. "So soft. Lush." He didn't hurt her with his claws. There was no pain. Just pleasure. Her nipple strained to his palm as he cupped her.

"I've waited ten millennia to see your breasts, picturing what they might look like." In a gravelly voice, he said, "I can scarcely believe how flawless they are."

When he removed his hand, she shocked herself by arching for more of his touch.

"Infinite times, I fantasized what color your nipples would be." He swirled his forefinger around one, making her jolt. "But I never imagined such a lovely shade of rose."

She started to pant.

"When I fantasized how sensitive they'd be"—he lightly pinched the other one—"I never imagined they would get so . . . very . . . stiff."

She couldn't bite back a moan.

Another pinch, another swirled finger. "Do you like when I play with your nipples, Lila?"

Her nickname, said in his accent, sent her heart racing. She nodded, biting her lip to keep from begging for more.

He sucked her earlobe, then rasped, "Am I making your pussy ache?"

She couldn't believe he was talking to her like this, but it only turned her on even more. *"Yes."*

He skimmed his hand down her belly, circling her navel. "Your skin is like silk." His fingers descended to her mons, lightly grazing it.

Just when he was about to make contact with her clit, he pulled back.

"What? Nooo."

"I thought you liked it when I played with your nipples." He pinched the puckered tips again.

"More." She yearned for this demon's hands on her, for the orgasm that danced just out of reach.

"That's it, beautiful girl. You need these sensations, do you not?"

She could only moan in answer.

"I can give them all to you, Lila." He sounded like a monarch, one seething with power. "Anything you crave can be yours." He rolled her nipples between the pads of his fingers.

Could he make her come like this? "Wh-what are you doing to me?"

He trailed a hand down once more. "Is the flesh between your thighs the same shade of rose as your nipples?" His own breaths grew heavier. Was his hand shaking as he teased her navel?

She murmured, "Lower."

"Tell your husband what you need."

"I need you to touch me more."

"Where? How? Say, 'I need my husband to . . .'"

Hearing him talk dirty was different from doing it herself, but she was too far gone to be embarrassed. She spread her legs and said, "I-I need my husband to stroke my pussy."

He groaned. "You make my cock so fucking hard." It jerked against her hip.

Would he want her to suck it? Right now she would. She'd do anything if he'd just let her come—

His forefinger covered her clit.

"Ah!" She rocked up to the contact.

"No, beauty. *Still.* You're not to come yet."

"Why?" she cried.

"I want you wanton."

"I am!" Her head thrashed against his arm. "Do you want me to ask for it?"

He nuzzled her ear again. "No, little wife, I want you to *ache* for it."

Focus. No battle had ever meant more to Sian. *Go slow with her.*

His forefinger dipped to her slippery entrance. *Slow, Sian!* To restrain himself, he called on every ounce of the strength he'd earned just by virtue of surviving for millennia. "You've never had anything inside you, have you?"

"N-no." Her eyes were ablaze—that sultry teal.

He watched her expression as he gently probed her. When her core clamped his finger, his engorged cock pulsed in response. *"Lila."*

Her lids fluttered. "Ohhh, demon."

He delved his finger deeper, his instincts screaming for him to put his seed inside her. To impregnate his mate.

Why would a demon like him be fated to a fey if the result was so bad? "You like being penetrated?" His breaths were now heaving.

When he stirred the tip of his finger, she gave a throaty moan. "I *love* that."

Though her channel was slick with welcome, she was *too* tight. He would hurt her if he didn't work with her. "I feel your virginity. You're going to give that to me, Lila. One day, you will." In Demonish, he told her, "I'll claim this hot, wet sheath with my seed."

But not until she asked. Which meant denying his most primal instincts and subjecting his cock and balls to excruciating pain. "Do you want your husband to keep fingering your pussy?"

Her breathtaking body writhed in the water, those flawless tits quivering. "Yes, yes!"

He wanted to roar his victory, but he was losing control. He'd been so confident that he could maintain it with her—because he had so easily with other females.

Once I enter my mate's body . . . His resulting culmination, spending in the throes, would rob him of sanity, not to mention all restraint.

His body had been built to kill; hers could barely accept one of his fingers.

He was glad he wouldn't be claiming her until she asked. They had time. Unfortunately, his instinct wouldn't rest until he'd marked her. Somehow a male like him would have to go through the most intense and powerful transition in his long life—gently.

Even now he teetered on the edge. Could she handle what was about to be unleashed?

This demon was a sex god. His voice, his reactions, and his sinful touch all combined to make Lila wild for him.

How had she lived without this?

At first, she'd been nervous about his finger inside her, but the pressure felt wonderful, *necessary*. Shameless, she said, "I-I need my husband to make me come!"

He rested his forehead against hers. "Look at me." Their gazes locked. His eyes were black as jet. "When I claim you, nothing will stop me from giving you this kind of pleasure."

Right then, she was ready. Sign her up. *Anything*.

In Demonish, he said, "We will wait until your body's prepared for me."

It was! Once she hovered on the very brink, he held his finger still inside her.

"Nooo!" She reached down, crazed enough to do it herself.

"Ah-ah." He gently captured her wrists with his free hand.

"Abyssian!" She rocked on his finger, sending it in and out of her, fucking herself.

His glyphs were on fire. "I can't take much more of this, beauty." *He* couldn't? "Nearing the point of no return. I'm going to bring you off."

"DO IT!"

He gave a strained laugh. "My fey mate loves her pleasure. Doesn't like to be denied it."

He released her wrists. With one forefinger still inside her, he used his other to cover her throbbing clitoris. "You want my touch here?"

"Yes!"

"On this needy little bud?"

She whimpered, tremors of her orgasm beginning. *"Pleasepleaseplease."*

"What will you do for it?"

"Anything, demon!"

"Good girl. Come for me." He rubbed her and finger-fucked—

"Ahhh!" Coiling pressure . . . released. Bliss exploded, sending her flying. She screamed as her core contracted on the demon's big finger.

He growled, "I *feel* you! Feel your tight pussy coming for me."

His voice spurred another series of contractions that went on and on. . . .

THIRTY-ONE

My mate's virginal sheath . . . milking my finger . . . as I bring her to come.

Too much . . . Sian nigh lost his senses. Had to fight not to spontaneously culminate. His hand—steady for lifetimes—shook wildly as he drew out her orgasm.

Once she was spent, she closed her legs and pushed at his wrist.

He shuddered as he removed his finger from her body, reluctantly surrendering his prize. He would never get enough of her quivering tits, her gripping pussy, her desperate moans. The way she called him husband and looked at him with trust. *Want her so fucking much!*

She was pleasure godsdamned embodied.

"Abyssian?" she said, her voice uncertain. "You look really . . . demonic."

The unbearable pressure racking his body demanded release. He'd be finished with one pump of his shaft. "Slake me, wife."

"How?"

He took her hand and raised it to his face. He kissed her palm. Flicked it with his tongue. Rubbed his cheek against it. Then he placed it high on his chest, dragging it down. "Touch me. Touch my cock."

Every time he mentioned his cock, her ears twitched, and her eyes grew brighter. Wicked little female. She rose to stand between his thighs. With a trembling hand, she caressed the length of a glyph.

He sucked in a breath. *Exploring me?* He'd expected her to tend him in a perfunctory manner. If she knew how close he was to coming . . . He was almost fearful of his impending release.

Eyes watchful, she did it again. "Your skin is hot like fire, and when these glow they look like flames." Another light stroke. "Are they sensitive? Do you like them to be touched?"

He sensed her rebounding excitement, and it made his shaft jerk in the water. "Yes." He stared into her eyes. Between breaths, he said, "No part of me . . . is off-limits to you. Touch where you will."

She surprised him by reaching for one of his wings.

Lila smoothed her palm over the exterior of a wing. That side was roughened like callused skin, yet he seemed to feel even the slightest contact. His muscles rippled when she lightly raked her nails across it.

After the orgasm he'd just given her, she was more curious about her new husband—about what made him . . . *demonic.* "You don't fly a lot?"

He shook his head. "I trace too easily. They're more for battle."

She let go of his wing. *Always back to war with this one.* The impulse to touch his horns struck her, but she held off. She reached down and began trailing her fingers up his neck. He swallowed thickly, his Adam's apple moving between her fingertips.

She grazed her knuckles along his wide jawline and his prominent chin. Tracing the piercings above the bridge of his nose, she asked, "Did these hurt?"

"Fleetingly."

She cradled his face, then smoothed her thumbs over his sharp cheekbones, his stern brow, his sensual lips. . . .

The gold band on her ring finger glinted in the firelight—a wedding ring of sorts.

Returning her attention to his chest, she traced a fingertip over one of his pierced nipples.

He inhaled sharply, nostrils flaring. His wings fluttered uncontrollably. Sensitive!

She grazed him again, and he groaned, his brows drawing together as if she'd struck him.

I can make this king quake with my tiniest touch! His response made her giddy. She wanted to test out her newfound power, to explore him all over and gauge his reactions.

He rasped, "You're figuring it out, aren't you?"

"What?"

In Demonish, he said, "That I'll command you, but you'll rule me."

She just kept herself from nodding. After he'd captured her earlier, she'd predicted a bleak future. Now hope glimmered. They would actually have mind-blowing pleasure between them—and she wouldn't be powerless.

Feeling bolder, she trailed a fingertip down his torso. Breaths ragged, he gripped the sides of the tub.

His lean sinews strained to her touch. Every inch lower increased his obvious agony.

Her hand descended beneath the water's surface. She gazed up into his eyes as she circled *his* navel. He gnashed his teeth till his jaw muscles ticked.

She grazed the length of his shaft, and a yell burst from his chest. *One tiny touch . . .*

"You won't accidentally hurt me?"

Sharp shake of his head.

She reached lower and cupped his heavy testicles.

His grip began to bend the copper. *"Lila . . ."* Black flooded even the whites of his eyes.

The texture and weight of his balls fascinated her. The demon must love having them stroked; he spread his knees wide and bucked. If he responded like this to her hands, what if she used her mouth? Her tongue?

Her fingertips alighted on his shaft. She gave a tentative graze along the slit of his cockhead.

"Uhn!" His body shook so hard, the tub vibrated.

Playing with fire, girl. But she was more titillated than nervous. She circled her thumb over the slit. "It's slick." Even in the water.

He'd tightened his grip on the tub until the contact radiated glowing white heat through the metal. "I make it . . . for you alone." The castle quaked, volcanoes threatening.

She should be afraid, but she was dizzy with discovery. *I'm already addicted to this. . . .*

Sian's mate was a born temptress. Her eyes were glittering. A flush of new arousal spread over her chest and breasts.

He'd never imagined she could be this sexually engaged with him—not so soon. He'd never expected *her*. A lusty fey firebrand named Lila.

How much more could he take before he sucked her taut nipples raw? Before he devoured her tender pussy and rubbed his horns all over her to mark her with his scent? "No more play." He gazed longingly at her pale neck, his fangs throbbing as badly as his cock. "Make me come."

Eyes watchful on his face—she had yet to even glance down—she stroked both of his nipples.

"Yes!" His groan grew constant. His heavy balls drew up, readying.

She dipped one hand. Simultaneously, she thumbed a nipple and his cockhead. His eyes rolled back in his head.

Over—

His back bowed, and he roared his release. *"Fuck, fuck, GODS!"* His

wings snapped open, cleanly slicing the sides of the tub; water sloshed out into the bathroom. His grip mangled the metal.

She rubbed the crown over and over, hurtling him to even greater heights, his roar deepening. Cracks appeared in the walls. Volcanoes heaved and spewed as his cock pulsated for her again and again. . . .

Once the explosions ebbed, he grabbed Calliope and collapsed back on the bench.

Legs sprawled.

Mate in his lap.

Shaft still pulsing.

Her name on his tongue. *"Lila . . ."*

THIRTY-TWO

The demon's arms coiled around her. He didn't appear worried that the ruined tub was leaking water all over the floor.

As if he could barely lift his hand, he laid his palm on her head.

She couldn't wrap her mind around what had just happened. She'd made Abyssian Infernas go into a frenzy, and he'd made her climb the walls.

The demon was some kind of sexual Jedi. No wonder females had fought for him.

No wonder, no wonder, no wonder. Tonight, she would've begged for him to fuck her. And he had to have known that—which meant he could've claimed her, but he'd held off.

He raised his head, giving her a crooked grin. "So far I like married life very well."

She almost grinned back. Her idea of him was getting rewritten.

He was a Møriør. He thought peace was overrated. He *enjoyed* war.

But maybe he was much more than a killer. His wickedness—and these hints of vulnerability—were drawing her in, seducing her.

Not to mention her newfound sense of control. Holding sway

over one of the most powerful beings in the universe meant *she* was powerful.

After his release, his lids were heavy, his face relaxed. His eyes were green once more, and he actually looked sleepy.

Seeing him like this tugged at her emotions. Though their marriage was loveless, a "mutually beneficial arrangement," the notion of him as her *husband* was messing with her mind. "A primordial can get tired?" *Maybe at heart he's just a Lorean like me.* Not some godlike Møriør. Not some bogeyman.

"My young mate has worn me out over this day. And before you escaped, I'd spent all my magic making a new dimension for the Vrekeners."

"You *made* a dimension?" Nope, definitely godlike.

"The Sorceri wanted land for their bounty." He kissed her neck. "I'd resented being forced into that situation, so I sent their new realm spinning into the ether."

Holy shit. "The trickster strikes again."

"Ah, but right now, I consider the magic I paid well spent."

She stiffened. Why'd he have to bring up the fact that he'd basically bought her—twice?

First, he'd paid with land. Second, he'd paid with peace.

She wriggled from his arms, and with a sigh, he let her go. In Demonish, he muttered, "Forever hot and cold."

Lila needed to remember an important distinction: *Liking the demon and liking the phenomenal orgasm he gave me are two different things.*

But then, she'd also liked the way his magnificent body had responded to *her* touch.

She'd liked his voice.

And his lips.

His eyes were kind of glorious.

She reached over him for the robe, earning a growl.

"I'm more exhausted than I've ever been—and I just came till my eyes rolled back in my head—yet you still heat my blood."

The garment was a female's, which soured Lila's mood even more. Who did it belong to? After appropriating it, she climbed from the tub to the slippery floor. "Please give my thanks to whichever demoness owns this robe."

"I conjured that for you."

Over her shoulder, she said, "Did you happen to conjure any other clothes?"

"We'll sort that out in the morning." Droplets of water flew through the room when he shook his hair and wings out. "For now, we'll sleep. Into the bed with you."

She tossed a towel back in his direction, hoping he'd wrap it around his waist, then padded out of the bathroom.

Resigned to sharing a bed, she settled under the luxurious covers far to one side, turning her back to him.

The demon's weight pressed down on the mattress beside her.

"Have you been with a lot of females in this bed?" Why did she even care?

"None. I've never brought anyone to my bedroom but you. By the way, wife, we sleep without clothes."

She tensed. "How do I know you won't do things to me when I'm asleep? Trusting you with my body when I'm awake is one thing. Being naked and defenseless with you is another."

He exhaled. "I vow not to 'do things' to you as you slumber tonight."

With a huff, she sat up and removed the robe, tossing it to the foot of the bed.

He pulled her against his naked body, spooning her. His dick pressed insistently against her lower back and ass, his intoxicating scent surrounding her.

"And you will sleep within my wings every night." He lifted her to slip a wing under her side, his other draping over them—which put one of his lethal wing claws in front of her face.

"Seriously, demon?"

He retracted it. "Better?"

"Must we do this?"

"We must." Each wing was warm and soft on the inside, like a blanket out of the dryer. Such a difference from the cold stone she'd slept on.

As a storm gathered strength outside, she felt safe and warm and found herself relaxing against him.

Too bad the Lôtān head was staring right at her. That mounted trophy must be a demon treasure beyond calculation, but did it have to look over the bed she'd be sleeping in?

As her lids grew heavy, she thought of a question she'd always wondered about. "Why did your ancestor come to this place?" *Abyssian's ancestors will be my children's ancestors.*

Then, with a pang, she remembered she wouldn't have children. Unless she became a widow.

His chest rumbled against her as he murmured, "A tale was passed down that he saw a strangely colored flame on the horizon, a flare of blue in the middle of blackness. He couldn't stop looking at that flame, dreaming of it, obsessing over it. He somehow understood that it was his beacon, a point of reference from which to view all other things. He knew that if he kept his eyes on that light, all would be well. The hellfire led him to Pandemonia."

Abyssian's line was legendary, his ancestors discovering new worlds. Her line was . . . shameful.

"Calliope, you were fated to come here. To come to me." He clutched her closer, exhaling as if with bliss. "You are now exactly where you belong." The satisfaction in his tone made her wonder if he'd been waiting ten thousand years to say those words.

Calliope's breaths had grown deep and even. His mate was sleeping in his arms.

Yet Sian felt as if *he* were the one dreaming.

I wed my female. I have her safe in my bed. Within the protection of my wings. He stifled a groan at the feel of her. Calliope's curves would bring a lesser demon to his knees.

Sian leaned in, greedily inhaling her scent. His mate's scent was ideal to him, at once soothing his mind and enlivening his body. In all his travels across thousands of realms, he'd never encountered anything like it.

Though fatigue weighed on him, his cock hardened even more. *By all the gods, she is . . . mine.*

He'd intended to maintain his distance with her, drawing on his long-seething hatred. Yet after what he'd experienced over the night—from their pleasure by the goldfall to their cataclysmic encounter in the bath—distance was the last thing on his mind.

He had no idea what tomorrow would bring, or how to be a husband, but he could try to prepare for his new bride's day-to-day needs: food, clothing, and shelter. His lips curved. *The care and feeding of my fey.* At last, he would fulfill his instincts to protect and provide!

Food. He would talk to his steward about smuggling in a steady supply of Sylvan fare.

Clothing. Already taken care of with a mystical dressing room. When the queen of hell entered her wardrobe, it would perceive her mood and provide whatever she imagined wearing.

Shelter. Perhaps her idea of luxury differed from his. She doubtless wanted his—their—bedroom to look different.

He gazed at the Lôtān that had hung above the mantel since the castle had been completed. She wasn't a fan. Granted, the head was grisly. And it *did* loom over the bed.

He'd remove it tomorrow, then ask her what other changes she might like. Just in case, he'd have her things brought from her apartment as well.

With her needs planned for, he racked his brain for anything—

anything—he and Calliope had in common. Not their species, ages, affiliations, backgrounds, cultures, political views, friends, or experiences.

Sian's likes—his alliance, demon delicacies, combat—would count as her dislikes.

He could come up with only two commonalities: they enjoyed reading. And they would both be in sore need of release again soon.

Pleasure would bond them, serving as their foundation.

All those years ago, when he'd been in Sylvan, he would lie in bed and dream that Kari was his. Staring at the ceiling, he'd imagined being able to touch her whenever he had the impulse.

To explore her naked body. Or bury his face in her hair for more of her scent. To kiss her lips and draw a moan from them.

His fantasies about her had changed, just as he had. Calliope too was different from Kari. He knew Kari would never have stroked his horns, receiving him with abandon. But Calliope . . . might.

He could almost be thankful to the hell-change curse for bringing him new ones.

If he was patient and gentle, in time he could train his wife's body to crave more of his—

She rolled over in sleep, turning to him. He smoothed a lock from her cheek. Her eyes darted behind her lids, her expressions shifting from happiness to a brows-drawn look.

What is she experiencing?

Her active dream life was yet another part of her held separate from him. He could probe her mind, but the idea sat ill with him. She was his wife now; no one should take advantage of her.

Including himself.

THIRTY-THREE

Lila woke from a deep, dream-filled sleep, her body warm and rested.

Where was she? Not the cold stone floor of the tower. Not her bed in her apartment.

She blinked open her eyes, squinting against a bright light. *Wait* . . . *That's a glyph.*

The demon lay on his back, and she was sprawled over him, her arm draped across his chest. Her knee was thrown over his torso, and her calf rested on his hard dick.

Her lips were an inch away from a pierced nipple; he had to feel her breaths. Her pussy pressed against one of his hips, and she might have been rocking her own.

Lazily petting her hair, he rasped, "In sleep, my wife can't get enough of me." His dick jerked, lifting her freaking leg.

She scrambled away from him, tripping out of the bed, too late realizing she was naked. She swiped her robe, yanking it on. "What were you doing to me?"

He raised his brows. "Doing *to you*? I haven't touched you. I told you I wouldn't."

This didn't even compute. A warrior demon would be expected to take what he wanted, especially from a female who was legally his. Especially when she'd been rubbing against him.

With his dick tenting the sheet, he put his hands behind his head, the corded muscles in his torso and arms flexing.

That body is too much. Demonesses must go crazy for him.

Smirk in place, he said, "I didn't touch you—even though you used me as a masturbatory scratching post all night and morning." Could he look any smugger?

"What are you talking about?"

"For hour after hour, you ground against me, moaning, all but coming. The worst torment I have ever known. Each time I attempted to get away, you would sink your nails into me and give this little growl of displeasure. I translated it to mean *Please, oh glorious demon, stay.*"

"I don't believe you," she said . . . though she *had* experienced graphically sexual dreams about him. Even now she was turned on like crazy.

"Yes, you do."

Her lips thinned. "Then you just lay there and took it?"

"I forced myself to relive my most grueling battle campaigns. During the Buthidae offensive, I went without water for weeks in a desert teeming with giant scorpions. In the Quotoh invasion, my allies and I seized control of a strategically favorable but noxious swamp. Those campaigns were less torturous than your attentions. When I was at war, I fantasized about my mate. Now that I have you in my bed at last, I must fantasize about war."

Again, does not compute. "Why did you?"

"The sooner you trust me, the sooner you'll ask me to claim you."

"So you were decent for calculating reasons?" Figured. "*If* I did rub on you, I probably mistook you for a body pillow."

"Do you often rub yourself against large pillows to orgasm?" He was clearly imagining the visual; his shaft jerked again, drawing her attention. "Female, I would take on an army to see that."

She made out the impressions of his piercings against the sheet before she focused elsewhere.

"Looking away? Even after last night?"

"Everything I see—or feel—just reinforces my belief that we are not anatomically compatible." *Among other issues.* He'd been waiting to lose his seal for ten millennia. All that pent-up need had built on itself, century after century.

She wouldn't visit a volcano that was overdue to blow, yet this demon was supposed to erupt *inside her body.*

What female wouldn't cross her legs tight at the thought? Much less a virgin. "If your marriage required you to get clubbed nightly, would you want to stare down the bat beforehand?"

"That analogy isn't flattering—or accurate. You'll get clubbed five times a day, minimum."

"You're taunting me? Anticipation of a blow is oftentimes worse than the hit."

"Since I refuse to claim you until I'm asked, that puts you in control. The club is in your hands." Smirk deepening, he added, "After last night, you've got me by the bat."

"You're impossible."

"Calliope, if you ever don't like something I do, tell me to stop. If you're not prepared for something, tell me to wait. If you have questions, I welcome them. It's that simple." He sounded so . . . reasonable. "Any questions so far?"

Before she could stop herself, she'd asked, "You truly got your dick pierced?"

"I am pierced. Three barbells of hell metal."

What would make him do that? Had a lover wanted it? A flare of jealousy took her by surprise.

"You look displeased. Come then, firebrand, don't knock my cock until you've thoroughly tried it. Especially since it's the only one you'll ever know for the rest of your immortal life."

"Can't you let me ease into all this? It's not as if I've spent oodles of time checking out dicks. Disney Wi-Fi is not conducive to exploring porn, much less supersecret Lorean porn."

He canted his head. "I'll take you to a pleasure dimension, and you can watch sex live."

"Really?" How did she feel about that?

"After last night, I'm inclined to take my passionate wife anywhere she pleases."

Glimpses of what this life could bring proved so seductive. She shook her head hard. *He's a Mørior, Lila.* Two orgasms couldn't erase that.

He sat up in bed and stretched his long arms. Even his wings expanded.

She'd bet those felt good to stretch. When his wing claws extended, she wondered if he'd kept them retracted all night.

Casting her a significant look, he said, "I'd love to know what you were dreaming about."

In between lifelike scenes of licking his nipples and sucking on his neck, she'd dreamed of the fawn again.

She'd been running with it across a green field that turned rocky and ashen. She'd slowed when it neared the edge of a cliff. Some kind of mysterious light had blazed up from below. She'd urged the fawn to come to her—but it'd walked right off the edge.

What was the dream trying to tell her?

Abyssian said, "I wager I was in your reveries."

Her cheeks heated, busting her.

"Good." In Demonish, he added, "You've been in mine every night for ten millennia."

His unguarded comments in that tongue gave her valuable insights about him, but eventually she'd have to tell him she spoke Demonish.

She would also need to disclose her royal status. Yet that news might convince him she was more like Karinna than he'd thought, and then he'd throw Lila back into the dreaded tower.

She felt safer overall, but her position here remained dicey. "If you expect me to do . . . queenly things, you should outline them for me so I know how to plan my time."

"If you're searching for something to keep you occupied, look no further than this bed. Your queenly duties will be found *here*." He patted the mattress beside him.

What have I done? That huge, smirking, smug demon was . . . her husband.

The harsh light of day flooded into the bedroom. *Now what?* For the first time in her life, she had no idea where to go or what to do. No schedule to maintain, no goals to achieve. The order and structure her fey heart craved was absent. "I'm being serious."

"So am I. You don't have to plan your time. You don't have to do anything. You answer to no one."

Because she finally had control over her destiny? "No one except you."

"Yes, but I suspect I'll be a soft touch where you're concerned."

How had her life gotten so derailed? She'd been born and raised for a specific existence, and now she was trapped in another one. The king she'd married was far from the king she'd expected. "Don't you have ruler stuff to do? I wouldn't want to keep you from your job. If you need to work late or go on lengthy campaigns, I'll be *completely* understanding. After all, you love your wars, and I want to be supportive of your pastimes now that Sylvan is out of the crosshairs."

"You and I are on our honeymoon. I have nothing but time to tease my bride."

"I thought the great Møriør would be defeating and governing all of Gaia."

"In time," he said. "For now, I need to make sure you are comfortable in your new home."

"What will my days be like here?"

"Until you wear my mark, I'll keep you separated from our subjects in the castle. Though I expect no problems, we don't want to advertise something that might be perceived as disunity between us."

Not only was she a foreign fey, she was an unclaimed mate. Lila appreciated his caution.

"But I'll take you out to explore less populated parts of the realm whenever you like."

She'd forgotten about this particular benefit of being the queen of hell. "Will we see the hellhounds? And the dragon roosts?" she asked, her excitement building. "Will you show me the hellfire your ancestor found?"

"I haven't a clue to its location. No one does." He gazed past her. "I have searched and searched, but unfortunately, I can't find that flame."

Her stomach began to growl. She'd slept so late, it must be well past lunchtime.

Facing her, he said, "For now, we'll dine."

"What do I wear?"

"The entrance to your wardrobe is across from the bathing chamber. I trust you can find something in there to suit you," he said with that tricksy look about him.

Wondering if he had some prank up his sleeve, she headed down the hallway. After her dreams, she was still in a state, her robe brushing over her nipples. She peeked into the bathing room, finding everything had been put to rights.

She opened the golden door opposite it, and stepped into a huge room with a plush divan in the center. Clothing racks lined the walls.

Empty clothing racks. Was this his idea of a joke?

Wanting to brush her teeth and wash her face, she continued through the empty wardrobe to an adjoining powder room with a large vanity. Various toiletries and a toothbrush had been set out for her.

After she'd readied for the day, she headed back through the wardrobe, wishing she had a comfortable outfit, like a flirty skirt and a peasant blouse—

She leapt back when two garments suddenly hung in the closet. The ones she'd just imagined!

A grin spread over her face. *Magic.* She pictured a pink bra and panties set, and it appeared on the divan. Footwear? A pair of strappy sandals materialized in a shoe rack.

She turned and found the demon leaning against the doorway, dressed in his customary leather pants.

She supposed leather would be the custom here since hell didn't exactly have fabric mills.

"You like your new wardrobe?" he asked, looking very pleased with himself.

"What's not to like?" His bare feet caught her attention. *Whoa.* Last night she hadn't noticed how beastlike they were. His toes had pointed black claws. A sixth one jutted from his inner sole.

Reminded that she and Abyssian weren't even the same species, she raised her face.

He was scowling at her, all good humor vanished.

If his mate was shocked at his feet, what would she do when he transformed even more?

Run screaming?

When he'd been making plans for their future, he'd imagined himself as he currently was—not as he *would* be. Yet his deterioration would continue, the years taking their toll.

Once again the hourglass was working against Sian, only now the sand spilled too quickly.

If he and Calliope shared more nights like the last, he would grow attached to her. But in the end, it wouldn't matter how he treated her. Eventually she would spurn him.

I've already been forsaken by her once. Frustration rose up like bile. How could he endure it this time?

Maybe he should separate from her, lest he discover more that he liked about his mate. . . .

No! The idea of separating made his agitation spike.

Gaze wary, she asked, "Can I have some privacy to get dressed?"

He crossed his arms over his chest. "We're wed now. What need have you for privacy?"

"So much for my power—and your soft touch. I don't even get to dress in private."

He supposed he should make allowances for her. She was a fey raised in Sylvan, and their culture was much more reserved.

Right now he didn't feel very charitable. If he couldn't separate from her, maybe he should keep animosity brewing between them, anything to maintain a boundary. "There's nothing I haven't already seen at my leisure. Except your ass. You put on that robe before I could evaluate it."

"Evaluate?" Her eyes flashed. "How would you like it if I evaluated you?"

"Go ahead. Of course, that would mean actually *looking* at my feet or my cock or my horns."

"Less than a *day*, Abyssian. That's how long I've had to get accustomed to you as my husband. Can't you be more patient?"

She was right. But no demon wanted his mate to have to "get accustomed" to him.

"Change. *Now*."

Shooting him a killing look, she tugged up her panties under her robe, followed by her skirt. She gave him her back as she donned her bra and shirt. She stomped her feet into her shoes. "Are you happy?"

Not once since you died, female. He frowned. Until last night.

THIRTY-FOUR

Their late lunch on the terrace was grueling.

As Lila and Abyssian shared their second meal ever—plates had arrived with both demon and Sylvan dishes—he continued to seethe. Because she wouldn't look at him?

She was half-tempted to say, *Whip out your dick, and I'll examine it for hours if that'll make you feel better.*

He expected her to get used to so many things at once! She'd told him she adapted. And she was ready to, but give her a freaking nanosecond to keep up.

She'd noticed that he'd donned boots. *Sensitive males.* She supposed this would be a bad time to ask him what in this hell he was eating? The dish kind of looked like eggs—if they'd been painted by a modern artist.

The demon's table manners were fine—his utensils were larger by necessity—but he and Lila would never be sharing a dish.

"Why aren't you eating?" he demanded, seeming eager to resume their hostility.

Since she'd officially tied her fortunes to his, she wasn't as keen to;

cooperation was a more logical route. But she would go toe-to-toe with him if she had to.

"It's Sylvan fare. Is that not even good enough for you, princess?"

She stiffened, hating when he called her that. "Are you always so moody?" Why did he have to spoil such a beautiful day? The ash had been tamped down by rain last night, and the late-afternoon sun was bright. When she'd gotten her first daytime glimpse of the Mercury Sea, the light had beamed across the water, reflecting off its silvery surface.

"Moody? Perhaps I already see the writing on the wall."

"Which is?"

"I doubt you will ever be satisfied here."

"So will you let me go?"

He leaned forward, his lips drawing back from his fangs. *"Never."*

She leaned forward as well. "Then fucking satisfy me, Abyssian. It's not difficult."

"Ah, this I must hear. How would one go about such an epic endeavor?" He settled back in his chair, as if he expected a long-winded reply.

"Play up your strengths." *Like the way you made me feel last night.* "And don't be a prick." *The way you are this afternoon.* "Simple enough for you?" She rose and headed for the terrace railing. *Gods, that demon gets my back up!*

Inhaling for calm, she gazed at the sea. Lila might not be getting along with hell's king, but his kingdom called to her.

What creatures lurked in those depths? The tide was lower than before, revealing the shoreline. Was the beach . . . *green*? Algae must cover it.

She had wanted to explore the castle; now she could. She had wanted to know more about this realm. He'd said he would take her out—

Some animal breached the surface of the sea! When its red scales glimmered in the sunlight, she sucked in a breath.

Abyssian was beside her in a heartbeat. "What?"

"A sea serpent!" She pointed, but it'd disappeared.

"You saw one?"

"I swear. It was right *there*," she said, her excitement dampening her anger. "I've read about them, but didn't know if the accounts were true. They're supposed to be like limbless dragons, right? Each one's bigger than a train, weighing dozens of tons."

With an unreadable expression, he said, "We should investigate." He took her elbow and traced her.

She blinked, getting her bearings. They'd appeared on the green beach.

Not algae. Eyes gone wide, she dropped to her knees to scoop up shiny grains of sand. Peering at Abyssian, she said, "Jade?" She sifted tiny pebbles through her fingers.

Nod.

"Get the fuck out!" A jade beach. Why not? As she stood to kick off her sandals, her attention strayed past the demon. Purple and orange fish leapt from the water. They each had a horn like a unicorn! She sprinted closer to the seaweed-dotted shore.

Abyssian traced in front of her, one arm outstretched, the other pulling her against his back. "Tell me before you run away."

"Is there some kind of danger—"

A gigantic serpent shot out of the water like a geyser and plummeted onto the beach, its body crashing directly against Abyssian.

The ground shook; she choked on a scream, but the demon hadn't budged a single inch.

She didn't know what shocked her more—Abyssian's show of colossal strength or that he'd started petting the great creature.

"I haven't visited here for a while, and they get excited," he said. "This one in particular." The creature's head coiled around, its slitted eyes taking her in. Its forked tongue—as long as she was tall—flicked with curiosity.

More serpents streamed out in the water. "They're tame?"

"They are with me. Come pet it. You'll like the sensation against your fingertips."

She raised her brows at him. *And for my next trick . . .*

He said, "It's safe."

She eased closer. He nodded again, encouraging her, so she reached for the creature. Muscles rippled beneath iridescent red scales the size of dinner plates.

She was about to hyperventilate from exhilaration/fear/*holy shit!* "I'm petting a *sea serpent*!" She grinned over her shoulder at the demon.

As if he couldn't help himself, his lips curved. His moods seemed to be as changeable as the sea's tide.

Her own irritation melted away. When her strokes slowed, the serpent shimmied for more, making her laugh.

In Demonish, Abyssian murmured, "Wants your touch as much as I."

Be nicer, and you might get it. "How many are there?"

"A hundred or so in the sea, more in the swamps to the south. This one was a hatchling when my brother and I were pups." *Sea serpents can live that long?* "Its dam died, so my sire gave us the egg. We kept it in our room, checking it every five minutes for weeks."

The idea of Abyssian Infernas as a little boy, waiting for an egg to hatch, softened her toward him. She imagined him with miniature wings, downy horns, and a missing baby fang.

When her smile deepened, he gruffly said, "What are you thinking about?"

"I bet you were a handful growing up. Were you forever getting into trouble?"

"Always the first to trace into danger. Everyone said my life would be short. Little did they know."

She smoothed her palm along a crease between the serpent's scales, and it twitched. Ticklish? "What do you call your large pet?"

"We named him Loki."

She raised her brows at the demon. "After the greatest trickster ever to live?"

"This one was a crafty hatchling, always figuring out ways to get free from his cage. Similar to my fey pet."

"Watch it, demon," she warned. "Here be dragons."

Another curve of his lips. "How *did* you escape?"

"My ring came loose, so all bets were off."

"And the vines?"

"I made wearable shields out of your gifts."

"I see." Seeming to make a decision about her, he asked, "You like to swim?"

"I love it. But I haven't been a single time in Gaia." She tapped the tip of one ear. "I could never hide these in the water."

"I'll take you now."

She surveyed the sea serpents. "Isn't it a bit crowded out there?"

By degrees, Sian's ill-temper had faded, his mate's excitement contagious.

There were so many things he could show her. Not just in hell, but in other realms as well. He wanted to experience these places anew with her.

Already he was viewing Pandemonia differently. The sea had never gotten him to raise a brow. It simply *was*. The same with the sea life and the jade beach. Yet she'd been breathless, her eyes flashing teal.

Hell was putting on a good show for its new queen. At least his kingdom *satisfied* her.

Could he? Again he wondered to what strengths she'd been referring. The way he'd pleasured her?

Maybe Sian should strive to live in the present, enjoying her for as long as possible. "If you want to swim, I could send them hunting. Not that they'd ever hurt my mate."

She bit her bottom lip. That Calliope was even thinking about getting in the water was a testament to his mate's courage. "I don't have a swimsuit."

He wanted to say, *This is hell! Not Gaia or Sylvan.* But she'd asked for patience; he could . . . attempt it. "You can leave your underwear on, and no one but me will see you. This is my—our—personal beach, and I'd sense any trespassers. In any case, most are terrified of the serpents."

"I'll swim. If you go first."

"Fine." He patted the serpent, and it lumbered off the beach into the water to join the others. They departed like a school of fish.

Sian reached down to yank off a boot. Pride still stinging from earlier, he couldn't resist saying, "You should turn away. I don't want to offend your fey sensibilities."

She narrowed her eyes at him, muttering, *"Moody prick."*

He turned to remove his other boot. As he was standing on one leg, something cold, wet, and slimy ran down his back. The little witch had used her speed to retrieve a clump of seaweed, then shoved it down his pants.

Yanking the mass free, he pinned her gaze. Her haughty smile faded when he grated, *"Run."*

THIRTY-FIVE

Heart racing, Lila tore off across the beach, sending up jade in her wake. Over her shoulder, she called, "Don't pull something, relic." Laughing, she faced forward.

He appeared in front of her!

She skidded to a stop, then sprinted in the opposite direction. Heading for the more compacted jade-sand, she ran through the waves, elation thrumming inside her. Her senses were on fire; everything felt magnified.

Lots of firsts today. Her first time to pet a sea creature. Her first day as an immortal. Her first relationship/husband.

He called, "You can run, little fey, but you can't trace." If those hints of vulnerability had called to her, this teasing from him was like a drug.

Just last night, he'd chased her. Last night, Sylvan had been in jeopardy—until she'd sacrificed all of her dreams for the good of her kingdom.

Now her realm was safe, and being married to the hell king wasn't as awful as she'd feared. She would learn how to manage him. It seemed *fucking with him* was the best way to tweak his mood. *I can totally do that—*

His arms wrapped around her waist. He tackled her into the waves, taking the impact.

She sputtered as he righted her. "Lucky catch!" They faced each other in the waist-deep water.

His lips were curling. "The luckiest."

Smoothing her hair off her face, she said, "Tracing isn't fair."

"You never said there'd be no tracing." The sun struck his green eyes, sending them aglow, the color as vivid as this beach.

She stared up at his gaze, briefly losing the thread of their conversation. What had they been talking about? *Oh, yeah.* "I would pound on your chest from the injustice of our race, but after seeing you repel that serpent, I don't have a shot of hurting you, do I?"

Voice growing husky, he said, "You make me ache in parts of my anatomy farther south. Just as you did all morning."

He'd been teased and denied for hours, which would help explain his irritability. When he'd done the same to her in the bathtub—for mere minutes—she'd been about to strangle him.

He nodded to indicate her clinging blouse. "You can't swim in that."

"Something tells me if I remove my clothes, I won't get much swimming done."

"Then you and I will promise to race to that cove"—he pointed in the distance—"and back before I get to pleasure you."

Pleasure me? Her lips parted. So that was a given on today's agenda?

She didn't stop him when he pulled her shirt off. She didn't resist when he used a claw to slice her skirt away. In fact, she was getting more turned on by the second.

He wadded up the remains of her clothes and tossed them to the shore, his torso muscles contracting. He ran his knuckle along her bra strap. "This should go as well."

"I thought I got to keep my underwear on."

"By royal decree, all beaches in hell are topless. As of today."

Dare she? Again she was reminded of the pomegranate lesson. "Topless, huh?" She reached back to unstrap her bra. "The king here must be brilliant."

"Equaled only by his clever queen."

"What's she like?"

"A lusty temptress. Subjects can hear her screams of pleasure coming from the castle."

Had they? Her face heated. "Can they hear the king's roars?"

He nodded. "And they envy him every one."

She removed her bra.

He rubbed his claw-tipped hand over his mouth. "If you knew what the sight of those does to me . . ."

Her nipples stiffened even more. She could feel the sun's heat on them.

"Also by royal decree, the beaches are bottomless."

Skinny-dipping with a demon in hell. What could possibly go wrong?

But she *was* starting to trust him more. Still high from all these new changes and sensations, she said, "I don't want to break the king's laws." She reached down to pull off her panties.

His eyes widened with surprise. "My laws are important."

As she threw her underwear toward the shore, his eyes locked on the movements of her breasts.

With a growl, he tore his own pants off.

Catching a vague glimpse of his dick through the waves, she dragged her gaze up. "When we race, will your wings slow you down?" She sized him up. "They aren't very hydrodynamic."

"I'll hold my own." He turned to toss his pants away.

"Oh? Then you better—" She dove, swimming for a head start.

Calliope looked like a sleek torpedo in the water. As Sian watched her, his mind was as blown as hers had been over the beach and serpents.

Then he remembered their race. Tracing to her side, he swam full speed to the cove, keeping pace with her. On the way back, he beat her.

She surfaced with a sputter. "You cheated!" Smoothing her wet hair back, she stood in water up to her chest.

"You *still* haven't said no tracing."

"Tricksy demon." She shielded her eyes from the sun. "How big is this sea? I came across different accounts in my reading."

"It would take weeks to sail across."

She blinked up at him. "And the dimension?"

"You are queen of a gigantic realm. There are many regions. The Badlands, the Highlands, the Stygian Marsh, Slaughter Gorge."

"Where you sent those legions of demon warriors for more punishment."

"Just so," he said, picking up on her undertone of censure. But he didn't acknowledge it. "Last week I ran for four days and covered only a fraction of the lands here."

"The days you didn't come to the tower?"

In a wry tone, he said, "I intended to be gone for months. I remained away from you for ninety-six whole hours. Even then . . ."

"Even then?"

"A demon doesn't like to be separated from his mate."

"Ah." Calliope waded, seeming to enjoy just floating in the gentle swells.

"To what did you attribute your interest in this realm?"

"I didn't know. My parents found my fascination disturbing, but nothing could stop it."

Disturbing. They sounded similar to her parents in her past. "Do you still disbelieve you're reincarnated?"

She shrugged. "I'm different. You're different. I care more about the future than the past."

Yet his future outlook was limited. *Enjoy this while you can, Sian.*

Her expression was relaxed, her eyes bright. In the sun, one was gold, the other amethyst. "I was deeply disappointed when I thought that your eyes matched."

"Why?"

"How many males have a female so unique?"

"I didn't even know you had green eyes until yesterday." His rage and lust must have kept his irises black for days. "What made you calmer?"

"A demon's mate is thought to center him." *After* the claiming, at least. Until then, Sian would be at the mercy of his mating instincts, battling them at every turn.

Calliope's cheeks, already pinkened in the sun, warmed even more as she asked, "Could people really hear my screams all over?"

"If you listen closely, you can still hear echoes." He would need an eternity just to steal blushes from her. How easily *tricking* had turned to *teasing.*

"Ha. At least I don't trigger earthquakes when I come. Or slice bathtubs open. What did that poor tub do to piss you off?"

His lips twitched. "That was my first time to pleasure my mate, and the experience affected my release *intensely.*"

She tapped her chin. "Did it? I wasn't sure until the tub murder. Have you always reacted that way with females?"

"Never. I've maintained strict control."

"How?"

"With ridiculous ease. Then you come along. . . ."

The seabed began vibrating beneath their feet. The waves rolling toward shore quavered and sloshed erratically.

"What's going on?" She sidled closer to him.

He faced the beach. "Hellhounds approach."

THIRTY-SIX

The silver and black brush lining the shore rustled, the larger trees bending.

Lila got goose bumps in the warm water when a pack of creatures burst onto the beach.

Though she'd seen illustrations of hellhounds, their appearance still shocked her. Each one was as big as a car, with bloodred eyes, dripping fangs, and spikes lining its back.

There were five adults and two puppies, all with charcoal-gray fur. Blood and bits of gristle covered their maws.

She sensed Abyssian's gaze slide to her, but she couldn't hide her wonder. Sea serpents and hellhounds and a playdate in hell. She muttered, "Holy shit."

"Did you read about these as well?"

"Yes, but the description didn't do them justice. Are they tame like Loki?"

"Somewhat. The pack recognizes my horns. I'm the alpha, I suppose. Still, they might challenge me if I were injured or compromised in some way."

The seven played in the sand, chasing and nipping one another. Their pounding paws shook the beach.

She was transfixed. "What do they eat?" Where'd the blood on their snouts come from?

"Reptiles and unwary demons. Last night, the pack could have happily varied their diet with you."

There's no outrunning hellhounds.

One puppy plopped over. Four legs in the air, it shimmied in the sand and chuffed at the others, as if saying, *This. Is. The. Best.* She knew the feeling.

Realization struck her: this might possibly be the best day of her life.

She was swimming naked with a demon in a foreign realm, yet she felt safe. Here she didn't have to worry about humans with smartphone cameras or bounty hunters or homicidal archers. Instead she was greeted by one wonder after another.

She gazed up at Abyssian from under her lashes. Her rapidly developing interest in him surprised her, but it made sense. She'd been solitary for so long, exiled to the mortal realm as if to a deserted island. All she'd known was loneliness—until an intense, powerful, sexy king focused his attentions on her.

She found it *thrilling*. Plus she was newly immortal, her every emotion amplified.

"What are you thinking about?" he asked with a sigh.

"Abyssian . . ." She trailed off. *This is moving fast. Don't hurt me. Let go of the past.* Dragging her attention from his face, she cleared her throat. "Is the pack not afraid of serpents?"

"The two species seem to have called a truce. Otherwise neither of them would really win, and both would lose."

His words brought to mind Sylvan. Though the fey overlords had the upper hand—at present—their use of slavery was corroding them, degenerating them. In the end, they would lose, even if Abyssian didn't invade with an army.

As quickly as the hellhounds had appeared, they vanished back into the brush, their fur camouflaging them.

Abyssian turned to her. "This can be an unforgiving world, Calliope. You have to respect the dangers. There are resin pits, quicksand traps, lava tides. I can go on all day."

"What about the dragons? Would they attack?"

"If we were separated, they might. But you're safe with me," he said. "If you'd like to become acquainted with the largest and oldest dragon shifter in existence, he currently roosts in our throne room."

"Uthyr."

"I haven't seen him in a day or two, but when he returns, I could set up a meeting." In a casual tone, Abyssian said, "You will have to meet my allies one day."

Didn't mean she'd be happy about it. "How did you get to be a Møriør?" *And can I make you stop being one?* Preferably before she had to meet any of them.

His expression grew more animated. He liked simply *thinking* about his alliance, as if the mere idea of the Møriør was a talisman for him.

"My sire was a member, so I was a legacy of sorts. After your death, I needed something to occupy my mind, so I sought out Orion. I was drawn to his views on the universe and decided to join him. He helped me through those first years." Abyssian added, "Now that we're wed, I will be more forthcoming about my alliance."

"Everyone talks about them as if they're larger than life. What are they really like? As people?"

Her interest clearly pleased him. "Blace is the primordial vampire, an expert swordsman and filled with wisdom. Darach Lyka, the oldest werewolf, is inconceivably strong, even more so when his beast rises. Allixta, the Overlady of Witches, is bent on imposing taxes on mystical expenditures. Before she became a Møriør, she hexed me with a pain spell so excruciating, I was surprised I emerged from it with my sanity intact." Yet he didn't seem to have any lingering resentment. "Uthyr has the power of invisibility and can vary the fire he breathes, using it for everything from portals to shields to spurts of time travel."

Time travel. Could anyone stand against them? Sylvan certainly couldn't have.

"That wise old dragon has a dry sense of humor and loves television. Especially soap operas." At her look, he said, "I swear it's true."

"And the archer?"

"Rune Darklight is a brother to me. Has been for millennia."

Ugh. A bromance. "You said his mate was a halfling. What kind?"

"Josephine is part vampire and part phantom, one of the rarest and most powerful combinations. She possesses many abilities: tracing, telekinesis, levitation, incorporeality. She can even drink Rune's black blood."

Lila had never heard of such a thing. "Is she a Møriør now?" Did that alliance just become stronger?

"No. And I don't know if she will be. She doesn't have much interest in politics." How nice that would be—to just *bow out.*

"What about your leader?" The one Nïx was particularly keen to hear about.

"Orion is an enthralling male. His appearance constantly changes—no one knows what he truly looks like." How odd. "You were right—he can detect the weaknesses in everything—from a castle's defense to the instability of a society's foundation." Like Sylvan's. "He sleeps now, will wake once Tenebrous reaches Gaia."

"What's it like to travel in a moving dimension?"

"You would enjoy it very much. I'll take you there in time. I want to see your face when you stare out at the black ether and watch worlds flash by."

Though she would kill to see that, to learn firsthand about such a place, she didn't foresee a visit in her future. "What about the others? I heard there were a dozen of you."

"Only ten. We have two seats remaining at our war-room table. My other three allies are . . . not as easy to explain. I would rather you just meet them."

"You said you would be a soft touch. Can I convince you to draw back from"—*quit forever*—"the Møriør?"

"They are my family. Just as they could never persuade me to relinquish my mate, you will never persuade me to relinquish my family. Mark my words, Calliope: I will *always* be a Møriør." Moving in closer to her, he said, "Tell me why you hate my alliance so deeply."

I can't! Not until she trusted Abyssian more. She would have to trust him *with her life*.

A shadow passed over them. She craned her head up. Five dragons soared above! They were much smaller than Uthyr and had black scales. To her delight, one shot a stream of fire, then flew into the flames. "Why did he do that?"

"Warming up for the night's hunt. This is my favorite time of the day. The dragons set out from their roosts. Creatures rouse in the wilds. Soon the hounds will howl."

"You must've missed this place when you were in the Elserealms." The dragons continued on, one of them trailing a wing tip across the water's surface. "Will you have to return there?"

"If I do, you'll be coming with me." With an inscrutable expression, he said, "We will never live apart."

"Never?" That was a word immortals didn't throw around lightly.

"Ever. As I said, a demon doesn't like to be away from his mate."

Sian was reminded of that last dance with Kari when he'd told her, *You will be mine, Kari. For all time. I will never be separated from you.*

But he had been. "Do you have a problem with a male keeping his wife by his side?"

Picking up on his change in demeanor, she glared. "Depends on if the male is a surly demon who gives his wife whiplash with his moods. Such a wife would wonder if such a husband recalled that they were skinny-dipping on a gorgeous day."

Fair point. *Just enjoy this, Sian. . . .*

A couple of dragon stragglers glided overhead. With her attention distracted, Sian decided on a prank to reclaim her good mood. He reached a wing around under the water and skimmed her calf.

Eyes darting, she eased closer. "What was that?"

Keeping his expression blank, he said, "What was *what*?"

"I felt something against my leg."

"Hmm. Could be a school of hatchlings."

"A *school*? Of baby *serpents*?"

"They're even more poisonous than the larger ones. Good thing you're immortal now." Unable to resist, he moved his wing again—

She screeched and leapt for him. Climbing him like a tree, she wrapped her arms around his head just below his horns. Her breasts pressed against his face, her legs locked around him. "T-trace us to the shore, Abyssian!"

He coiled his arms around her and turned his head, which put one of her nipples just out of his tongue's reach. So close, yet so far. *The prank's on me.* In a muffled voice, he said, "*Or* it could be your husband's wing touching you underwater."

"Oh, you dick!" she cried, releasing her grip on him. "You will *pay* for that one. Now put me down."

"Of course." He let her slowly inch down his body, her nipples raking his chest.

She sucked in a breath.

Already he could scent how aroused she was. His shaft throbbed for that honey. But he had to behave—somewhat—until she invited him to claim her. And right now, Sian felt a hot, aching hope that an invitation would be forthcoming soon.

Halfway down his body, she gasped, parting her glossy lips.

He was helpless to resist them. He cupped her ass, holding her aloft, then leaned down. She must know he was about to take her mouth, to kiss her tongue with his pointed one.

Her lids went heavy, and she raised her face.

She wants my kiss! Sian hesitated, savoring that he was *about* to take her lips.

After lifetimes of waiting, he'd wondered if his mind had exaggerated how intense their one kiss had been.

He eased toward her mouth . . . an inch closer. He could feel her exhalations. Closer . . . Their lips met.

When his tongue touched hers, pinpoints of light exploded behind his lids. Heat and need erupted inside him. His mind had *not* exaggerated.

Kissing my mate. Lightning and balance. The rightness.

She moaned against his lips, wrapping her legs around his waist. *Lusty female!*

He squeezed her closer, kissing with all his longing, his ages-old yearning. If his first taste of his mate's lips had ruined him, this resurrected him.

Was she just as affected? He needed to see her ethereal face, to behold her reaction and commit it to memory. He drew back.

"Abyssian?" Her teal eyes were hooded and locked on his lips as she licked her own.

Between breaths, he said, "That was—"

"More, demon." She tugged on his hair to yank him back.

And all of a sudden, Abyssian Infernas comprehended the meaning of joy. . . .

THIRTY-SEVEN

Here are my fireworks! Lila returned the demon's blazing kiss.

Their tongues tangled, their breaths mingling. She fed on his groans, shivering when the tip of his pointed tongue teased her. She rubbed her body against his, undulating right as he thrust—

The tip of his dick met her entrance. They both froze.

She broke the kiss with a gasp. "Demon!" The crown lodged against her.

His eyes had flooded black, his horns shooting straight. With a shudder, he clamped his hands around her hips, holding her in place.

She didn't think he'd meant to hit the bull's-eye, but he wasn't in any hurry to right the situation either.

Was she? That pressure felt incredible. Even *tempting.*

Voice harsh, he bit out, "Closest I've ever been . . . to spending. Need—to—thrust. To *fuck.*" He rocked his hips a touch, just as his hands pressed down. "Ahh! My mate's so *tight.*"

She gasped at the new sensation: unbelievably good—laced with a definite twinge. Reminded of her overdue-volcano analogy, she said, "Abyssian, not here. Not now." Logic told her she would need a vat of wine, a lot of preparation, and a somewhat calm partner when losing her virginity.

"Then you must get . . . away. From me." Gnashing his fangs, he lifted her off him, setting her down. "Or I'll claim you . . . right here . . . wedge my cock so deep inside you."

Her body ached with loss, but she gave him a shaky nod and hurried through the currents.

As she climbed out of the water, his groan sounded over the waves.

On shore, she could feel the heat of his gaze on her, the first time he'd ever really seen her naked from the back. She *might* have slowed her steps to give him a good look at her ass. *Evaluate this, demon.*

He yelled, *"Stop."*

She froze. Had he spotted some danger? A heartbeat later, he traced directly behind her, then dropped to his knees.

She peered over her shoulder. "Abyssian?"

His brows were drawn, his expression lost. With shaking hands, he reached for her, palms easing closer to her ass. "Beautiful mate. Maddening me." His lean body quaked—and his huge cock strained.

She sucked in a breath at the sight of it.

The rigid length jutted upward from his groin, straight as a rod. The crown was broad and pulled taut. Two raised veins twined over the thick shaft.

Her pussy went wet for it—though her mind doubted the logistics. He hadn't even gotten the head inside her before she'd felt pain.

Yet his dick riveted her. She licked her lips when moisture beaded the slit. Could he feel the breeze glide over that tip?

What would it be like to suck him? She'd never given a blowjob before, but she was game. She knew the basics, and he'd said he would welcome questions. They'd figure it out.

His hands finally reached their destination, his growl giving her shivers. His splayed fingers squeezed. In a dazed tone, he grated, "Fuck me, Lila."

I'm contemplating it.

He moved his grip to her hips. Her eyes widened when he rubbed his horns over the curves of her ass. Sounding as lost as he looked, he muttered in Demonish, "Desire me, beauty, as I desire you."

She couldn't answer, wasn't supposed to understand him. She jolted when he nipped her with his teeth. "Oh!"

Then came more rubbing with his horns. They were shockingly warm. From the sun, or were they always?

The tower's engravings had featured horns again and again; demons seemed to revere them. A male demon was supposed to love it when his partner steered his course with them—or held on to them for dear life.

I really want to touch Abyssian's horns.

He froze. "I heard that thought."

Shit! She'd have to be more careful with her blocks.

He spun her around, putting her sex in front of his face. Would he go down on her right now?

"Gods almighty, what I wouldn't do for a taste of your sweet flesh." Seeming to give himself a shake, he rasped, "But first my mate will have her wish. Touch me."

"Will you lower your head?"

He did. Signs of Abyssian's might surrounded her. He had dominion over lethal predators, volcanoes, *her*. Yet the legendary king of hell was on his knees, making himself vulnerable to her. That concession meant so much.

His chest was still—holding his breath? When she ran the pads of her fingers across the base of one large horn, he loosed a ragged exhalation.

Again that heady sense of power swept her up. "I didn't expect it to be so warm." The length straightened even more. "How well can you feel through them?"

He tensed, as if her question had provoked him. "They are extremely sensitive organs. I feel pleasure—and *pain*."

"Do you want me to stop?"

He hastily said, "Keep touching me."

Her fingers were stark against the black smoothness. Growing more aroused, she caressed his other horn, and it straightened as well.

"Lila . . ." He bowed his head even more. "I've no defense against you." Though he quaked harder, she felt as if she were gentling him. A small fey's touch was taming this great beast of a demon.

When she impulsively leaned down to press her lips to one horn, he made a broken sound.

"Was that wrong?"

"Right." He reached around to grip her ass. "I just don't know how much more I can take."

A thought blasted through her mind. And it wasn't *hers.*

—She will be the death of me.—

Moments ago, he'd picked up one of her thoughts; had she just read Abyssian's mind?

Or was she losing her own?

Maybe the throne of hell brought more perks with it than she'd ever expected. . . .

Kneading her ass, he said, "Now I want you on my tongue. Knee over my shoulder, Lila."

She swallowed. "Um, okay."

Before she could lift her leg, he muttered, "Wait." He canted his head, seeming to listen for something. "Godsdamn it, I have to return." He shuddered as he rose.

"What's wrong?"

"I've sensed an entry into our dimension."

He could do that? "An enemy?"

Abyssian grated, "As of this moment forward, yes."

THIRTY-EIGHT

Of all the bloody bad timing . . .

An entry into Sian's realm had pinged his consciousness. Muttering a vile curse, he grasped Calliope's elbow, teleporting her to their room.

He'd just been a heartbeat away from tasting her, inhaling his mate's tantalizing scent—about to feast on her.

While she'd been stroking his horns! How many times had he fantasized about that same scenario over the last ten millennia?

Fuck the defense of Pandemonia.

No, no, he now had a mate to protect; defense was more important than ever.

After steadying her, he traced to his dressing room. Brushing sand from his knees, he stabbed his legs into trews, struggling to tie the laces over his bulging cock.

Had he really been partway inside his mate?

She'd donned her robe by the time he returned. "What's going on?"

"Kingdom concerns. Stay here. I'll be back to escort you to dinner." He briefly took her lips again, reluctant to release her.

Sudden impact rocked the castle. From the throne tower?

She grabbed his hand. "What concerns?"

"There's no danger to you. I'll take care of this."

"Okay. Go. I can keep myself occupied."

"That's what I'm worried about. Don't take the edge off your need." He pressed a kiss to her palm. "Wait and allow me to tend to you."

She nodded breathlessly.

He traced to the throne room, baring his fangs for a confrontation.

Uthyr had just collapsed onto the terrace. Scorch marks covered him. He was missing scales and looked exhausted.

"What happened to you, dragon?"

Uthyr's chest heaved, emitting wheezing puffs of smoke. —You *happened to me, demon!—*

"Explain."

—I flew to the Vrekeners' mountain to watch the queen's television, a season finale. *But when I was ready to return here and check on your progress,* someone *had decided to lop off that realm. With me in it!—*

Sian pinched his forehead. "My apologies, Uthyr. How did you manage to get back here?"

—Let's just say it involved a lot of firepower and many transdimensional connections.— His streams of fire burned tunnels to other worlds. *—Since I was already out, I journeyed to Gaia to visit Rune in Louisiana. But weakness hindered my invisibility. I was seen by drunken mortals! They called me a* Mardi Gras float. *What in the hells is that?—*

Sian shrugged, eager to get back to his mate.

—When I didn't give them moon pies*, they hurled beads at me!—*

Indeed Uthyr had colorful beads dangling from his horns. The dragon's scaled brow furrowed as he took in Sian's expression. *—Why do you look* not *miserable?—*

"Much has occurred here as well." Shoulders back, he said, "I wed Calliope yesterday." He needed to get her a wedding gift. He'd procure jewels for her from one of Graven's rooms.

Setting aside his ire, Uthyr said, *—She accepted your appearance? Your past treatment of her?—*

Sian rubbed the back of his neck. "I made a bargain with her not to invade Sylvan. I vowed that the Møriør would leave those inhabitants in peace."

Uthyr rolled his golden eyes. *—Still playing your games?—*

"Maybe I know of no other way."

—Wait, all *of the inhabitants? Some of Magh's line reside in Sylvan. Rune will go apoplectic to be denied his vengeance.—*

"I'll make him understand."

—Let me know how that works out for you.— He sighed. *—Of all the times for Orion to sleep.—*

As if Sian and Rune would need some kind of intervention?

—Have you claimed your mate?—

He shook his head. "She will let me know when she is ready."

—Finally, an iota of sense from you. I don't suppose you've told her your appearance will continue to change.—

"No. I want to give her a chance to cleave to me, if that's possible. And it might just be." Her smoldering sensuality had staggered him. "She is demonstrating facets I never saw before."

She'd wanted to touch him! Her tender caresses on the beach had set him aflame. He could scarcely believe she'd *kissed* his horns. And all the while, the maddening scent of her arousal had deepened.

Maybe she did belong here in hell. With him.

—What facets?—

Sian couldn't stop his grin. "She's a lusty one."

—Lucky demon.—

"Gods, dragon, that female is bliss embodied." She'd already ruined him for all other females.

—You've forgiven her for everything in the past?—

Sian's grin faded as if never there. "I try to turn my mind from it, but I fear the past will be like a drop of acid, seething forever." Even in the midst of such pleasure on the beach, he'd been reminded of losing his horns. "I can't relive certain memories without erupting into a rage." The amputation and her reaction . . .

—Excellent foundation for an eternal union. What will you do about heirs?—

When Sian tried to picture his offspring—a possibility that was actually in reach—he couldn't see anything but pups with pointed ears and demonic tempers.

Yet he knew such thinking was idiocy. "I'd never pressure Calliope to bear a dark fey. She'd probably be horrified if I brought up the prospect." She'd reached for that contraception ring quickly enough.

—Tell her how you truly feel, even if your pride fights you.—

"I will. In time. I have this under control."

—Of course you do. Why listen to a wise dragon like myself?— With a surly look, Uthyr licked a gash across his forepaw.

"I am sorry about your troubles, brother."

—I'll need to sleep this off for a couple of days.—

Sian nodded. "How are Rune and Josephine?"

—Settling in nicely, and so in love it'd be sickening if Josephine didn't "jank" on him so much.— She took zero guff from Rune, keeping him in line with her brash attitude. *—I told them you have found your mate. They plan to stop by soon to meet her.—*

Which would give Sian scant time to get through to Calliope, to change a view she'd held all her life. . . .

THIRTY-NINE

Lila crossed to the terrace railing, unable to summon a flicker of worry about Abyssian's *kingdom concerns*; she knew he would take care of any trespasser. Only an idiot would attempt to breach this castle.

The sea serpents had returned to frolic in the waves, their scales aglow in the setting sunlight. She'd witnessed fiery sunsets in Florida, but this was ridiculous. Feverish red and orange battled to steal the sky, the sight mind-boggling.

And I'm queen of this place. . . .

Eager to try out her new closet again, she headed back inside, replaying the way Abyssian had kissed her palm earlier. What had that look in his eyes promised?

Though they'd almost had sex, she wasn't ready for more of that. Yet. But oral? *Sign me up.*

At the fireplace, she drew up short. The Lôtān head was gone.

Her gaze took in the bare stone above the hearth. The spot where the Lôtān had hung was darker than the rest. That thing must've resided there for eons.

Yet Abyssian had removed the *sacred demonic trophy*. For her.

Pang.

An existence here would be far different from her dream existence in Sylvan, but what if two beings as dissimilar as she and the demon could eke out a future together? If she could manage his moods . . .

Getting attached to him wasn't the smartest thing she could do—not with her background—but she couldn't just turn off her feelings, despite how little she knew about him.

I know him as well as he knows me. A sobering thought.

She meandered down the hall toward her wardrobe, but two gold doors past her own beckoned. Feeling like Bluebeard's wife, she opened the first one. Abyssian's dressing room.

Inside, she found pairs of his usual leather pants and boots, and a few more formal garments. Several white tunics had fastenings on the back to accommodate his wings.

Along the farthest wall, he'd organized swords and other medieval weapons, but an ax held a place of honor among the rest.

Abyssian Infernas's legendary battle-ax.

No one would ever believe how close she'd gotten to it. She tentatively touched the dark metal. As cool as he was warm. She sensed the history of this weapon, but couldn't imagine how many lives it'd taken.

She traced the edge of the blade, testing its sharpness. Blood rose along a thin slice. Regeneration began to tingle.

Immortality had its perks.

What would she find in the other room? Bluebeard's wife wanted to know. Lila might no longer be in hell as a spy—she'd fulfilled her role—but she still had a fey's curiosity.

She exited the dressing room, then tried the second door. *Open.*

His study! She breezed inside, raising a brow at the Lôtān trophy hanging on a wall. Better here than in the bedroom. She made a face at the monster head.

Atop a large stone desk were stacks of papers. An antique hand mirror served as a paperweight. Why would he have a mirror like that on his desk? She couldn't see him gazing at his reflection.

Going through Abyssian's things might jeopardize their fragile new start . . . but his papers were *on top* of his desk, weren't they? She wouldn't go digging to get to private stuff or anything.

Of course, he would feel comfortable leaving everything out in the open because he didn't know she could read Demonish. She was going to have to tell him about that soon.

She sifted through his letters, all handwritten—because the Internet didn't exist here. A definite strike against Pandemonia.

E-mail vs. sea serpents . . .

Several letters were in languages she'd never seen. She'd have to ask Abyssian how many he knew.

A note with dainty writing caught her attention. Definitely a woman's hand. But Lila couldn't make out the language.

When she thought of all the females he'd been with over his lifetime, the sheer number, jealousy scalded her.

She recalled her emotionless mother telling her that Saetth would keep a mistress after the wedding, because "that's what kings do."

Through calm, logical reasoning, Lila had concluded that his keeping a mistress wouldn't work for her; in her mind, a king and queen needed to be a unified front—without others' interests coming between them.

When Lila imagined Abyssian with other females, nothing felt *calm* or *logical.*

A scroll of paper caught her attention. She removed the ribbon and unfurled the page, finding Demonish written in another woman's hand.

Lila read:

Felicitations on your marriage to your fey mate, my great king. Your harem humbly beseeches you to visit the Tower of Lusts in order to begin seeding your line of succession. The Infernas Dynasty awaits its illustrious continuation.

Tower of Lusts? How freaking cute. The joke was on them; he still had his demon seal.

Once he was free of it, would he go back to his harem? Though she'd become convinced of his growing attachment to her, Lila couldn't give him red-blooded heirs.

He'd said he wanted pups but would never father a baneblood. She gazed down at her ring. It *wasn't* a wedding band; it was a contraception method.

Not only that, he'd warned her that he liked challenge and variety. He'd point-blank told her he intended to keep a queen *and* a harem. That'd been *last night*.

Her eyes widened. He hadn't been speaking hypothetically! He'd known she was his mate from the start, so he'd been referencing *her* as the queen in question.

She'd been so confident when she told him that hell would freeze over before she became one among his other females. As of today, he might have put her into the rotation. He could be in the Tower of Lusts with one—or more—of them right now.

Inhaling a deep breath, she rolled up the page and returned the ribbon. Maybe she was jumping to conclusions. Having never felt jealousy before, she had no idea how to handle it.

Be logical, Lila. But logic backed up her conclusions! How many warrior kings would go without heirs? Why would Abyssian stop seeing professional lovers who kept him "very satisfied" and catered to his "every filthy desire"?

He had a freaking tower in his castle devoted to lust!

His dynasty did await, and once he lost his seal with Lila, he could—as he'd put it—plant his seed in every field but a fey's. *Her* field. Again, he'd known she was his at the time.

She imagined him having young with those twelve females and grew queasy. Abyssian would never let her sleep with another male, much less have a baby with one. Would she be forced to live in a castle with all her husband's children—and none of her own?

Fuck that. The need to lash out at him burned inside her. Perhaps she could use her newly discovered power over him. . . .

You can look, demon, but you can't touch.

She hastened to her dressing room. The closet produced one brazenly sexy dress after another.

She settled on a scandalous number, a backless ruby-red gown with a halter top. The material of the halter was no mere silk. . . .

After bathing, she drew on black hose and red garters, then slipped on the gown. She wore her hair up. He seemed to love nuzzling her ears, so she accentuated them with dangling onyx earrings.

What would he think?

Half an hour later, he appeared in the bedroom, freshly showered and formally dressed.

She purred, "I've been waiting for you."

His sharp exhalation was worth any embarrassment.

FORTY

My mate has discovered her wiles, Sian thought as he surveyed her at the dinner table.

From the waist up of her red dress, the material was transparent, and gods help him, her breasts were free. How was he supposed to make it through this meal?

Seated to his right, she sipped her wine, gazing around the room with an air of boredom. She'd barely touched her plate.

She was angry with him, but he had no idea what could've happened in the interval between when he'd left and when he'd returned.

How easily she could shut him out. He could stand it no longer. "My compliments, Calliope. You found a gown sure to please your husband."

She leveled her gaze on him. "My husband seemed so enamored of my breasts that I displayed them to their best advantage."

"My clever wife is *displaying* my dessert."

She arched her brows. "You assume an after-dinner treat is being offered?"

"Another advantage to your dress—I can see your *treats* responding to me. They want me to savor them." A flush spread over her chest.

Yet more signs of her arousal. As if he wasn't aware of how aroused she'd grown! He could detect the mouthwatering scent of her need. He doubted she wore panties.

He imagined tossing her on the table, shoving up her skirts, and feeding his length inside her. She'd be so wet and tight for him. . . .

"I'm still getting used to my new immortality and its effects. At this point, I'm as discerning as an alley cat."

Which was the only reason she'd responded to him during their encounters. For just a short amount of time—a couple of godsdamned hours—he'd forgotten his looks.

She added, "But I've gotten a handle on my need. You won't have to worry about 'tending' to me ever again."

"So that's it? I got to share pleasure with my wife twice?" He shook his head. "The signals I get from you baffle me—yet you called *me* moody? As ever, you burn hot and cold. My tolerance for it hasn't improved over the last millennia."

"*Kari* burned hot and cold."

"*You* were hot when keen to get my secrets, then cold as ice afterward. You shut down your emotions utterly. I'd never seen anything so unsettling." When he'd offered up his most dear sacrifice to her, she'd coldly given him her back.

As blood ran down his face, he'd willed her to turn around and see him. To comprehend that he would do anything for her. *Turn around, Kari. Look at me. . . .*

He gritted his teeth, shoving aside that memory.

Calliope said, "Fey have that talent."

"Talent? You mean *curse*." He swigged demon brew. "I'm used to hot and cold from you—but never at the same time. That dress does not fit with your sudden bout of pique."

"You continue to bring up the past, but you'd have me believe you've let go of your revenge?"

"My vengeance against you is done. And I am trying to keep my mind from the past. There is a memory, a haunting one that tries to surface. . . . I turn from it every time."

"Why?"

Because it will make me hate you anew. "As you said, I want to look to the future instead."

"You want to, but you *don't*."

"For ten thousand years, I was one way. For a couple of days, I've been another. I'm a very old demon unused to change."

"Oh, I believe that more and more," she said. "Speaking of which, did you visit your concubines earlier?"

Concubines? What other surprising subjects did she ponder when he was barred from her thoughts? He steepled his fingers. "Would that bother you?" *Say yes. . . .*

"All monarchs have them. And you did warn me."

"What are you talking about?" Actually, he *had* visited them.

"Since you knew I was your mate from the very start, I've been thinking about our previous dinner conversation in that context. You smugly told me you would have your wife *and* your harem. I realized you were referring to me all along."

Again, not his best moment. "Then ask me to get rid of them," he said, though he'd paid them off and released them earlier. "I can be accommodating with my new bride."

"So you had no plans to send them away on your own?" Her pink nails drummed on her cup. "You make it sound like I could ask you for that *favor*. And you might be magnanimous enough to grant it."

Could Calliope possibly want him only for herself? If she could feel for him even a fraction of his bone-deep possessiveness toward her . . . "You hold sway over me. Bid me to send them away, and I will do it."

She flashed him a look of disgust. "If I have to tell you, then the gesture is meaningless."

"No? I thought you would never share a male."

"I'd been talking about my fiancé."

His gut clenched. No one could wound him like this female. "So you wouldn't have shared *him*, the male you chose for yourself. The one you wanted."

"In all ways, the life I had planned with him is different from the life you've offered me."

Sian lowered his hands, digging his claws into his palms. *I know this!* Some things couldn't be changed. His looks, his home, his alliance. The type of babes he would give her. And just like all those years ago, it was *killing him* that he couldn't be what she wanted. "Yet I have it on good authority—my touch—that you're still a virgin. You weren't tempted to give him your innocence?"

"Just the fact that you called my virginity 'innocence' shows how incompatible we are."

He ground his fangs. "I might enjoy bedding you so much that you wouldn't even have to *ask* me to be true. And once I claim you, Calliope, I promise you'll want my attentions focused solely on you."

"I already expressed doubt that you could satisfy twelve females, much less a baker's dozen. This marriage is a joke. I'd ask you for an annulment; unfortunately, I'm the protection price for my kingdom."

"You mention annulment because you still hope to be with your fiancé!" His wife, his *mate*, longed for another. That crimson haze covered Sian's vision. "I haven't waited ten millennia for you just to hand you over to another male. I should find him and take his head with my bare hands." As Sian had her first husband.

She bit out, "Spoken like a true Møriør."

"Maybe your former betrothed *did* try to seduce you, but you resisted his charms. You haven't resisted me though. When you were in the bath, I had you begging for more though I'd barely lifted a *finger*." He smirked—

Wine splashed his face. She'd tossed the contents of her cup at him? Through the drops he spied her haughty smile.

FORTY-ONE

"You little witch!" the demon sputtered, swiping wine off his face.

"You needed to cool off." Lila's grin deepened.

He narrowed his gaze at her smile. "You've had your fun." He traced beside her, sweeping dishes off the table. "Now I'll have mine." Before she could blink, he'd lifted her to the table, wedging his body between her legs.

"Enough, demon," she said, sounding breathy and excited—not resolved and indignant. Over their meal, she'd reluctantly gotten turned on each time he'd gazed at her breasts with his penetrating green eyes.

He eased down to kiss her, but she averted her face. With a growl, he turned to nuzzle her ear—*not the ears*—till her lids fluttered shut. He'd figured out her weakness before she'd even known it.

He kissed her neck, nipping the skin there, scorching a path down to her shoulder. "Tit for tat," he rasped.

Her eyes snapped open when cold liquid poured over her breasts. "You asshole!" He was holding a bottle he must've conjured from somewhere. Chilled wine? She shoved at him, didn't budge him.

"The better for you to feel the heat of my tongue. We'll see how well *you* like hot and cold."

He leaned down, his warm breaths caressing a stiffened nipple. Her own breaths shallowed.

He licked the tip through the thin material, sending a bolt of pleasure through her. His tongue *was* hot. He took the peak between his lips, into his searing mouth.

"Oh, gods!" Her back arched sharply, the sensations dizzying.

He suckled on that nipple. Nuzzling it. Groaning around it. He moved to her other breast, starting his attentions over. All the while, he pinched the nipple he'd left aching. Between sucks, he said, "I scent how wet you're getting for me."

She needed to tell him to stop. Her pride urged her to reject him, but her body disagreed.

Just a few moments more, and then she would push him away. Any second she would.

He drew back. "You've teased me with these breasts all night. And you accuse me of unfairness?" He unfastened her halter at her neck, and the sodden material fell to her lap. She parted her lips to tell him no, but then he cupped her with his big demon hands.

She pressed herself against his roughened palms. She forgot to breathe when he leaned down again. He sucked one nipple and flicked it with his tongue at the same time.

"Oh. My. Gods." Each pull of his lips made tension coil low in her belly.

Kneading her, he moved to her other breast, playing with the peak, tonguing it and suckling. When his suction tugged harder than before, she started to pant.

He poured more wine over her, drinking it from her breasts. Then he kissed up her chest and neck till his lips were beside her ear. He breathed against it until she was squirming. "Have you ever had a tongue against your pussy?"

Her ears were twitching like crazy. "N-no." Was she about to? There was a reason this shouldn't go any further. Why couldn't she remember the reason? Her nipples throbbed so hard, she couldn't think.

He turned to pull up a chair before her, then sat. Because he was going to be down there awhile? How *titillating.*

He began easing her skirts higher, revealing her garters and hose. "Are you curious what this feels like?"

She nodded. But she shouldn't let him do this. Should she?

With her skirts bunched in her lap, he laid his palms on her thighs and eased them apart. "I'm going to show you what a demon can do with his pointed tongue. I want your honey all over it." She felt air against her soaked curls just as he growled, "Gods almighty."

She knew he'd make this act heart-stopping, but what if she got even more addicted to him? Would she turn a blind eye to the others he slept with?

Fuck that. She shoved back and snapped her thighs closed.

What the hell just happened? "After I've fantasized about this for ages, you wait until I'm breathing your arousal, and then you bar the gates to heaven? Unnecessarily cruel, Lila."

She crossed her arms over her breasts. "I refuse to be in the rotation among your many females."

He drew back in bewilderment. "What's brought on this concubine talk?"

"You said you pursued me because you liked variety and a challenge; I don't want to be a challenge for you, and you don't want to give up your variety." She exhaled. "Maybe we should just get rid of your demon seal, and then you can be with others. You can have heirs with them."

Though he'd planned this exact scenario, his stomach clenched. "Is that what you want?" His wife would rather he fuck others than share his bed? *After she's ruined me?*

Giving himself a shake, he said, "You know what—it doesn't godsdamned matter what you want." He stood, staring down at her. "I won't share you, and you will not share me. There will be no others for either of us. I demand total fidelity."

She gazed up at him. "You're the one who told me to expect the opposite!"

"I said careless things to get a rise out of you. I haven't been with another since you came to this castle."

"Now I know you're lying. You roared right after I arrived, and it sounded sexual."

"Oh, it was."

Her lips thinned. "So I heard you coming with someone else."

Could she actually be . . . jealous? The possibility made his heart thunder. "Did you know that I got your silk shift from the Sorceri?"

"What does that have to do with anything?"

"I roared because I was stroking off with *your* godsdamned shift giving me the scent I needed. You heard me pleasuring myself to memories of our first kiss all those eons ago."

The pulse point in her throat fluttered. "Really?" she asked, her anger seeming to dissipate.

By all the gods, she had been jealous! She hadn't been pining over a fiancé; she'd been bristling. "I inherited that harem with the crown, but I have no desire to bed someone because she sees it as her duty. I've never been with any of them."

"You made it sound like you had. You said they catered to your every filthy desire."

"At our dinner, I enjoyed getting a rise out of you. Otherwise, my pride made me goad you," he admitted. "Calliope, I already released those females earlier. You and I have issues between us—but infidelity will never be one of them. You've gotten yourself a very faithful husband."

At least *that* would always remain constant. *Unlike my appearance . . .*

Lila thought back to the first time Abyssian had mentioned a harem. *Oh, yeah.* It'd been right after she'd scoffed at the idea of sleeping with him.

She'd stung the demon king's pride, so he'd reacted with a lie. This again made him seem . . . normal.

With all the lies she'd told, she could hardly be upset about his.

Had he truly used her lingerie to masturbate? She would have liked to see him, naked, stroking his hard length. . . .

She peered up at his proud face. His gaze glimmered in the firelight, filled with hunger and promising wicked things.

Things only *she* would get to enjoy.

Her jealousy vanished, and in its place rose an undeniable lust for him. He'd said all the right things, sending her back to where she'd been before she'd read the invitation.

"Your irises are bright teal. Are you relieved I'm all yours?"

She lifted one shoulder. "Maybe."

"You *were* jealous!" He looked delighted.

Chin jutting, she said, "I'm proud, and I respect myself."

His eyes grew lively. "My fey mate refuses to share me with others, and she'll let me know her wishes forcefully."

She sighed. "What are you talking about?"

"Would I have gotten a glass of wine in the face if you hadn't been bristling? You snapped those lovely thighs closed because my mouth is to pleasure *you* alone. Message received, little wife."

She hadn't thought he could look smugger than this morning. Wrong.

"You will never have reason to bar those gates again."

"Very well. I was jealous." She blew a curl out of her eyes. "Are you done now?"

He shook his head, his lips curving. "Oh, not by a league."

"While you're busy gloating, I can go masturbate."

"Ah-ah." He pressed closer to her. "Not a chance. I was a tongue's touch from where I'd kill to be. Now that I've soothed your anger, I want to soothe other parts of you."

Curiosity seized her, and she uncrossed her arms. "Okay."

His delight deepened. "My fey mate loves her pleasure. And my jealous hell queen won't share me. I'm a very happy male."

He was never going to let her live this down. But she could take his ribbing.

He pressed his mouth to hers for a tender kiss. Then he grazed his lips along her neck, to her breasts, to her navel. . . . He rubbed a horn against her torso, murmuring, "Want my scent on you."

She was panting by the time he took his seat once more.

"I'm truly about to taste my female." He was usually so arrogant, but in this, he let down his guard. "I'll have you in nothing but those garters and hose." With one claw he sliced off the remains of her dress, leaving it for her to sit on. His gaze roamed over her, and he cast her that awed expression. "If I live another ten millennia, I'll never forget how you look at this moment."

When he licked his lips with that pointed tongue, urges gripped her. Instinctive needs. She craved her lips on him. Her tongue on his fiery skin. . . .

"It'll be everything I can do not to come the instant I taste you. My cock's about to explode."

"Well, *don't* come. I have plans for that cock."

FORTY-TWO

Sian's jaw slackened. He tried to answer her. Failed. In a strangled voice, he finally managed, "At your service, beauty."

Somehow he'd have to hold back his release. Envisioning more of what she'd done to him last night in the bath, he vowed not to disappoint her. For now, he would enjoy his treat. . . . "Show me where you're wet."

Eyes ablaze and locked on his, she opened her thighs.

He groaned at the sight. Her little clit was so swollen, it must ache. She rolled her hips, and her plump lips parted for him. *Fuuuck.*

In the firelight, her glistening sex was a vision. "Spread your legs wider for me." She trustingly did. With a broken sound, he parted her with two fingers. *"Lila."* He could see inside her pink sheath. His cock *strained* for it.

Sian could tease her until she asked to be claimed. This very night, he could know what ejaculating felt like. The mystery would be revealed.

No, Sian! She might resent him afterward, and he desired far more from her than just sex.

He settled between her legs. Trailing his lips up one thigh, he flicked her supple skin with his tongue. Kisses up her other thigh made her rock her hips again, offering up his destination. "Your pussy's getting wetter before my eyes." He inhaled her delectable scent, letting her feel his exhalations against her clitoris.

"Don't tease me. I want to know what this is like."

"*You* want to know? Every night of my life, I've imagined licking an orgasm from you." His tongue lashed her bud.

She cried out, undulating for more.

He nuzzled her drenched lips, growling, *"Worth the fucking wait."* Tasting his mate. Rightness. The balance. She was soft as silk against his mouth.

Her breaths had shallowed, her breasts quivering. *Already on the edge.* Surrendering to him, she murmured, "Demon, I'll never get enough of this."

He briefly pulled back to rasp, "Me neither." He set back in, laving her rosy flesh.

She gave a sharp moan. "About to come!"

He nipped her thigh. "You'll come when your husband says you can. Not till you get wanton for me." He covered her entrance with his mouth, his tongue penetrating her.

"Abyssian!" Her whimpers made him crazed. *"Pleasepleaseplease."* She grasped his horns.

He jolted with shock. *Don't come! Gods, don't come!* When she gave a tug on his horns and rocked to his tongue at the same time, Sian lost his mind.

"Uhhhhnnnn!" Burying his mouth against her, the demon roared, sending vibrations into her flesh.

As she gripped his horns, he dug his claws into the stone table, and his wings snapped wide, billowing the hearth fire. He brought his lower wing claws down hard, sinking them into the table on either side of her hips. *Thunk, thunk.*

"Abyssian?" She used his horns to raise his face.

Mouth seamless with her flesh, he gazed upward. She watched as his eyes flooded with black.

The sight made her even wetter, his wildness spurring hers. "Need to come, Abyssian!" She shamelessly undulated, stroking his horns, desperate to ease this pressure.

He growled as he tongued her inside.

"Yes!" Her core tightened, her body readying. "Oh, gods, oh, gods! I'm going to come . . . come so hard."

He gave her clit a suck.

Her eyes shot wide. The world tilted until all she knew was his hot, hot mouth. She threw her head back and screamed.

In a frenzy, he shook his head between her legs, snarling against her.

Her sheath clenched, contractions seizing her again and again as he devoured her. She tightened her grip on him and moaned, *"Abyssian."* The tremors began to subside, but he kept kissing her.

Releasing his horns, she fell back on the table, arms thrown over her head. "My gods, demon . . ."

The king of hell sat at his dining table feasting on *her*, and she was tempted to let him continue. But she was more tempted to reciprocate. His wildness had called to hers. Now his hunger did.

Pleasure was rewriting *her.*

She sat up and pushed at his head; he continued to lick. She murmured his name. He wouldn't stop.

Before she got swept back up, she said, "It's—my—turn."

FORTY-THREE

As he lapped at her luscious orgasm, Calliope's voice carried as if from a distance.

Tasting her release was a baptism of fire. His demon instincts roared with fulfillment, yet his cock throbbed for relief.

When she pushed at his horns, he reluctantly drew back from his prize. How he kept from falling upon her again, he didn't know.

He'd pleasured his female well, and it showed. Her eyes were bright, her skin flushed. His chest bowed with pride even as his body pained him beyond measure.

She wanted to touch him, had vocalized her wish. He rose to stand before her.

Reaching for his shirt, she unfastened a button, then another. When she opened his shirt, his raised glyphs burned, reflecting in her hooded gaze.

His brows drew tight. "Don't know how long I can last. . . ." His cock was so swollen, she couldn't get the ties of his pants loose. He slashed them open.

"Thanks." She gave his pants a decisive yank, shoving them down his thighs. When his length sprang free above her lap, her eyes glittered as if with greed.

His lust-fogged mind couldn't quite wrap around this. She took her time staring, and he let her look her fill, his shaft jerking under her gaze.

Don't come! "I could go off just from your eyes upon me." Clenching his jaw, he willed himself back from the brink. When she grasped him, his hips bucked uncontrollably. Her fingers were so pale against his demon skin.

Her soft palm roamed downward to his heavy balls. He opened his stance for her, choking back yells as she fondled his aching testicles, tugging on them, hefting them.

So close . . . He could easily come from this, but he must know what she had planned! If he could last long enough for her to reveal her intention, then he would know what had been going on in that mysterious mind of hers. . . .

"You need to sit." She shoved against his chest, and he didn't resist, collapsing back into the chair, his shaft bobbing. He maneuvered until he'd freed his trapped wings behind him.

What will she do?

She hopped from the table, then knelt on the floor between his legs.

He froze, scared to spook her. Had she . . . had his mate been thinking about *sucking* him?

"I've fantasized about what your skin would taste like."

Gods almighty! Somehow he had the presence of mind to conjure a pillow under her knees.

She peered up at him with that soft look.

He was defenseless against it. "You look at me like that, and I grow as malleable as lava."

"I'll remember that." Her voice was throaty from her screams. Her gaze raked over him, from his balls to his face. "I'd heard females fought over you."

They used to. Until . . .

"I didn't see why before." Meeting his eyes, she said, "But now it's so clear to me."

He swallowed thickly. *Lila . . .*

Her attention dipped, then locked on his cock. The tip was wet, more moisture arising each time his shaft pulsed. She licked her lips for it.

Do—not—come. "I'm dreaming this. Have to be."

"What would I do in your dreams?"

He cradled her ethereal face. "You would feel comfortable and go at your own pace. You would—"

Her tongue flicked his sensitive crown.

"—keepdoingthat, keepfuckingdoingthat!"

She did, wrenching a growl from his chest. Too soon, she drew back. "You even *taste* like fire." She blew on the tip.

He shuddered with pain/pleasure.

She returned her mouth, enclosing the head with her lips, then began to dart her tongue.

It moved as quickly as the rest of her! *"Lila,"* he gasped when a deluge of little licks covered the crown. "Your tongue is . . . like a vibration. . . ."

Pausing, she murmured, "That a bad thing?"

He grated, "Fuck. No." He drew his hands from her, gripping the chair. "Never felt . . . anything like it."

She grinned up at him; he gaped down at her. She set back in.

"Fuuuuuck." Her tongue made him twist. His instinct commanded him to thrust between those plump lips.

Her pink nails dug into his torso, reminding him to stay still. She was on fire, uninhibited. Lila was a gift. He could enjoy her innate passion for an eternity—if he didn't do anything to dampen it.

With enough fire, even rock will melt. His firebrand burned so hot she could make even his stony heart soften and beat again.

Abyssian had teased her, holding all the cards. *Turnabout's a bitch.* Now *he* was desperate to come, his every reaction giving her a toe-curling high.

When she licked the underside of his pierced shaft from the base to the crown, he bit out oaths. His mighty body quaked as she traced the slit of his cockhead with her tongue.

Her mouth against his heavy testicles stopped his breath. When she leaned down to nuzzle him there, unintelligible sounds left his lips.

Aside from power, she felt an overwhelming tenderness toward him, her *husband.*

This act would be *between them* alone.

He clutched the stone armrests, seeming determined not to touch her. "You don't know what you're doing to me!"

She had a good idea; his dick *throbbed* against her tongue. "Mmm. Your taste makes me crazy, demon." Those hints of salt . . . she couldn't get enough.

She fed on his raw reactions until her pussy ached. Needing to come again, she reached her free hand between her legs and rubbed her swollen clitoris. Her lids grew heavy.

"Fingering yourself? Now I know I'm . . . imagining all this." His intensity warred with his vulnerability.

She had to slow her fingers, holding off the orgasm that threatened at any second. She drew him deeper into her mouth. When she sucked and licked at the same time, she watched in delight as his eyes rolled back in his head.

Helpless against pleasure—against *her*—his knees fell wide in surrender.

Sian wanted this never to end, but couldn't withstand her kiss any longer. "About to come!"

She suckled him with greedy pulls, her lids fluttering. Her tongue lapped hungrily, her moans getting louder. Her arm twitched as she fingered herself.

"I-I'll try to keep still, beauty." As he fought not to buck his hips for more of the wet heat of her mouth, the stone in his grip started to crumble.

She took him deeper, drawing on his shaft till her cheeks hollowed.

Fuck, gods, FUCK! Each suck racked his body, a fresh torment.

She began to orgasm—and his shaft muffled her cries.

Done. "Defeated me, Lila. Coming. *Coming. Coming! COMING!*" He yelled so loud, the walls cracked. In his palms, the armrests disintegrated to sand.

Pulsations seized his cock over and over and over.

Pleasure rocked him. Ripped through him. Robbed him of all tension and concerns.

He floated while his mate still languidly kissed him. . . .

In time, he pulled her away, dragging her into his lap. With his legs sprawled and his body limp, he pressed kisses to her hair.

His culmination of the godsdamned ages had just shattered everything he thought he knew about sex.

She sighed. "I take it I did okay on my first attempt. Wait till I practice."

"Little wife," he groaned, "if you get any better at that, I'm a dead demon."

FORTY-FOUR

Later that night, Lila and Abyssian lazed in bed. She lay within his wings, facing him. He threaded his fingers through her hair, his expression relaxed.

The sea breezes had picked up until she could hear the surf crashing. . . .

After their dining room encounter, Abyssian had traced her to the shower to rinse off wine. As he'd rubbed his callused palms over her, he'd said, "You can't be done after coming two times. A third will make you sleep better, and you'll be less likely to use me as your body pillow." One thing had led to another. And another.

The promise of a life with him was seductive. Life in the fey court had once been seductive as well. She'd been protected from the Møriør, yet vulnerable to infighting royals. Now she was protected from other fey, yet vulnerable to the Møriør.

She'd learned never to lower her guard in the Sylvan castle. Could she with this demon?

How exactly would she tell him her secret?

You remember Magh, the evil bitch with the tainted line? Surprise! Your fated female is one of those disgusting descendants of hers that you think should die. On top of that, I was Saetth's fiancée. S'posed to be his queen. I vowed to him that I'd deal you a blow, then I lied to you from our first moments on. See, I was a spy, just like Kari. Now I know history repeats itself, but I'm totally different from her—aside from being the same person engaged in the same type of scheming. . . .

What if he locked her in the tower again?

"Tell me what thoughts are hidden behind those spellbinding eyes." Gods, the way he was looking at her . . .

With his millennia of yearning, the demon tugged at her heart.

She didn't want to ruin this. She'd never been in a real relationship, just wanted to explore it a little more. She drummed up a question: "Why did you move the trophy? It must have hung on that wall since the first days of this castle."

"The Lôtān served his watch commendably, but my wife is not a fan. So off he goes." The demon pinned her gaze. "Just because I don't adapt well doesn't mean I'm incapable of it. I will adjust to sharing my life. As you're adjusting to sharing yours."

The great king of hell was *trying*. That sense of hope hit her with all the finesse of a charging hellhound.

"There's your soft look, the one that twists my horns into knots. I'm defenseless against it."

Was a soft look all it took to manage him? Maybe this big dominant beast *could* be tempted by sweet things.

"But, Calliope, I too ask for patience. It will take me time to get this right. I want you to give me some leeway."

"Like a get-out-of-jail-free card?"

A lock of hair tumbled over one of his eyes. "I suppose you could say that."

"I'll give you a card if you give me one too." Or an entire deck.

"Agreed," he said. "On that note, I have a wedding gift for you."

She popped upright. "Ooh, what is it, what is it?" A rock? Emeralds?

He sat up and conjured a weird-looking . . . wand thingy? "Here." He handed it to her.

She accepted the strange piece. It looked kind of fey in origin. "I . . . thank you." She was grateful for his thoughtfulness, but she *did* wonder what message he wanted to convey with such an unromantic present.

"I was guided to give you that. Graven kept putting it in my path."

"What do you mean?"

"With jewels in mind for my new bride, I traced to one of the castle's rooms, a chamber I remembered for its copious riches. The area was empty except for this: a scepter wrought of gold and Titanian steel."

Titanian? The Ancestors' Sword had been forged of that metal.

Abyssian continued, "Not exactly what I'd had in mind. So I went to a second room. Again, I found it empty except for the scepter. The third room was the same. Graven wanted you to have it." He curled his finger under her chin. "Calliope, never refuse the castle more than three times."

"Why not?"

He shrugged. "My father told my brother and me this rule. Even he didn't understand Graven. Which meant even he feared what it is capable of."

She glanced around, wondering what her new home had in mind for her. "How would a fey scepter end up in a demon castle?"

"With Graven, who knows?"

"Thank you for the gift, demon." She leaned forward to press her lips against his cheek. "Will you put this on the mantel?" She handed him the scepter.

With a nod, he rose, unfolding the long length of his body. She'd seen his ass in the shower, but she hadn't gotten a view like this.

My, my, my. Sculpted rock-hard muscles flexed with each of his steps. In the shower, when she'd been on her knees giving him another blow-job, she'd dug her nails into those muscles; he'd cradled her face with shaking hands and stared down into her eyes, rasping in Demonish, *"How I've yearned for you . . ."*

On his return to the bed, he treated her to even more magnificence.

Her gaze traveled up his lean body, lingering on his sigh-worthy dick, roving over the chiseled ridges of his torso, before settling on his smirking face.

He joined her in bed, then situated her in his wings. "My jealous hell queen can't get enough of me."

Fighting a grin, she turned over, giving him her back. "Shut it, you smug prick."

He clasped her waist, drawing her against him. At her ear, he said, "If I even look at other females in front of you, I'll be endangering lives. My Lila does *not* share her toys."

"Fuck off, demon."

She dozed off to the sound of his chuckle.

Over this night, the female in Sian's arms had delivered more bliss than he'd known existed.

As he stroked her shining hair, her breaths were deep and even. His young mate needed more sleep than he did.

Hours passed, but he found it difficult to close his eyes. He was half convinced this must all be a dream.

A hundred things had rendered him dumbstruck tonight. Among them: when she'd gazed at him with desire and told him she understood why women fought over him.

And she'd bloody *leered* at him when he'd returned naked to bed. His lips quirked just to recall that.

Everything Calliope had objected to initially had been because of his treatment of her—not necessarily his looks.

Possibility glimmered on the horizon like a flame. *Could* he let go of his lifeline?

As he'd told her, he'd been one way for so very many years. And he still dreaded how the hell-change would affect their future. But for now he wanted to savor a night like this.

Her body twitched against his. Such an active dream life. Was he about to be tortured once more?

He frowned when she gave a distressed moan. Instead of sexual dreams, she was plagued with a nightmare.

He brushed his knuckles along one high cheekbone. He sensed her blocks weren't as impenetrable as usual. Maybe she was beginning to trust him. Though tempted to delve, he would respect her privacy—

She shot upright with a scream.

"Lila! I've got you." He dragged her against his chest, tucking her head under his chin. "It was just a nightmare. Shh." Protectiveness surged inside him. His mate should never be afraid. Rubbing her back, he said, "Tell me what you dreamed."

Shuddering, she murmured, "I couldn't run fast enough."

"Shh. You're safe here with me." He rocked her. "You have nothing to be afraid of."

Sounding dazed, she said, "There's a face to the violence you love so much, a cost that the Møriør never have to pay. Why *wouldn't* you love war? You never feel the toll like the rest of us."

He lowered her back to the bed, holding her.

In time, she drifted to sleep again.

As he listened to her breaths, his mind raced. She was right: the Møriør lost nothing with each battle, just seized one victory after another.

He couldn't do anything about war out in other realms, but could he change his own? Calliope continued to bring up the legions. Even by punishment standards, their two strongholds in Slaughter Gorge were disgraceful, festering with hatred and violence.

Sian and hell were symbiotic; so what did those hellholes represent within him?

He could alleviate the worst through magic—changing doom to fortune—or he could give those demons a purpose.

Sian thought of his brother. Goürlav had wanted commerce and prosperity to be his legacy. He'd been such a young king with so many dreams for Pandemonia.

If Sian took up the mantle, his twin's life wouldn't have been one long tragedy.

Sian wanted this kingdom to be his mate's home, but was he ready to make it the home she needed?

FORTY-FIVE

You don't write, you never call . . ." Rune drawled, giving Sian a crooked grin. "Hitched three weeks, and you never got around to inviting us to meet the missus?"

Sian had just been overseeing his new project when he'd sensed arrivals. He'd found the archer seated in Sian's throne, sharpening his claws with an arrowhead, and Josephine kicked back in Calliope's throne.

Uthyr slumbered like the dead nearby.

Sian had a little time to talk with them since Calliope was in the library, buried in books.

Rune pointed the arrow at the sleeping dragon. "I've been reading Uthyr's mind, trying to get caught up on your marriage, but mainly he's been dreaming about plump cattle."

"Careful that we don't get our feelings hurt," Josephine said, her pale face glowing. The longer the halfling was with Rune, the happier she appeared. "Couldn't spare five minutes to draw summoning runes?"

"I've been busy."

"I'll bet you have been, old boy." Rune waggled his brows, his craggy features showing his amusement. "So where's the slip of a female who brought down hard-ass Abyssian Infernas?"

"She's not ready to meet anyone yet." With a sigh, he admitted, "She fears the Møriør, has heard only the worst about us." Every time he assured her of her safety, Calliope refused to listen.

Josephine said, "You want me to go inform her how bad the Vertas is? How Nïx kicked my ass?"

"Calliope isn't pro-Vertas." Yesterday, she'd told him, "Let's bow out and not pick sides. You and I can be allies, just us." She had no idea how futile her attempts were. He would always be a Møriør. "I will make her understand, but it will take time."

Rune dropped the arrow into his thigh quiver. His ever-present bow was strapped over his back. "So she's truly a fey? Pointed ears and everything? Don't know whether to congratulate or console you."

Sian scowled. "I wouldn't have her any other way."

Rune held up his palms. "To each his own. So how's she settling in?"

"Very well. Though getting used to life in a castle like this has its challenges." Three days after their wedding, he'd heard her screech from the bedroom.

He traced and found her staring up at the Lôtān trophy—which had just reappeared above the mantel.

She raised a brow at Sian. "Yet another prank, demon?"

"The castle did this. I have no idea why. I'll take it away again, but if the head continues to return, we must accept Graven's will. . . ."

Rune said, "I can't imagine a Sylvan female appreciating the wildness of hell."

"In fact, she enjoys exploring the realm." She loved everything new he showed her, but especially the animals.

One day when they'd been hiking through the steamy Stygian Marsh, he'd sensed a litter of hellkittens nearby.

As their wary mother looked on, Calliope had cuddled the cannonball-size runt, stroking its red and silver pelt. The kitten had purred loudly, and a drop of drool had clung to one saber tooth. . . .

"I don't suppose I could have this little guy?" Calliope asked.

She could have anything in this world she wanted. Still, he said, "You shouldn't separate him from his litter."

"Oh, of course." She'd put the kitten back with the others, giving it a scratch and a look of longing.

"We will take all of them, mother and kittens alike—it's not as if we can't spare the room."

Calliope had leapt up and wrapped her arms around his neck, kissing him soundly. He'd needed ever more of her, deepening the contact. Against his lips, she'd murmured, "Not in front of the kittens. But definitely somewhere, demon!"

As he'd gazed down at her bewitching face, he'd thought, *I am so fucked if this ends.*

Josephine said, "I see that look in your eyes. You're done for. It's the look this one"—she hiked her thumb at Rune—"sports twenty-four/seven. It's getting embarrassing."

The archer nodded. "Too true."

Sometimes Sian had the urge to throw a wall up between himself and Calliope—anything to keep their bond from solidifying more. If his new existence with her *was* going to end, he needed the divide to happen now—not in a century or so, when his appearance had changed so drastically that she finally hit her limit.

Rune said, "I know you haven't claimed your female yet, or you would've been bursting—pun intended—to talk about the experience. You'll *need* to talk to someone. Trust me."

"Trust him." Josephine tossed her legs over the throne's armrest, the first to sit there.

Sian had had no choice but to separate Calliope from his demon subjects. He didn't anticipate any danger, but she wouldn't be fully protected until she wore his mark. "I'm in no rush."

"Liar." Rune filched a flask of demon brew from a jacket pocket and raised it in offer to Josephine.

Her expression said, *You've gotta be kidding.*

Rune took a pull, then tossed it to Sian.

He caught it and swigged. "Do I imagine what it would be like to claim my mate? Constantly." Despite the devastating pleasure they'd been sharing.

She was open to anything. Earlier today, they'd relaxed on a blanket at the beach, lounging naked in the sun. His mind had wandered, wicked fantasies arising.

He'd realized there was nothing to stop him from taking a taste of his mate.

Without a word, he'd lifted her to straddle his face. After a hesitation, she'd gotten caught up. Her fists had moved on his horns, jacking him as she'd shamelessly ground against his mouth. She'd screamed, climaxing right upon his lips.

And his mate was all too happy to reciprocate, using her life-altering little tongue to render him mindless.

Just when he swore their bedsport couldn't possibly get hotter—quite a thing for the king of hell to think—they would reach new heights. Yet at no time had she said those four words: *Will you claim me?*
"But I also imagine a future with her." Sian coveted what Rune and Josephine had. "I won't push Calliope before she's ready."

Rune plucked his bowstring. "Gods, man, you really do like her."

When Sian nodded, Rune and Josephine both raised their brows, waiting for more.

He exhaled. "Can't stop looking at her. Or touching her." If he could take relationship advice from a dragon, he could be forthcoming about his feelings. "I watch her when she sleeps and dreams. The sound of her laughter makes my wings unfurl, like I'm godsdamned flying." He scrubbed his palm over his face. "When we talk into the night, I get to see inside her dazzling mind, and I can never get enough."

Tough-talking Josephine sighed. "How did your girl react when you told her about the hell-change?"

Sian took a drink. "Haven't told her." Not only was he selfishly keeping the curse a secret, he'd been taking out his frustration on her.

Yesterday, he'd asked what kind of tattoo she'd make him get once he marked her.

"No tattoos for you." She kissed one of his glyphs. "I would never change a single inch of this skin."

Body gone tense, he drew back, cursing his future.

She blinked at him. "Did I say something wrong?" When he didn't answer, she muttered, "Moodiest male . . ."

"I wanted Calliope to feel more for me before I revealed that." Sian believed her attachment grew, but he also suspected something was holding her back.

"No offense, demon, but she's going to know soon." Josephine tilted her head. "I can already see a difference from the last time we stopped by."

Truly? Their previous visit had been only a couple of months before Calliope's arrival here! "I will tell her soon."

"I wouldn't sweat it. She married you, so obviously looks"—the halfling gestured to him with a careless wave—"aren't that important to her."

Sian scowled. "She likes my looks." Whenever Calliope gazed up at him from under her lashes, he could *feel* her attraction to him—and her growing possessiveness. The proprietary light in her eyes made him stand taller. Made his cock harder than stone.

To his surprise, she couldn't keep her hands off him. The more she explored his body—and she adored exploring it—the more aroused she grew by his form. "But not for long."

How much time do I have before she doesn't even recognize me? Would he recognize himself? Even now the low hum along his spine, that engine inside him, roiled on.

"It doesn't matter what you look like," Rune said. "You're still my brother. Win her over, and she'll be just as loyal."

"Easier said . . ."

"Has she told you anything about her life on Gaia?" Rune asked. "Her family?"

Sian capped the flask, then tossed it back. "She doesn't like to talk about it. Probably because I forced her to abandon her fiancé."

Rune and Josephine winced.

"Exactly." Did that male still stand between them? Sian had finally brought up the subject.

"I know I took you from your intended. Abruptly. Tell me what I can do to help you put him in the past."

"I might pine for the family I thought I'd have. But not him in particular."

Sian had thought, *I could give her a family*. But they'd be dark fey. Considered abominations by most.

Then why did he *feel* like they would have young between them? "My spies found out nothing about her in Gaia. Next I will dispatch them to Sylvan."

"Josie and I can dig into Calliope's background there. My female's interrogation techniques are improving every day." She gave a queenly wave. "And my connections are still in place."

"Even though *Rune the Insatiable* isn't trading sex for secrets anymore," Josephine said in a pointed tone. "Funny how that worked out, huh?"

Rune nodded easily. "I trade exclusively with phanpires now." He turned to Sian. "We'll begin at once. In any case, I'd be less worried about a fiancé and more worried about her reaction when the Møriør conquer Sylvan."

As good a time as any. "About Sylvan . . . I vowed to her that as long as she is my wife, none in that kingdom will fall by a Møriør's hand."

The color of Rune's irises shot from magenta to black. "The fuck?" He traced to his feet. "With zero warning—or discussion—you made vows for me?"

Josephine swung around and sat on the edge of the throne. "Demon, you're in troublllle."

Striving for calm, Sian said, "Calliope kept attempting to escape me, endangering her life. So I bargained with her, giving her incentive to stay."

"Your bargain includes the royals in Sylvan!" Rune traced in front of him, fists clenched like he was about to take a swing. Sian would welcome it. "You undermined my entire life's goal. Everything I've worked for. I've craved revenge against that bloodline for millennia!"

Sian squared his shoulders. "This is what I had to do to secure my mate," he said simply.

"And I want you to experience matehood, brother. I do. But you have to know Nïx set you up like a bloody line of dominoes." Sian nodded. "How do you know Calliope isn't working with her? Was Saetth involved? He benefits most from your . . . arrangement."

"Calliope had a job in Gaia for years, living as a human. She wasn't immersed in the Lore whatsoever. But I do wager Saetth is in league with the Valkyrie."

Rune's lips parted, revealing his fangs. "And you still went ahead with this?"

When Sian recalled the night Calliope had escaped him, how frantic that chase had been, his calm deserted him. "I would have done *anything* not to lose my mate."

Rune stabbed his fingers through his hair. "You don't have the right to make vows for me."

"You of all people should comprehend my motivations. Put yourself in my place." Sian grabbed his friend's forearms, needing him to understand. "Would you have hesitated to protect Josephine—until you could discuss your actions with me? Could you live with her death not once, but *twice*?"

Rune turned to Josephine. They shared a look that was fraught with emotion, communicating so much, though not a word was spoken.

Will Calliope and I grow that close?

Rune faced him again. "You know I couldn't."

"Then back me in this." Sian released him.

"Godsdamn it, demon." Rune exhaled. "I will make . . . sacrifices for you to keep your mate safe. But if you'd found your female before I found mine—and I didn't know what this bond felt like—we would not be having this conversation."

"I believe that."

"What about the demons enslaved in Sylvan? I know you have zero intention of leaving them to that fate."

"I will come up with something." *Put it on my list.* "But first I need to complete an undertaking in my own kingdom." He'd announced his ideas to Uthyr:

"I'm going to engage my legions in something other than war."

—Begone, chimera! Do not return without the real Abyssian Infernas.—

Rune sat once more. "What bloody undertaking?"

"I've ended the legions' battles forever."

"What will you do with such bloodthirsty subjects?"

They'd been created to war. "They will mine ore." Gold abounded in Slaughter Gorge.

Sian had considered telling Calliope about his work, knowing she would be pleased, but he'd decided to keep it a surprise. He'd prefer to garner some success with his first societal transformation before he revealed all to her.

Though the legions had liked his vision for them very well, converting the battle-happy demon warriors into workers was taking some effort.

He made daily trips to oversee progress, reluctantly leaving Calliope. She would relax in the library with hellcats, spiders, and books piled up all around her. She read as fast as she did everything else, the pages flying. . . .

Rune said, "Your mate's had some effect on you."

"I want to rid her new home of conflict." Her censure of his royal record still affected him. "But it's not just her. My brother once dreamed of peace."

"Any other changes on the horizon?" Josephine said. "Maybe like . . . kids?"

"Unlikely." How could Sian ask that of Calliope? "Aside from obvious concerns, what if they look like I do now?"

Rune shook his head. "The hell-change curse would remain dormant, no? As long as you live, your pups wouldn't be affected."

Josephine rolled her eyes. "So what if they look all demonic? You said your chick digs your appearance."

"And about those other concerns," Rune said, "don't let my millennia of bitterness influence your decision. All I needed was a mate who worships me as I am."

"Worships?" Josephine made a hand-job gesture.

"Will you two have children?" Sian asked.

Rune nodded. "I warned her they'd likely be banebloods."

Josephine said, "So I told him our kids would just have to find wicked-cool mates like their father did."

"Mates? Though dark fey are so few?" Before Josephine, Rune had searched the worlds over for a female of his kind. If Sian and Calliope had children, would they be setting up their offspring for misery and loneliness?

Rune chuckled. "Hell, Sian, maybe your baneblood spawn will date ours."

He'd never considered that.

Rune traced forward to slap his shoulder. "My sons could mate your daughters."

Knowing his friend's past with females, and already protective of any future daughters, Sian grated, "If your sons wish to die. . . ."

FORTY-SIX

Abyssian could sense whenever someone crossed the barrier into Pandemonia.

Weirdly, *Lila* had gotten that sense not long ago, glancing up from her book. Though her ears had twitched like crazy, the hellcats all around her had snoozed without so much as a whisker twitch.

Either Lila was developing the Force, or her queenly gifts were expanding. Maybe she could do even more than reading Abyssian's stray thoughts and seeing hallucinatory deer.

Tempted to go investigate, she closed her book—one of *millions.*

In their first week of marriage, Abyssian had told her he had a surprise for her. . . .

He traced her to a different part of the castle, squiring her through an arched double doorway. "This is the Tower of Learning."

Her jaw dropped at what must be one of the largest book collections in the Lore.

Balconied landings were spaced every twenty feet or so, ringing the inside walls of the tower, with the center open. She could see straight up to a painted ceiling, soaring above them.

"You like your new library?"

"It's unbelievable!"

"The tower holds nothing but books," he said. "Most of them were in Demonish, so I implemented a spell for you. Whenever you enter, all the text will change to your tongue of choice."

Guilt had dampened her excitement, her lies and secrets weighing on her. She'd nearly blurted, *I know Demonish.*

Damn it, she'd never expected to develop lasting feelings for Abyssian Infernas.

The temptation to confess everything continued to grow. Yet always, she would recall the tension at court on the heels of one of Rune's assassinations.

Had she learned nothing from the past? Secrecy meant survival.

Take it from my parents. . . .

Part of her longed to grab Abyssian's brutal demon face and say, "I want you. I want a future with you. I need to be honest with you."

Another part of her would look in the mirror and say, "I want to live. I want a future. I need to protect myself."

Would she feel differently once he claimed her? Would that bond them so much she could relax her guard and confess all?

One way to find out. She'd decided tonight was the night. She remained nervous about the actual deed, but she trusted him, and she didn't want him to have to wait any longer. . . .

Stretching her arms over her head, she asked her heavy-lidded pets, "Should I investigate any new arrivals?" The hellcats were snuggled up with her on the comfy couch in the library's reading den.

Purrrrrrr, they answered.

She'd released them into this tower. The little spazzes had gone nuts, treating the place like their personal jungle gym. But as long as they continued to go outside to do their business and didn't shred any more books, all was well.

She'd even coaxed Chip and Dale to visit. After a tense introductory period with the cats, they'd gotten more comfortable. Presently they were napping in front of the den's fire.

After peeling cats off herself, she made her way from the library to the candlelit corridor. Fluttering drafts made the flames dance. Shadows leapt.

Sometimes this mystical castle could be spooky as fuck. Earlier today, the Lôtān head had come back—for the third time—which meant it'd be staying. *Great.* She'd glared at the creepy head. "Are you happy now?"

Though her life in hell was turning out to be both provocative and dreamlike, part of her still longed for Sylvan—

Clickety-clack sounded from behind her. She pivoted around to find the fawn standing in the hall.

It blinked its lustrous eyes.

She often saw Bambi. Sometimes it followed her around the library, going still whenever she peeked over her shoulder, like a supernatural version of the red-light/green-light game.

Was Graven supplying this illusion? And if so, *why*?

She hadn't told Abyssian about the fawn. It always disappeared right before he appeared, so she'd stayed mum, figuring what would one more secret hurt?

She still saw Bambi in dreams as well. Each time, it would bound toward the edge of that desolate cliff as some light blazed from below. No matter how much she urged the fawn to come to her, it headed right off the cliff.

Lila had no idea what the dream meant, but it made her hesitate to trust the creature now.

The fawn turned in the opposite direction, glancing back at her. Lila vacillated. . . .

Screw it. When Bambi started down the dim corridor, she trailed behind. She passed dozens of doors, each leading to one of Graven's treasure-trove rooms. She and Abyssian had explored many of them, investigating chests of jewels, wardrobes, art, antiques, and more.

A couple of days ago, she'd modeled old-fashioned dresses for him, and they'd waged mock battles with weapons they'd found. "En garde, relic," she'd cried as she launched a sword offensive with her speed.

He'd teleported behind her, lightly swatting her on the ass. "You *still* haven't said no tracing."

Later when he'd closed the door to the room behind them, he'd gruffly admitted, "I haven't had this much fun since I was a boy. . . ."

He'd also shown her all over the dimension. After each dinner, he would trace her to some new wonder. He'd taken her to a woodsy glade where raindrops fell *up* and to an ancient temple made of solid gold. He'd introduced her to the hellhounds. . . .

The pack rushed to his side fresh from a hunt. She was baby-talking one of the puppies—"Who's a cute doggy-woggy? You are!"—when it sneezed on her.

A spray of reptile blood and bits of gristle spattered her shirt.

The demon had looked surprised when she'd laughed it off and named the puppy Sneezy. She'd named each of the other pack members after one of the seven dwarves as well.

Abyssian mused, "I don't know why those dwarves are noteworthy among other dwarves, aside from their ridiculous names."

"Ridiculous, huh?" She ripped off her soaked shirt and flung it onto one of Sian's horns like a ringtoss.

His response to that: "Run."

She and the demon did have fun together. Among his other roles—as a hell guide and bedmate—he was becoming her best friend.

Abyssian had turned out to be playful, off-the-charts intelligent, protective, and sexier than any male she'd ever encountered.

A hell demon with a raspy voice and a downright sinful tongue.

If only they didn't have so many barriers between them. The Møriør. Rune. Her background and lies. Their species. The prospect of dark fey children.

Abyssian might not be bedding other demonesses, but that didn't mean he wanted to bring banebloods into the world. He'd made his thoughts on that clear. Yet she still longed to have children. Would Rune target *them*—

Bambi slowed. With another glance back at her, it took a sharp left—into a wall. The fawn disappeared as though sucked into the stone.

Lila raised her hand to the wall. Instead of solid rock, air met her palms. An illusion concealed a hidden doorway.

Squaring her shoulders, she passed through the opening.

Pitch blackness greeted her. Even her immortal eyesight couldn't penetrate it. "Oh, hell no." She turned back, colliding face-first into stone. "Ow! Fucker."

She was trapped.

Abyssian had told her he believed the castle liked her, but what if it *didn't*? Had Lila just made a fatal error?

Clickety-clack, clickety-clack.

The tiny hairs on her nape rose. She had no choice but to follow the sound. As she fumbled through the dark, the passageway ascended for what felt like miles. . . .

Her ears twitched again. She could hear Abyssian's voice! The fawn disappeared, just as Lila spied a muted light shining from ahead.

She eased closer, discovering a secret nook that overlooked the throne room. The castle had wanted her here! Though a screen concealed her, she could see below.

Abyssian leaned against a wall, drinking from a flask. Uthyr the dragon slept, his body and tail stretching the length of the room. A stacked brunette with pale, luminous skin and bright hazel eyes slouched in Lila's throne. Her legs were crossed over an armrest. She wore a miniskirt and combat boots.

A tall male with fangs, pointed ears, and long black hair sat in Abyssian's throne. A bow was strapped over the male's back, a quiver around his leg.

Lila stifled a gasp. The fey-slayer.

Rune the Baneblood was *here*. The star of her nightmares. Her heart pounded so loudly she feared they could hear it.

She'd never seen a dark fey in person before. He was lean, his build similar to Abyssian's. His eyes were magenta, his features roughhewn. But altogether he was moderately attractive. Tattoos marked his tanned skin, a band of them encircling one of his wrists.

The arrows in his leg quiver looked color-coded. Which arrow decimated armies? Better question: which one *didn't*?

That female must be Rune's mate, Josephine—the halfling with all the abilities.

Lila had known the archer would show up sooner or later, but had hoped on years later.

Josephine asked Abyssian, "Is your chick pretty?"

"Calliope Infernas is exquisite," he replied. *They're discussing me?* Was this why Graven had led Lila here?

Or had the castle wanted her to face her fear?

Rune didn't appear so otherworldly and ominous right now. He looked like a regular guy—one who needed a shave and could barely keep his eyes off his mate.

Lila's feelings toward the Møriør had been a mix of resentment and terror. With a mystical castle on her side, that terror dwindled. . . .

"What's her personality like?" Rune asked. "Uthyr spoke of a fiery temperament."

"Her temper is as sharp as her intellect—and her ears," Abyssian said, his tone proud. "She's a firebrand."

Lila had never seen him juxtaposed against humanoid beings. As she gazed over his horns, claws, and wings, tenderness bloomed in her chest. She was growing to love everything that made him demonic.

She'd gotten used to sleeping in the protection of those remarkable wings. They were soft on the inside and deadly everywhere else.

Like Abyssian could be. . . .

"Why don't you let me go talk to her?" Josephine said. "I hated all of you freaks at first, but now I tolerate you. And if I can, *anybody* can."

Lila kind of liked this girl.

"She wouldn't want to meet anyone connected to a Møriør." Abyssian traced to take a seat on the dais steps—instead of commanding Rune to vacate his throne. A testament to their friendship. "Not yet at least. It will take time."

"Good news, brother," Rune said, "we've got nothing but time."

Uthyr's tail twitched, and he growled in sleep.

Josephine murmured to Rune, "Hey, sport, watch this." She waved her hand in the dragon's direction.

Uthyr immediately scratched his earflap.

"Worth the trip to hell, right there." Was the female using telekinesis to screw with the Møriør's almighty dragon?

Abyssian raised his brows. "Surely you've heard the saying: Never wake a sleeping dragon."

Rune apparently hadn't. "Do it again, Josie."

She did. When Uthyr scratched and smacked his chops, Lila found herself almost grinning. They all seemed so deceptively normal. *Too bad one of them has vowed to murder me.*

Another wave of Josephine's hand.

Uthyr scratched so hard that scales popped off, pinwheeling in the air.

The halfling and Rune cracked up. Even Abyssian laughed.

Rune turned to him. "I haven't heard you laugh since you took the throne." Tracing to sit beside Abyssian, Rune clamped his shoulder, the two demonstrating such an easy camaraderie. "Like I said, your female is already affecting you."

Lila thought back to some of the first times she'd heard the demon laugh. He'd definitely seemed rusty at it. No longer.

"Didn't I tell you? There's nothing better than matehood." Rune's contentedness surprised her. Abyssian had confided more of what

Magh had done to the archer, and it'd been horrific. Did Rune deserve revenge? Gods, yes.

Just not against me.

When Josephine joined Rune on the steps, he wrapped an arm around her, pressing a kiss into her hair. So clearly in love.

Lila gazed from them to Abyssian. Though the demon continued to reveal those hints of vulnerability to her, something was weighing on him. Did he have a secret of his own?

Abyssian asked the two, "Have you ever heard of the seven dwarves?"

Josephine grinned. "Yeah, they sound a jot familiar. Why do you ask?"

Frowning, he said, "My mate named a pack of hellhounds after them, but I'm baffled why those seven are significant among all other dwarves in the Lore. If she admires them, I would like to understand better."

Lila sighed. *That demon.*

Josephine said, "They're a band of miners who aided and abetted an endangered royal named Snow White. They're basically revolutionaries."

Hey, I'm the only one who gets to fuck with him over mortal-realm references.

"I see," Abyssian said, no doubt thinking the dwarves had gone by code names. "That makes sense."

"Is your mate really a reincarnate?" Josephine asked.

Nod. "She lived ten millennia ago."

"How weird." *No kidding.* "Does she have memories from her past life?"

"No. Nor does she want them."

Lila had told Abyssian as much a few days before. . . .

He asked her, "Have you accepted you are a reincarnate?"

"I . . . have. I've also accepted that I probably won't ever remember my previous existence."

"I could use magic to help you."

She exhaled. "Why would I want to, Abyssian? And more, why would you *want me to remember my own death?" As well as the death of her child. Considering she would never be pregnant in this life, that memory would be all the more devastating. "I don't even want to think about it."*

"How did she die?" Josephine asked, seeming absorbed with the subject of reincarnation.

His expression darkened. "Childbirth. She . . . she wed another."

In one of Lila's late-night talks with the demon, he'd told her about her first husband. . . .

"That fuck couldn't wait a few months for her—you—to transition? I . . . it never made sense to me. How could he risk you?" The demon's thought hit her. —When I would've done anything for you!— *"I was supposed to protect my mate, but that sealed portal kept me from reaching you. He as good as killed you, and there was* nothing *I could do to save you."*

"Did you confront him?"

"I did. His assassination was my first act as a Møriør." Gaze gone distant, Abyssian said, "They never found all the pieces of him."

So much rage. How could he not always resent the past—and therefore her? Already he would hate her for her very blood.

Rune told him, "I'm glad you've forgiven your female for the past." When no response came, he said, "You *have* forgiven her, right?"

Lila held her breath, though she knew the answer. No, he had not.

When she'd asked Abyssian what his life was like before he'd taken the throne, he'd answered, "I thought I'd found a measure of contentment. Now I know I'd just been numb since your death."

For ten thousand years.

Yet he wanted her to believe that he'd relinquished his anger against her?

Abyssian was a proud trickster. She hoped the joke wasn't on her, because she was falling for him hard.

At length, he said, "It's complicated."

Actually, it was really simple: too many things stood between them. As long as he resented her for deeds done in the far-distant past, he would never give her a fair shake in this present.

If she confessed the truth to him, she would be vulnerable. The tower awaited.

But if she kept concealing her identity, he would find out eventually.

Lila couldn't see a way out of this bind. Pain was inevitable, no matter what course of action she decided on. Unwelcome realization struck her. . . .

I can't *figure this the fuck out.*

Abyssian stood. "I'm keen to return to her."

Shit, shit! Got to get back! Would the secret opening let her out this time?

Lila hesitated when Rune said, "Will you tell your mate we were here?"

"I won't lie to her if she asks. But I don't want to distress her unnecessarily either."

Josephine said, "She might put her foot down and forbid us from returning. If I didn't know Rune, I sure as shit would."

Abyssian straightened. "I will never bar my friends from this castle."

Good to know . . .

"One last thing," Rune said. "I accept—grudgingly—that we're not to harm the inhabitants of Sylvan." *He did?* "But I've got leads on a few of Magh's descendants who live outside the kingdom." *Like . . . me?* "Are those outliers included in your vow?"

Abyssian shook his head. "If they're evil, take them out."

Before Sian returned to Calliope, he traced to one of Graven's many echoing corridors in search of a mirror.

Josephine had spoken about his appearance deteriorating. He needed to see how bad the hell-change had gotten since he'd last assessed his looks. How quickly was he failing?

Though Sian was transforming parts of his dimension, he couldn't transform himself. The hourglass kept pouring.

He found a mirror. *How much time do I have left with Calliope?* Inhaling, he faced the glass.

My gods. His fangs were longer, his horns even larger. The mask around his eyes had spread outward, becoming more prominent. Another line of hell metal had appeared between his brows. So the number of his piercings would keep increasing?

If all of his demonic features continued to grow more exaggerated, a time would come when things he took for granted became impossible.

Such as speech. Or pleasuring his mate.

The patience he'd demonstrated toward Calliope's claiming was replaced by urgency.

He conjured a picture of himself and Rune from not so many months ago. *My former likeness.* Sian would've made a fitting partner for a beauty like Calliope.

He focused on the picture, noticing the deadened look in his eyes. *Sleepwalking . . .*

Before Calliope, he'd been handsome, but empty. Now he was wide awake.

All the better to feel my coming misery.

He punched the mirror, shattering the glass.

FORTY-SEVEN

"*Where are we going, demon?*" Calliope asked him, having to raise her voice over the pounding waves.

Sian and his mate walked along the jade beach, the tumultuous night reflecting his mood. "It's a surprise." He was taking her to see a Pandemonian phenomenon that happened only during the full moon.

He could have traced them, but she didn't seem to mind the blustery weather, and he needed the time to clear his head.

A week had passed since Rune and Josephine had first come to Graven, yet something was keeping Sian's mate from surrendering to a life here with him.

She still talked with him into the morning hours, still loved exploring the realm, still responded to him just as passionately. But . . . he sensed her distance.

Earlier today, he'd found her on the terrace, gazing out over the sea with that analytical look in her eyes. She was working out some puzzle.

What? What? What? Their days were simple and undemanding. She woke. They ate. They pleasured each other. They explored. Not necessarily in that order. What possible conundrum could she have?

He couldn't read her thoughts, couldn't predict her moves. Her mind had always been a mystery, and she continued to hold him separate from her musings. He handled that as well as he had when he'd been sixteen.

In other words, she was making him *crazed.*

"Did you have visitors this morning?" she asked.

"I did." Rune and Josephine had stopped by to bring word on Saetth. . . .

"My half brother was indeed in league with the Valkyrie," Rune said. "The soothsayer must've predicted you'd make that vow if they sacrificed Calliope. They set her up, sending bounty hunters after her."

So she'd been a virgin offering to appease the king of hell and keep the beast out of their lands.

Rune added, "Tomorrow night, Saetth's hosting a gala—in Sylvan—to select a queen from a different fey realm, strengthening his alliances. Considering how emboldened he's become, he must know you've vowed not to attack."

Sian gritted his teeth. Something needed to be done, but he had effectively tied the Møriør's hands. His allies were to meet the following week to discuss what their next move would be. "And what have you learned about Calliope?"

Rune shrugged. "We came up empty. Couldn't find anything on her."

Odd. "Should I send my generals?"

"I wouldn't if I were you. Getting to know your mate is the fun part. Let it happen, brother."

Sian was surprised a spy like Rune would advise against digging for more background. Matehood must be changing him. . . .

"It was nothing pressing," Sian told Calliope.

"I see." She frowned up at him. "Demon, have you slept in the past month?"

Not once. "I've been half asleep for far too long already." He watched over her all night, wanting to be there when she had bad dreams. Plus he suffered his own waking nightmares that he would lose his mate again.

He'd survived before; he would not now. *Why is she holding back from me?*

Would this distance disappear once he claimed her?

In each of their encounters, he took her with his fingers, teaching her to relax and accept them, preparing her delicate fey body for his hulking demon one. She'd grown to crave penetration, especially when he tongued her at the same time.

Last night, he'd attempted three fingers inside her, but she'd climaxed too quickly. . . .

Why wouldn't she ask him to claim her? That humming sensation down his spine continued, reminding him that time was running out.

Enamored females could overlook a lot of things. If he earned her love, could he keep it no matter his appearance?

"Are we almost there?" Lila asked Abyssian.

"Soon," he answered absently, continuing on as if they were enjoying a tranquil evening stroll. The wind whipped his black hair over one lean cheek, his eyes flickering from that vivid green to onyx.

"Why is the weather like this, demon?" Tonight was the full moon, but the clouds were too dense to see it.

He didn't answer, lost in thought. Today was their one-month anniversary, yet he'd barely spoken to her over dinner.

"You've been acting strange all week." Since the day she'd spied on Rune and Josephine's visit.

Though Lila had planned for Abyssian to claim her that night, he'd been agitated when he'd finally returned to her. He hadn't improved much since.

She'd decided to wait for a sign, telling herself she'd know when the time was right. . . .

"Hey, big guy"—she bumped her hip against him—"I thought full moons were supposed to make *werewolves* get testy."

No response. Okay, this was more than mere Abyssian moodiness.

She'd grown convinced that he was keeping something big from her as well, and his behavior tonight only reinforced her belief.

She'd gone a little nutty trying to suss out what, until she'd managed to let it go. For now.

Dragging her gaze from his stark face, she surveyed the storm-tossed sea. Off the shoreline, water spouts swirled atop the towering swells. Yellow lightning forked out, illuminating serpent scales. Thunder roared.

Mind-boggling.

Hell would never be orderly. Or meticulous. This realm was harder, wilder, crazier, and more brutal than Sylvan.

Yet for the first time in her life, Lila felt as if she'd found her true home here.

Not that she could ever ignore the problems in Sylvan. Why had her cousin never considered ending the slavery? Or her parents?

Though Lila needed to right these wrongs, she didn't know how to start. How could she expect to figure out a solution for an entire fey kingdom when she couldn't even untangle her own life?

She planned to ask Abyssian for his advice—once she'd disclosed all. *One obstacle at a time.*

He tightened his wing around her, buffering her from the gale. Turmoil rolled off him like those waves. She could relate.

I'm really falling for him.

Whenever he was in a good mood—and she could ignore her secrets for a time—they laughed and played. Each night when she drifted off to sleep within his wings, he would rasp Demonish endearments. Last night he'd told her, "I didn't know my heart could beat this madly or grow this full."

With her loneliness finally at bay, she'd never been happier. In fact, she couldn't imagine a life without him.

She didn't want to lie to him anymore. She wanted to protect him, to ease the worry on his brow. Yet she still hadn't *fitfo*'d their relationship.

Other worries plagued her as well. The castle still gave her those dreams about Bambi, the same scene at the desolate cliff. But for the last three times, the fawn had expected her *to follow* it off the edge.

Each time, she'd balked. What would happen if she refused Graven a fourth?

The winds gusted even harder. Surf crashed, pelting Abyssian's wings. Foam floated in the air. He seemed not to notice it.

"Abyssian, why are we walking instead of tracing?"

"Increases suspense." *And for my next trick . . .*

What if he'd *already* discovered her real identity? Her gaze widened. One of his visitors this morning might have brought word about her!

She'd continued picking up on the demon's stray thoughts, but what if she *tried* to listen? Closing her eyes, she concentrated. . . .

—CLAIM POSSESS MARK.—

Her eyes flashed open, and she yanked herself away. *Whoa.* His mind was a battle zone, his demonic instincts uprising. No wonder he was troubled.

She'd hoped he would be calm and controlled for the deed. But the longer she waited . . .

Maybe we should take this step before he gets worse*?*

He guided her off the beach toward the base of a mountain that meandered down almost to the sea. He escorted her into a darkened cave, releasing her inside.

She scanned the area. Faint light shone from an opening above. The wind and waves rocked the mountain. Spray hissed inside. "What is this place?" It looked like a regular cave to her.

He gazed up at the opening and waved a hand. Clouds dissipated, like stage curtains drawn back.

The full moon appeared. Light flared down into the cave, illuminating thousands of . . . diamonds. "Oh, my gods." They studded the cavern ceiling like a starlit sky and twinkled from the walls. "This is the diamond volcano!" Abyssian had told her about it. Dormant now, this vent had once been a perfect storm for creating stones.

She raised her hand to one of the infinite streams of light. "Demon, this is amazing." Abyssian was such a fierce warrior, yet he'd taken her to see this wonder.

She'd been looking for clarity and illumination about their relationship; diamondlight beams surrounded her.

Is this my sign?

He didn't share her giddiness, still just as restless. He opened his mouth to speak. Closed it. Tried again: "Why are you holding back from me?"

Because there's no solution! "What do you mean?" Specifically.

"You won't surrender to me, to our life." He swiped a palm over his weary face. "Why haven't you asked me to claim you?"

"I've been nervous." Not a lie.

He narrowed his eyes. "You spoke of an annulment. Perhaps you still think to walk away from this marriage?"

"What are you talking about?"

"You're pulling away from me, and it's making me insane! Tell me why."

"Why?" She exhaled, feeling just as frustrated as he was. "Because I can't figure out how to make our relationship work."

"That is what you've been musing?" His lips parted, as if she'd struck him. "*We* are the conundrum? And your incisive mind can't determine a solution for us to be together?"

"We have so many obstacles. The Møriør and Rune and our species." He didn't seem to be hearing her. "Abyssian, I need your help, your advice. I want to figure this out, but I can't do it alone."

He laid his palm over her nape. "You were thinking about leaving me, weren't you?"

Her temper was peaking. "I don't want to leave! But I can't keep paying for my previous life. How are we going to work on the issues we have *now* if you can't get over the *past*? You'll never give me a fair chance." His mind would immediately connect Kari's betrayal to Lila's desperate actions.

His hand tightened. "You've got my fucking heart in your clutches, and you planned to desert me?" He appeared more demonic than she'd ever seen him.

They were getting nowhere. What would happen if she asked him to claim her?

Sex was a variable, an unpredictable one. But if she expected heartache from every other avenue . . .

What in this hell did they have to lose? Maybe the claiming *was* a magical relationship cure-all.

Horns straightening, he demanded, "How did you think you could get away from me, little wife? All I'd ever needed to do was get you back to my realm. You're trapped in hell with me forever—"

"Shut up, demon."

Growl.

"And claim me."

Groan . . .

Calliope gazed up at him, her ethereal face bathed in the moon's glow and caressed by the diamondlight. She clamped his shoulders to pull him closer, standing on her toes to get to his mouth.

She kissed him hard, and Sian returned it. Their teeth clicked, their tongues twining.

Calliope wanted him! So why did this hollowness within him remain?

Because he'd been falling more and more for her, and she'd been looking for an out? He reached around her, gripping her ass, grinding against her. He needed closer to her, inside her.

What if she can't figure out the conundrum?

Then he would be cursed with emptiness, his heart returning to cold, black stone forever.

He broke away from their kiss, chest twisting at her lovely face. Teal blue eyes, kiss-swollen lips. "You're a godsdamned part of me, yet you would willingly leave me?" Just like in her past life.

While Sian had been dreaming of taking Kari back to hell—*you will be mine, Kari . . . for all time*—she'd been dreaming of another.

He'd thought of Calliope as his, but she hadn't been. After tonight, she would be.

"I want you," she murmured. "Now. Here."

This was her invitation. But it wasn't enough to soothe the desolation churning within him. He kissed her again, harder, savoring her breathy cries as their tongues tangled.

Make her understand. Between kisses, he said, "You don't know what it's like to *yearn* for ages without end. To see what you want so clearly—and be denied it. *Violently denied it.* Never again." His claws sliced through her blouse. He stripped them of clothes. Fabric ripping.

As they traded hungry kisses, he conjured a fur to spread over the sandy floor of the cave and a small fire to warm her. Before she could change her mind, he broke from the kiss to lower her down.

This will happen. At the realization, he seethed; the dimension seethed. Winds picked up, battering the mountain all around them. Waves crashed, sending spray inside the cave.

His gaze roamed over her trembling body. Droplets of water misted her naked flesh, making it shimmer. Her breasts were swollen, her stiffened nipples begging for a suck. *Can she feel the fire's heat through those tips?* Her hips subtly rocked.

He must be dreaming. If so, he would never wake.

Were ten millennia of his fantasies about to come true at last?

FORTY-EIGHT

Lila stared up at Abyssian's onyx eyes. The fire set the diamonds ablaze with all new prisms, the flames reflected in his gaze.

Before she'd known it, he had them naked on a fur, his massive frame levered over her. "I've never felt so alive." All of her senses sang. She could *taste* the fire and *feel* the mesmerizing lights. Awareness of him overwhelmed her.

When she grazed her fingertips over one of his bright glyphs, he held himself motionless, a primordial gentled by his mate.

She smoothed locks of his black hair away from his brow, then traced the rugged line of his jaw.

She was nervous, but . . . "I trust you." She did—with her body. So why couldn't she make the leap to tell him everything? The confusion roiling inside this demon made her chest ache.

No longer could she wonder about their fated connection; his pain was her pain. They were connected.

He's my mate too. "Abyssian . . ." *I'm falling for you.*

"I won't let anything divide us." Burning in his gaze was that bone-deep yearning, calling to hers. "I can't ever lose you again. You are a part of me, Lila." His forehead met hers. For long moments, they stayed like that.

How to voice all the thoughts whirling in her head? *I need you to show me this. To accept me as is. Please let this bond us enough to last.*

He leaned down to nuzzle her breasts, and her lids went heavy. "Sweetest nipples. They swell to my tongue." He took one and suckled with a growl. Against her damp skin, he said, "Never get enough . . . of your soft breasts. Never get enough of you. . . ."

His erection captured her attention. The veined length strained even harder. A bead of moisture clung to the head, pearlescent in the firelight.

He muttered words in Demonish, his voice so hoarse she had trouble understanding him. Something about watching her walk away.

She wanted to pay attention, to ask him to explain, but that bead taunted her. When she reached for him, he caught her hand.

"No, I won't last." He sat back on his knees, retracting the wing claws and the ones tipping his fingers. "I'm going to get you ready."

Would she *ever* be ready enough to receive his size? They'd soon find out.

When she spread her legs for him, he licked his lips. "My mate's so *wet.* I see these soft petals part, and I am stricken with need." His hand skimmed up one of her thighs. "This will truly happen."

She gasped when he cupped her pussy, slipping his middle finger inside her. "Yes, *yes* . . ."

"Look at you, beauty." His eyes turned solid black as he studied her expression. His gorgeous skin sheened. His piercings glinted, and his straightened horns shone.

Her primordial sex god. Firelight *loved* Abyssian.

"Shall I give you another?" He started wedging a second finger into her sheath. "Take them both for me."

"Ohhh." She writhed to accept them, about to climb the walls.

He slowly thrust. As he'd been doing over these past nights, he spread his fingers inside her, twisting them. He teased her until she could hear how slick she'd grown.

When she rocked on his fingers, his aggression started spiking. "You'll surrender to me tonight. I want *everything* from you—and I'll have it."

No longer nervous, she did surrender to him. Despite the turmoil he'd been suffering, he would never hurt her.

He withdrew those fingers and raised them to his mouth to suck. She moaned at the sight.

"Never get enough of this honey." Another dip, another taste. As if he was drinking her one drop at a time. His big fingers filled her . . . then withdrew.

Fullness. Then emptiness.

Heat. Then achy coolness.

Torture.

He worked his fingers even deeper. "This is what you need." He pumped them into her core until she grew light-headed. "Made for me." He sounded like he was unraveling—but still he fought for control.

She was struck by his contradictions. The demon had been built to kill. And to pleasure. He was tender, yet carnal.

His lust was palpable, but his body told the story of his restraint: bulging muscles, heaving chest, shaking hands. Voice raw with emotion, he said, "I will be your first lover, Calliope. And by all the gods, I'll be your last."

Sian's demon instinct roared inside him. CLAIM. POSSESS. MARK.

Her pink nails bit into his shoulders. "I can't take much more." Her swollen little clitoris pouted for his tongue. Her glistening entrance begged for penetration.

He'd trained her pussy to crave it. Even so, he drew on the powers of their realm to infuse her with protection magic, anything to keep her from feeling pain.

"Abyssian! I'm about to come!"

He withdrew his fingers. "No." *She's ready. This will happen.* He swallowed. *Now.*

In a daze, he maneuvered over her, his slick cockhead gliding across her leg. His heart thundered as he settled between her thighs. In Demonish, he said, "From the instant I first saw you, I knew."

His gaze roamed over her, from the shiny tresses spread around her head to her lustrous eyes and sweet mouth. Her full breasts and puckered nipples. The dip of her navel. The curls on her mons. Her pinkened flesh. . . .

She cradled his face with her soft hands. "Demon, is something wrong?"

"Want to remember this for our next ten thousand years." As he gazed into her heavy-lidded eyes, clarity hit him with the force of a lightning bolt.

I don't cherish her because I desire her; I desire her because I cherish her.

He'd battled his instincts for so long; he couldn't fight them a moment more.

Inside her. The balance. All will be well.

Grasping his shaft, he guided it toward her virgin sheath. When the crown kissed her wetness, he bit out a curse. "So lush."

He ran the tip up and down between her flaring lips until she was rolling her hips to meet him. "No more teasing!"

He nudged the head against her entrance, pressing forward.

She spread her knees wide for him. "Yes, yes, *inside me.*"

Her wet heat squeezed him so tightly, he wouldn't last even two thrusts! "Lila, I will put my seed in you. And I will mark you with my fangs." A quake rumbled. Primal forces swirled around them. Hell demanded its due. "We cross the point of no return. . . ."

FORTY-NINE

"Do it!" Lila all but begged. "I'm ready."

Abyssian rested on his forearms, leaning down until their faces were inches apart. As he eased deeper, feeding her his cock, the realm seemed to hold its breath. . . .

She gasped from the stretching sensation, but it didn't hurt. Pressure gave way, and his shaft sank farther inside. She hissed in a breath, expecting pain. None came.

"Virgin no more." He cupped her face, brushing his thumb over her cheek. "I was losing you—didn't know why. But now you've surrendered to me." His hips tilted forward, his muscles straining with barely harnessed aggression. Sweat dampened his skin.

As he inched deeper, his smoldering gaze scanned her face, gauging her every reaction.

She bit her lip. *So far, I'm undecided about this.*

"Give me time, love," he said, as if he'd heard her thought. Then she heard one of his: *—Last, Sian!—*

Staring into his eyes, she grew centered. Steady. They could do this. She relaxed a degree.

"That's it." He took as she gave, filling her even more. "Surrender everything to me." Once he was seated as deeply as he could go, his wings extended wide, and he bit out one word: "Mine."

She maneuvered under him, adjusting to the fullness. "Oh!" *Better!*

With every beat of his mighty heart, his cock throbbed inside her, but he somehow kept himself from thrusting. "Are you mine, Lila?" He reached between them to rub her clitoris.

"I'm yours!" she cried. *Much better!* As his fingers made slow, slippery circles, she dug her nails into the rigid muscles of his ass.

"Holding on by a thread." His onyx eyes flickered dangerously. "Fondle your breasts for me."

She released him to pet herself.

"Good girl." His fingers were sending her closer to the brink. "You're mine now. You can't ever go back. You will belong to a demon . . . forever." His shadow loomed on the wall—all forbidding horns and wings—as if his darkest self was in the cave with them.

She didn't want to go back! "Abyssian . . ."

"Pinch your nipples harder."

With a moan, she did.

"Harder."

"Ah!" Her hips bucked uncontrollably. Which felt *unbelievable*. She rocked on him again—sending his shaft in and out of her. "Nothing can feel this good!"

He gnashed his teeth. "Still! You have no idea what forces you toy with."

She couldn't remain still. Too much sensation danced just out of reach. She undulated on his cock again . . . and again . . . faster . . . faster . . . until *she* was fucking *him*.

Seeming incapable of speech, a growl rose from his chest. But his thoughts blasted her. *—Stop, Lila! No, do NOT stop. Mercy!—*

Stopping wasn't an option; she chased her orgasm.

"You're—*uhn!*—about to—*ah!*—come."

"Yes!" She pinched her nipples to the point of pain.

A drop of his sweat ran off his forehead to hit her breast. Even his sweat was searing. Pleasure built and coiled deep inside her.

Building . . . coiling . . . building . . . coiling.

"Then come hard." His fingers sped up. "Wring my cock."

"My gods!" *Sexy fucking demon.* "You make me feel so—"

RELEASE.

Her inner walls clamped down on his thick length, her back arching. Her breasts swelled beneath her palms. When she caught a breath, she loosed it on a scream.

"Lila! I feel you . . . feel you coming on me!"

Needing to touch him, her hands flew to his back, nails embedding under his wings. Another convulsion hit, and she scored his skin, drawing a roar from his lungs.

His cock stayed wedged deep inside her, the unyielding pressure forcing her to climax harder than she ever had. Shattering spasms gripped her. . . .

Sian's breaths heaved as he fought not to come. *Must mark her.*

But Calliope's sheath tightened even more around him, the rhythmic contractions nigh irresistible. *Last!*

The urge to thrust lashed him like a razor whip—but he'd be done with a single plunge! She was so tight around him, he wondered if he *could* thrust.

She sank her teeth into his shoulder in abandon, screaming against his muscles.

I am *in hell. Heaven! No, hell.* For so long, he'd longed to release his seed; now he was frantic to hold it back.

He perceived volcanoes in the distance readying to explode. He invoked dark forces in the realm, anything to maintain control.

Though he still hadn't dared to move, semen ascended his shaft, rising against his will. His heavy balls drew up, aching in a way he'd never experienced. *Laden with seed for my mate.*

The tug of her sex demanded it from him.

The heat of her . . .

Get control! His claws bit into his palms, his body suspended on the brink.

As she came down, she caressed his shoulders, his chest, his sensitive pierced nipples. Her hands sped up until they seemed to be touching him everywhere at once.

Instinctive drives surged inside him. To thrust. To *fuck*.

To bite.

His eyes were drawn to the flesh between her neck and shoulder. Her misted skin beckoned his fangs.

She turned her head away, baring herself for him. "Do it."

"Can't. Not yet." He didn't recognize his voice. "Must—keep—control."

Her glowing gaze locked on his horns.

"No!" Just from her look, his hips jerked between her legs. A guttural sound broke from his chest. *"No."*

This dream female reached up and *clutched his horns*. She yanked him down to her neck.

"LILA!" He sank his fangs into her. *"Uhhhhnnnn!"*

He *felt* her scream as she came again. Her arms fell limp over her head, and her spasms rippled up and down his cock. He scented her orgasms, and knew he couldn't resist her this time.

He snarled against his mate's neck as her sweet pussy milked him. . . .

Ah, gods, ah fuck—

Semen *erupted* from him.

He released her neck, throwing back his head. The force of his ejaculation wrenched a bellow from his lungs. *"COMING."* His back bowed, his wings snapping open. Shudders seized him, and his vision blurred. *"LILA."*

His mind turned over. His psyche. His heart in his chest.

Euphoria. Floating.

The need to fill her overpowered him. He helplessly plunged, fucking his mate to relieve lifetimes of pressure.

"It's so hot!" Head thrashing on the fur, she met his thrusts, sending him into a frenzy.

In burst after burst, he emptied himself into his female's body. . . .

Muscles whipcord taut, the demon pistoned between her legs. His cataclysmic bite had forced her to come again, his body escalating her climax. *Too much, too much . . .*

Sensations engulfed her. His blindingly bright glyphs, the fire flaring, the intoxicating taste of his sweat-slicked skin. The stunned look in his gorgeous eyes. *"Lila?"*

With a last shudder, he collapsed over her. All around them, aftershocks rocked hell.

Mind-blown, she took stock of her body. No pain. Just satisfaction.

Demonish left his lips: "Gods almighty . . . never knew." He buried his face in the hollow of her neck, his breaths heaving against her mark. But he didn't stop lazily thrusting his still-hard cock inside her.

She smiled to feel his cum mingled with hers. As relaxation spread over her well-loved body, she wrapped her arms around him, giving him adoring kisses.

He raised his head, gazing down at her with hooded eyes. "Did I hurt you?"

"No, I'm fine. Better than. I feel thoroughly mated."

"Even when this bite heals"—he grazed his teeth down her neck—"demons will see my mark on you forever. My *claim*."

They were bonded. Optimism surged inside her. They could fix anything amiss between them—because they were one entity now.

As he slowly thrust, his chest skimmed her swollen nipples. "You belong to me. Around me. Connected to me."

Connection. "Yes, yes." She tilted her hips up to meet his movements.

He raised his brows. "You're not nearly done, are you?"

"Oh, not by a league, demon."

Lips curving, he covered her breasts with his palms. "My fey mate loves her pleasure." Rubbing his thumbs over her nipples, he rasped, "Made me come so hard I lost my mind. Could you feel it?"

She excitedly nodded. "It was searing inside me." The demon's rich essence.

His eyes gleamed with triumph. "I can give you younglings now."

Her excitement dimmed, and she gazed away. "You could have red-blooded children with a demoness."

He pinched Lila's chin, forcing her to face him. "At the height of my anger, I plotted to use you, then go to others for offspring."

In a deadened tone, she said, "You can plant seed in every field—except for mine."

"Total fidelity, wife." Voice rising with each word, he said, "I will have sharp-tempered, sharp-eared little pups with my cherished queen, or I will have none at all!" A wave crashing outside punctuated his statement.

Cherished queen? He wanted the two of them to have kids? "Truly?"

"Your choice, Lila."

Her heart stuttered as she breathlessly stared at him. He looked so menacing and demonic and sexy. Her core reflexively clenched him.

His shaft pulsed in reaction. "Good. I have your answer. Inform me whenever you're ready."

She grinned. "I will." When light beams struck him, she said, "What a place to lose my virginity."

"And to lose my seal."

"So after all the pressure and fury have churned in this volcano for millennia, diamonds appear?"

"Just so."

"Then this place is just like your life. The diamonds could be . . . your future."

He cast her a brows-drawn look. *"Yes."* With another wave of his hand, he used magic to pluck a huge diamond from the ceiling. When he offered it to her, the stone refracted the light from his glyphs, illuminating his hypnotic eyes. She saw so many things in his expression.

Hope. Need.

Love.

She raised a hand to trace a beam gliding over his face. "Can you let go of the pressure and fury and forgive the past?"

Abyssian nodded. "I can. I *will*." He placed the diamond into her palm and closed her fingers over it. "My future is yours."

FIFTY

Her demon was asleep.

Lila sat up in their bed, surveying Abyssian as sea breezes and moonlight stole inside their tower. The storm from earlier had ended.

Eyes shut, he lay on his back. His face was at peace, his breaths deep and even. She'd never seen him like this.

After another bout in the cave, he'd traced her back here. Then he'd taken her once more, slowly. He'd pressed kisses to the corners of her lips, her lids, her cheeks—adoring her.

Then he'd laid his big hand over her belly, gazing at her with a question in his eyes.

She'd simply nodded.

Though she'd been ready for another round after that, he'd refused, saying, "We need to pace ourselves in the beginning. We have time."

Now she leaned forward, ghosting her fingers just above his face, tracing his features—his stern brow, his proud nose, his lean cheeks. Those sensual lips.

This male, so different from her, was her soul's match. He'd shown her what being treated like a queen felt like.

Her former fiancé Saetth could never have given her that. Fresh from a night with Abyssian, she comprehended all the more just how cowardly and selfish Saetth had been.

She shuddered to think how close she'd come to missing out on Abyssian.

Tomorrow, she would tell the demon everything, revealing all about Magh and Nïx and Saetth.

Lila would confess her feelings for Abyssian, knowing he felt the same. She gazed at the mantel. To the right of the scepter sat their diamond. If he truly let go of the past and embraced their future, he would understand what had driven her to undertake Saetth's mission.

If the demon loved her, he would accept her bloodline.

Once she and Abyssian worked through her secrets, she would ask his advice on what should be done about her kingdom. She had a feeling her cousin's days as ruler were numbered. . . .

The demon's eyes darted behind his lids, his breaths growing erratic. His fist clenched and unclenched, as if grasping for her.

Heart aching, she smoothed his brow and whispered, "You are the most beautiful male I've ever known."

His eyes opened. "Calliope?" He blinked as if surprised to find her beside him. He reached for her, his strong arms enfolding her. "I never want to wake up without you." He kissed her neck—her marking.

"Abyssian . . ."

"Yes, love?"

"You're my mate too."

She heard him swallow thickly as he pulled her closer. In Demonish, he murmured, "And that is why you own my heart."

As she drifted to sleep in the shelter of his wings, she thought, *I'm in love with Abyssian Infernas.*

Sian remained awake after she'd fallen asleep.

Savoring this satisfaction, he gazed at her mark. His possessiveness surged again, but so did his tenderness toward her.

He would replay her words for eternity. *You're my mate too.* After so much misery, his mind could barely reconcile a life with a passionate, brilliant mate he adored.

And with their children as well. She *wanted* younglings with him!

In every way, Calliope had been worth the wait. He could've gone *twenty* thousand years if he'd known this night awaited him.

At last he understood what spending felt like: inconceivable ecstasy. But more powerful than the physical pleasure was the feeling of connection with Calliope. Sian now comprehended the bond only a mated male could experience.

Maybe their history was supposed to have happened—to lead them to this present. Without Kari's betrayal, he never would've sought out his father's former alliance and been received into the Møriør. Sian might not have matured from a cocksure and conceited demon prince.

He was different, stronger. Calliope was as well. *Maybe we are both better.*

Her limbs started to twitch. More dreams. He delved, finding her blocks wavering. He'd hesitated to probe her dreams before, but she was his claimed mate now. They were one.

He dipped into her thoughts. Flashes of scenes raced through her mind. She dreamed as quickly as she ran!

In one snippet, she sat in the grassy yard of a mansion, playing with her dolls. She was miserably lonely, already knowing that she needed more love than her precious dolls could give her. She heard a male's deep voice from a distance, and she gave a cry. *It's him! My betrothed has come to see me!*

Sian could *feel* the love she had for that male.

His instincts warned that he didn't want to see whatever might follow. He told himself to get out of her thoughts.

Who was her betrothed? Damn it, who?

The dream began to speed up even more, her memories bombarding him. They arose from all different times in her life, in no order.

One face stood out among many. A male. Blond and tall. Handsome.

Wait, was that . . . *Nïx* in one of her memories?

Calliope must be experiencing imaginary scenes. She'd told him that she didn't know the Valkyrie.

But how could Calliope dream what Nïx looked and sounded like unless those two were acquainted?

Why would his mate lie unless . . . ? He gazed down at her sleeping face. *Lila, I beg: please don't have betrayed me.* He could not have waited all this time only to be deceived again.

No, no, no. This wasn't possible. *I must be sure. . . .*

Just as he delved into her dreams again, he placed that blond male.

Calliope's betrothed, the one she adored, was . . . the king of the fey.

FIFTY-ONE

Lie-la. How fitting a name.

As Sian sprinted through the farthest reaches of Pandemonia, winds gusted around him. Boiling rain hissed against fire tornadoes, and quakes devoured terrain.

Calliope's dream had been just as chaotic, but he'd managed to piece together many of her secrets. . . .

He turned toward the shore, running for what felt like days. His mind was more disordered than when he'd learned of his mate's death—more disordered than when he'd learned another male had impregnated and killed her.

The crimson haze had returned, coloring the entire world.

When he reached the Mercury Sea, the depths were murky, like his thoughts. Eddies swirled and huge breakers crashed, just as the truth had crashed upon him, pulverizing his idyll with his mate.

She was *still* a princess. Still a liar and a spy. Only Calliope spoke Sian's tongue! She was not only King Saetth's fiancée; she was his gods-damned cousin, part of the line Rune had vowed to stamp out.

One Møriør's mate was another one's prey. And Nïx and Saetth had delivered her into Sian's home like a ticking bomb.

Calliope had vowed to Saetth, "I won't rest until I discover a way to hurt Abyssian Infernas. I'll figure out what his weaknesses are and how to exploit them. I'll do anything I can to destroy him."

Anything for Saetth, the male she adored. She considered him *the epitome of masculine perfection* and saw him as her ideal match. *Socially, royally, sexually.* All she'd ever wanted was to be his queen and have children with him.

I will gut that fuck so slowly.

Mist from the waves sprayed Sian's face, reminding him of his own appearance. He pictured his recent reflection, ashamed that he'd believed a female like her could want him.

How she must have inwardly laughed at him! How he *should* be laughing now. Her fiancé had betrayed her. On this very night, the king of the fey would select a new bride.

In both of her lives, Sian's mate had fooled him. He recalled the day of Kari's surprise wedding, finally giving free rein to that harrowing memory.

She'd stood upon the dais, so lovely she'd stolen his breath. . . .

With zero emotion, she said, "I am marrying my fiancé because I want him. *I have loved him since I was a little girl."*

Sian's stomach lurched as if it'd been punched. "Do not do this, Kari. You love me!" Hadn't she told him as much? The tender regard I feel for you . . .

"I do not—and could never—love an animal with horns." She returned her attention to her reflection.

He gaped in disbelief. But their kiss . . . the way she'd responded . . . their plans . . .

Adjusting a lock of her shining hair, she asked, "Can I make it any plainer, prince of beasts?"

Guards entered, but he was too stunned to fight as they forced him outside.

Frantic to stop the wedding, Sian raced back to his quarters to determine his next move. Replaying her words again and again, he realized what he had to do.

With grim resolve, he collected his battle-ax. He took it into the forest she loved so much. Sweating, eyes watering, he rested his face on a tree stump. He raised his weapon above his head.

This is forever, Sian.

So will her marriage be.

There is no future without her.

He let fall the ax. Pain. Unimaginable. He silently screamed. Consciousness faded in and out.

But somehow he managed to amputate his own horns. In shock, he sheathed his bloodied ax and collected the remains.

He sneaked back into the castle, then slipped into her room once more. Uncaring of all the attendants, he offered Kari his once-noble horns. "You told me you could never love a male like me. These will not ever grow back. I will look as your kind do. I will live *as your kind do."*

He thought he saw a flicker of emotion in her eyes, but then she glanced around at her scandalized attendants. Her expression was cold when she faced him again.

"Kari, I would do anything for you. I would take out my heart and give it to you if I could."

"Demon, you will regret this deed for the rest of your life."

He squared his shoulders. "I am proud of my pain. Of my loss." He raised his sacrifice to her. "Proud that my actions are in the service of a cause so precious."

She simply tilted her head. As if he'd presented her with an unknown variable. "You almost look like a person now. But I should have said: I do not—and could never—love you. *In any guise. You are a fool if you ever thought otherwise."*

Bile rose in his throat. "Then why act as if you cared for me? Why lead me to believe . . . ?"

"Young lovers tell each other secrets, do they not?"

Comprehension: nothing between them had been true. "You . . . you spied for your parents."

"Indeed. Come now, you had to know deep down that you are beneath me." She was *like all the other fey, able to turn off her emotions. She'd evaluated her involvement with a young demon prince and rationally—coldly—concluded he wasn't worth the bother.*

With a shrug, she picked up the skirt of her wedding gown and gave him her back as she traipsed away.

While blood ran down his face, he willed her to turn back and see *him. To comprehend that he would do anything for her.* Turn around, Kari. Look at me!

She never did.

Millennia later, Sian bellowed with rage. When would he learn? He tore at his hair, bashing his fists against his head.

His mate's past and the present swirled together in his mind, her statements melding.

I do not—and could never—love you. . . . I won't rest until I discover a way to hurt Abyssian Infernas. . . . You are beneath me. . . . I'll do anything I can to destroy him. . . . You're a fool. . . .

His legs buckled, his knees meeting the shore.

Before he'd left Calliope earlier, he'd stared down at her. Hating her. Loving her.

He'd fallen for her utterly. And now that he knew what love felt like, he realized he hadn't yet been in love with Kari. Maybe he'd been too young, or he'd needed more time. Maybe Calliope's passion had pushed him over into the brink.

I loved her.

He swiped at his face, surprised to find two humiliating tears running down his cheeks.

The last time he'd learned that she loved another, he'd disfigured himself and offered up the remains. Now he would spurn Calliope, behaving as coldly with her as Kari had with him. Never would he let his mate know he'd been stupid enough to fall for the same trick twice.

The more pain he felt when he confronted Calliope, the calmer he would be.

He envisioned his revenge. It was because he'd set aside his trickery that he'd left himself vulnerable. Now she would pay—as she should have from the beginning.

His wrath knew no bounds. So hot, it felt . . . freezing.

He held his breath, and the sea stilled. Ice formed around his knees. A sheet of it crept out from him.

Cold. Like his crumbling stone heart. . . .

FIFTY-TWO

Abyssian wasn't there when Lila woke the next morning. Disappointed, she looked for his note.

He always left a note.

She frowned when she didn't find one. Maybe he was talking with Uthyr in the throne room. Strange, the weather had grown blustery again, the temperature dropping.

As soon as Abyssian returned, she would sit him down. Her resolve to tell him everything hadn't wavered over the night.

After dressing, she gazed in the mirror and traced her neck. She couldn't see his mark—only demons could—but she felt different.

Bonded.

Last night, she'd dreamed about her past, reliving milestones in her relationship with her former fiancé. Her mind's way of severing all ties with him?

About time.

Though the specifics of her pie-in-the-sky wishes had changed, her hopes would all come true—with Abyssian. Unable to stop grinning, she stood in front of the fire and rubbed her hands together.

"Good morning, love." He appeared in the bedroom. He was freshly showered, his hair still wet.

Her heart pounded just from the sight of him. *My mate.* "Good morning," she said. "Were you outside? It's really cold."

He leaned in and pressed a kiss to her neck. "Is it?" Even his lips were cool.

"What were you doing?"

"Arranging a surprise for you."

"*Another* one? You're spoiling me, demon. But maybe we could—"

"I can't wait to show it to you."

"Um, okay." But after this, they *would* have their talk.

"Are you ready?" He clasped her elbow, his hand as cold as his lips. "Close your eyes."

She trustingly did. He traced her somewhere musty and dank. Her ears twitched. Were those . . . rats squeaking?

"You can open your eyes."

She frowned to find them inside a cramped cell in some kind of dungeon. "What is this, Abyssian?"

Face expressionless, he traced to the other side of the bars. "Your new castle accommodations. The tower was much too nice for you."

And for my next trick . . . "This isn't funny."

"Isn't it, *Princess* Calliope?"

Oh, shit! Her breath caught in her lungs. She finally managed to say, "Just wait, and let me explain."

"No explanation necessary. I know you're a spy for Nïx and Saetth—your fiancé. You came here determined to destroy me."

"Yes, I did." Surprise crossed his expression. Had he thought she'd deny it? "But then I got to know you. I learned not to fear you, learned to trust you."

"If true, then I won this round, and all the rounds."

"What are you talking about?"

He leaned his shoulder against the bars. "You always suspected I was setting you up for some trick, but you still let me enjoy you, let me use your body to rid myself of that problematic seal. You fell prey to the ultimate setup. Now that I have no seal, I have no need for you."

How could he act this way just hours after what they'd shared? Could he truly have faked his feelings all night? She shook her head. "Bullshit. You feel more for me. Just like I feel more for you."

Switching to Demonish, he said, "You were particularly suited to spy here—since you know my tongue."

In English, she said, "I do. And I was sent here as a spy. But that doesn't change what happened between us. Look at me, demon." She pinned his gaze with her own. "I'm in love with you."

Seeming to grow even more bored, he said, "Save it. I've heard all your lies. And I know that you've loved Saetth since you were a little girl. Just like Kari loved her fey king. History does repeat itself."

"I did love Saetth. But then he killed my mother and father and exiled me to the mortal realm. He didn't come see me there for that entire time."

Abyssian exhaled. "More lies, princess? I delved into your dreams. I saw you kissing him in the mortal realm. Recently, in fact."

"He finally showed up my last night there—the exact same night the Sorceri caught me," she said, realizing that her story sounded far-fetched. "And I did kiss Saetth, to see what it'd be like. I found it lacking, but I didn't care, because I was desperate to return home—so I wouldn't be vulnerable to Rune. Saetth and Nïx offered me a deal. I would journey to hell to spy on you, learning about your alliance and Orion. After they extracted me, I would get to go back to Sylvan as queen."

"I hate to be the one to tell you this . . ." Abyssian trailed off. "That's not true; I relish telling you this: I have it on good authority that Saetth, the male you love, your 'brave' king, was in league with Nïx to *sacrifice* you. You were his virgin offering to the king of hell. No one was ever coming to extract you."

So her cousin had known everything. She'd figured, but it still stung.

"Tonight he's hosting a gala for the most powerful families from all the fey kingdoms. He'll select one daughter from among them to be his bride."

That prick had *never* intended to marry her. He'd sent her out to do his dirty work, then sat back to reap the rewards!

"What do you think about him now?"

"If all of this is true, then I think I'm going to kill him."

"I'm not one to get in the middle of a lovers' spat. I'd tell you that you two will work it out—but you're never leaving this dungeon again." He ran the backs of his claws across the bars. "Actually, now that I think about it, I should imprison him in here with you. After all, you are made for each other—socially, royally, sexually."

She was too pissed to flinch. "Another prison? That's your solution?" She bit out, "Get this through your thick demon skull: I—love—*you*."

"It isn't returned, little fey. Fooling you is my greatest trick of all. In this life, you are the one who'll yearn for me. Do you really think I'd want something more from you—one of Magh's descendants?"

"I'm so sick of paying for that!"

"Hmm."

What did that mean? Grappling for control, she said, "Abyssian, you're only saying these things because you're angry. I get it—my temper's about to blow. And I don't do my best thinking when I've just been locked in a creepy dungeon. But let's talk about this."

"Angry? Do I look it? What color are my eyes?" They were green. And his lips curled with amusement. "I'm in a great mood. I always am on the brink of war."

"What are you talking about?"

"Sylvan blood is soon to wet my ax, and I can hardly wait." He conjured his weapon, twirling it in his hands.

No, he wouldn't. . . . "You vowed to me—"

"That I wouldn't attack your kingdom as long as you were my wife in truth. You no longer are, because we are no longer married. I have forsaken you forever."

Shock stole her breath. Tears threatened, but she would never let him see how much this was breaking her heart. Karinna had gone emotionless with this demon? Lila could too.

Abyssian had seen *nothing.*

"You went from prisoner to queen right back to prisoner." His grin deepened. "You wanted to match wits with me? You lost, Calliope. You lost everything."

"We won't come back from this." She strode up to the bars, her teal eyes glinting. "Think very carefully about what you say next."

When will I learn? He'd been tempted to seize on certain things she'd said, ignoring her blatant lies. "I'm only speaking the truth," he told her. "Take comfort that you're still a princess, because you're no longer a queen. Of course, once I invade Sylvan, you won't be a princess even there. In time, I'll install one of my many demon heirs on the throne."

She gripped the cell bars. "I'd planned to talk to you about this today."

"After a month in my company, you'd selected this very day? How convenient." He shook his head. "You were a liar in your last life, and nothing's changed."

"This is exactly why I couldn't tell you—because your eyes only see the past. I knew you'd never give me a chance to prove myself, and I was right."

"Alas, I can't stay and talk. I'm off to Tenebrous to meet with my allies." Now that Sian considered the situation more closely, he realized Rune *must* have known Calliope's identity. The archer had kept tabs on that bloodline for ages. In investigating Saetth anew, Rune couldn't have failed to put everything together.

Yet Sian's closest friend had concealed that knowledge. *Why?* He blamed Rune for his pain almost as much as he did Calliope!

Sian would send a message, calling the archer to Tenebrous. After confronting Rune, he would rally the Møriør to action. "The time has come to plot our Sylvan invasion."

"Abyssian, you're hurting a mate who adores you. You're killing my love with your stubborn distrust—with your inability to see anything other than the past. My only mistake was falling for you." Releasing the bars, Calliope said, "But I can remedy that. Just as Kari did, I will shut down my emotions. I will strangle my feelings for you until they're dead forever." The teal faded from her eyes. "Remember what could have been, demon."

Though the change gave him chills, he shrugged. "You would say and do anything to get out of your cage, my fey pet."

In an eerily monotone voice, she said, "You tricked me, just like Saetth did. You're no better than he is. Anything Kari did to you—anything I did—wasn't nearly enough. I only wish I could remember."

That bitch! Somehow he kept his expression impassive. "I did try to warn you, my queen of nothing—my soon-to-be princess of nowhere. Any who challenge me *will* lose."

"Demon, you've lost this round just by virtue of one fact."

He ground his fangs, but the words still escaped: "Which—is?"

"You think the game is over."

He stiffened. On the verge of losing his composure, he traced to his tower.

He surveyed his bedroom. Her scepter rested on the mantel, the diamond beside it. Her robe lay across the foot of the bed. He inhaled her scent on a pillow.

Their existences had become intertwined.

When will I fucking learn?

FIFTY-THREE

That asshole!

The master of trickery had struck again.

Now that he'd gone, Lila thought of all the things she could've said. She could've reminded him about the promise represented in that diamond and about his vow never to hurt her again.

Not that she would have made a difference. When he'd first busted her, she'd regretted not coming clean—until he'd revealed his true feelings. He'd never intended something more with one of Magh's descendants.

So why play with her? Why not just bargain to lose his seal?

Maybe he'd been so warped from losing his mate that he'd turned evil. Maybe he just loved his games. Maybe he was a typical Møriør.

Why *would* she have rushed to volunteer information about her identity when he was such a fan of Rune's mission?

Fists clenched, she paced, her attempt to shut down her emotions failing epically. *Think about escape, Lila.* Anything other than Abyssian's treatment of her.

If she couldn't divert her mind, she would lose it. Once she started crying over him, she might never stop.

Even as her heart was splitting, fury inundated her. Fury was easier. It kept her standing. *I fucking fell for him.*

Abyssian wasn't the only target of her hostility. Saetth and Nïx had set her up, leaving Lila at the mercy of a cruel demon. If Abyssian was to be believed, Saetth had been fine with damning her. No one had expected her to like it here in hell, trapped with a hated Møriør.

She'd once been a powerless "hothouse rose." Then a pawn of Nïx and Saetth. Then a demon's prisoner. Now she was queen of nothing.

After all of her struggles, was she right back where she started?

She stopped pacing. Saetth and Nïx had targeted Lila because of her association with Abyssian in a past life. For deeds done eons ago, the demon had happily punished Lila.

She kept paying for Karinna's sins while enjoying none of that princess's advantages.

Karinna had been the *heir* to the Sylvan throne. If she and Lila were one and the same . . . then Lila had precedence over even Saetth.

Which meant Lila was the rightful ruler.

Which meant . . . Saetth was sitting on *her* throne.

I want it back.

Rulers who returned from war or exploration after being assumed dead always fought to reclaim their thrones.

Maybe I've just been exploring *for ten millennia. I took a tour of the afterlife.*

And those rulers executed anyone standing in the way. Would Lila? Could she finish the job her parents had started?

She had the mettle to become a king killer—her life in the fey court had been good for one thing—but logistics presented a problem. She'd have to escape this prison, then figure out how to reach Sylvan, even *before* she could face off against a lethal swordsman.

If she somehow defeated Saetth to take the throne, she'd then have to prepare Sylvan's defense against the Møriør.

She'd figure it the fuck out. *Step one, Lila. Escape.* She inspected her cage for weaknesses—

Clickety-clack.

Her gaze whipped up at the sound. The fawn appeared not far down the dungeon corridor. They stared at each other.

Pulse racing, Lila asked, "Can you . . . free me?"

The cell door groaned open. *Whoa.*

When the creature seemed to be awaiting her, Lila swallowed. Three times in her dreams she'd refused to follow the deer over the edge of the cliff.

Something told her she was about to get one more chance. Could she accept whatever fate Graven had planned for her?

Lila sensed she was on the verge of discovering a great truth. Or at least of understanding why she'd been reincarnated.

The feeling that everything was connected struck her. Did the solution shimmer just beyond her fingertips?

Anticipation mixed with uneasiness as the fawn led her out of the dungeon. In the main part of the castle, the moving doors and corridors and stairways of the labyrinth took them deeper into Graven's heart.

At the lowest landing, the fawn disappeared into a wall. Lila didn't even pause, just walked right through it.

Her eyes adjusted to the light, her mind slow to register the sight before her. *"Oh, my gods."*

Within a massive atrium burned a blue inferno. The flames must be eight stories high! Black blooms swirled above them. Dark drops—blood?—rained down from some unseen source, hissing in the heat.

The fire seemed alive. Ancient and primal. Its shape swelled and contracted, like a beating heart.

How could anything be so beautiful?

Awestruck, tears welling, she breathed, "You're the hellfire that beckoned Abyssian's ancestor."

The flames soared even higher.

The fawn approached the inferno, never slowing as it continued into the fire. Blue flames closed behind it, the creature consumed.

Fear skittered up Lila's spine. She was supposed to . . . follow.

In a daze, she started forward. Was this a gallows walk? Or the solution to all of her problems?

At the edge of the hellfire, she squared her shoulders and ignored her pounding heart. She wouldn't refuse Graven again.

Holding her breath, she took that terrifying step. . . .

FIFTY-FOUR

The dimension of Tenebrous
Perdishian Castle

"You *knew*," Sian bit out as he swung his fist into Rune's face. The archer went reeling from the unexpected blow.

Eyes black with rage, Rune charged him. Sian charged back. They collided in the middle of Perdishian's empty war room with the impact of two dragons.

"You knew she was Saetth's fiancée," Sian yelled. "And a spy!" This would be a close fight. Both could trace, both were around the same size. Sian was stronger than he'd ever been and older than Rune, but the archer was quick.

"Not at first." Rune traced forward, his fist a blur as it connected with Sian's throat. And again. "But I found out in time."

Bellowing, Sian blocked and struck.

Pummeling each other, the two crashed into the walls until the black-stone keep quaked. Their blows echoed throughout the room.

"Why would you not tell me?" Sian swung, catching Rune in the jaw. "You were my friend!"

Rune bared his fangs, shoving Sian back. "I still am!"

"Then why?"

"Because I wanted to give her time to tell you." *Strike.*

Block. "I never would have let myself feel more for her!"

"I didn't do this lightly. You forget—I wanted to put an arrow in her heart."

"You won't godsdamned touch her!" Sian roared and traced, launching his fist with all his new might.

Rune hurtled across the room, crashing into the glass wall.

A crack forked out across the blast-proof expanse. If that glass broke, they would be sucked into the ether. . . .

Lila woke to the plaintive howls of hellhounds.

Blinking open her eyes, she sat up. She was naked on the floor of the bedroom?

The last thing she remembered was stepping into the fire. She patted her arms, legs, and face. Not burned? How long had she been out?

The sun was low in the sky. She must've been unconscious for hours. So what had happened to her during that interim? And how had she gotten here?

She stood unsteadily, her head as heavy as a bowling ball. Courtesy of the fire, her brain had been saturated with new information, her body with magic.

Lila was . . . *changed.*

In her mind's eye, she could see every inch of this dimension and castle as though looking into a terrarium. This was how Abyssian viewed his realm! No wonder he'd been able to find her so quickly after her escape.

For some reason, she knew Graven hadn't *transferred* Abyssian's abilities to Lila. No, she had her own, equal to his—because she was the queen of hell, and Pandemonia was half hers. She felt it in every cell in her body.

Using her new talents, she searched for his presence. She detected Uthyr in the throne room, but the demon was gone. No doubt off to plan his fucking war.

The ground trembled as if with *her* fury. She frowned. Could she learn to control her surroundings? Closing her eyes for focus, she imagined one of Graven's staircases sweeping left. It obeyed! She shifted another one to the right.

As she got the hang of this power, she opened and closed moving walls like a kid playing with a car window.

She made a small volcano erupt—with just a thought. *Amazing!* She fanned the winds over the sea. When the terrace curtains fluttered, the late-afternoon sun struck the diamond on the mantel, the concentrated sparkle catching her eye.

The demon had pledged his future to her. He'd promised to let go of the past. How could he break her heart, without a seeming care?

What if he returned and tried to imprison her again? *This is* my *home now.* The castle had chosen her to challenge, and Lila had boldly stepped into an inferno. In reward, Graven had anointed her with power.

If Lila wielded magic like Abyssian's, then maybe *she* could banish *him* from this realm. Hell hath no fury like a hell queen scorned. She burned to make him pay.

He possessed no magic outside of Pandemonia, so how could he defeat hers? She recalled him telling her about one of his battle campaigns, stressing that field advantage was key in war.

Only one of hell's two rulers is currently in this advantageous field.

She pictured the invisible border of the dimension, then imagined sheets of hell metal covering it, locking the boundaries down.

Locking *him* out. Only she had the key.

"Pandemonia is *mine*," she murmured, hands balling into fists. "I control it." She concentrated harder. "I want him gone. Lock him—and any who would help him—out. I forbid Abyssian to return."

The hellfire had blessed *her*. He didn't deserve this place.

He broke my heart.

Power thrumming through her, she swayed on her feet, sensing . . . success. She'd barred him from this dimension!

Though she savored this electric feeling of connectedness to Pandemonia, wanted to explore it even more, she had a mission to challenge her cousin.

But if she couldn't wield hell's magic in another realm, how could she defeat him? He would have the upper hand in every way.

He's stronger. Faster. A legendary swordsman. Protected by guards. Backed by an army. Field advantage. More experienced. More devious.

In one of her many late-night conversations with Abyssian, Lila had said, "Maybe a more levelheaded fey regent could overthrow Saetth."

He'd answered, "That king's the strongest of his kind. He's too powerful to be routed by another fey."

She'd bitten her tongue, instead of voicing her thought: *And Saetth* knows *it. Which is a vulnerability in itself. . . .*

Her attention was again drawn to the mantel. The Lôtān head and the scepter seemed to call to her.

The moment grew dreamlike; yes, everything felt connected. This was why she'd been brought back for a second life.

Fate *wanted* Lila to be queen.

Suddenly she knew how to defeat Saetth.

She laughed at the solution, stamping her feet. By not *defeating* him at all. . . .

FIFTY-FIVE

Sian and Rune stilled, waiting to see if the glass would hold.

Tense moments passed. The fracture began to slow. *By all the gods, stop.*

When it finally did, they both exhaled a gust of breath.

"Are you done with this?" Rune traced to his feet, adjusting his jaw.

Now that the heat of the fight had ebbed, Sian was left with . . . emptiness. He gave a faint nod.

"I truly thought she would tell you." Rune shoved his hair out of his face. "I read your mind when Josie and I stopped by, and I saw how happy your mate was making you. I wanted that for you."

"She did make me happy. *Before* I learned of her treachery."

"I didn't do this to harm you. Think, Sian—can you comprehend how difficult forgoing my own revenge was? She's been one of my targets since her birth."

"How did you forgo it? You vowed to yourself, to Orion. Even to Magh."

Rune crossed to the war room's table, then dropped into a seat. "I vowed fealty to my allies. That comes before all others." He rooted in his jacket pocket and produced a flask of demon brew. He took a swig, then offered it.

After a tense moment, Sian joined him at the table. He accepted the flask and drank deep.

"I agonized over this decision, talking out all the ramifications with Josie. Who, by the way, will hand me my ass for not bringing her with me. But I figured something was up when you summoned me here."

"What if I'd never found out?" Sian passed the flask back. The two sat side by side, gazing out at the galaxy. "How would you have gotten past the fact that my mate and I might've added to Magh's line?"

No matter what he'd said to Calliope, Sian wouldn't have cared who her ancestors were. Last night, he'd felt the possibility—no, the *certitude* of children between them.

He mourned the loss.

"Josie reminded me that every other fey in that line might be evil, but if Calliope isn't, then my reasoning would be flawed. She also pointed out that my father was evil, but I'm not. We're not our parents." Rune took a generous swig. "I never thought I would still have so bloody much to learn at my age. . . ."

They both fell silent at that, wordlessly drinking. *What am I going to do now?* Sian had no appetite for war, no interest in combat.

Earlier, when he'd stopped by the throne room to tell Uthyr his plans, the dragon had been pacing, already aware of what had occurred. . . .

—*Free your mate!*— he'd demanded.

"She stays where she is, dragon. Do not interfere."

—*Have you finally lost your demonic mind?*— Uthyr had loosed a stream of flame beside Sian. A dragon's way of snapping his fingers? —*What if she did set out with ill intentions but grew to love you?*—

"Over the adored king of her kind? I couldn't win Kari's love when I'd been as handsome as Saetth. Now . . ." Sian had gestured to himself. "You told me to accept my curse. She's my second one. I must accept that she is vicious down to her soul, and nothing will change that."

Uthyr's parting shot: *—Mark the words of a very old dragon: this will not end well for you.—*

How could it? Sian's dreams were dead. Matehood was an impossibility. Just as he'd always known.

Minutes passed, maybe hours. The pull to return to his mate intensified. *I fucking miss her.* But the time they'd spent—filled with laughter, play, and pleasure—was over.

Allixta, the Møriør's spellcaster, sashayed into the room, her oversize witch's hat covering her long raven hair. Curses, her enormous otherworld panther, slunk beside her. The towering Darach Lyka followed. Though the full moon had been last night, Darach looked to be on the very edge of turning, his eyes ice blue, his beast barely leashed. But then, he was like that most nights.

"We couldn't help but delve into your minds," the witch said unapologetically. "Such turmoil, demon." She sat at the table, Curses leaping atop the surface.

Sian could feel her prying into his thoughts for even more detail. He gave her free leave.

Speech proved difficult for Darach when he was this far gone, so he used telepathy. *—Betrayed again?—*

"Yet again." Betrayed and tricked.

Allixta asked Sian, "How could your mate stomach sleeping with you when you look like that?" Leave it to the witch not to sugarcoat anything. "The fey king, for all his faults, is sublime. To go from him to you . . . I feel for her."

Sublime? Sian would kill that prick. *Soon.*

Rune grated, "You're not helping things." He and Allixta were forever quarreling. When they started up again, Sian tuned them out, his gaze shifting back to the glass.

A starburst at the center of a fracture caught his attention. It reminded him of the diamond.

He focused on that starburst. Little by little, the crimson haze seemed to disperse. As his clarity returned, he recalled something Calliope had said last night.

You'll never give me a fair chance.

She'd asked him how they could work on the issues they currently had when he couldn't get over the past.

Had his rage against Kari colored his judgment of Calliope? Would he have viewed her dream differently had she never betrayed him in the past?

Maybe he wouldn't have jumped to the worst conclusions.

With this growing focus, he pictured Calliope's breathless wonder when he'd claimed her. She'd *wanted* him to. Why? She'd had no reason to up the stakes between them, no reason to offer her neck so trustingly.

Curious, he dug deeper into his memories of her dream, experiencing impressions he hadn't before.

Her outrage at her treason trial . . . her bewilderment at losing her cold parents . . . the horror of their beheading . . . her resentment over her exile . . .

Saetth had to have weakened her attachment—just as she'd said earlier. Enraged at the idea of her kissing that fey, Sian had hardly listened to her.

As if a band had tightened around his chest, Sian's breaths shallowed. He'd made a pledge to her—an understanding represented by the diamond—to forgive the past and move forward.

But he hadn't.

He murmured, "I broke my pledge."

Dimly, he heard Rune tell Allixta, "I shouldn't have concealed my knowledge of Sian's mate. Maybe nothing good will ever come from that line."

"Bravery did." Three heads swung around in Sian's direction. "A powerless fey, not yet immortal, marched into my hold to take down a Møriør. She braved the lion's den—in hell. Even though she knew Rune could appear at any time to assassinate her."

Allixta said, "Did she brave such risks out of love for the male she'd always wanted?"

Reluctantly agreeing with the witch, Rune said, "Love can make beings do crazy things."

Sian nodded. "That's true. In fact, *I* am going to do something I would've thought impossible just weeks ago. I am going to have faith in my mate." Saying those words bolstered his resolve. Calliope couldn't have feigned that wonder in the diamond cave. She and Sian had *begun* something. "My female told me she loves me. I'm going to believe her."

"According to your memories, she said that after you locked her in a dungeon," Allixta pointed out. "What *wouldn't* she have said to get free? Didn't she lie to you repeatedly?"

Sian stood. "She had no choice. But I do."

"For gods' sakes, demon, your female admitted that she sought to destroy you."

"Until she learned to trust me."

Allixta's lips thinned. "Your decision affects more than just you. If she speaks Demonish, she could have read your correspondence, or overheard you talking."

Rune added, "We have no idea how close she is with Nïx."

"Then my mate and I will both have an alliance that our partner hates." *If I haven't lost her.*

Allixta made a scoffing laugh. "Now you're just being silly. Why would she prefer a hell-changed demon over the gorgeous, golden king of her own kind? One she's loved since her earliest memories?"

"Brother, if Saetth is what she desires . . ." Rune trailed off, searching for the right words. "You can't *force* her to want you."

Sian heard his allies' thoughts.

Allixta: —*Delusional demon.*—

Rune: —*Desperate male.*—

Darach: —*Unstable. Like me.*—

"Damn it, I'm not seeing this situation wrongly! Am I desperate not to be mateless? Of course. But if I'd kept my mind from the past,

I wouldn't have reacted like this." He stabbed his fingers into his hair. "She knew I would think the worst. She predicted my behavior like a bloody soothsayer. Yet she'd still broached talking to me last night."

Her words: *I need your help, your advice. I want to figure this out, but I can't do it alone.*

She must have dreaded his reaction to her bloodline. How could she *not* have after the things he'd said about it?

Now that he could think clearly, he realized Calliope had been longing to tell him everything—despite his idiocy.

That was the reason for her distance. *That* was the conundrum.

How to fix his colossal mistake? He would return hat in hand. He'd admit how stupid he'd been. Once more he would plead to her. . . .

Rune said, "But won't you always react like this? Your mate's betrayal will continue to influence your view. This will just happen again."

Darach nodded. *—Stuck in rut.—*

"No. Because I forgive her for the past." Sian rasped, "I forgive her down to her very soul. From now until I die, I'm going to believe in her." But could she forgive him?

Allixta sighed. "You can't argue with the deluded. . . ." She trailed off, her eyes widening.

"What?"

"Well, look at you, Mr. Man."

Sian frowned, turning to Rune and Darach. Both were slack-jawed.

"What is it?" he demanded. Was that . . . ash wisping in front of him?

Rune's shock gave way to a grin. "You might want to take a gander at your reflection."

Sian raised his hands to touch his face, freezing at the sight of them. They were transforming into . . . into his *former* hands. A thin line of fire bordered each of his lengthy claws, scorching them away.

He teleported in front of an undamaged part of the glass. Gaped at his reflection.

His face had morphed back into his previous guise, his piercings gone. His glyphs faded, his skin growing smooth and tanned. That simmering heat singed away his wings. Would those proud horns remain?

They too burned to nothing. . . .

Rune traced behind him. "Your curse is being reversed."

How? Why? As Sian's thoughts raced, his dam's words flickered through his mind: *Find the fire, and your appearance will be pleasing.*

He'd taken her words literally, scouring his realm for the hellfire.

Though his reflection tried to hold his attention, Sian peered past it, gazing out into the black ether. Was this what his ancestor had seen?

Suddenly Sian understood the moral of the hellfire tale passed down in his family. If the universe hadn't been dark, his ancestor would never have spied that fire in the distance.

It took darkness to see the light.

For Sian, *Calliope* was the fire on the horizon. He'd dreamed of her, obsessing over her, searching for her in every era.

He hadn't been *sleepwalking*—he'd been immersed in darkness. He'd vowed to survive long enough for her to return to him. Which meant the promise of reuniting with her had gotten him through all those years, leading him forward.

Calliope had become his beacon, a point of reference from which to view all other things. If he kept his eyes on her . . .

I'll always know my way.

But he hadn't. He'd taken his eyes off her to look to the past.

Never again. His search had prepared him. By forgiving her, he'd *found* her. His heart soared. . . .

Then it sank. "When I left Calliope, she was strangling her emotions." *That chilling blankness.* Kari had walked away and never looked back. "I told my mate it was all a game with her. I told her . . . I would war on her kingdom."

He recalled his father's advice: *Only hit hard if you aim true, son.* Sian's aim had been false, and he might've swung a deathblow.

"You left her with nothing to do but sit in hell's dungeon and solidify her hatred of you." Allixta stroked behind her panther's ear. "All the best with your reconciliation."

Was he too late? A short jaunt to Tenebrous would equal hours gone by in Pandemonia. "I go now." He traced home—

And came shooting back into the black-stone keep, hitting the wall. "What the fuck?" He tried again. Boomeranged right back. "I can't trace into my kingdom!"

"Let me." Rune teleported. A split second later he flew through the air, slamming into the glass, which began to crack anew.

The others stilled, but Sian couldn't be bothered with that threat. His mind was too busy conjuring one nightmare scenario after another.

What if hell had been attacked? What if one among his countless enemies had taken Calliope? Killed her? Uthyr had better be giving his dragonic life to protect her!

"I can't get to my mate!" Sian snapped. "What force is keeping me out of my own realm?"

FIFTY-SIX

If I'm going to visit the neighbors, I've got to look fabulous.

When Lila entered her wardrobe, a purple gown appeared across the divan, a pair of glass slippers beside it.

She'd never seen such an exquisite garment. It was sleeveless with a stiff, raised collar and a neckline that would plunge almost to her navel.

The color was royal—and *defiant*, reminding her of her treason trial.

"Why shouldn't I believe you were involved in your parents' plot to take my crown?"

"Because it still sits upon your godsdamned head."

She pulled on the gown with a shiver. The material—one she'd never encountered before—had such a pronounced sheen, it looked black in certain lights. She stepped into the glass slippers, and they molded to her feet.

After pulling her hair into a loose updo, she assessed her reflection. *Not bad.*

In the mirror, she caught sight of a box on the top shelf of the wardrobe behind her. She imagined the box disappearing and reappearing into her raised hands.

It . . . did.

Her lips parted at its contents: an eerie black headpiece—a crown. Power seemed to flow from it.

On either side of the circlet, a proud black horn jutted upward. Over the front, long fangs crisscrossed. Wispy vines twined around the crown. Like black fire vines!

Queen of nowhere? Not quite. Her inauguration wouldn't coincide with her wedding or claiming.

But with her *crowning.*

She donned the piece, eyes going wide when it tightened to fit her head. Those vines slithered down, plaiting into her hair.

She faced the mirror once more. Her eyes glowed with purpose. That crown made her look as if *she* had horns. A true queen of hell.

Now for her accessory. She turned to the scepter she'd modified and lifted it.

Carefully. Her scepter wasn't normally a weapon, but tonight would be no normal night.

Abyssian had made it sound like Saetth's strength was something to be feared; she was *counting* on it.

Now all she needed was transportation. One of Uthyr's portals would do nicely. With her new power, she no longer feared the Møriør dragon.

As she set out from the tower, the castle assisted her, its clockwork pieces shifting to provide the most direct route to the throne room.

When she entered, the imposing dragon was leaning against the terrace doorway, a contemplative expression on his scaled face.

"King Uthyr."

He went motionless, except for his rippling tail. Then he turned his great body toward her and eased closer.

"I'm Queen Calliope."

His brow furrowed as his gaze lighted upon her crown. He extended his long neck, leaning in, far too close for comfort. She cringed when he sniffed the crown. After lingering on the horns, he drew back his giant head with a thunderstruck look.

She'd sensed the uniqueness of her crown, but hadn't thought other creatures would. "Abyssian told me you can create portals."

He nodded. She could have sworn she saw both approval and amusement in his expression.

"I'm late for my fiancé's gala, so you are going to open a rift to Sylvan for me."

His canted head so clearly said: *I am?*

"I'm the queen of hell, the sole sovereign of Pandemonia. Abyssian won't be returning. You may stay in *my* kingdom, if you serve me."

Golden eyes gleaming, he drew back his wing and made a flourishing bow. —*Then your wish is my command.*—

She jolted to hear his strangely accented voice in her head. She'd understood his telepathy? She supposed it made sense, at least here.

—*If you'll just step back, my fair queen, I'll get started on a pumpkin carriage. Of sorts.*— He steered her aside with his tail. Inhaling a deep breath, he loosed a stream of white flames across the throne room.

After the smoke cleared, a circular portal remained, like a tunnel of fire. She could see Sylvan on the other side! Traitorous feelings arose. As much as she loved hell, she'd missed Sylvan.

Lila would seize both realms, uniting them under her rule!

Uthyr must've opened his portal into the royal gardens; the stunning castle lay just beyond, haloed by portentous gray clouds.

Torches lit the structure, candlelight beaming from the arched windows of the throne room. She gazed with longing at the ivy-covered spires, the giant evergreens flanking the palace, the trellised roses that painted one wall bloodred.

In Gaia, she'd dreamed of that place, yearning for her childhood home so much she'd haunted a facsimile of the castle. Memories from those years surfaced, dividing her focus, but she ruthlessly shoved them away.

Just as she shouldn't think about Abyssian. Whatsoever.

But how could he have said those things to her? When she'd told him she loved him?

The dragon leaned in again. *—Be back before Sylvan's clock tower chimes midnight.—* He winked at her. *—In all seriousness, my portal will extinguish itself on the final stroke of twelve.—*

She raised her brows, surprised yet again by a Møriør. Like Rune, he didn't strike her as very vicious or monstrous.

—You are teeming with power here, Queen Calliope, but outside of hell, you won't be. If you go to confront Saetth—perhaps for double-crossing you—he will prove far too strong and fast for you to defeat.—

"Precisely," she said with utter confidence, practicing for what was to come. "As long as we're all on the same page about that."

Expression merry, he said, *—Anything else, my queen?—*

"Yes. I'm going to conjure a note for you to deliver to my ex-husband in Tenebrous. I would like him to read it aloud to his allies."

The dragon looked delighted. *—This is better than my soaps.—*

Pacing the war room, Sian racked his mind for a way to reach Calliope. Every back entrance and secret portal into Pandemonia had been blocked. An impenetrable barrier had hurled him back onto his ass a dozen times—

White flames appeared out of thin air. Uthyr's rift! When the smirking dragon strutted from a fiery tunnel, Sian dove to return through the portal, but the edges sealed behind Uthyr's tail.

Sian scrambled back to his feet. "Is Calliope safe? Why can I not trace to hell?"

Uthyr cast him a broad smile. *—Look at you! You've returned to your old form. Which is good, since you won't be returning to your old home.—*

"What are you talking about?" Sian bit out.

—You've been barred from Pandemonia. I did warn you that your plan would end badly, did I not?—

"I can't be barred from hell; I *am* hell."

—*Well, apparently so is Calliope. She's brimming with magic.*—

How? He'd figure that out later. For now . . . "Tell me how to reach her!"

—*She sends you a message.*— Uthyr lifted a forepaw. A small scroll had been tied to one of his talons. —*You're to share it with your allies.*—

"Give it to me!" Sian nearly shredded the page in his haste. He read aloud:

Demon,

Hell is now mine. You locked me in a dungeon; I locked you out of our godsdamned house. In the immortal words of a very wise mortal: everything you own in the box to the left.

Field advantage is key, and the joke's on you.

Game, set, and match,
Calliope I, Queen of Sylvan and Pandemonia

P.S. If you or your allies make any move on Sylvan, I will retaliate against the Møriør tenfold. Do not test me.

"*Queen* of Sylvan?" Sian clutched his chest. "She must plan to go back to Saetth. Must not have believed what I said about him." Why would she when Sian had been bragging about all his lies and trickery? "I told her that we were no longer wed. That I'd forsaken her. She could marry again. I drove her straight to him."

Would Saetth want her hand—or her head?

"What does that part mean about the box to the left?" he demanded of his allies. "Does she reference Pandora's box? Or the mystical Nagas box? Maybe—"

"Brother, it's a song lyric," Rune said. At Sian's blank look, he added, "Just trust me when I say it's the funniest shit you've ever read."

Sian turned on Uthyr. "She can't get to Sylvan, though. Because you would never create a portal for her. Correct?"

—She demanded one. Who am I to deny a queen in her own castle?—

His stomach dropped. "Tell me everything!"

—She was dressed in a ball gown, wearing the most fascinating and historical crown you can imagine.—

As if Sian cared what she wore!

—Also, she had no intention of wedding Saetth.—

"I have to reach her in Sylvan! She's going to challenge him. She told me she was going to kill him."

"I like her more and more," Allixta said. "You are sure to be attacked by Sylvan's army. Shall we provide backup?" Blue light blazed from her palms.

He shook his head. "I vowed to her that no Sylvan would fall by a Møriør's hand." He couldn't kill a single fey, nor could he risk his allies harming anyone. "I have to go alone." He would keep his word if it killed him. And it might.

Damn. This is going to hurt. . . .

FIFTY-SEVEN

Sylvan Castle

"*Queen Calliope the first of Pandemonia and All Hells.*"

The liveried herald announced her in a booming voice that carried throughout the court.

Lila loved how quiet the crowd got. Only the sound of the fountains could be heard. The scent of roses and candlewax permeated the opulent throne room.

The last time she'd been here, Saetth had cast her out for a crime she'd had no part of. At least now she intended a coup. Even better, she was *in charge* of her own political plot.

Courtiers and attendees parted for her as she made her way toward the throne dais, cradling her scepter. The tall fey males wore formal suits and the customary sword belts. The willowy females were clad in airy pastel gowns and glittering jewels.

They all stared at Lila, a royal wearing such a brazen dress—and a devil's crown.

She spotted her cousins. They were gathered like hyenas off to one side, wide-eyed with shock to see her. She gave them a chin jerk in greeting.

As she took in faces, she recognized the shallowness of this extravagant affair. Lila knew make-believe when she saw it. Compared to so much superficiality, her existence with Abyssian felt rich and deep.

Already rooted.

But had it been? He'd called her the queen of nothing.

Should she believe his behavior this morning—or his tenderness toward her over the days and nights of their short marriage?

Now that her anger was cooling, she could so clearly recall the look on his face when he'd handed her the diamond.

That freaking demon *was* in love with her. He'd been lashing out—which he had a bad habit of doing—to hurt her.

He'd left her to rot in a dungeon, and he'd lied so convincingly. How could she ever trust anything he said?

Focus, Lila. She refused to let Abyssian break her heart *and* ruin her one-woman revolution.

If she lived through the next half hour, she might dissect her relationship with him and figure out whether anything could be salvaged between them.

That was a big *if.*

Across the room, Saetth came into view. He sat upon his throne, flanked by guards and a collection of fawning courtiers. Attired in a taupe formal suit, he wore his scabbard and replacement sword. His golden crown perched securely upon his head.

His narrowed gaze took in Lila's own crown and dress.

Trying to appear relaxed—her plan and her life depended on convincing Saetth that she was all-powerful—she called to him, "My invitation must've gotten lost in the mail. Because I know you wouldn't be searching for a queen when you've already promised me the position."

His lips curled. "How many husbands does my greedy cousin desire? I heard you wed the king of hell, but could scarcely believe it. Even more surprising is your arrival here. How dare you enter my kingdom before I've lifted your exile?"

"I dare easily. Since you set me up. Do you deny it?"

His smile was no longer handsome, just sinister. "Not at all. You're a traitor to the crown, just like your parents."

"Not to the crown. In fact, I've come to collect it from you."

Amusement. "Have you, then? You and your demon spouse? You forget my castle is mystically protected against any and all Møriør. He'll never make it past the barrier."

"No, it's only me. I seized Abyssian Infernas's kingdom—just as I'll seize yours."

"I confess I'm intrigued. Why would you ever believe you could best me?"

Because I learned trickery from a master. "Because I was anointed by hellfire as the true Queen of Pandemonia. Saetth, you cannot begin to understand my power. Not only do I wear the crown of hell, I wield the scepter of the primordial fey."

His covetous eyes locked on it.

"It should look familiar to you," she said. "It was forged of Titanian steel, at the same time your sword was created." She tapped her chin with her free hand. "Oh, wait . . . you lost the Ancestors' Sword to Rune the Baneblood—when you targeted that male's mate in a cowardly attack."

He didn't deny that, just said, "A loss which makes me particularly interested in your scepter."

So predictable. "I'm giving you one opportunity to abdicate. This is your only chance to leave this kingdom alive."

"Indeed?" He shared a laugh with his courtiers before addressing her again. "I'm a warrior king, and you're . . . you. We all know you're better suited to modeling ball gowns and traipsing across a dance floor."

Lila smiled pleasantly. "And still I'll make a better ruler than you."

"You continue to look at me as if *I* am the villain. You have yet to understand that I did what I had to in order to protect Sylvan."

"Say that were true, *you* have yet to understand that if two alternatives are wrong, you don't pick the least wrong, you figure out something right. *That* is what makes a monarch."

She turned to address the crowd, giving him her back, hoping he'd take the bait. "I'm Queen Calliope, ruler of hell and heir to Sylvan's throne," she declared, her voice ringing. "When I defeat Saetth, you will all acknowledge my rule. Or I'll end you." She addressed the king's guard. "You'll vow fealty. Or you'll die." She told her cousins, "You'll flee this kingdom. Or you'll share Saetth's coming fate." Facing him once more, she said, "Don't challenge me, cousin."

The scepter drew his eyes again. *That's it, asshole. Take the bait—*

Shouts sounded from the castle's grounds. Soldiers? They were yelling for backup, the commotion growing louder. Fey archers started to fire, their bowstrings going *twang, twang, twang.*

Abyssian had come.

Inside, the crowd surged to the castle's arched windows to look.

"A Møriør!"

"The handsome primordial!"

"Will the barrier hold?"

When a demonic battle roar carried through the night, she raised her gaze to the ceiling. "Fucker."

FIFTY-EIGHT

The castle was as protected as hell had been, an invisible shield blocking Sian's way. No tracing inside.

In front of that barrier, a line of soldiers with swords and spears mounted a defense.

Sian had charged them. All of them.

Poisoned arrows rained down from the castle's battlements, crossing the shield though he could not.

He swung his ax over and over, not to strike soldiers—but to deflect arrows. He bodily knocked down swordsmen, clearing enough of them out of the way for him to reach the barrier.

He sank his ax into the mystical shield. It wavered. Held strong.

His opponents regrouped, attacking his back. He warded off strikes, but they were fast. Soon the small number of swordsmen gave way to troops hundreds deep.

Every time he raised his ax, soldiers landed blows, piercing his torso. Pain flared over every inch of his body. Archers continued to target him. Arrows jutted from his shoulders, glancing off his skull, lacing gashes with poison.

Wings and horns would come in really fucking handy right now.

A different kind of pain erupted. In his jaw. His temples. The tips of his fingers. He chanced a look down. His hands and arms were darkening, claws protruding from his fingers. Glyphs began to glow.

He gritted his lengthening fangs when his wings burst free and his horns emerged from his head.

The guards hesitated, stunned by his transformation.

They went flying when his wings flashed out. *Missed those.* Seizing room to move, he swung his ax against the barrier.

Why would he return to this form? Maybe Calliope *had* gone cold forever. Had he lost the fire?

Just get to her. Where was she? He scanned the windows. Didn't see her amid all the fey gazing out. Another sweep of his gaze . . . There! He spied his mate just approaching the glass. She was alive! He didn't see Saetth near her.

Others seemed to dart away from her. "Lila, get out of there!"

Their eyes met. His steps faltered at her appearance. *Mine. My queen.* She wore . . . a crown of hell. Did she comprehend the extraordinary significance of it?

He yelled when a volley of arrows plugged him. He ducked under a spear's trajectory, narrowly missing the tip of a sword. Another glance at Calliope.

She looked uncaring as she gazed at him. *No, I can't have lost her. . . .*

Roaring with frustration, he rammed his horns against the shield. His bellows reverberated off it. *Get to her.*

With her shoulders squared, she picked up the skirt of her gown and turned her back on him.

Just like the last time he was in Sylvan. His breath shuddered from his lungs. *Noooo!*

While blood ran down his face, he willed her to turn back and see him. To comprehend that he would do anything for her.

Turn around, Calliope. Look—at—me!

And then . . .

She did.

Lila needed to keep her focus on Saetth, but she couldn't drag her gaze from Abyssian.

He was fighting off hundreds. He used his battle-ax—but only to hack at the barrier and ward off attacks. The blade didn't have a drop of blood on it.

His wings knocked swordsmen over like bowling pins and deflected spears. Yet he never beheaded a single fey.

She watched his wing claw stop short at one soldier's throat. Abyssian could have decapitated the male easily. Instead, he took blow after blow without killing. His blood poured as he proved himself.

The lesson of the pomegranate. He'd yearned for carnage against the fey, but he'd surrendered his need—and the look in his eyes said he expected to get *her* back.

That demon was so totally in love with her.

Didn't mean she wouldn't kick his ass.

In Demonish, he yelled, *"Hold on!"* His bloodied horns were straightened, his muscles bulging. He was magnificent. Power incarnate. His gashed skin sheened under the torch flames.

Firelight loved Abyssian.

The soldiers had regrouped. Even a Møriør couldn't fend off onslaught after onslaught—not without thinning those numbers.

Multiple spears sank into his torso. He gnashed his fangs from the pain.

She yelled in Demonish, "Fight back, you idiot!"

That could *not* have been a hint of a grin on his face.

It disappeared when swords sliced his wings apart.

"Trace away!" Lightning flared outside, and rain started to fall. It strengthened until blood washed away from him, revealing the extent of his wounds. *Dear gods.*

"Behind you, Lila!"

She whirled around. The crowd was parting for Saetth and his courtiers to close in on her.

Abyssian yelled, "Do not challenge him! *Get the fuck away from him!*"

Uthyr must've told the demon her intentions—and Abyssian believed she was about to be lost once again. He battered the barrier with his horns, his blood smearing the surface.

Saetth said, "You *did* bring a friend, cousin. Surely that can't be the handsome hell king."

She held her ground. "I don't need help defeating you. I have this." She gestured to her scepter.

Saetth's gaze followed her every movement.

"Oh, cousin, if you try to take this from me, I vow to the Lore I will use my darkest powers to smite you down—"

He snatched the scepter from her.

The bait.

She could hear Abyssian frenziedly grappling to reach her. While Saetth laughed and gloated with his courtiers, she peered over her shoulder at Abyssian. As if in slow motion, the demon swung that ax overhead, rotating it, building momentum with all the strength in his primordial body.

Yelling, *"Aim true!"* he whaled the ax into the barrier. The blade ruptured it. A shock wave blasted out from the impact, leveling trees and sending fey flying.

The shield was no more.

He traced inside a split second later, weapon at the ready, drenched in rain and blood. "Lila!"

Before she could blink, Saetth had unsheathed his sword and raised it against her throat.

FIFTY-NINE

Sian quickly holstered his ax, raising his palms. That fuck was the fastest of his kind; Sian couldn't even trace to intervene.

Saetth beheaded his victims with such speed they could still be talking after the deathblow.

Calliope held herself motionless, but she didn't look afraid.

In a menacing tone, Sian said, "If you hurt her, I will snatch your godsdamned spine from your body. I'll take your throat with my teeth!"

She blasted out a thought: *—I have this under control.—*

Sian drew his head back in confusion.

"*You* are the demon husband?" Saetth said with a sneer. "Not quite the ladies' man I was expecting. Really, Calliope, there's no accounting for taste." His courtiers laughed. "I didn't think I'd get to end the king of hell today as well." Without lowering his blade, Saetth twirled a scepter. *The one I gave Calliope?* Voice dripping with arrogance, he said, "Tsk, cousin, was *this* the source of your power?"

"My source of power is my wits. Always has been." *What is her plan?* "Do you remember what you told me the day you exiled me?"

"Ah, I remember that day vividly. I told you I wanted to see if my hothouse rose could survive."

Did I actually believe she could still love this prick?

"And I said, 'Careful, cousin, this hothouse rose intends to flourish and grow sharp thorns.' Saetth, you've run afoul of them, and you don't even realize it."

From his experiences with her, Sian knew two things.

Calliope had laid a trap. She'd already struck.

How? He could only imagine. But he needed to trust that she knew what she was doing. Which meant . . . *Do not take Saetth's throat with your teeth.*

"I admire your unfounded optimism," Saetth said. "In reality, you're about to share your parents' fate. You'll die like them, your body burned like a traitor's. *After* I behead this Møriør." To Sian, he said, "If you don't kneel before me and surrender your life, I'll take Calliope's pretty . . ." He trailed off, clearing his throat.

Sian bit back a growl, claws sinking into his palms.

"With one flick of my wrist, I'll cut off her . . ." Saetth coughed, his brows drawing together. His face began swelling, veins ticking in his forehead. "Calliope?" His skin was turning as purple as her dress. He released the scepter to clutch his throat.

She assumed a thoughtful mien. "Something more to say, cousin? Hmm?" More loudly, she called, "I told you I would smite you down with my powers! I wield the very fires of hell!"

The fey in attendance retreated even farther.

When Saetth dropped his sword and stumbled back, Sian traced to her. He murmured in Demonish, "The fires of hell? What did you do?"

"I've got this," she replied in the same tongue, stepping away from Sian. "Obviously."

Still, he used one bloody wing to ward off the king's guard, telling them, "You do not want to anger her. Lay down your weapons and back away."

When their king fell to his hands and knees, they did.

"No, *no*." Saetth's features bulged grotesquely, his face mottled. Reaching for Calliope, he collapsed to his front.

His crown tumbled from his head, rolling across the marble floor like a loosed coin.

In a lower voice, she told Saetth, "Oh, cousin, that Titanian steel was laced with lethal venom harvested from a Leviathan's fang."

Sian's gaze snapped to her. The scepter. The Lôtān head.

Chin raised, Calliope lifted one pale shoulder at him.

Sian gazed at her in awe. *Mine.* "My clever queen." With her hell crown.

If he had known all those years ago that his sacrifice wouldn't be wasted . . .

She returned her attention to Saetth, watching his death with disdain. The Møriør had tried to kill him for ages. A twenty-four-year-old fey with no fighting skills had taken him out.

In seconds, the unending millennia of King Saetth's life drew to a macabre close. He took a last gurgling breath. His body spasmed before going still.

The remaining attendees screamed and fled the room.

Only a few guards lingered, looking wary of Sian and Calliope.

In an authoritative tone, she commanded them, "Collect the body and that spent scepter—without touching either. Burn both, and secure the castle."

"Yes, my queen," a senior guard said.

As Sian tore free one of the dozens of arrows in his body, he probed the male's mind. That guard and the others had hated Saetth, were relieved another ruler would take his place; not to mention that she was next in line of the succession. *Good.* They intended to do her bidding.

Unfortunately Sian wasn't faring much better than the corpse they carried away. A snapped spear tip had lodged near his heart, and the mass quantities of poison were starting to hit—not lethally like Lôtān venom, but enough to affect even him. It prevented his wounds from mending, which meant blood continued to drain from him.

He held out till the guards had gone, then lurched on his feet. One of his legs, sliced from the back, buckled. "Calliope . . ." He dropped to his knees in a pool of blood.

SIXTY

"Abyssian!" Lila rushed to his side, trying to steady him, but he fell backward onto his ravaged wings. "Damn it, I told you to fight back." She cradled his head in her lap.

"They are your subjects. I can't hurt my queen's subjects." He weakly reached for her face, brushing the backs of his claws over her cheekbone. "You were amazing tonight, love. I am so proud of you."

Her chest twisted. All her big talk about wanting nothing to do with him faded. He'd come for her, believing he would save her. He'd fought off an army—without harming a single soldier. *For me.* "You look awful." She started yanking arrows from him. He must have twenty broken shafts jutting from him, and at least a hundred more arrowheads embedded inside him. "We've got to get you back to hell." *Yank.*

He grimaced at her less-than-gentle ministrations. "Can't trace there. You barred me." And she couldn't *un*bar him until she returned to that realm. "How did you do that anyway?"

"I found the hellfire. Or it found me. I got some powers and figured out how to use a couple."

A gust of breath left his lungs. "My beautiful, brilliant wife."

Yank. "*Am* I still your wife?" Her temper simmered.

"Always. Even when I'm acting like an idiot."

"I thought you had forsaken me." *Yank*.

Shaking his head, he tried to help her with the arrows. "Don't touch the poison. You can sicken."

She slapped his hand away. "Uthyr left the portal open for me until twelve." Could she get Abyssian out of the castle and across the grounds to reach it? "But I ought to let you bleed out for that bullshit you pulled today."

He nodded. "I broke my pledge. Did just what you feared I would. I should not have taken out my pain and resentment on you."

"Well, I did agree to spy on you." *Yank*. "I lied repeatedly."

"Your deception was born from desperation and longing for a better future. Mine grew from bitterness."

"I *was* desperate. I would've done anything to be free from the Møriør's threat."

"It guts me that you were terrified of us all. I want to make up for every second you lived in fear."

"That doesn't change my blood." *Yank*. "I belong to the line Rune wants to wipe out, the one *you* said deserves its annihilation. The tainted one."

He flinched.

"Still want to have kids with me?"

"It would be my honor to." He reached for her, but she slapped his hand down again.

"Would Rune put *them* in his sights?"

"Never. He's known who you were, but he didn't tell me because he wanted me to discover happiness with you." That surprised her. "He was hoping you would confide your secrets to me."

"I wanted to make sure of your feelings for me before I risked everything on you." *Yank*. "After last night, I'd planned to confess. You never gave me the chance because you invaded my privacy!" Of course, she'd never revealed that she could read *his* thoughts in hell.

"I fucked up again and again. Tell me I'm not too late. Tell me I haven't ruined everything. Can I play that . . . get-out-of-jail-free card?"

Her anger began to cool, but she didn't want it to. "I can't keep paying for crimes I don't remember. I'm done with that." *Yank.* "What happens the next time you fly off the handle? Will you lure me down to your creepy dungeon again? The days of me trustingly closing my eyes for you are over."

He winced. "I am so sorry for that. It's no excuse, but I relived a memory today, one that has always made me crazed. I'd tried not to think of it. . . ."

"What memory?"

"Our last day together." His words were starting to slur, and his wounds weren't closing. "I couldn't handle the rage. Couldn't think. But now I see it's all connected."

"What is?"

"In Tenebrous, I decided that I was going to do something I'd thought impossible: believe in you—despite the past. I finally let go of my bitterness. Once I did, I found the fire, Calliope. *I found it.*"

"What are you talking about?"

"You changed me." Ash wisped in the air. His horns started burning away. His wings! "My gods, Lila, I can do it at will."

"What's happening to you???" His skin was losing all its color, the glyphs disappearing. "The poison is burning you up!" *Yank. Yank. Yank.*

He grunted in pain. "Little wife, you are the hellfire for me. My beacon in the dark."

Was he going to die? Maybe the fey archers had found something equivalent to the Lôtān venom for their arrows! Tears blurred her vision. *Yank. Yank. Yank.*

"Lila, no. I'm fine."

"Clearly you aren't! We need to get to hell—"

The clock tower began to toll midnight.

Her heart stopped. "Up, demon!" She wrapped an arm around him, helping to haul him to his feet. "NOW, Abyssian."

They careened out of the castle's entrance as the third tolling sounded. . . .

Sian dazedly stumbled with his female out into the rain and wind.

"We've got to beat the clock!" she cried. "Keep going."

If they ran into more soldiers before they reached the portal, he might need what was left of his wings and horns. As he lurched beside his mate, he imagined his transformation stopping.

His body ceased its transition. He pictured himself with his hell-change fully in place. The edges of his wings and horns reformed.

Just as he'd once dreamed, he *could* change back and forth between his guises—like a shifter.

Though he was in his hell-change form, the thrumming along his spine had disappeared. Which meant the deterioration had stopped, that engine dead.

Find the fire, and your appearance will be pleasing. In Old Demonish, that could also be translated as *Find the fire, and your appearance will please you.*

Sian had control over his own form.

"I can see it!" Calliope increased their pace. The fiery white outline of Uthyr's portal hissed in the rain. "We're almost there, demon." She murmured to herself, *"Nine clangs."*

They blundered around shrubs. He'd forgotten how many bloody plants were in this realm.

"Ten clangs," she cried. "Hurry!"

He and Calliope barreled through the portal just before the fire dwindled to nothing. . . .

As soon as Sian crossed into hell, he began to strengthen. He drew on magic to protect his mate against any poison transference, then turned to his own injuries.

"The arrows, Abyssian."

With a nod, he willed them to disappear. One by one, his wounds sealed. As she checked him over, he healed completely, stretching his regenerated wings for good measure.

Her face was pale, her skin damp from the rain. Confusion filled her eyes.

"Need to get you warm." He grasped her elbow, then traced them into their room before the hearth fire. He raised his brows at the Lôtān's single remaining fang, then gazed down at his mate. Her worry had heartened him. "I haven't lost you. You can't deny that you still care for me."

She crossed her arms over her chest. "Okay, so maybe I didn't want you to *die* from that poison."

"I wasn't dying. I was changing. Or reverting."

"I don't understand."

"When a demon inherits the crown of hell, he transforms into his most monstrous self. I didn't always look like this. . . ." He explained to her about his own hell-change, that ever-present feeling of deterioration, his fears that she could never want him.

Or that she wouldn't for much longer.

"As soon as I let go of the past, I reverted to my former guise. But when I was trying to reach you, I lamented the lack of my demonic features. Suddenly they started to grow."

She appeared skeptical.

"I can show you what I used to look like." He willed himself to shift forms.

Her eyes went wide when his horns and wings burned once more.

With a cocky grin, he said, "I think you're going to like the old me very, *very* much." His claws disappeared, his facial structure changing. He popped a crick in his neck when he'd completed his transformation.

Her lips parted as her gaze roamed over him. "More trickery?"

"I had no control over this. I should have told you, should have warned you that my appearance would keep getting worse. But I was selfish; I didn't want to scare you off."

In a measured tone, she said, "This is what you looked like for almost all of your life?"

"Not bad, huh?" His cocky grin faded when she shrugged noncommittally.

"You don't have horns in this form? What happened to them?"

He raised his eyes to her crown. "You're wearing them."

SIXTY-ONE

"Pardon?" Lila was still reeling from his appearance. The male before her was just as Nïx's dossier had described: physically flawless.

He had the same raven-black hair and green eyes, and his frame was still leanly muscular. But his smooth skin was tanned. His features were chiseled and masculine, his face beyond breathtaking.

Yet to Lila, he was a stranger with her husband's eyes and voice. He didn't even look like a demon!

"My old horns are part of your hell crown."

"How did they get from your head to this crown?" she asked, but she had a suspicion.

"Graven gets the thanks for that. When they were severed ages ago, I had my brother cast them away. All this time, I assumed they'd been lost forever. But now the sight of you wearing them fills me with satisfaction," he said, his tone indicating the greatest understatement.

"You're hedging, demon. *How* did they get severed? Keeping secrets is how we both got into trouble in the first place."

"You're right." He exhaled. "I cut them off during your past life."

"Why would you do that?"

After a hesitation, he grudgingly said, "You told me you could never love an animal like me. One with horns. You were about to wed another, and I would've done anything to stop you. So I took my ax . . ."

The dimension seemed to spin. He'd carried out that grueling amputation to himself?

For her.

"I brought them to you, vowing that I would look as your kind and live as your kind."

But she'd still spurned him for that other male. This day began to make more sense. "You relived that memory after you delved into my dreams."

He nodded. "It maddened me. I wish I'd reacted differently, but in the end, I needed to acknowledge that memory, to face it." He ran his fingers through his hair, seeming surprised not to find his horns. "Lila, I'm a demon grown, have lived lifetimes, but I would do the same thing today. And I will make the same promise: to live as you do. In this form. In your realm."

"That is *not* what I want." Yes, his looks were stunning. But so had they been before.

"Tell me what you do want. Whatever it is, I will give it to you." He curled his finger under her chin. "I'm in love with you."

"I kind of figured." She gazed up at this strange face, trying to lose herself in those familiar eyes, but the situation didn't feel right—as if she were cheating.

He smoothed his thumb over her cheek. "I will do anything to win you back."

With a challenging lift of her brow, she said, "Anything?"

"Anything."

"Quit the Møriør."

Abyssian went still. "And you will be mine once more? Forever?"

He'd actually do it? "I was just fucking with you." Maybe she *was* a fitting queen for Abyssian Infernas. After all, Lila had used trickery to take her own throne.

He exhaled a pent-up breath. "You got me."

"Considering that Uthyr helped me, and that Rune wanted to give us a chance, you should stay in the Møriør."

"So what do you truly want?"

"*If* I forgive you, I will want you to change back to the demon I love."

He cocked his head. "Ah, my wife is having another go at me."

"I'm not joking."

His expression grew baffled. "You . . . you prefer me like that?" She heard his thoughts: *—All that worry for nothing.—* Then: *—She's saying she loves me!—*

"Yes." She sidled closer to him. "I want you to be comfortable, but I also want me to constantly dream about kissing your gorgeous skin."

He jolted straighter. "At your service." He began his wondrous transformation. Glyphs arose and started to glow, stark against his bloodred skin. He gritted his teeth when his wings and horns emerged. As his facial structure transformed, he wagged his jaw. "Better?"

Heavy-lidded, she said, "Better."

He wrapped his arms around her. "You can forgive me, again?"

"How can I be pissed at your trickery today when I was such an apt pupil?" Everything was connected. Every lesson learned, every wrong soon to be righted. "But we still have a lot of things to work out. Establishing boundaries, for one. If you look into my thoughts, I'll look into yours."

His arms tightened around her. "You can . . . ?"

"Oh, yeah."

"I suppose it's only fair since I spied on you with a mirror."

"You were watching me?" The hand mirror on his desk. "I sensed something! You were *always* watching."

He shamelessly admitted, "No demon has ever looked into a mirror as much as I."

"You'll have to teach me how to do that." She now had a ton of untapped abilities. Then she frowned as a thought struck her. "Why do you think Nïx assisted us? She had to know I'd kill Saetth."

"And that I'd send the Vrekeners' realm spinning. I have no idea why she's steering fate this way—and that will make more than one Møriør uneasy. But whatever comes, we'll weather it."

"Are you sure, demon? Dealing with two realms, two different species, a queendom *and* a kingdom could get really complicated."

He lowered his forehead to hers. Lips curling, he said, "Or, for the first time, it could get really easy."

SIXTY-TWO

Pando-Sylvan Trade Negotiations
Round 1

Sian bowed his chest up for more of her touch. He lay in their bed with his exquisite mate atop him.

Calliope's eyes flickered as she greedily surveyed his body. Meeting his gaze, she told him, "I need gold, love." She rose up on his length . . . then slowly . . . so slowly . . . slipped back down.

He gripped her hips, shuddering with pleasure. "Then this is coercion."

Calliope shook her head, her hair a glossy tangle around her head. Her face was still pinkened from their afternoon at the beach. Though they worked hard, they played hard as well.

Throwing his words back at him, she said, "Consider it a mutually beneficial arrangement."

Anything in the worlds she desired was hers, but he liked withholding concessions—just so she would coax them out of him.

Knowing his clever mate, she'd long since figured that out, which meant she was playing along with him.

Which meant she was *perfect* for him.

She rose up again. "To make the changes I have in mind, I'll need a mountain of gold." Surprisingly, many demons wanted to remain in Sylvan as long as they could earn a fair wage and enjoy all the rights they'd been denied.

"A *mountain* of it??" Sian demanded, making his tone stern. "You're worse than a sorceress. And what will I get in return?"

As she lowered her body, she purred the words, "A dinner."

He was having difficulty following the conversation, his mind absorbed with her tight heat. "Wait, you mean with my friends? Let me get this straight: I have to pay a fortune in gold for you to attend a meal with Rune and Josephine?"

"Of course not, demon. You have to pay a fortune in gold, if you want their meal to be venom-free."

"Is that so, firebrand? And of course, you wouldn't use your powers to play pranks on them?"

She cast him an innocent look. "Define *prank*."

Calliope needed to meet them—since he'd already invited them to the surprise coronation he was hosting for her in two weeks. He figured if she got along so well with Uthyr—Calliope had gotten him a battery-operated flat-screen TV for the throne room—she'd eventually come around with Rune and the rest of the Møriør.

Time to use his bargaining chip. He started to shift, his horns and wings burning.

"No fair!" she cried. "Okay, okay. I'll . . . limit the pranks."

"Good enough." He transitioned back, loving her relieved expression. She truly preferred him demonic. Considering her wholehearted approval of this form, he'd even begun to see himself differently.

She grasped his hand and kissed his palm, her eyes shimmering teal.

The color would always remind him of the hellfire tale passed down through his family.

Calliope had taken him to see the towering blue inferno she'd described, but the hellfire had disappeared, its light unnecessary.

Calliope was Sian's fire, and he was hers.

He muttered in Demonish, "How can I resist you?"

She replied in the same, "But we're just getting started. . . ."

Pando-Sylvan Trade Negotiations
Round 2

Sprawled on their bed, Lila and the demon stared at the ceiling with their limbs tangled.

One of his wings gave a halfhearted flutter, then drooped over the side of the mattress.

She stretched, loving her new role as her queendom's chief negotiator. Though she'd much preferred to live within Graven, commuting to Sylvan via Uthyr's portals, she'd acted put out to Abyssian. "Must we live here?" she'd asked. He'd answered, "We must."

She'd scored all kinds of concessions for Sylvan in that round. She suspected her husband saw right through her, but, man, did he like the games they played.

Now she asked him, "How much did the legions strike today?"

"I fear telling you lest you bleed me for even more." Abyssian's peace project was a success. The legions had already hit the mother lode.

Slaughter Gorge was now officially known as the *Orelands*. Arm in arm, Lila and Abyssian had gazed out over the valley. In Demonish, he'd said, *This is for you, brother. My queen and I will honor your legacy and care for hell in your stead. . . .*

"They did that well, huh?" Though she acted mercenary about the gold, both Pandemonia and Sylvan benefitted as trade partners and allies. Sylvan had limited gold to pay for imports and no ore for weapons. Pandemonia had no crops and only one slow-growing forest for lumber.

The two realms fit as well as Lila and her demon, needing each other to a symbiotic degree.

"We had a banner day," he admitted. "So I have much to negotiate with."

She walked her fingers up his chest. "Then where were we?"

"I was about to mount you from behind and pound your flesh till you scream for me." He rose up on his knees, reaching for her.

Sexy demon. "I meant with our negotiation."

"So did I." He flipped her over on her belly, then maneuvered her to all fours. She could feel his heated gaze as he murmured, "So fucking beautiful."

Wriggling her ass, she said, "I'm taking a bold position this round. Do you think it'll pay off?"

Gripping her hips, he gave her curves a light slap. "I'll make sure of it."

Pando-Sylvan Trade Negotiations
Round 10

With a groan, Abyssian collapsed onto his back. "Mercy, firebrand! You'll get your gold. You'll get anything in the godsdamned universe."

Lila curled up against his side as they caught their breath. "Then these negotiations have officially concluded." At last, she had power over her own destiny—and others' as well. Her pie-in-the-sky dreams weren't so far-fetched after all. "I'll send you a memo."

He groaned again.

"Demon, you really do love me, don't you?"

His thought hit her. *—She has no idea.—*

She rose up to slide him a grin, her heart ridiculously full.

"There's that soft look. You really love me as well, do you not?"

—Duh, relic.—

He chuckled, the sound making her toes curl.

She rested her head against his chest. "There is one other boon I'd like from you."

"Name it."

"I was really angry at those Sorceri bounty hunters at first, but now, I want to thank them. I'm not saying we should send them a fruit basket or anything, but could you make their dimension stop spinning?"

"I can look into it. And I won't even demand anything in return from you. I'm thankful as well."

She lazily grazed her nails over his torso. *Wait . . . where's my*— "Oh, shit." She shot upright. "Have you seen my contraception ring?" She rooted through the tangled sheets.

Abyssian helped her, but they couldn't find it. "Let me check something." He traced away, then returned a split second later with the ring. "It was among your jewels."

"How? I never took it off. . . ." Her eyes went wide. "You think Graven did this?" Was the mystical demonic castle influencing their lives like a fairy godmother?

Abyssian nodded, sitting against the headboard. When he reached for her, she crawled across the bed to him. "I suspect our home would prefer to be filled with younglings sooner rather than later." He pulled Lila across his lap, then handed her the ring.

What a wild, incredible place for kids to grow up. Hellcats and spiders, hidden corridors and a jade beach, sea creatures and hellhounds.

Uthyr had already volunteered for "pup duty."

"But I was hoping to enjoy you all to myself for a while." She slipped the ring back on. "Will Graven take it again?"

"I believe so. It might not happen for a century, a year"—he nuzzled her ear—"or a day. But when it does go missing three times . . ."

She sighed. "We would never refuse a fourth."

EPILOGUE

The storyteller noticed that her audience had grown, and she was pleased that her listeners clamored for the ending of her tale. She told them: 'You see, our truehearted fairy princess and that cunning dame of darkness clashed—figuratively—and became one: a fitting mate for an adoring beast king with two faces. She would be his consort of Pandemonia, and he would be her consort of Sylvan, two united halves of one whole—for the betterment of all elven- and demonkind. And they lived happily ever (after a bitch of an Accession) after.' The moral of the story is that the Sylvan fey just allied with Pandemonia and the Møriør."

The Valkyries who'd gathered to listen to Nïx's tale exchanged looks, then broke into heated discussions about this development.

"But all fey are *our* staunch allies!"

"This is how alliances crumble: one power at a time!"

"I would do the dragon. What? Don't fucking judge me."

"Why would Nïx aid them?"

"We must take back Sylvan before this hell queen solidifies her rule!"

Amid the chaos, Nïx rose and slipped outside. Gazing up at the stars, she whispered, "Your move, Orion."